THE BURNT SUNSET

CHRIS LEDOUX

Acknowledgments:

Celeste, Zacharie, Aurelie, Ranger, and Summer.

Dedication:

For Z.

BURN

BURNT SUN RISING

June 21st. Portsmouth, New Hampshire.
BAERAN

THE STREET WAS LITTERED WITH TREE LIMBS AGAIN. Baeran Sheridan rode his skateboard toward Portsmouth's downtown, throwing in carves and grinds, dodging debris from the previous evening's windstorm. Selene, his yellow Labrador retriever, trotted alongside. He encouraged her, "Come on girl, let's race."

Baeran kicked off the pavement in the dim light of the streetlamps. An easterly gust blew into his face, and Selene surged ahead. At the public gardens by the river, fourteen-year-old Baeran hopped off the longboard and tossed his backpack under a park bench. A sketch pad fell from the bag, and the breeze flipped through the drawings of his family, Selene, Portsmouth buildings,

1

and portraits.

Baeran surveyed the bench with his gold-speckled brown eyes, determined to hurdle it. He often spent early mornings in the commons, practicing parkour before the windstorms rolled in. He stepped backward, leaving fifteen feet from the park bench and his launching point. He extended his left leg and crouched into a runner's stance. An imaginary pistol fired, and he bolted toward his target. Selene pranced to his right, with her mouth open and her ears flapping. He landed three strides and bounded over the four-foot-long wooden slats, smirking. A gust slowed his progress, and his trailing heel caught the iron handrail. His right leg buckled, while his body continued toward the dewy grass.

Baeran tumbled, coming to a stop on his back near the dog's feet. Selene pounced on his stomach. He gasped and forced his hands under her chest. She leaned forward with her tail wagging. Baeran rubbed the scruff of Selene's neck and she pawed at his chest. He sat up, forcing the dog off. Selene took a step backward. She danced out of Baeran's reach, moving from side-to-side, taunting him. He lunged for the dog, ready to chase her, but a gust forced Baeran back. He reached for the bench arm rail to steady himself while he leaned into the dry wind.

The weather had been like this for months, and the media took to naming the storms. Lupe had rattled the trees and windows on the previous night. The windstorms were fan-like, spinning and picking up energy over the Atlantic Ocean, but with little moisture. Gusts of 50 mph were common, as were power outages. Baeran's father had purchased a generator two months ago when wind season began. Spring used to usher in torrential rains, and the locals had once described the soggy period as mud season, but not anymore. Wind was the dominant weather feature along the Atlantic Seaboard in the first half of the year. Rain had been scarce, and the entire region suffered under a drought.

Thunder rumbled and Baeran looked up at the elder birch tree leaning over them. Through the leaves, he saw the dark gray clouds descending on the city. Lightning crackled, striking the birch tree. Baeran and Selene scooted backward, but a white-black branch gave way, crashing onto them. Baeran let out a nervous laugh and hugged Selene, certain, for a moment, that another lightning strike was imminent. Unhurt, he rose, pushing the leafy branch off himself. He stared at the smoking birch tree, his ears still ringing from the strike. Two blocks away another lightning bolt struck, and the boy and dog jumped. "Let's move," Baeran said as he grabbed his pack and longboard.

While the pair jogged, Baeran glanced at his phone, eager to track the squall. He selected The Weather Channel icon. It indicated the latest gale, Maximus, the thirteenth named seasonal windstorm, would intensify as the day progressed.

At the park's edge, Baeran heard the familiar siren sound. He held Selene's collar, gawking at the firetrucks racing toward a glow in southern Portsmouth. He gauged the wind, weighing his options and he resolved to check out the emergency before heading home.

Baeran bounded onto his longboard and rode toward the fire with Selene. As he got closer, the sound of sirens increased. All around him Portsmouth was coming to life, as residents spilled into the street with their phones in their hands.

After two blocks, he stopped across the street from a half-dozen emergency vehicles. Sparks rained from a telephone pole transformer onto the historic Johnston House. The three hundred fifty-year-old clapboard-home centered a Portsmouth historical exhibit. Three dozen colonial-era buildings, occupied an entire city block in the Clipper Harbor neighborhood, serving as living museums during the daytime. The curators maintained the structures to approximate a seventeenth-century neighborhood.

Firefighters scrambled to connect hoses while the colonial-era wood kindled, and the flames spread across the structure, burning it like paper. The fire crew was outpaced and within minutes, the fire jumped from the Johnston House. Gusts fanned the fire, and the blaze intensified, igniting a dozen nearby structures.

The water cannons came to life, manned by the Portsmouth Fire Department. Streams of water arched into the air, deflecting off the buildings as they glistened in the orange glow of the rising sun. But the raging fire boiled off the water and kept the building materials at ignition temperature, sending black and white smoke and steam billows into the air.

Baeran shielded his face as he felt the heat wave from the flames. He stepped back, scared and awed all at once. He knelt with his arm around Selene. Ash flew into the air, flashing off the Johnston House. It fell from the sky like gray fallout, swirling in the gusts before landing onto Baeran and Selene.

The wind-driven blaze chased a firefighter across the street. She pulled at Baeran's arm, forcing him back into onlookers that had gathered. She yelled, "Back up!"

All around Baeran, residents watched the spectacle with their phones raised, filming the blaze.

The firewoman raised her arms, gesturing. "Everyone back to your houses!"

Her walkie-talkie crackled, "Sarah, are you there? Get rid of that crowd now."

Sarah leaned into Baeran. "You heard the man. Go home."

Lightning flashed in the distance, striking buildings, telephone poles, and cell towers across Portsmouth. The throng ducked, grouping closer together. Selene cowered while Baeran held her close. Baeran scanned the crowd and he felt his chest constrict. With each breath he tasted the coffee, cigarettes, and sweat of those around him. He deliberately controlled his breathing, forcing air deep into his lungs, like his doctor had once shown him. But he coughed, sucking in smoke. The world closed in on him, and he had to escape. Baeran pushed his way through the onlookers. "Excuse me. Please move."

The crowd ignored him and looked south as one, when blocks away, sirens from other firehouses answered the blaze.

Sarah yelled, "Move it now!" She spread her arms and advanced forward, walking the crowd backwards.

Across the street the fire spread, threatening the fire engines. The flames danced, shimmering in the wind before leaping onto roofs beyond the Clipper Harbor neighborhood. Overwhelmed, undermanned, and outmatched, the firefighters fought the blaze, but despite their efforts, the flames sustained.

Baeran and Selene turned their backs to the fire and raced the rising sun and the burgeoning gale home. As the power lines and tree branches bent with each gust, the wind propelled Baeran down the street on his longboard. Behind them, dry lightning struck, and thunder roared, chasing the boy and dog. Poor Selene struggled to keep pace, her tongue hanging from her mouth as she galloped at his side. Debris from the windstorm—tree limbs, signs, toys, roofing and siding—littered the street, obstructing him. Baeran grabbed his longboard and ran alongside Selene.

The wind strengthened when he arrived at his street, and Baeran held the skateboard over his head. As he ran parallel to his own yard, leaves spun in swirls in the roadway, and bark mulch from the family's street-side gardens formed blinding, dusty whirlwinds.

Baeran and Selene sprinted through their fence gate and up the cobblestone walkway, bursting through the front door. They slid on the entranceway hardwood floor, and crashed into the coat stand, sending the jackets airborne and toppling the rack.

From under the fleeces and windbreakers, Baeran looked at Selene with wide eyes. He laughed, releasing his nervous energy. The dog stood and shook the clothing off, wagging her hind quarters. A gust whipped through the open doorway, and Baeran trekked to the door. Enthralled and alarmed by the whirlwind in the street, it was the strongest storm he had ever seen. Selene trotted to his side and leaned into the squall with her ears blown back. Lightning crackled, striking the nearest pole, and Baeran shielded his eyes. Blinking through the flash, he heard a girl's voice call to him in his mind. He stared at Selene, as he contemplated the girl's lyrics rattling in his head: "Baer leave Portsmouth, now it is time, for a new road, soon you must find."

GLISTENING GLOW FLASHES
June 21st. Lexington, Kentucky.
SOLSTICE

SOLSTICE DAYTON EXTENDED HER LEFT ARM and raised her right leg straight up, stretching after ballet at the Lexington School of Dance. She fought back a headache and eye-balled the competition next to her. The new girl with the ripped tights had raw talent, but lacked the discipline required to succeed at Ms. LaMerde Femme's Affected Academy of Dance, Solstice's concocted name for her dance school.

HolesInHerTights stretched, raising her arms over her head. She said, "Are you alright? You've got a weird constipated look going on."

Solstice positioned her right heel on the barre handrail attached to the mirror. She grimaced and touched her forehead to her knee. She flexed her back and turned toward HolesInHerTights. Ignoring a sharp flashing pain behind her eyes, she activated her inner princess-mean-girl. "Love the donation dumpster leggings. Did you study dance at a tavern? Your pirouettes on pointe are dreadful. I give you a week. BTW, Alexander Graham Bell called your phone, and he wants it back at the museum."

Solstice didn't wait for a response as a wave of pain rolled over her. She stumbled toward the exit, leaving the new girl speechless.

Bright yellow lights glistened in her blue eyes, and the headache intensified to the tips of her blond hair. It had been half a lifetime, but the migraines and glowing auras had returned. When the flashes sparked, she lashed out at the unfortunate girl next to her. Taken aback by the intensity of the pain, she already regretted her words.

Solstice's mother, Elle, stood near the coat rack. It was Wednesday, and she always picked her daughter up mid-week. Elle overheard the drubbing and grabbed Solstice's arm. "Come with me, young lady."

Elle led Solstice from the studio to her vehicle. "Honestly, Solstice, what was that about? Get in."

Solstice sat in her mom's powder blue Scout pickup.

Elle turned on the ignition. "This will not happen again. Not everyone can afford what you have. Am I clear?"

Solstice leaned back into the seat cushion, trying to relieve the pressure building in her head. "Yes."

Elle shook her head. "Is this how fourteen-year-olds treat people? I'm in town for one day, and I see this. God, I hope you're not like this all week."

Solstice stared at the dashboard, ignoring her mom. She fought back tears, holding in the fear, as if not acknowledging the flashes wouldn't make them real.

Elle looked over her left shoulder, seeking a break in the traffic. "I don't know where those comments even came from. The poor girl has zero friends, and you're twice the dancer she is. Why bother? Why bring her down?"

Solstice rubbed her temples. She said, "She's not in my squad."

As Elle merged the truck into traffic, she replied, "Neither will you be, dear, if you don't change. You can do other things in Lexington besides dance. If this happens again, you won't be spending any time with your squad. Clear?"

Solstice didn't want to be alone, ever. "Crystal."

"All right, take it down a notch next time or try making a friend."

Elle weaved between traffic. The top was down on the Scout, and the wind blew in her blonde hair. She grabbed her sunglasses from under the visor. She switched on the radio, flipping between country music stations before settling on NPR. The news woman was wrapping up a story about the storm on the east coast. "Have you heard about that fire..." Elle stopped as she glanced at Solstice. "Are you alright?"

Solstice glared out the window, biting her lip. She held back tears, while fighting off the throbbing headache and nausea. "I'm sorry, Mom, my head's killing me. I'm not myself today. They're back—the flashes."

Elle's eye's darted between the mirrors, looking for a parking spot. "Are you sure?" She reached for her phone, typing in 911.

"Mom pull over, it's coming."

Elle swerved toward the curb and came to a stop. She reached for Solstice's left hand, but it was clenched, grasping the tan bucket seat.

Solstice closed her eyes. Her head drooped to her right and came to a rest on the window frame. The sound of Elle's voice faded. Lightning flashed behind Solstice's eyes and a dreamvision formed. She saw herself dancing with a boy under the moonlight in a burnt-out forest. The image swirled, replaced by jumbled words swaying through rainbow-colored images. Like a psychedelic virtual reality episode of Sesame Street, numbers and letters danced, floating in out of her dreamvision line of sight. Solstice's head rolled from side to side and she reached out to touch the imaginary letters. Her fingers bumped into Elle and the dashboard. She saw a younger version of herself, clutching a pink plush unicorn blanket. The voice that had haunted Solstice as child spoke to her. She grimaced as the words became lyrics, sorted and sung by Melody, Solstice's imaginary friend.

Solstice opened her eyes and screamed, "Baer!"

"What are you saying? Who is Bear?"

"It's Baer. Mom, Melody is awake. Get my notebook from my sack and write this down." Earlier in the day, when Solstice awoke at dawn the words were on her lips, but she had lost them as the dream world slipped into the real. Now the lyrics were back with Melody's help.

Elle frowned and grabbed the journal and pen.

Solstice sighed and released the tears and the tune, dreading Melody's return after seven silent years, while whispering the harmony to Elle:

Baer leave Portsmouth
Now it is time
For a new road
Soon you must find

I am Solstice, the Sun
Singing, kindling, sighting
A seer with visions
Of powers igniting

The tale of The Burnt Sunset
Firegale horizon blaze
Teens are destined to survive:
Burn, evolve, or daze

Sun igniting
Aether throwing
Air whirling
Earth growing
Fire burning
Water flowing

Soon will rise
As the world is dwindling
A pentad of
Ancient elements kindling

9

FIRE DAWN

June 21st. Portsmouth, New Hampshire.
BAERAN

BAERAN SHUT THE FRONT DOOR. He scanned the open concept room. Like a family room, kitchen, entry way, and breakfast nook, all in one, this was the room the family gathered most often. To his right was a hallway leading to the stairs in the center of the house. He heard his half-awake dad shout from his parents' bedroom upstairs. "Baeran Sheridan, knock it off!"

"Dad, you need to get up. Look out your window."

Baeran waited a moment, but only silence answered. Convinced his dad, Cole, would be awake soon enough if the gale continued, Baeran shook his head. Traces of the girl's lyric still lingered. He searched for an explanation to the voice echoing in his mind. It could be a trick of the wind or his phone. He reached into his pocket, wondering if he had pressed play on a long-forgotten song. He pressed the home button and only the weather app was open.

The adrenalin surged in his body. It wasn't just the jog home, or the storm. It was awe combined with the anticipation of meeting her, like an old image he had deep within his memory, suddenly sprung to life.

Baeran stood completely still near the overturned coats. His phone dropped from his hand onto a fleece. He closed his eyes. He pictured the contours of the girl he had never met. She was a sketch coming to life in his mind. He felt the eureka like he had so many times before when he drew in his pad—that moment as an artist when the essence of a subject was suddenly revealed and the pencil danced across the paper, knowing full well what to do, before his mind could think it.

10

But moments are fleeting, especially those born from the dream world.

Selene nudged Baeran. She pointed her nose towards the kitchen sink.

The image of the girl faded, like dreams do at the crack of dawn when they are confronted with the cruelness of an alarm waking.

Baeran picked up the coats and headed into the kitchen with Selene to wait for his father. The dog panted as he poured water into her bowl. He whispered, "Sorry, we cut that a little close."

Selene wagged her tail, still excited from the race home.

Baeran grabbed the remote, hoping to catch the Portsmouth blaze and lightning storm on WMUR. He repeatedly pressed the power button, to no avail. He flipped the light switch, but nothing happened. He dashed to the hall, and yelled upstairs, "Mom, Dad, Lani, wake up!"

Baeran greeted his family at the stairs. "You guys have got to see this. There's a fire downtown, and a new windstorm with lightning strikes everywhere. Plus, the power is out."

"Slow down, son," Cole responded. "Let's get the generator running, and we'll see what the news says. Lani, go with your mom and find the emergency supplies. Fill the water jugs, too. Kay, anything else we should do?"

"I'll make a list." Kay replied, "We may want to go to the store in a bit, when the storm lets up. Who knows how long the power will be out this time?"

Baeran helped Cole fire the generator on the back deck and sprinted into the house when the windstorm rose again. He watched the wind and lightning strikes intensify through the kitchen window as Cole sorted through a tangled web of TV wires.

Kay walked into the kitchen, with Lani trailing her. "We've got the flashlights, candles, matches, and batteries."

Cole plugged the TV into the extension cord leading to the generator. He pressed the remote, but the screen was blue. "Cable's out, too. The generator won't help with that. Kay, where's the battery radio?"

Kay replied, "Got it."

Lani complained. "My phone keeps losing reception."

With the constant wind, Lani hadn't had a good hair day in months. Baeran had tormented his older sister all year, leaving combs, a hairnet, and caps in her room. He smiled at his sister, offering Lani a pair of scissors from the knife block. She shook her head, declining. She grabbed a hair tie from her wrist and tied up

her bed-headed brown hair. Like her brother, Lani was an athlete, excelling at soccer, volleyball, and lacrosse—making her current hairstyle typical. She embraced its functionality, downplaying her beauty, preferring to focus on her strength. Lani's gray eyes glared at Baeran. "Nice. Super thoughtful, but don't you know? Ponytails are all the rage."

Near the kitchen sink, Kay tuned the radio. Storms were common, and she was used to adjusting her routine during the worst weather. She kissed Cole as he joined them, smiling. She ran her fingers through her brown hair. "Thanks for setting up the generator. Did you see the birch tree in the yard?"

"Yes, the grill and deck are in bad shape." Cole replied. "I'll call the insurance agency, but I'm worried about the fire."

Kay looked back down at the radio. "Me too."

CYBORG
June 22nd. Portsmouth, New Hampshire.
BAERAN

THE NEXT DAY, BAERAN AND HIS FAMILY SAT IN SILENCE around the breakfast table, listening to a battery-powered radio. The deep speaker voice sounded like a cyborg, speaking in clipped anchorman tone. "Superstorm Maximus has brought the entire Atlantic Seaboard to a standstill with downed trees, lightning strikes, and wind-damaged property. While the power failures spread overnight, the fire continued to grow."

Black smoke billowed from downtown, whirling in the wind, as the fire advanced several blocks overnight. Already New Englanders marked the days in relation to the superstorm Maximus. June 22nd also became M2.

The cyborg continued, leaving dramatic pauses, "As exhaustion and injury began to overtake the fire fighters, the Portsmouth fire chief was caught by the blaze as it jumped between buildings. Moments ago, his body was removed from the rubble. Chief Hierholtz gave his life to bring a young man to safety. Volunteers, policeman and firefighters are overwhelmed by flames as they continue to spread."

Baeran gazed out the windows surrounding the table, forcing himself to comprehend the news. He caught his own reflection framed by the fire off in the distance. "Do you guys hear that?"

The four Sheridans stood and leaned into the window. They gawked as rays from the sun mingled with the glow in the old church steeple, and an emergency warning siren echoed through the city, signaling the call to evacuate.

The Cyborg continued reciting the news, "At daybreak, it has become clear the Firegale ruled the night. As the sun rose, so did the flames. Portsmouth is lost. Leave now."

FLASHED BACK
June 21st. Lexington, Kentucky.
SOLSTICE

Solstice reclined in the tan passenger seat, contemplating the dream-vision—the boy, moon, and fire—while waiting for a response from Elle about the lyrical revelation.

Elle turned off the truck. Like Solstice, Elle was petite with blonde hair and blue eyes. "It'll pass. It's been years since your last episode."

"What about the voice—Melody and the song?" Solstice groaned.

Elle rubbed her temples as she watched a bus switch lanes. The words "Central Kentucky Children's Hospital" hung over a young girl. She stood smiling, holding her mom's hand as a doctor examined his clipboard. The advertisement implicitly assured a victory against a horrible childhood disease. Solstice had been a surprise, a detour just as Elle's career was getting started. After attending the University of Kentucky, Elle had taken an internship with the state's senior senator. She advanced within his staff over the last fourteen years, stopping to take care of Solstice after her daughter's first vision at age seven. When the apparitions ceased after a few months, Elle returned to work.

"Let's call Doctor Johnson," Elle said, watching the advertisement. "He helped us years ago. He'll know what to do."

Solstice closed her eyes, recalling her own previous victory. She had buried the memories like a childhood trauma, but now they flooded back. She involuntarily rubbed her forearms and her shins, remembering the straps holding her down seven years ago. Headaches, flashes, and blackouts ruled those days. Later, Solstice ate mush with her scarred tongue, and she spoke senseless words, dreaming of places she'd never been.

"Mom, I can't go back to being that girl." Solstice pleaded. "The seizure was bad enough, like a lightning bolt down my spine, and the leg braces were intolerable. But the voice-," She paused, searching for her words. "Melody. She was the worst. I can't let her back into my head."

Elle reached over the stick shift, grasping Solstice's hand. "I know."

GEAR
M2. Maximus plus two days.
BAERAN

BAERAN LOOKED TO COLE FOR A PLAN. The words "Portsmouth is lost" hung in the air. Tall and muscular with blue eyes and dirty-blonde hair, Cole had a mustache and goatee with a bit of gray. He glanced from the flames blocks away to the radio and then to his family. Finally, Cole spoke.

"We need to leave. Baeran, you're with me. We'll load the camping gear in the garage." Cole reached for the girls, grasping their hands. "Kay and Lani, pack the suitcases and grab all the food."

Kay responded, "Got it."

Baeran dashed with Cole to the garage.

"Baeran, I want to put the plow onto the truck.

"Why the plow, Dad?"

"There's debris on the roads."

Cole climbed into the truck and pulled the truck forward to the back of the garage. "Line me up with the plow."

The truck snapped into the plow frame and Baeran pulled the lever locking it in place.

Cole hopped out, checking the pins and wiring. "Looks good, Baeran. Pull the truck out of the garage and help me attach the trailer and load the ATV, garden trailer, and scooter on it."

Baeran backed the truck out of the garage, careful to clear the edges of the door frame. Once the truck was completely out of the garage, Baeran leaped out, scanning the street. The entire neighborhood was on the move, packing their vehicles. Next door to his left, Mrs. O'Dillian was yelling at her son to move faster, while her daughter cried. To his right, a black SUV backed into the street, screeching away. An ambulance swerved to avoid the collision, racing in the opposite direction. Baeran chased it for a few steps, tracking the emergency vehicle until he lost the red lights in the black smoke of downtown.

Cole yelled, "Baeran get back here and help me with this."

Baeran hustled to the back of the truck and helped Cole attach the trailer.

"Dad, the neighbors--they're all doing the same thing."

Cole hopped on the ATV and drove it onto the trailer. He shouted over the engine, "I know. We need to hurry."

Cole strapped down the ATV. "I'm putting the Remington shotgun in the truck. I engaged the safety and trigger lock. Gather the ammo in the safe; it's open."

"Why?"

"We may have to camp for a few days if the hotels are too crowded in Kittery. We'll do some hunting. It's time you learn."

Baeran carried the ammunition over while Cole put containers of water, gas, and propane on the roof rack alongside the generator.

"I'm going inside to find a map and check in with Mom." Cole scanned the garage. "Grab a few of your things. It'll be a little while before we can return. And tighten everything down."

Baeran tossed his hockey stick, baseball glove and bat into the truck, while Cole ran in the house.

As Baeran was finishing tightening the straps of the roof rack, Cole lugged two suitcases into the garage. "Mom's ready. Got your stuff?"

"Just a few more things, Dad." Baeran added his polished birch wood stick from Boy Scouts, the Wayfarer sunglasses he found on the sidewalk grass last week, and a black backpack.

Kay stepped into the garage and walked to the open door. A few blocks away, smoke billowed from downtown, while fire whirlwinds danced among the buildings. "Oh my. Baeran and Cole, come get the coolers. We need to leave now. Kids, do you have your journal and sketch pad?"

The kids joined Kay, focusing on the flames downtown. "Yep."

Baeran, Lani, and Selene hopped into the back seat while Cole and Kay climbed into the front seats. Cole explained the plan, "We head north into Maine and monitor the radio for instructions."

As Cole pulled out of the driveway, the old white clapboard church steeple, a few blocks away, succumbed to the Firegale and toppled into the downtown square.

PRIMA

June 22nd. Lexington, Kentucky.
SOLSTICE

SOLSTICE AND ELLE SPOKE WITH DOCTOR JOHNSON over the phone, and he encouraged Solstice to remain active until he returned from a conference in a week. After Solstice lied, insisting that she was fine, Elle returned to Washington, D.C., at the senator's request to help address mounting concerns over the East Coast fires.

Solstice attended dance class the following day, despite the continuing headaches. Her head pounded as if worker bees with hammers were banging the inside of her skull, making sparks and buzzing while they attempted to tunnel out to release their queen, Melody, and her song.

Solstice stumbled through her routine as Ms. LaMerde Femme unleashed a tirade like the one Solstice MeanGirl had done on HolesInHerTights.

"Hold. Hold it. Arms raised. Allongé. Straighten your leg. Raise your right leg back. Parallel with the ground! OK, hold it. Wait. Hold. Ahh. No. No. No! Mon Deiu. What is wrong with you?"

Solstice stood motionless, staring at her pink ballet slippers. "My head is killing me."

"A headache, are you serious? A hundred other girls would kill to have your spot, prima. Don't think for a second, I'll put on a summer performance with a lead who can't hold an arabesque. And your pointes and your pirouettes, both are dreadful today. Do you want to return to being a virtuoso? I should call your mother and tell her you're wasting her money and my time."

Solstice ran from the dance floor, as her fellow students snickered.

Ms. LaMerde Femme continued, "Leaving? Are those tears? Merde…"

Solstice snatched her coat and sling sack. She dashed from the studio, bolting toward the street and stumbling into a pothole. She fell onto her knees and hands; the concrete ripped holes in her tights.

Tears streamed down her cheeks, and mixed with the cool, muddy water. She leaned onto her palms and forced herself to stand. Lexington hadn't seen rain in weeks. She must have found the only puddle in the city. Down the street, A-frames with flashing lights marked off an open manhole as filthy water gushed upward.

Solstice wiped her face, tasting the dark water on her lips. She plodded back to the curb, rung the water from her coat, and brushed off her knees. From the studio window above the street, she saw Ms. LaMerde Femme glaring at her.

Solstice gathered herself and crossed the street at the crosswalk. The headache departed, and the words came. Solstice bit her lip, holding the rhymes inside, fearful of what may follow. Her pain had a pattern years ago: flashes yielded to headaches, and when they passed, songs formed in her mind with visions. On her seventh birthday a seizure followed the apparitions.

21

THE BURNT SUNSET

As Solstice hurried past the bustling storefronts, she disciplined her mind and envisioned the harmony. She realized the song wasn't a revelation. Thankfully, not every song predicted the future, nor did it belong to Melody. Sometimes songs were only songs, as was this one. At the bus stop, she allowed the lyrics to develop in her head, and the tune formed. She dropped her head and sang softly to herself.

"Trill"

Falling down
My sweet trill
To the ground
Becomes a shrill

Off the curb
Into the puddle
I roll around
All wet, I muddle

Loathing, I'm
Such a loser
Loud whispers
Why choose her

Falling down
My sweet trill
To the ground
Becomes a shrill

Her legs, weak
Classmates say, graceless
Did you hear? She
Once walked with braces

Her voice, in doubt
They say, it's small

Can't hold a note
Ever, at all

Falling down
My sweet trill
To the ground
Becomes a shrill

Should she let them
Should she even care
They don't know the
Burden she must bear

It is not for them to say
Will she stay or runaway

Rising like the sun
My sweet trill
I'm not close to done
Back off—chill

Rising like the sun
The fire within, burning
Watch me now not run
Jealous, you're all yearning

For mad skill
Wait for it
My sweet trill

SNOW IN SUMMER
M2. Maximus plus two days. Portsmouth, New Hampshire.
BAERAN

BAERAN SAT IN THE LOADED TRUCK WITH HIS FAMILY. Cole pulled out the driveway and merged into a half-mile-long motorcade waiting to cross the Piscataqua River bridge into Maine. Cars lined up on both sides of the divided highway in the north and south lanes to drive northward.

Baeran fidgeted in his seat near Selene. He could barely breathe, and the humid air stifled him. Already he was feeling it, the world closing in. Cars surrounded the Sheridans on all sides. Baeran took short quick breaths, and his eyes darted back and forth, desperate to find an exit.

Kay turned around to check on the kids and caught Baeran's worried look. She tied back her highlighted shoulder length brown hair and reached back to touch his knee. She whispered, "Baeran, take a breath. Look around. It's only us four and the dog. You are safe. Remember what Dad taught you. Break it down. Focus on us, your family, and you'll be fine."

Baeran's face reddened, but his mom meant well, and her advice did help. He turned away from the window and focused on Selene and regulating his breaths. He inhaled, held the breath, and counted to six. He exhaled, blowing out until a count of nine. He paused for a four count. He repeated the process. Six-nine-four.

Baeran continued measuring his breaths while scratching behind Selene's ears, seeking to distract himself. His pulse slowed, and the blood left his face.

The wind shifted, and ash smoke from downtown Portsmouth settled onto the truck. Cole closed the windows and switched on the air conditioner and the windshield wipers. Lani stared out the windows, her mouth dropping as an ash cloud descended on the motorcade. "Mom?"

Kay forced a grin at the kids in the back seat. "I know you're old for this, but why don't we play the alphabet game."

"Mom, you're not serious?" Baeran complained.

Kay snapped, "Yes, I am, Baeran." She whipped her head around, eyeing the kids in the back seat. "We're a bit tense, including your father, and I want to play a game to pass the time!"

Cole glared at Kay, but he forced a smile and said, "I've found an *A*."

Lani joined in, "I get it. Like old times when we used to go to the beach as a family." She scooted up in her seat, scanning the stopped cars through the ash flakes. "I miss those trips."

"Me too," Kay grinned. "But not the traffic. This backup is as bad as when they were working on the highway when you kids were toddlers."

"This is worse," Cole said.

"There's nothing like the hot cinnamon buns from Camp Ellis near Old Orchard Beach. Remember how much stuff Dad used to lug from the car to the ocean?" Lani joked. "We'd park the car, and Dad would unload forever."

Cole smiled, "Four chairs, Selene, a cooler, the game bag and the portable speaker, and the umbrellas." He scanned the rear-view mirror. "And that giant sack of toys!"

The truck crawled forward in the stop-and-go traffic, traveling only a few feet per minute. All around the Sheridans overloaded vehicles waited in line, filled with desperate families hoping to cross into Maine.

"And we had that foldable table," Baeran remembered, jumping in. "I bet it used to take Dad one hour to set up on the beach."

Lani added, "He had that old plastic *Star Wars* Han Solo cup and he'd sneak a beer in it... Oh wait, there's a *B*."

"What? Where?" Baeran smushed his head against the window, scanning the bridge. "It's a bit hazy."

"BMW right there, silly," Lani grinned.

Kay interrupted, "*C*" as she beamed at Cole and squeezed his hand.

Baeran played the game but couldn't block out the Firegale.

At the bridge's center, between New Hampshire and Maine, Baeran glanced back at Portsmouth, a half-mile away. The boardwalk snaking along the Piscataqua River below burnt from the salt piles near the bridge to the park beyond downtown.

Thirty minutes later, around the letter R, as the Sheridans negotiated the stop-and-go traffic on the mile-long bridge, Lani's phone rang.

"Go for Lani." She answered the phone. "Hi...Jordin. Hi Annie."

Lani looked up at Cole. "They are with their grandfather. Jordin says she can see us from a few cars back. Dad, can you see them? They are in the red Prius."

Cole adjusted his rearview mirror; northbound traffic was stopped on both sides of high. "Yep. Got it. Wait. What the..."

A box truck rumbled forward, slamming into the jammed traffic, forcing itself between the long row of cars, striking the Prius.

Lani shouted, "Jordin's grandfather is yelling in Chinese. Now Jordin is doing that... Jordin, speak in English. I can't understand you... Wait. Jordin, are you okay? Dad! They're screaming. Jordin! Jordin!"

Lani released her seat belt and spun around on her seat, peering out the driver's side rear window. Flames were spreading onto the cars closest to New Hampshire side of the bridge. The blaze raced along the river's bank, igniting ships, structures and vehicles. Trapped between the stopped traffic and the flames, families closest to the riverbank jumped from their vehicles, running north towards Maine. Ahead of them the box truck pushed cars aside as in barreled down on the cars closest to the Sheridans.

Cole yelled, "Buckle up!" He reached behind his seat and grabbed Lani, forcing her away from the window.

Vehicles swerved left and right, like they would have for an ambulance, finding every last bit of space in the crowded highway. Cole steered their truck, jumping the sidewalk curb and hitting the bridge railing. The box truck scraped the side of the Sheridan's truck, shearing off the driver side mirror and continued bumping vehicles as it made its way to the northern bridge side.

Kay dug her fingers into the tan truck seats, "Oh, my God."

Lani picked up her phone from the floor mat, listening to screams. "Dad, Jordin and Annie are stuck. That truck rear-ended them and

26

pinned their car against the rail. They can't open the doors."

Baeran spun around, looking out the back window. Jordin was his friend, too. "Cars are on fire. Dad, we got to help."

"Where are the police?" Kay leaned forward in her seat, scanning the roadway. "Cole, can you see them?"

"Hold on a minute." Cole stuck his hand out the window, pulling off the side mirror. "Is everyone okay?" He handed Kay the broken plastic.

"Dad! Jordin!"

"Lani calm down. I'll check on them, but we can't turn around. Everyone stay with the truck."

Cole jumped from the truck. "Kay, hop in the driver's seat and keep moving. I'll catch up on foot." A car beeped, and he leaned against the truck, as cars moved back in the lane.

"Get in your car, asshole!" A man screamed, honking at Cole again.

Cole scanned up the roadway, "Take it easy buddy, no one's going anywhere."

As ash flakes rained down, Cole hastened toward the Prius in the breakdown lane, avoiding the stopped traffic. Behind the Prius refugees scrambled to avoid the flames jumping between cars. Jordin and Annie's grandfather, Wàigōng, was trapped. The old man screamed in broken English and Mandarin for Annie and Jordin to leave the car. Wàigōng pounded the front windshield with his feet and hands. When the bloodied windshield gave way, Wàigōng forced the girls onto the car hood.

The girls slid off the hood, rolling onto the tar as the hatchback caught fire. Wàigōng shouted, "Run!"

The flames climbed toward the front seats. Jordin and Annie screamed as the flames enveloped the car. Jordin ran toward the car, desperate to help her grandfather, but Cole grabbed her arm.

"Stay back!" Cole yelled.

"We can't leave him," Jordin screamed at Cole. "Call the police!"

"Help him," Annie screamed.

Cole grabbed Annie and Jordin's hands, pulling them away from the vehicle.

Wàigōng screamed in agony as the flames encircled him. He

27

flailed his arms against his window, jerking himself back and forth, in a last-ditch effort to extinguish the fire.

Cole forced the girls farther from the vehicle, gripping them by their waists.

Inside the Prius, the flames raced through the trunk into the underbody, igniting the rubber wire-reinforced hose leading to the gas tank. The flames burnt the hose, stalling for a minute waiting, until the rubber melted, releasing the gasoline vapor. The Prius exploded, front to back, toppling end over end landing just feet from Cole and the girls.

Cole, Annie and Jordin fell to the tar on their stomachs, as flames blew by them. Cole rolled over. All around the Prius, other cars caught fire. People scrambled from their vehicles, dashing by Cole and the girls, running and tripping over them.

Cole stood, forcing the girls up. He grabbed Jordin's coat, ripping it from her back, and tossing it to the ground, extinguishing the flames dancing on it. "Girls move it," Cole yelled.

Cole, Annie and Jordin dashed to the truck, leaving deep footprints in the ash settling all around them. They sprinted between the slow-moving cars until the caught up to Kay, Lani and Baeran.

Cole ran to the passenger side of the Ford truck, as it crawled forward. Kay put her foot on the brake.

"Keep it moving," Cole yelled and grabbed the door handle. He swung it open, forcing Annie and Jordin into the back seat. He jumped into the front passenger seat. "Don't stop!"

Lani pulled Annie and Jordin. She asked, "Are you OK?"

Annie lowered her head. Tears dripped down her blackened cheeks. Jordin took her older sister's hand and responded between sobs, "*Wo hen hao.* I'm okay. So is Annie."

Lani's eyes lit up when she saw Jordin was okay. Lani loved how Jordin mixed Chinese and English. Usually Jordin would repeat the translation to English immediately following the Mandarin Chinese word. Jordin had done it since the girls were kids, and Lani liked it. As did Wàigōng.

Lani wiped Jordin's tears. "Where's Wàigōng?"

Jordan shook her head. "*Wo de* Wàigōng, my grandfather is gone."

ALL THAT YOU CAN'T LEAVE BEHIND
M2. Kittery, Maine.
BAERAN

BAERAN STARED OUT THE REAR WINDOW. He watched the flames jump from car to car in the wake of the Prius explosion, and cut off the traffic in the northbound lane. Gray ash swirled over the bridge in advance of the Firegale, falling like snow. On the other side of the divide, the northbound traffic slowed in the southbound lane, shifting away from the flames dancing near the meridian.

On the Maine side of the bridge, the northbound traffic expanded into the breakdown lanes on both sides of the roadway, quickening the exodus as each car left the bottleneck of the bridge.

Tears streaked down Lani's face. "Poor Wàigōng." She had known the old man since the girls were in preschool.

Lani held her two friends in the back seat. Like Lani, Baeran knew the girls from school. Annie was Lani's age, sixteen years old, while Jordin, like Baeran, was fourteen. Both girls had raven hair, brown eyes, and their grandfather's dark skin and features. Jordin had a faded-purple streak in her hair.

Lani gripped Jordin's neckline and hugged her, forcing Jordin's shirt down around the collar and exposing her scars. Baeran had seen the scars on Jordin's neck, shoulder, and arm before at the public pool. She never hid the burn marks. At five years old, she had reached for a pot handle overhanging the stove. Too curious, she overturned the boiling water and suffered for months in a burn center. But she turned her pain into a passion, visiting and volunteering in the trauma center long after she healed. Earlier in the year, in eighth-grade civics class, she had talked about her hopes for medical school.

Baeran turned away from Jordin. The traffic was crawling

forward. Instead of stop-and-go, they were moving steadily at about five miles per hour, but, still, the truck was feeling smaller by the moment. He thought, "Six-nine-four. Break it down." He inhaled as he counted to six in his mind. He exhaled, blowing out a nine count. He paused for a four count and repeated the process. Six-nine-four.

Years ago, Baeran had gone to the doctor for what his mom thought was asthma. After a few tests, Dr. Lydia informed Baeran and Kay that it was anxiety and not asthma that plagued the boy.

"What can be done?" Kay asked.

Dr. Lydia replied, "While there are pharmaceuticals I can prescribe, we should focus on two non-drug solutions initially. First, immerse Baeran in what he fears most—crowds. The more he is exposed to the fear, the better he will deal with it. Secondly, we help him cope, and breathing exercises are the answer."

Baeran had sneered at the doctor's ridiculous advice, but gave the breathing a try after several embarrassing panic attacks at school and church.

After a few minor successes, Baeran heeded Dr. Lydia's advice, focusing more on the breathing and changing Dr. Lydia's number counts to a sequence that worked best for him, six-nine-four. Later, Cole helped him prevent symptoms by "breaking it down" and focusing on the people closest to himself. But the phobia still appeared under stressful or new situations.

In the truck, Lani leaned over Annie and Jordin. "Baeran, are you okay?"

Baeran forced a smile. "I'm working on it."

Off in the distance, Portsmouth burnt. As Cole sped away from the river's edge into Maine, Baeran imagined the Firegale consuming his home, burning all he had left behind, including the longboard he had forgotten.

BUS STOP JABBER
June 24th. Lexington, Kentucky.
SOLSTICE

EACH DAY, SOLSTICE RETURNED TO DANCE CLASS, despite the dust-ups with HolesInHerTights and Ms. LaMerde Femme, and the headaches. She continued to perfect her part as prima for the summer performance.

After class, Solstice walked to the bus stop wishing her mom would have stayed in town. Elle spent most weekdays absent from Lexington, while Mrs. Consquento did Solstice's laundry, helped her with homework, and fed her. Solstice had to be the one teen girl in Lexington with her own condominium. Elle flew home Wednesday night from Washington, D.C., spent a few hours at home, and took a red-eye back, sleeping on the short flight. She returned home on Friday night and left on Monday morning. Elle had a special security pass, and on a good day, the commute took 210 minutes including the ride from the airport.

At the bus stop, Solstice waited under the LexTran #5 sign for her bus to arrive with two elderly women and a boy a few years older than herself. Plugged into his headphones, College Boy ignored the crowd as the two old ladies jabbered on.

Solstice listened to the conversation. She knew the strangers enough to invent names for them. Solstice had played the game for many years. Her first name had been for her dance teacher, "Ms. LaMerde Femme"—the crappy French woman.

RedWoolCoat croaked, "Have you seen it on TV?"

"What?" BlueWig leaned toward her friend, pulling back her scarf from her ears. "This damn wind."

Solstice smiled, shuffling her feet near the bus awning, as she sought refuge from the wind. BlueWig never wore her hearing aids.

"The fire burning in Boston and New York." Red raised her voice.

The shouting didn't help. "Where will the people go?" Blue answered, forgetting the original question.

"I'm not sure." Red replied, "Vehicles are stuck on the highways. The pictures are miserable. First the Maximus windstorm and then the Firegale."

"I'm worried about Washington," Blue added. "What will happen to my checks if D.C. shuts down?"

Red clasped Blue's sleeve.

Solstice glanced at CollegeBoy; his headphones were pulled down. Solstice smiled at him acknowledging the eavesdropping.

"I've been carrying home an extra beef stew can from the store each day," Blue continued. "You need to be prepared too."

Red answered, "I don't care. If the Firegale comes to the city, I'm staying put. My cupboard's already full. After seventy-nine years, born and raised in Lexington, I'm not running, Martha. Where would I go? My son never calls."

"Liza, do you have room for an old friend?" She tightened the gray collar on her coat. "This damn wind. I'm too exhausted to run, and I have a Canadian Club jug."

Solstice laughed, a little too loud.

"Martha, I would like that." She glanced back at Solstice. "Aren't you cold, Dear?"

Solstice pulled her coat closed, covering her tights and leotard. "I'm fine, thank you."

The bus pulled into the stop and LizaRedWoolCoat stepped onto the platform. MarthaBlueWig followed her friend but spoke to Solstice before stepping onto the bus, "Aren't you coming, Dear?"

Solstice replied, "I'm waiting for the #5. Thank you."

CollegeBoy strode past Solstice. He made a goofy face, whispering something to her before stepping onto the bus. Solstice stared at the #23 bus departing, forgetting Liza and Martha's names or who was Red or Blue, as she contemplated CollegeBoy's words, "Leave now, before the panic."

BUCKETS FOR BATHROOMS

M3. Maximus plus three days. Kittery, Maine.
BAERAN

BAERAN'S NEWLY EXPANDED FAMILY SLEPT NEAR THE ROADSIDE at the rest area in Kittery. After waiting for hours in the traffic-clogged highway, Cole had pulled off Route 1 and parked the truck under a Maine, The Way Life Should Be sign. The parking lot overflowed with vehicles. Refugees parked along the roadway and lawn that bordered the rest area and the surrounding woods.

As the sun rose, Baeran saw Portsmouth glowing as it continued to burn across the river. When dawn yielded to daylight, the group exited the truck and stretched their legs. Baeran climbed the truck rack and lowered a water jug to Cole. Kay found two hand towels in back and wet them.

Kay tended to Annie, wiping her face with the wet cloth.

Lani washed Jordin's tear-streaked face, removing the soot and blood, "This will make you feel better. I know it's cold, but let's scrub that blood and dirt off. Wàigōng wouldn't want one of his princesses looking like this."

Jordin wiped away her tears, "Wo zhidao, I know, Lani. You were one, too. He used to call you San-Nuer."

"What does that mean?" Lanie asked, "Is it little bugger?"

"San-Nuer," Jordin smiled, "Means third daughter."

Lani pulled Jordin closer and hugged her.

Annie asked, "Where's the bathroom?"

"You're looking at it." Baeran pointed at the woods. "We're going to check the forest for trees and water them."

Baeran and Cole headed for the woods with Selene to pee. When they returned to the truck, Kay asked, "What are we sup-

34

posed to do?" She gestured to herself and the girls.

"We don't have a choice right now." Cole pointed at the bathroom line snaking around the rest-area building. "That will take forever. We'll follow you girls into the woods and ensure no one is around."

Jordin glanced at Annie and shook her head. "No." Kay and Lani put their arms around the girls, expressing their solidarity.

Baeran reached into the truck cab and emerged with a five-gallon pail with a lid and a toilet paper roll. He pulled out his bowie knife, a gift from Cole, and cut a circle in the lid, leaving a two-inch border around the edges. "Here you are, girls."

The group ambled into the woods.

Baeran and Cole whistled and waited for the girls with their backs against a tree. Selene cocked her head sideways at Baeran, as if to say, "What gives?"

"You can leave now. We're set. Nothing to see here." Lani growled, "Go away. We'll get the bucket. Baeran Sheridan, are you laughing? I can hear your smile. Scoot, and don't come back."

Baeran and Cole strolled to the truck with Selene.

Lani and Jordin returned minutes later and handed Baeran the heavy bucket with smiles.

"Hey, you should have dumped this!"

"Serves you right, Baeran. I swear you are enjoying this," Lani replied, pointing at the bucket. "Won't be so funny once you have to squat. Have you thought about number twos?"

"No." Baeran laughed.

"Try to sit on that." Lani tossed the toilet paper at Baeran, hitting him in the face. "Peeing is bad enough but wait until you have to empty the number-two bucket. It's going to get real personal around here."

Baeran grabbed Cole's arm, turning his face away, holding in his giggle.

"I hereby nominate Baeran Sheridan for bucket duty." Lani raised her hand. Jordin and Annie raised theirs too. "Laugh it up, bro, but you are going down to shit-bucket town."

Baeran stared into the bucket at his feet, expecting floaties.

Cole laughed as the girls darted away. "Time for a lesson, son. Don't mess with women. You can't win, and they travel in packs."

PANICWAVE
M3. Kittery, Maine.
BAERAN

BAERAN HEADED INTO THE WOODS with Selene to dump the bucket. What would the girls do to him next? He returned to find Cole scanning the roadway with binoculars.

Cole handed the binoculars to Baeran. "Do you see it?"

Baeran scanned to the south. "Black clouds over Portsmouth."

"Look north, Baeran."

Baeran focused the binoculars, scanning Route 1 North. "Pushing, fighting, yelling, and lengthy lines at stores that don't open for hours."

"Your mom and the girls have been talking to families along the roadside and at the rest area."

When Kay and the girls returned, Kay grinned at Baeran. "Did you empty the bucket?"

"Yes, Mom. It was the worst."

"Get used to it. Lani says you're in charge of it."

"There was a vote and everything," Lani quipped.

Jordin and Annie nodded.

"Now that is decided," Cole jumped in. "What did you find out, Kay?"

Kay added, "We could see Portsmouth." She pointed to the ash clouds lingering near the river. "The flames are everywhere."

Cole hung his head and replied, "People are getting rough around the stores, eager to buy supplies."

Kay said, "If you head south a mile down the road, you can see fire burning along the river. Folks are restless, too. A man knocked Lani over."

Cole surveyed Lani and asked, "Are you hurt?"

"Na, fine." Lani pointed to the overflowing parking lot. "It's like a football game; everyone is tailgating. We saw a hundred cars between us and the riverbank."

"*Geng duo.* More," Jordin added.

"Way more, Mr. Sheridan." Annie blurted out. "I bet there are thousands of cars."

Kay interrupted, "Cole, those cars will come this way."

"Mom is right." Cole sighed. "It's time to go."

Kay leaned into the truck and switched on the radio.

Baeran whispered to Lani, "It's the Cyborg."

"The Firegale has crossed the river."

Cole increased the volume on the radio, and the Cyborg droned on, "...the burning bridges, wind, and the shipping traffic have contributed to the Firegale's spread. Several tugboats drifted from Portsmouth when their mooring lines burnt through, preserving the Firegale as it crossed the river."

The words "crossed the river" hung in the air, like the fog from their breath. Baeran and Lani stared south, searching for the flames, while Jordin reached for Annie and placed her hand in hers. Kay put her hands to her face and gazed at Cole.

The Cyborg said. "Cell phone service is failing."

Baeran gawked at Lani, while she desperately sought for a signal on her phone.

The voice continued, "...the Firegale cannot be contained by natural boundaries or by our brave firefighters. The electricity will continue to fail as the Firegale spreads westward. The lightning and windborne debris from Maximus has sparked fires from the Carolinas to Maine. For those living along the coast, it's time to acknowledge despite the efforts of firefighters, policemen, and the national guard, we have failed as a nation to contain this fire. Delaware and the Chesapeake Bay area have struggled to manage the Firegale as it spreads west, forcing the President and the government to evacuate the capital..."

Cole lowered the volume on the radio. "Crap. In the truck, now! We'll cross the river upstream back into New Hampshire."

Kay, the kids, and Selene stared at Cole, stunned. Cole shouted, "Move it! Now! Get into the truck; minutes matter. We must cross the river before cars clog the road again!"

Baeran closed the tailgate while Kay loaded Selene into the front seat. The girls hustled to the back seat. Cole started the truck and yelled at Baeran, "Move it!"

Baeran hopped in, and Cole slammed the truck into drive, sending dirt flying as the truck and trailer fishtailed onto the road. Baeran scanned the roadway behind the truck, hoping to see the skid marks on the tar, but instead he saw the steady stream of vehicles moving toward them. He felt the panic wave overtaking him, and whispered to Selene, "Six-nine-four. Break it down. Repeat."

MELODY
June 27th. Lexington, Kentucky.
SOLSTICE

Solstice hummed a new tune to herself on the bus ride home from dance class, relieving her migraine aura. The words came to her, and she blended the lyrics and harmony. Often the song emerged from her mind formed, like another person did the challenging work and fed her the words. A talent she had tried to forget, ignore, oppress, and refused to cultivate. This song, unlike "Trill," was a vision, and Solstice closed her eyes to see it.

Solstice saw an inversed mirror image of herself, like a negative photography print. In a field, under the noonday sun, a solar eclipse was underway, and the negative—a girl much like herself but with darker skin and raven-black hair—approached. As the eclipse reached totality, the girl, Melody, moved closer, until she blocked the blackened sun, touching Solstice's nose to her own. Melody stared into Solstice's dreamvision eyes, piercing them. "Release me!"

Solstice opened her eyes, stared out the window and sang.

"Melody"

My old friend
Lives in my head
My Melody
Back from the dead

Welcome home
I have missed you so
Where you went
I don't want to know

THE BURNT SUNSET

Missing
My melody
Returning
My remedy

I remember when
I was on the breather
You left me
Before that car seizure

In the back seat
You spoke your task
The accident
It came so fast

Missing
My melody
Returning
My remedy

What will you bring?
Me, I don't want to know
How much time do I have?
Don't say it's time to go

Melody, Melody
Not yet, don't take me
Melody, Melody
Please, you can save me
Melody, Melody
No, you can't have me

Returning
My Melody
Becoming
A part of me

CACOPHONY

June 27th. Lexington, Kentucky.
SOLSTICE

SOLSTICE STOPPED SINGING, as the LexTran #5 bus rolled on. She smiled at her bus-buddy across the aisle, embarrassed. She didn't always notice when she sung out loud.

"My daughter used to sing." CoffeeShopMan interjected. "You have a lovely voice. Who's Melody?"

She's the super-secret voice in my head, awoke from the dead. Solstice replied, "Thank you, she's no one," to the fifty-ish man in the seat next to her. "Does your daughter attend school in Lexington?"

"No, she lives in New York City. I haven't heard from her."

"I'm sorry." Solstice peered out the window, watching pedestrians battle the wind. "Is she staying?"

"Hopefully, she will head south and stay until the Firegale..." CoffeeShopMan leaned over the aisle. "I'm worried about the riots up north."

Solstice asked, "What do you mean?" She had seen the pictures on the news. Supermarkets running out of food. Long lines at gas stations. It reminded Solstice of a couple years ago, when it snowed a foot in Lexington. "Won't the police just take care of it?"

"The unrest is about fear—not injustice or politics. I'm not sure the police care enough. They've got family too." CoffeeShopMan lowered his voice, whispering, as he waved his phone. "These riots are living on our phones, recorded and accessed at will. I'm afraid the panic will spread to Lexington. People are worried about food and survival. They see these videos and that just makes it worse."

A gust shook the bus, rattling the windows, rattling Solstice. "But everything will be okay, right?"

The bus stopped, and the door opened.

CoffeeShopMan stood. "This is my stop. Watch the news tonight. I'm betting the riots, looting, and the Firegale will be worse in the north. Any time they name a wildfire, it's bad. If the Firegale reaches the Capitol and D.C. falls, Lexington can't be far behind. People don't understand yet. We're used to watching wildfires burn out on TV. There's no putting out this one. I'm preparing to leave before everyone else decides to."

"How can you be sure?"

"I'm not. But why risk it? Good luck and go right home to your mom."

See my mom? Not today.

Solstice watched her bus-buddy walk down the sidewalk. She slouched in her seat, clutching her sling sack.

Stops later, she heard Bus Drivin' Man yell, "Miss! Miss! Isn't this your stop?"

"Yes, thank you." Solstice exited the bus. She walked down the sidewalk for a half-mile, but lingered on the last block to her condo, knowing her home would be empty, cold, and dark when she arrived.

SHATTERED

M3-M8. Maximus plus three days to eight days. Maine and New Hampshire.
BAERAN

COLE LED THE GROUP WEST FROM KITTERY, MAINE, back into New Hampshire over the Salmon Falls River, a tributary of the Piscataqua River, at the town of South Berwick. Determined to avoid the main highways and its standstill traffic, Cole abandoned the crowded state roads for backcountry roads while Kay plotted their route westward. Miles downriver, Baeran imagined Portsmouth smoldered.

The Firegale creeped westward, northward and southward. Held back by the heroic efforts of emergency personnel and the armed services, the Firegale slowed along the Atlantic Seaboard. Like tentacles, the fire probed in spurts, exploiting weaknesses away from population centers. The government's response was uneven to the disaster. National resources were thrown at the great cities populating the Interstate 95 corridor, but northern New England was left to its own defenses. The Sheridans were forced into a narrow corridor a couple hundred miles wide, lined by the fire on both sides.

Traffic converged onto back country roads bringing the exodus to a standstill. In order to conserve fuel, the Sheridans pulled off the roadway frequently, camping out of the back of their truck. They traded goods and information with families along the road, hoping for news, while only covering a few miles per day. But there were no friends along the road, and distrust ran high. The refugees were anxious, and fights broke out. Gas stations ran out of fuel while store shelves were stripped clean west of the advancing fire.

The Sheridans snaked their way northwestward on a sparsely populated road, stuck in stop-and-go traffic. Power continued to fail

43

along with cellphone service. Guns were openly displayed. Slowly emergency personnel and policemen slipped away from their posts, worried for their families.

On the sixth day since their escape from Portsmouth, M8, a thin ash layer coated the gear on the truck roof. The family gathered near the truck, waiting for an announcement from the government. The eastern horizon glowed, like a second sun setting. The Sheridans set up camp along a quiet country road in a small clearing, while traffic slowly moved forward on the next closest road. Cole was concerned about consuming the family's fuel, and with Kay had elected to wait for long periods along the side of the road, hoping the traffic would eventually thin. They studied the map to navigate a way westward that took them through sparsely populated areas believing the roads would be less crowded. The highways, state roads, and backroads were not equipped to handle the two million residents from Maine and New Hampshire on the go at the same time, and the Firegale had limited their options by burning southward and northward as it crept west.

Cole poured fuel from a gas can into the tank. "Is it time?"

"The President should be coming on any minute." Kay replied, staring at the map laid out on the tailgate.

"Where are we, Kay? What's the closest town?" Cole asked.

Kay checked the map and replied, "Midway between Rochester and Woodstock."

Baeran stood near Kay; he tossed a stick to Selene. As she fetched it, Baeran peered over Kay's shoulder at the map. "West Sumwhereorother."

Kay smirked, mouthing the imaginary town name. She pulled out a battery-powered radio and the group sat on a rock, listening to the President's broadcast.

"My fellow Americans. We come together today to discuss the great challenge ahead. Like so many generations before us, I call upon us to be extraordinary. We cannot fail.

"Superstorm Maximus struck this country's East Coast eight days prior. As you know, several fires ignited, many because of dry lightning. The windstorm debris hampered emergency personnel. Within days, the wind-blown fires burnt westward and southward.

"I implore you to remain calm and lawful. Criminals—and let's make no mistake about it, looters are criminals—have used this opportunity to take what is not theirs. Let me be clear. It is stealing. The riots in Baltimore, Detroit, Cleveland, and Chicago must cease, so I can direct available resources to combat the fires. I have authorized local, state, and federal law enforcement to impose curfews. We must respect the rule of law.

"I pledge to you, my fellow Americans, we will beat back this fire.

"To guarantee continued governance, I will relocate the executive and legislative branches to Lincoln, Nebraska.

"Northern New England—Maine, New Hampshire, and Vermont—must evacuate immediately. Do not wait for help. I repeat, leave when this broadcast concludes. The national guard will manage the evacuations of Philadelphia, Trenton, Washington, D.C., and other cities along the Atlantic Coast. The army and national guard will station fuel, food, and water ahead of the fires along the main roads.

"I implore you as Americans to remain peaceful and respectful of other citizens' property. I hereby declare martial law and will execute the additional powers granted to my administration.

"Good luck, Godspeed, and God bless America."

The Sheridans stared at the radio, waiting for more.

THE CODE

M12. Maximus plus twelve days. AKA July 3rd, Lexington, Kentucky.
SOLSTICE

SOLSTICE SAT ON HER BED AT THE CONDO and called her mother. "Can you connect me with Elle Dayton?"

"She's unavailable. Who's calling please?"

"This is her daughter." Solstice moved her hair behind her ears, pressing the phone, straining to hear the operator through static interference.

"I can take a message, if you like."

"This is an emergency," Solstice pleaded.

"Please hold."

Seriously? She paced the room, allowing her nervousness to slip into her voice. "Thank you. Yes, I'll hold." *Please hurry. Music? Who picks the soundtrack to panic?*

Her cellphone made a clicking noise, signaling a new voice on the end of the line.

"Solstice, what is it?" Elle asked.

"Hi, Mom. The counselor let us out early from Total Drama Teen Camp."

"Is that the camp's real name?"

Solstice sat on the edge of the bed. "No, I invented the name. I saw a wildcat today. The mascot from University of Kentucky explained improv at camp. I kept an open mind and it turns out she had innovative ideas. She deals with rowdy fans. She used to be a gymnast and did flips for my class."

"You're not calling to tell me you want to be a mascot, are you?" Elle joked.

Solstice looked at her phone—one bar. Solstice sighed. "No, I don't want to be a mascot. My instructor cancelled class because

46

of the President's speech. Can you take me off speaker phone? Have you seen the news?"

"No, we are busy here."

"Put it on. What's this about Japan, Mexico, and Germany? The Firegale is worse, too. The President left D.C. for Lincoln, Nebraska. Mom, are you there?"

"Solstice, I'm listening. I know this. Why are you calling?"

"Mom, I need you to come home."

"Solstice, can you hang on a minute? I need to get these containers shipped now."

"Sure."

What does the senator have Mom working on? The silver fox, Elle had once called him after too much wine at the condo. Solstice had seen a picture, years prior, in a box in Elle's closet while rummaging for a scarf. He was tall and yes, handsome, with flowing silver hair and piercing blue eyes.

Elle lowered her voice. "Solstice turn on the news and keep it on. Listen carefully. The power will be out soon in Lexington. I am working on a plan for us. I will be home late tonight. I would have been home sooner, but we need this."

"What plan, Mom?" Solstice stood and moved to the window, pulling back the shade. Down below, the courtyard was darkened.

"It rhymes with 'drunker'."

Solstice stepped away from the shade. "I need another hint, Mom"

"Unkerbay omplexcay."

"Nice, Mom. *Igpay Atinlay*. You've fooled the I-F-bay. The government will never crack our code."

"Quiet, Solstice, the phones are being tapped," Elle whispered.

"Why would the FBI tap the phones? Is the Firegale close to your office?"

"Yes."

"You need to leave. I don't want to be alone. My friends are with their families. Mom, what are you working on?"

"I am working on a trade to help us."

Solstice sat on the bed and pulled open the bottom drawer of her nightstand. "What trade? Please come home. Don't wait for the last plane. Leave now." Solstice removed a handful of notebooks. In the bottom of the drawer was an old keepsake, her baby blanket, pinky-binky. Solstice ran her fingers along the plush fabric. She hadn't thought about it in years.

Elle continued, "I'll be leaving soon with Senator Adena. He is flying home to Lexington, overnight."

"Are you sure you'll be on the senator's plane?" Solstice closed the drawer, leaving the blanket in its resting place. She laid back in her bed, staring at the ceiling.

"Yes. I must go, Solstice. Stay with Mrs. C."

"Mrs. C.'s next door. She has family, too, Mom. She called you. She made me dinner. I gave her this week's check. I'll be fine for a while by myself." Solstice's eyes welled. "I'll slide over if I need anything."

"Have you had any episodes?"

"Not since the truck last week." Solstice sniffled. "I'm frightened, Mom about the Firegale and Melody."

"I'll be home in the morning, and we'll talk. Keep the radio on. Put some clothes, water, and food in a backpack and keep it by the door."

"Mom, you are scaring me." Solstice rolled over to her side on the bed, pulling her knees to her chest.

"I have to go, Solstice. I'll be home soon, and we'll talk. I love you."

"I love you, too," Solstice said, and ended the call.

SOLA

M12. Lexington, Kentucky.
SOLSTICE

SOLSTICE PUT HER PHONE IN HER SWEATSHIRT POCKET. She already regretted sending Mrs. C. home for the night. The trees rustled outside her second-story bedroom window. She sat on the bed edge, slipping on warm socks. A lone light shone from the courtyard below, casting long shadows of tree branches onto her window-shade.

Solstice shut off her bedroom light and left her door open a crack. She left her laptop open on the kitchen counter with the CNN.com feed streaming news. She needed to keep hearing the reporter's voices, drowning out the silence of her loneliness until Elle returned home in the morning.

Solstice peered out the shade, watching the activity below. TwoDogsSmiles-A-Lot wandered the courtyard with a Jack Russel Terrier and a Labradoodle, grinning at Butt Cleavage Gardener. Solstice smiled too. The old guy needed a belt or suspenders. The butt-show should have been a bullet point at a condo board meeting.

Despite the wind, Solstice cracked her window and listened in on the courtyard conversations. Mrs. C. joined TwoDogsSmiles-A-Lot and Butt Cleavage Gardener. Soon, Average Joe joined the conversation. There was nothing special about AJ, other than the fact that he married Gorgeous Jane, GJ.

Solstice preferred not knowing them or learning their names. That way they could never leave her.

Puzzles strolled into the courtyard with a newspaper under one arm and nodded at TwoDogsSmiles-A-Lot and Butt Cleavage. He put his left hand on Mrs. C.'s arm and kissed her cheek.

Intrigued, Solstice moved closer to the window, whispering to

herself, "Mrs. C.!"

The five adults sat on park benches on a slate patio framed by lavender bushes and ornamental grasses, engaging in pleasantries.

Solstice guessed their thoughts and invented a conversation. She beamed, proud of her inside jokes and the made-up dialogue, until her cheeks reddened. Her face burnt, when she realized the engrossing conversational topic. The five adults focused on her second story window, as Mrs. C. pointed.

Solstice retreated from the shade and into the darkened room. She sat on the bed, cupping her hands over her nose and gaping mouth. The owners were worried about her, the girl with the part-time mother and the friend in her head.

Solstice crawled into her bed and gathered the covers. She removed the old folded pink unicorn blanket from her nightstand. She clutched pinky-binky in one hand and her phone in the other. She closed her eyes as the hallway light flickered, and the branches scraped her window. "Mom will be home at first light and she'll have a plan," she whispered, and willed herself to sleep.

SHAFTED

M16. Maximus plus sixteen days. Halfway across the state of New Hampshire.
BAERAN

BAERAN SAT ON THE TAILGATE, anxiously awaiting Cole's return. With all the stop-and-go traffic, the truck overheated, blowing the thermostat. The Sheridans pulled off the roadway, parking along the edge of the woods. The caravan of refugees continued to push westward, leaving the Sheridan's behind. While Cole struggled to diagnosis the problem for a day, he missed the opportunity to ask for help. Once he discovered the problem, Cole left the family at their campsite on country road on the scooter, in search of gas station or tow truck. He was unable to locate help or the part for several days. Without cellphone service and GPS, it was difficult to locate a store, let alone find one that was still open.

The flames pushed northward, consuming much of the state of Maine. Emergency personnel held the Firegale back around New Hampshire's population centers, but the blaze advanced around the cities. Many refugees were able to escape southward, below the fire, but the Sheridans were in the center. At night they could see the Firegale on the horizon, surrounding them on three sides, miles away.

Kay sat on the truck tailgate next to her son. She recited facts from a folded paper map. "Did you know New Hampshire is eighty-nine percent forest and about five percent is settlements?"

Baeran asked, "What's the rest?" He guessed his mom was trying to distract him, and he played along.

"It looks like northern lakes and ponds," Kay replied, tapping her finger to the blue spots on the map.

"Why not head for a lake to ride the Firegale out?"

"Remember traveling in Sumwhereorother?"

"Yes." Baeran smiled.

Kay answered, "I spoke to another family. They drove for a hundred miles, but despite light traffic, they couldn't find a break in the fire." She ran her fingers over the map. "North like East is too dangerous now."

"What about the cars, Mrs. Sheridan?" Annie asked. "We haven't seen any in a day, not since we turned off the main road."

"I haven't decided if that's a good thing." Kay folded up the map and hopped off the tailgate. "It took two weeks to get this far, and we've reached our limit on traffic jams. We could have walked faster."

Lani shook her head. "No way and no thanks, I don't want to walk. I heard you say Lincoln was like six hundred miles."

Kay replied, "Lincoln is fifteen hundred miles, but we only have gas for six hundred miles."

"What does Dad think?" Baeran glanced over at the trailer. The scooter was still gone, as was Cole.

"Your father and I decided, last night, if he can't find the part today, we will abandon the truck."

"I'm sure Dad will fix the truck," Lani said, "but there's no way I want to get back in that caravan."

"Let's follow the back roads west," Kay said.

"Traffic jams are worse than bucket duty." Lani smiled at Baeran. "The middle seat sucks."

Jordin chimed in, "Baeran's got to give up his window seat."

Annie smiled, agreeing.

"Fine, but if you three are going to talk over me the whole way," Baeran replied, "I'm going to ride on the roof rack."

Kay smirked. "Let's get moving on the chores. I'll get the water from the stream over there." She handed Baeran the map.'"Baeran check the oil, the straps on the roof rack and see how much gas is left in the spare cans. Girls, you've got the campsite. Pack it up."

Baeran opened the truck hood, checking the oil and transmission fluid. He removed the air filter and blew out the ash dust.

Baeran's next task was cleaning the Remington shotgun. It leaned against the truck plow. Cole hadn't used it in years and when he cleaned and oiled it last week, he gave his son a lesson in gun safety and maintenance. Baeran repeated Cole's words in his head, *make sure the chamber is clear before you start.*

Baeran strode to the tailgate to collect the cleaning kit. He gazed eastward, seeing the burnt sunrise. The light from the Firegale grappled with the sun but yielded to the dawn. He blinked his eyes, as they watered from staring into the light. A man approached. "Dad is that you?" Baeran cupped his eyes, shielding the haze.

Selene barked, as a stranger rushed Baeran at the tailgate. Baeran stretched into the truck, and his hands found the familiar grip of his hockey stick. He pulled the stick from the truck and slapped it at the stranger's shins. The blade shattered. Baeran lost his grip on the shaft, and it fell to the ground. The stranger hobbled for a minute and punched Baeran in the chest, knocking him to his butt. When Baeran struggled to stand, the stranger crossed checked Baeran with the remainder of the stick, breaking the shaft in two.

Lani, Annie and Jordin gawked at Baeran and the stranger.

Kay heard Selene barking, and bolted to the truck. The man, similar in height and weight to Cole, sneered at Kay. "It's not safe to leave these kids alone." He grinned through his crooked, stained teeth and added, "Do you have any supplies to spare?"

"Please leave. My husband will be back any minute."

The stranger barked, "You're camping alone with these kids."

"Leave now," Kay repeated. "My husband is on his way back."

The man approached Kay, pushing his greasy dark hair behind his ears. She backpedaled, but he grabbed her wrist and struck her, knocking her to the ground. "You will give me your food and drink now! And when I've had my fill, we'll talk about how I can protect you and your family."

Baeran rose to defend his mom. The stranger removed a rifle slung over his back and jabbed the butt end into Baeran's stomach, knocking him to the ground.

"Stay down, kid, and knock it off."

The stranger peered into the truck, to glimpse its contents.

Baeran removed his bowie knife from his belt sheath. Gripping the blade, he leaned back and hurled it. The hilt glanced off the stranger's head, and he shook off the blow. "I told you to knock it off!"

Kay lunged for the Remington shotgun near the plow. She unlocked the safety and pumped it.

The stranger stopped in his tracks and gawked Kay's way. Kay fired the weapon. She fell backward with the discharge, but the pellets struck the attacker below the knee. The man jerked into the flamingo pose, removing the pressure from his damaged leg. He hopped on one leg toward the front of the truck. Selene pounced, hitting the man in the waist. He fell, striking his head on the plow, and his body slumped to the ground.

Kay shouted, "Girls open the back and find duct tape! Check Cole's toolbox. We need to tie him up before he wakes. Baeran, help me get his rifle."

Cole approached on the scooter. He saw the struggle from the roadway and raced back to his family, skidding to a stop near the truck. He dropped the scooter and checked on Kay first.

"We're okay, but a bit shaken." Kay hugged Cole.

Cole tested the stranger's restraints and dragged the man by the wrists to the closest tree. He leaned the stranger against the tree and slapped the man in the face, waking him.

Cole glared at the stranger. "This ends right now." He pressed the shotgun muzzle against the attacker's forehead. "Right here. Right now!" He pumped the shotgun.

Cole's hand shook as he placed his finger on the trigger.

The stranger forced a mumbled, "No," from behind the duct tape on his mouth.

"Cole!" Kay yelled.

Cole glanced at Kay and the children, their eyes wide and their mouths open.

"Cole," Kay repeated, lowering her voice, "you are not that man, not now, not yet."

Cole swallowed his rage and slipped on the safety. Flipping the shotgun over, he struck the stranger in the face with the butt of the gun, knocking him out.

Baeran and Cole tied the stranger to the tree.

Cole moved to Kay and kissed her. "If anything had happened to you, I don't know what we would have done." He hugged her, examining the mark on her face.

She reassured him. "I'll be fine." Kay released Cole. "Baeran, are you okay?

"Yep. I feel like I got boarded at the rink." He raised up his shirt, displaying red welts. "Just don't make me laugh for a bit"

Lani blurted, "How's your underwear?" as she giggled."

Baeran chuckled. "Ugh. Just fine," he said as he held his ribs.

The family regrouped by the truck.

"Well I've got the part, anyway," Cole offered. "It shouldn't take long to install. The Firegale is building on the horizon, too. Another ash cloud is pushing this way. I can taste it, before I can see it." Cole coughed.

Lani asked. "Won't he try to hurt someone else? We should call the police. That is, if we had working phones and police."

"We'll leave him right here, tied to a tree." Cole replied. "Screw him. Where's the map."

Baeran picked it off the ground and handed it to Cole.

Cole unfolded the map. "We must avoid the interstates and the eastern cities while we outrun the Firegale."

Baeran peered at the map. "You could take it off road. My friends and I rode our bikes on trails, bike paths and power line right-of-ways in Portsmouth."

"It's about eighteen hundred miles between New Hampshire and Nebraska. Avoiding the cities will add three hundred miles to the trip." Cole lined up his thumb with the map scale, and moved it across the paper, estimating distance. "It would take thirty hours travel by car under perfect conditions, if we drove nonstop.

"If the roads are backed up again, what will we do?" Kay asked. "I'd rather walk or ride."

"If we take back roads," Cole replied, "and avoid the highways, it will take a week. If the traffic jams force us to abandon the vehicles and hike, we could travel about ten miles per day, which would take one-hundred-eighty days."

Lani asked, "Dad, drive, ride and hike?"

"If we can use the trucks, ATV, scooter, and hiking," Cole replied, "the trip may take two months. Baeran, if we have to stay off the roads, how would we find the trails, power lines, or old railroad lines?"

55

"Try the TrailBlaZers App. I downloaded the data the last time we had cellphone service." Baeran pulled out his phone. "It's like this open source App where kids, hikers and bikers dump information about trails, abandoned rail lines and powerlines." Baeran pressed the App, showing Cole some the trail maps. "Plus, it links in with the major public trails, like the Appalachian Trail or the Eastern Seaboard Trail."

Kay, Annie, and Jordin joined the other three around the map. Cole explained the plans to his wife and the two girls.

Kay put her arms around Annie and Jordin, kissing each on the cheek. "What do you want to do, girls?"

"Whatever you think is best Mrs. Sheridan." Annie murmured.

"Girls call me Kay, and tell me your opinion, please."

"*Wo hen kaixin.* I'm so happy to be with you," Jordin admitted. "To have someone besides Wàigōng who cares for me and Annie. We never had a mom or dad. Honestly, we'd follow you anywhere."

"Girls, I know you miss your grandfather, but I'm thrilled we can be together, as a family." Kay hugged Jordin and Annie. "Call us Cole and Kay."

Annie smiled. "Okay, Mrs. Sher...Kay."

Cole and Baeran installed the thermostat while the rest of the group finished packing the gear and climbed into the truck.

Cole turned the key, and waited a few minutes, checking to see if the truck would overheat. Satisfied the repair was made, he crowed, "Let's go."

Kay placed her hand on Cole's cheek. "What about him?"

Cole glared out the window at the man roped to the tree. "Screw him." He pulled the truck back onto the road and turned on the radio.

Baeran recognized the Cyborg voice coming from the truck radio.

"...We have not heard from the President for eight days. FEMA, government officials, and armed service personnel are leaving their posts. Avoid Boston, New York, D.C., and Philadelphia. Fires and riots rule those cities..." The truck lost the signal for a moment as ash snow fell. Cole switched on the windshield wipers and closed the windows while Kay adjusted the tuner. "This reporter will be signing off now. Move west ahead of the Firegale and be careful. People are getting sick. Beware of Dazers."

NVRMND

M14. Maximus plus fourteen days. Lexington, Kentucky.
SOLSTICE

SOLSTICE HEARD THE KEY IN THE LOCK and ran to the front door at the condo. She opened the door. "Mom! You're home. How was the flight?"

Elle dropped her bag in the doorway and grasped Solstice. "There was turbulence, and I could see the Firegale off to the east at takeoff."

Solstice squeezed Elle. "I'm worried about the Firegale, too. In town, people are already acting weird. Old ladies are buying extra groceries, I saw a fight in the street, and people are skipping work-,"

Elle interrupted, "Turn on the news while I wash. After, we'll talk." Elle closed the bathroom.

"Mom? Are you coming out? You have to see this."

"Be right out, Solstice."

Elle opened the bathroom door and joined her daughter at the bar counter in the kitchen; they watched Firegale related news. Atlanta was in flames, and the Firegale was threatening Nashville. Elle turned up the volume on her laptop.

A youthful woman stood on the rooftop of the CNN Center in Atlanta, Georgia. The camera zoomed in on her and panned three hundred and sixty degrees, revealing ordinary staff, the TV crew and two other reporters. In the background, the Georgia Dome burnt, as did the city. Dark smoke surrounded the group. The reporter pushed back her blowing hair and spoke into the camera between coughs. "The Firegale swept through South Carolina, reaching Atlanta yesterday, and we are trapped. So much has happened with the superstorm, the dry lightning along the coast, the riots and looting, and the Firegale. It came on too fast. We leave you now today, not with the pictures of a dying city or the tough questions

58

concerning the failure to contain this disaster, but with ordinary people, ordinary Americans, frightened, like you."

Ash snow swirled around the rooftop. The reporter stepped closer to the camera. "To my mother and my family, I love you."

The camera lens roamed from the reporter and focused on an older man. Against a background of burning buildings and black smoke, he stammered, "I love you my dears. Be safe."

A woman stepped into view, tears streaming down her face. "Goodbye, Phil. Give my love to Becky and Jim. I love you."

Another woman spoke, "I'm Janice." She looked over her shoulder, tracking the flames. "It's too late now, but if you are watching Pat, I love you."

A man with a tie, in his thirties spoke next, "Tracy, name him after your father." He loosened the tie and tossed it to the wind. "I love you. I wish I could see him grow up. I love you."

Elle placed her hand on the top of the laptop to close it. Solstice put her hand on her Elle's. "No, Mom, leave it."

A man with gray hair, his janitorial suit had the name Pete on it, spoke next, "To my boys, Tim and Jack. Head to the mountain cabin above the tree line. Take my Chevy. Under the seat, I have a rifle with ammo. Take the fishing gear and warm clothes. Watch out for your mother. Bring her pills with you and anything you can, like fuel, food and water..."

The camera man switched from Pete to give another person a turn, revealing flames dancing on the opposite end of the rooftop near the double doors marked "stairs."

An older woman placed her hands together and began, "Hail Mary, full of grace, the Lord is with thee." She stopped to wipe the ash snow sticking to her tears, before continuing. "Blessed art thou amongst women, and blessed is the fruit of thy womb, Jesus. Holy Mary, Mother of God, pray for us sinners, now and at the hour of death. Amen."

The camera operator pointed the lens downward for a minute and handed it to the reporter. A woman with her hair tied back in a ponytail, and a harness over her shoulders stepped in front of the lens. "I'm Christa, your camerawoman. Mom and Dad, I love you. Watch Whiskers for me." Christa added with a smirk, "Steve and

Scott, you're both asses and you know why."

The lens pointed downward as Christa replaced it on her harness. Christa raised the camera and focused on a man with skinny-jeans.

"I'm John. Good luck. Um... Oh...excuse me." John rambled toward the female reporter who had led the broadcast and he took her in his arms. She nodded, yes, and John kissed her.

Christa yelled, "Woot! Woot!"

The reporter grinned at John, and the rest of the rooftop group circled behind her. She patted back her blowing hair and let her tears flow. "Reporting live from downtown Atlanta, this is... Oh, no!"

The reporter dropped the microphone and darted toward the rooftop edge. Flames shot through the rooftop from the floor below. The camera fell to the ground, and the roar of the flames competed with screams and prayers. Fire filled the sideways lens, as the rooftop tar ignited. Framed by the flames, a pair of hands interlocked. John and the reporter hastened from the lens and stopped at the rooftop edge. They kissed and then jumped.

Elle shut the laptop and hugged her daughter. "Pack your bag. We leave tomorrow."

SUMTRAIL

M15. Maximus plus fifteen days. Lexington, Kentucky.
BAERAN

Solstice and Elle loaded the powder-blue International Scout with camping gear, food, and water. The entire neighborhood was on the move, and an emergency warning siren echoed in the courtyard of the condominium complex.

Elle drove west on Route 57 until it intersected with Interstate 64 and Interstate 75, in Lexington. By noon, traffic was jammed for miles in both directions. Elle pulled off Route 57 before merging onto the interstate. She parked the scout.

"We don't have time to wait on the highway. We'll hike the Summer Trail."

Solstice complained. "Are you sure, Mom?"

"Yes. I don't know another way out of town." Elle put the keys under visor.

Solstice hopped out of the vehicle. "Well that sucks. This is worse than my seventh birthday."

"What would you have me do?"

Solstice kicked the Scout door shut, but the latch stuck, and the door swung open. "How about Senator Adena?"

"I'm sorry." Elle grabbed her sunglasses and clutch. "For forgetting about your birthday, Solstice. For not being there for you. But Senator Adena can't help us, not yet anyway. We need to stay ahead of the flames."

Solstice closed the truck door, clicking the latch. She considered her words. Elle was not a traditional mom. Close in age, Solstice often felt Elle treated her like a younger sister, merely tolerating her. They had spent much of the last few years apart while Solstice stayed with Mrs. C. and Elle was in D.C. Solstice had no father, and her mother was a stranger. Their conversations were flat, devoid of emotion, but Solstice couldn't risk alienating Elle. She had no one else. Solstice bottled her anxiety about the fire and the return of Melody. "Don't worry about my birthday, Mom." She peered through the open window across the seats at her mom. "Mrs. C. forgot, too. I'm worried about her."

"Me too, but let's worry about you and me."

Elle and Solstice removed their bags from the Scout.

Solstice slipped her sling sack over her shoulders. "Where to?"

"We take the trail until we can see the old quarry. The trail takes a hard-right turn ahead and the quarry should be visible through the trees. The tunnel entrance to the bunker complex is located near the senator's office." She tightened the straps on her backpack. "Do you have everything?"

"Just my phone and journal." Solstice unzipped her bag. "I got a pink sharpie, too."

"Oh, my Solstice. That's it? What about underwear and clothes?"

"I don't know, Mom." Solstice smiled, lowering her sunglasses. "We'll shop, or I'll borrow yours."

Elle walked toward the trail entrance. "Come on. I don't know what you were thinking." She stopped and read the sign.

Solstice put her hand in Elle's and the two walked down the path. "Remember that time I went with you to D.C. and they lost my bag?"

"Yes."

Solstice smiled. "It will be like that trip. We'll travel light and adapt."

Elle shook her head. "I packed an outfit for you."

About ten-feet wide, the trail was made of hard-packed crushed stone and gravel, no doubt from the quarry, and was lined with trees on both sides.

While Solstice and Elle hiked the trail, Solstice peppered Elle with questions. "The senator has an office at a quarry and he has a bunker? Why didn't you tell me?"

"I'm telling you now," Elle replied. "It was secret. His family money comes from the quarry, but it's a cover for a government installation."

A handful of bicyclists zoomed by. Elle and Solstice moved to the side, staring at the cyclist gear. Each one was overloaded with a pack, tent and sleeping bag.

"Geez, they got a lot of stuff." Solstice asked, "We don't need any of that stuff, right? Because we are going to be with your boss. Can you tell me about the bunker? What was it for?"

Elle stopped and pointed to the bald hill in the distance. "See that? The bunker was built under the original hill as a secure location for a military conflict. Senator Adena's father did the work for the government after the war. The quarry provided a reasonable explanation for the excavated material. But there's nothing special about this one. Bunkers were built all over the country."

Solstice stopped to remove a rock from her sneaker. Elle moved closer and Solstice leaned on her for support.

"Mom, will they let us in?"

Elle hesitated. "We'll see. If we can't get in, we'll try for the back door near Fort Hillock in Brankfort. Do you remember Fort Hillock?"

Solstice opened her sling sack and took a sip of water. She offered it to Elle, but she declined.

"Yep. We traveled to the fort last year for school. Fort Hillock is where the Union soldiers beat back the Confederates," Solstice replied. "What's that have to do with our plans? We took a bus. It's a half hour ride from the condo."

"Under Fort Hillock is the back door to the bunker." Elle replied. "The back door faces the forest and, beyond, the river."

"No way!"

Elle continued, "I've seen the plans in the senator's office." She stopped and knelt, drawing in the gray dirt. "The tunnel is twenty-three miles long from the quarry to Fort Hillock. Six short bunker tunnels are located under the Lexington Quarry, but the seventh tunnel leads from the quarry to the fort."

"Can't be." Solstice smiled. "You just drew a giant octopus."

Elle stood and rotated around her drawing, examining her stratchings from Solstice's angle. "It's true. We can approach the quarry three separate ways: the highway..." She pointed to the elevated roadway to her left. "...or through the woods or across a lake. Vehicles are jamming the highway, otherwise we'd be driving the Scout." She waved her arm towards the dense brush. The woods will take forever, and we'll have zero visibility at night. And we won't be anywhere near them, if the fire is near. We'll have to cross the lake."

"Seriously?"

Elle pointed again to her left. Up above the tree line, the elevated highway was visible. The traffic was stopped, and people were ambling about their vehicles, waiting for a break in the congestion. Elle replied, "Yes. Listen, I didn't accept it at first, but I saw the map and I researched known tunnels around the country on my phone, like subways. Did you know New York City has over four hundred miles of subway track?"

"Sure. Well, four hundred miles, no, but I figured it was a lot."

"These are huge tunnels built under the city while the city conducted its business." Elle continued, stretching her arms out as they walked. "The Lexington to Fort Hillock tunnel is hardly wider than a car, eight-feet tall and it's under woods and fields. The government can do anything without us finding out."

Solstice asked, "What about hiking the shoreline?"

"It's double the distance and rocky with no cover," Elle replied. "In some spots, there's only a cliff face and no shore at all. Plus, there is a fence with razor wire around the property."

"Are you sure, Mom? Why not walk to the front door? You know the senator."

Elle stopped and grasped her daughter's hand, looking into to her eyes. "We are not on the list—despite all I've done for him over the years. There's a disease forming in the Firegale's wake, and the people that can help cure the disease are supposed to be at the Lexington Bunker Complex, and no one else."

Solstice pulled away, walking faster.

Elle hustled to catch her daughter. "People are dying with the Firegale, riots and now a new disease." She slipped her hands in Solstice's as she matched her pace. "Two lives, like yours and mine, don't matter. We're on our own." Elle continued, "Solstice listen, our best hope is to sneak in and hide. Once they lock the doors they'll quarantine the place. They'll have to keep us."

The pair continued to hike the trail throughout the day, seeing only sporadic foot traffic. Most refugees continued to travel by car, and the crowded highway was occasionally visible through the trees lining the trail. As the afternoon waned, ash filled the sky, and dusk came early.

Solstice coughed, "Mom, how far?"

"We should be there in fifteen minutes if we jog."

They jogged to the trail's end. Elle directed Solstice through the woods for a couple hundred feet. Once they reached the shoreline, Elle paused and spoke to Solstice. "I have a zip-bag for your phone and for your lyricbook. Put them in your sling sack. Pull the strap as tight as you can around your chest."

"Mom are you sure about this?"

"Yes. We swim seventy-five feet from the trail shore to the island shore." Elle dropped her pack. "Then we sprint across the island, and swim seventy-five more feet to the quarry."

"I can't do that, not in the dark." Solstice dipped her foot in the water, testing it. "It's freezing."

Elle stepped in the water. "Solstice, the moon will rise soon." She urged Solstice forward, hiding her shivers. "We have to swim now."

"But why the water?" Solstice asked. "Is there no other way?"

"Not without getting caught." Elle replied, "It's our way to circumvent the razor fence and sensors. They are around the property, except near the cliff. We can't come from a direction the guards would expect. Once we climb the hill, hundreds will be waiting at the door, including workers from the quarry, guards, the senator's people and other important government personnel. People may have passes, but others like us must take our chances." Elle waded up to her knees, waiting on Solstice. "It will happen fast. People will be panicking."

Elle walked back to the shore, gripping Solstice's hand. "Listen to me at the door. It's a sizable iron drop-hinged door with hydraulic cylinders on each side, built into the sidehill. The guards will shoot anyone rushing the door. Did you hear me?"

Solstice turned away.

"People will die. No matter what happens listen to me." Elle continued. "You'll walk in front, and I'll hold onto you in line. I know a man at the gate. Now, deeper into the water."

SPLASHES
M15. Maximus plus fifteen days. Lexington, Kentucky.
SOLSTICE

SOLSTICE WADED IN THE WATER TO HER KNEES, hesitating. Elle clutched her daughter's hand in the hazy light of the rising moon and the Firegale glowing on the eastern horizon. She led Solstice until their legs and chest were immersed. Elle released Solstice. "Swim. Count your strokes. It will keep you focused."

Solstice pushed off with her feet and dove, dunking her head. She resurfaced and inhaled. She kicked her feet and counted her strokes, peering left to keep Elle in view. One, two, three... After a count of thirty, Solstice's finger tips scraped the shallow shoreline of the island. She stood and snuck onto the beach with Elle close by.

Solstice jogged near her mom on the rocky beach toward the trees along the eastern shoreline. The moon rose higher in the sky, and the pair did their best to move between the shadows. As the far shoreline grew closer, Elle signaled for Solstice to stop. "The wind is causing the water to be choppy. Stay close to me while you swim."

Elle and Solstice waded in the chilly water. Elle asked, "Ready to swim?"

"You bet, Mom. Anything to leave this water."

Side by side, mother and daughter swam from the island toward the quarry cliff. Solstice struggled through the choppy waves, counting the strokes. She felt her strength ebbing by the tenth stroke in the cool water. By the fifteenth stroke, she gasped, "Mom, shouldn't we have reached the cliff by now?"

Elle replied between strokes, "We're drifting, and we are in the shadow of the cliff. The moon's low on the horizon. Just keep swimming."

Solstice resumed counting her strokes, but the wind driven waves separated the two swimmers. At a count of twenty-nine, her hand scraped a rock. "Mom, where are you?"

"I'm close!"

"I'm at a sheer rock face." Solstice cried." I can't find a footing."

"Move to your left, Elle replied. "Follow my voice. You can't be far from me."

With her left hand in a crack on the rock face, Elle stretched, reaching out for her daughter.

Solstice touched Elle's fingertips. "Mom, what are you standing on?" She pulled herself closer, grabbing Elle's arm.

"Nothing, my hand's in a crack. Lean on me." Elle squinted, struggling to find the shoreline. "Grip my shoulder and rest a minute. Are there any foot holds from the direction you came in?"

"None I can feel." Solstice pulled herself up, putting her full weight on Elle. "Mom, I'm so cold."

The waves rose with the wind, slamming Solstice into her mother. Elle groaned, holding her daughter close, absorbing the impact.

"Mom, I can't feel my thumbs."

"Swim with me to the left." Elle released her hand from the crack. "Follow me."

Solstice followed, stopping to rest along the rock face after a dozen strokes. "I'm slipping Mom!" Exhausted, she ran her hands along the cliff, desperate to find a hold.

Elle doubled back, finding a crack in the quarry cliff along the way. "Twist your hand and make a fist. Hold yourself in place. Count to sixty. I'll be back." She grasped her daughter's hand and placed it in the crack.

"Mom, no." Solstice closed her eyes, fighting off the cold creeping over her while she counted alone. At thirty-nine, she groaned, "Mom, please hurry."

Solstice struggled to keep the count as the waves smashed against her. Had she already counted forty-five? She leaned her face against the cliff, and stammered, "Forty-six."

The next wave slammed Solstice's head against the rock face, and she lost her grip, sinking below the water line. As the water enveloped her, a migraine formed, along with an aura and flashes. She closed her eyes, sinking. The headache faded, revealing a dreamvision.

Melody swam toward Solstice and clutched her hand. The pair sunk to the bottom of the pond and found their footing. The water drained away, and Solstice stood in a meadow. The sun shone against a cloudless sky. Melody held Solstice's hand and led her through the tall grass.

After a few paces Melody stopped at a bare spot and reached down to grab a handful of dirt. Melody placed the warm earth in Solstice's hand. Melody smiled, but Solstice recoiled as the dirt turned to fire and burnt her palm. Melody grabbed Solstice's wrist and with her other hand poured out a handful of water, dousing the flames, revealing a handful of ash. Melody grabbed the ash and tossed it upward. The ash fell, but blew away with a sudden breeze, revealing a bright blue sky. Solstice stared at the sky, the blueness looking familiar, but it too faded revealing the stars, moon, the sun and space.

Melody turned and faced Solstice and she sang:

"Sisters, Black and Bright"

Sun, Aether, Air, Earth, Fire and Water
For them you shall search daddyless daughter
Find within yourself a new rising sun
Call Aether above all he is the one

I am Melody, a negative you
Raven instead of blonde, eyes black not blue
After Firegale and ash snow weather
Seek dark I would choose and find him, Nether

Sisters are we
Dark and light
You and me
Black and bright

Join me, become me and seek not the light
Silenced for seven years, accept me, don't fight
Two halves come together if you allow
Solstice and Melody can be one now

Sisters are we
Dark and light
You and me
Black and bright

Melody pulled Solstice into an embrace. Thunder roared above, and rain fell on the meadow, drenching Solstice. Melody faded, melting into the meadow. The meadow filled with water, rising above Solstice's head. Solstice involuntarily gagged, sucking in the icy water.

Elle pulled Solstice to the surface. "Are you okay? I thought I lost you. I found the shore. Keep counting."

"I'mmm stttucccckkk attt fottttty siccckkkkss."

Elle sputtered, "Move your legs. Kick." She coughed, having swallowed a mouthful of water. Her strength was ebbing too.

Elle stroked with one arm around Solstice's chest until she found the rocky quarry shoreline. She pulled Solstice onto the beach, gasping, "Sit. Put your hands under your arm pits. Let your body shiver." Elle stood, placing her hand on her knees, searching for air and resolve. She looked over at Solstice, watching her shiver and struggle. "I'll be right back." She ran towards the hill.

Solstice lay on the crushed rock beach as the waves lapped her shoes, counting to nine before she shut her eyes.

Elle came back a few minutes later and found her daughter asleep. She placed Solstice over her shoulders. Her daughter's sneakers bounced against her back as she closed the distance to the slope. Elle placed Solstice down. "Sweetie, I have to remove your wet clothes. The air is warm."

Solstice didn't answer, the cold had taken her.

Elle stripped Solstice down to her bra and panties and did the same to herself. She rubbed her hands along Solstice's back, arms and stomach, while placing her daughter's head against her chest.

Elle spoke to Solstice, recalling the struggles her daughter had overcome. "Solstice, remember the physical therapy and Dallas? Remember the braces, the visions and the voice? You can do this, come back to me."

Solstice gasped. She opened her eyes and hugged Elle.

Elle replied, "Thank God. You were so cold." She held Solstice tight, transferring body heat.

Solstice blurted out. "Forty-seven."

"What?"

"It comes after forty-six. I couldn't remember in the water."

"Thank God, you are okay. You counted to forty-six?" Elle ran her hands down her daughter's arms, rubbing them. "I counted to seventy-three before I came back."

"I was stuck at forty-six." Solstice shivered. "How come the water was cold, Mom?"

"I'm not sure. It could be the wind or water depth, or natural springs." Elle replied. She picked up her shirt and rung it out. "It couldn't have been rain water. It hasn't rained in a month at least. I'm hiking the slope to check the bunker door. Stay here."

"How long, Mom?"

"I'm sorry, I'll be gone to a count of a thousand."

Elle dashed up the slope, her squeaking shoes revealing her location long after she faded into the shadows. Solstice counted to seven hundred twenty-nine before the squeaks returned.

"We need to climb the hilltop before dawn breaks, join the line and blend in until the guard gives us the signal."

Solstice asked, "There's a line?" She stood, trying to see the top of the hill.

Elle pointed to her left. "I could see the headlights on the highway." Elle grabbed her shorts and slipped them on. "The cars aren't moving. Thousands of refugees are climbing down from the roadway, heading toward the quarry gate."

"Mom?"

As Elle weighed the options in her mind, she peppered Solstice with instructions. "No matter what, listen to me at the door. Put your clothes on. I know they're wet and cold, but we got to go. Put this water bottle in your sling sack. Are your phone and journal still in there? Did the zip-bag keep them dry?"

"The journal's fine. I can't find the phone."

"Okay. Listen. If we are separated, dash for the door." She rung out her daughter's shirt and handed it to her. "We'll have help. I sent word. A guard, his name is Chief, will help you, I mean us, enter, I know him from the senator's office. Put your leggings on. Once you are inside, trust no one, stay in the shadows and try to find me. Not all the supplies were delivered. Solstice, we need to move now."

THE FALL
M23. Maximus plus twenty-three days. Near the Vermont border.
BAERAN

BAERAN, LANI, COLE, ANNIE, JORDIN AND KAY DROVE WESTWARD, covering one hundred miles in a day on deserted back roads, outpacing the Firegale. The Sheridans, having fallen behind the westward migration of refugees when the truck broke down, no longer suffered from traffic jams. Homes and businesses were mostly abandoned in the small towns they traveled through. Cole knocked on few store fronts, but the doors were simply locked, with notes expressing that their owners hoped to one day return.

One afternoon, near the border of Vermont, Kay made a right turn onto a dirt road and pulled into an isolated campground. The owners, Bob and Sal, an elderly couple, were staying, planning on waiting until the last minute to evacuate. They greeted the Sheridans with a shotgun.

"We're leaving. Sorry," Kay pleaded as she raced to turn the truck around.

"Put that down," Sal scolded her husband. "Bob, it's a family."

Kay stopped the truck.

The old man lowered the weapon. "Listen no one has come through for a few days." Bob took off his hat. "I'm sorry. We've had some trouble. Please stay awhile. Be our guests and get cleaned up. We have hot water."

"What do you think, Cole?" Kay asked. "They've sold me on the hot water."

"Cole replied, "Let's stay the night."

The kids cheered.

Baeran scanned the campsite, excited to explore it. He sighed. He was relieved to have fresh air and some space away from the rest of the family.

—

Later, as Baeran off-loaded camping gear, he asked, "Dad, where's the police? How come no one is telling us what to do?"

"I don't know," Cole mumbled. "There's questions that the government needs to answer. How come the electrical grid failed so fast? What about the policeman and the armed services? Didn't the president say he left men and supplies behind to help everyone? How could a country, that took two hundred years to build, fall in two weeks? I don't know, Baeran."

"Dad?"

"Honestly, I can't accept it. Things fell apart fast. America wasn't prepared for a disaster like this. Your mom and I are worried about food. She's been studying the books we brought about harvesting and planting in the wild."

Baeran asked, "How about traps and hunting, too?"

Cole grabbed a sleeping bag and tent from the truck. "Yes, maybe you can come up with something."

Baeran hesitated. Something in him was excited about living off the land, but a bigger part of him was anxious about the possible loss of accessible food. "They'll be other stores, right?"

"We can't count on anyone anymore." Cole put his hand on Baeran's shoulder. "Enjoy yourself. We'll have a break for a few days. But things are different now. All of you kids are going to have to do things that you never thought you'd have to do."

Kay yelled, "There's beer, Cole!"

Cole smiled, dropping the sleeping bag at his feet. He walked towards the store and Kay.

Baeran stood there watching Cole walk away, absorbing his words. He felt older, but not any wiser.

Kay said, "Come on over Baeran, we'll set up later."

The family had their pick of food from the camp store and spent an ordinary evening around the campfire. In the morning the kids played near the river while Cole and Kay showered.

The Firegale stalled for several days while winds blew eastward. It wasn't until the Sheridans had spent five days with Bob and Sal that the ash clouds returned, and Cole and Kay decided to leave. They used the last of their cash filling the gas cans and their coolers. Baeran took a few moments choosing a handful snacks, coming to the realization that food supplies were dwindling in the advance of the Firegale.

When the family was loaded in the car, Bob and Sal came to wish the Sheridans well. Bob sighed, "Are you sure you won't stay? We enjoyed the company. It's just some ash."

Cole replied, "Are sure you don't want to go?" He turned on the windshield wipers, whisking the ash build-up away.

"Na. We've been here for forty-eight seasons." Bob offered his hand to Cole through the window. "We're going to wait it out."

"Good luck. Be safe. Thank you so much for your hospitality," Cole said, and the family pulled the truck of the campground.

"Where to Cole?" Kay asked.

"We head west and look for more good people and help."

FORSAKEN

M28. Maximus plus twenty-eight days. Eastern Vermont.
BAERAN

BAERAN HELPED THE GROUP STRIKE THE CAMPSITE in the morning. From eastern Vermont, the Sheridans continued to drive westward, along back country roads, but the traffic hindered their progress when they caught up to the caravan. The Sheridans avoided population centers as conditions worsened. Fuel had become scarce, and fights broke out over resources. For several days, Cole and Kay stopped to camp in secluded woods, letting the refugee caravan slip away, in order to conserve fuel. Cole was concerned too, the goods the Sheridans had gotten from Bob and Sal would provide a tempting target for the desperate.

Once the Sheridans assembled the campsite gear, Baeran left to scout the surrounding area. He hiked through the forest and found a neighborhood, observing it from afar. He placed his birch stick at his side and took off his backpack. He put his Wayfarer sunglasses on his head and pulled out Cole's binoculars.

From a woody hill, Baeran scanned the neighborhood. Ash snow covered a half-dozen houses. The fire had crept into this area, before moving on. The Firegale was not linear. It burnt some homes and trees but left others untouched, as if it probed areas with its tentacles, before racing away. The prevailing winds and the fuel type dictated the direction and speed of the flames. The fire could race through brush and grass but linger around bodies of water or in towns and cities that were defended. Old growth, new growth, hard wood and soft wood burnt at different rates. The moisture content of the forests, and the heat of the sun also affected the speed of the Firegale, while embers traveled on the wind with the ash snow, sparking wildfires ahead of the Firegale.

Baeran surveyed the neighborhood with the binoculars. Half the homes were burnt, but the trees around the neighborhood stood. The blaze had been caused by embers drifting ahead of the Firegale. He scanned each home looking for activity; he found a survivor separated from a larger group near the forest. Even from a distance, she didn't appear healthy. Bloody and burnt with ripped clothes, the woman darted from a house to the road, stopping to lean over and grasp a bloody teddy bear. She lingered around a dead boy in the street. She stared at his body, bent down, stroked his hair, and let the teddy bear drop, focusing on the nearest trees. She gazed at a group in the distance, meandering on the forest edge. She jogged to the other side of the neighborhood, slowing her pace to theirs, and the cluster surrounded her. Dazed, she lowered her head and trudged onward with the herd of people.

Baeran stowed his binoculars, as he watched the group fade into the woods. They were filthy, in shock, leprous and stunned, and he remembered the Cyborg had warned on his final broadcast, "Beware of the Dazers."

Baeran returned to the campsite, and when the family gathered together, he described the Dazers. "They were far away, but I wouldn't want to see them up close."

"Are you sure they weren't just dirty?" Cole asked. "What did they look like?"

"Dad, I had the binoculars, I'm telling you they were sick. Their skin was yellow and rotting with open sores."

"Okay. I'm not sure what you saw," Kay admitted. "But they were leaving the town. How about you and I check it out in the morning, and search for supplies?"

"Kay, I'm not sure..." Cole stopped, trying to swallow his words.

Kay glared. "You stay with the truck and the girls." She spread her feet and put her hands on her hips. "Later, you can head to the town with them after Baeran and I get back."

Cole had seen that look many times from his wife when she fought off stereotypes back in the world that once was. Kay was determined, and unswayable once her mind was made up. She was equally capable as Cole in the wilderness and had been a den mother for Baeran in the Boy Scouts. Cole smiled. "You got it, Kay."

The next day Kay hiked back with Baeran and Selene to the neighborhood for supplies, while Cole and the girls stayed with the truck.

From the hill overlooking the houses, Baeran pointed, "Mom it's like the people abandoned the neighborhood."

"Let's look."

Baeran and Kay ambled between the six unburnt homes, scanning each one for supplies. Two hours later they left the

neighborhood and jogged to the truck. The family sat in a circle near the tent, listening to Kay and Baeran.

Baeran told Cole, "It's like a jackpot: food, fuel, clothes, shelter, well water and a half-dozen cars. I opened the gas caps. I can smell the fuel."

Cole replied, "What do you think, Kay?"

"I don't know Cole. Are we looters?" Kay asked. "Didn't the President say..."

Lani interrupted, "We could live in the houses! OMG. There'll be showers. We could fire the generator and heat the water. We could pick one with a fence, so we could keep people out. What do you think? Does anyone else want to live there?"

Jordin and Annie simultaneously blurted, "*Shi!* Yes!"

Jordin laughed and pointed at her sister. "*Eyun!* Jinx!"

Cole rose. "First, we are not living in the neighborhood. Who knows when the Firegale will reappear? We keep moving west, even if they have hot water." Cole saw the frowns on the girls faces and continued, "This is not a democracy. It's more like a benevolent dictatorship, with your mother and I taking turns at the top. But I want to hear everyone's opinion."

Cole grinned at his son, Lani and Kay, and at Jordin and Annie. But the sisters stared at the ground. Cole continued, "But first, I want to deal with an important item. Jordin and Annie, I know I speak for Kay when I say this. You two are family now, like daughters."

Kay scooted over, wedging herself between the two girls, as she put a hand around each. "Cole is right. We love you. I know it's been four weeks since you lost Wàigōng but every day in the wild is like a week. I've come to know you girls as a mother."

"Thank you, Mrs. Sheridan," Annie replied.

"How about Kay and Cole for now and Mom and Dad when you are ready?"

"Mrs. Sher... ahh. Um. Kay. Jordin and I had no one besides Wàigōng." Annie confessed. "We miss him but thank you. We love being with your family. Lani is like a sister, and Baeran and Selene aren't too bad. You too, Mr. Sheridan, I mean Cole."

Jordin added, "*Qunian*—Last year, on parent's day at school, you remember Baeran, when I brought Wàigōng to history class. You know I loved him, but there's nothing like seeing your grandfather, standing with the youthful parents, to show his age. I wish he had died peacefully at home before the Firegale...but I'm grateful he's passed."

Annie gripped her sister's hand.

Kay squeezed the two girls. "It's settled. You're Sheridans." She gleamed at the two girls.

"Sisters! I am so happy." Lani cheered. "I've got big plans, and most involve annoying Baeran."

"Super, spare sisters." Baeran groaned. "Welcome, I'll show you the secret Sheridan hand shake later. Now, how about the supplies back in the neighborhood?"

Jordin giggled. "*Ai ni.* Love you too, Baeran."

Cole stopped the laughter. "Plain and simple, are we looters? Do we head down that path?"

"Cole, can we find a compromise?" Kay offered. "We need the food and the fuel. Baeran saw those people wander away, in a daze, from how he described them. How about being polite thieves? Let's take a bit from each house."

"I can live with polite thievery," Lani jumped in. "If it involves bagels and cream cheese."

"I'd eat some bagels," Annie blurted.

"I agree with your mom," Cole stated. He stood in front of the group, formulating a plan. "We'll take turns ferrying the gear through the woods, starting with fuel first. Keep adding fuel until the truck and gas cans are full. After, we'll fill the water jugs, and search for can goods."

Kay added, "One adult stays at the truck, and the other adult carries the shotgun." Kay hopped to her feet. "This time, Lani, I want you to take a full inventory of the food, so we can ration it."

"Any questions?" Cole asked. "No? Good. Kay and Baeran, you hike to the town first with Jordin and Selene. Baeran, do you know how to siphon the gas from the cars into cans?"

"Dad, the first house on the left had a pump siphon near a lawn mower."

"It would be nicer than sucking on the end of a garden hose." Cole smirked. "Steal the siphon, Baeran."

By nightfall, the group had filled the truck, gas cans and water jugs. Lani estimated, based on serving sizes, the Sheridans had procured a month's rations.

The Dazers never returned to the neighborhood.

TWENTY

M35. Maximus plus thirty-five days. Halfway across Vermont.
BAERAN

BAERAN SPOTTED A WRECK ON THE ROADSIDE, from his seat in the truck, a week after the Sheridan's restocked at the burnt-out neighborhood. Kay pulled over, letting the long lines of vehicles pull away. Along the tree line, a mangled olive-green motorcycle leaned against a tree. Cole examined the vehicle. "Baeran get the hose and gas can and check the tank for fuel."

Baeran removed the gear from the roof rack and brought it to Cole.

"Baeran, can you do this one with the garden hose?"

"Sure, I can try. Why not use the new siphon?"

"Because you need to know how to siphon with a hose, too." Cole replied. Cole place the can on the ground. "We need the elevation." Cole held the bike.

Baeran ran the hose from the gas tank to the gas can.

"Suck the lower end of the hose for a minute and insert it into the can." Cole made a fish face.

Baeran sucked and coughed, "Yuck. Tastes heinous," spitting out fuel.

"Pull the hose out of your mouth sooner next time." Cole laughed.

Lani, Jordin and Annie picked through the debris while Baeran and Cole talked. Lani pulled a pack from under the bike and a notebook dropped out.

Baeran grabbed a water bottle to rinse out his mouth and asked the girls between swishes and spits, "What's that?"

Lani scanned the pages. "It's a logbook from a soldier, Staff Sergeant Baker. They guarded the road from Trenton, NJ. I'll read it, but it's a bit choppy."

"What's it say? "Baeran asked.

"They saw the city burn and people getting sick, dazing, two or three out of every one hundred aimlessly walking. Dazing at the sky, despite the flames and chaos." Lani replied. She flipped through the pages.

"*Jixu*. Go on, continue." Jordin pleaded.

Lani read more, "They decided to go back to their base." Lani flipped through the pages. "Fort Dixon was burnt to the ground, so they headed west to Lincoln." Lani closed the log book. "Dad, how do you think the logbook travelled to halfway across Vermont?"

Cole replied, "I don't know Lani, maybe he sent a soldier northward."

"Why?" Baeran asked.

"Who knows? At least we know the soldiers tried. The motorcycle wreck can't be more than two days old."

"This account is incredible," Lani said. "I want to keep the logbook and add the information to my journal. Mom, what do you think? Like a scrapbook, like when we went to Disney."

"That sounds like a promising idea," Kay agreed. "Like, a record, so we remember what happened."

Baeran opened his pack and pulled out some sketches. "Here add these."

Lani flipped through the stack. "Baeran these are incredible. Here's me! Jordin, Selene, and a Dazer too! I knew you were doing them, but you so rarely give them up. Wow. Jordin, have you seen this? I know it's pencil, but with the shading I can almost see the purple streaks in your hair."

Baeran smiled sheepishly.

The family gathered around Lani and the sketches.

Jordin grabbed hers, stared for a moment and sprung toward Baeran, planting a kiss on his cheek. "*Xiexie*. Thanks, new bro."

Kay looked over Lani's shoulder. "Here's a sketch of the old church, the fire, and wait, who's this? She's beautiful. Baeran Sheridan, do you have a secret girlfriend, or did you have one from before? Did you lose one?"

Baeran replied, "Damn, I didn't mean to include those."

Kay continued, prodding Baeran, "Who is it?"

"Don't laugh. I have no idea. Except sometimes I hear her voice. And I dream about her. Maybe she's not real—just a combination of every pretty girl I've ever met."

Jordin grinned. "Oh. She has my eyes."

"My hair, but lighter." Lani laughed.

Annie grinned, "My smile."

Kay choked out between giggles, "My boobs."

"Enough!" Baeran yelled. "That is the worst, Mom! Everyone drop it, or I take them back."

"No way." Lani insisted. "These are going in the journal."

"Back off girls," Cole interjected. "Baeran doesn't like the attention."

Jordin couldn't resist, holding a sketch of the mystery girl, and added, "*Huo*. Ooh. I bet he'd like some of her attention."

Baeran chased Jordin back to the truck, yelling, "You're as bad as a sister!"

THE VALLEY

M39. Maximus plus thirty-nine days. Western Vermont.
BAERAN

BAERAN STUDIED A MAP FROM THE BACK SEAT in the truck, convinced Cole was lost. The Sheridans, isolated for days having lost the refugee caravan, had driven beyond the edges of the New Hampshire map about ten days prior, and the family's single-sheet USA map didn't show enough detail for Vermont.

When the country road the Sheridans drove along departed from a valley stream, Cole stopped the truck. Ash snow settled onto the truck's windshield. "The wind is changing, and we're losing the stream. Let's refill the water. There might be game along the water's edge."

Kay asked, "How far is the Firegale, Cole?"

"I'm not sure." Cole scanned the hills. "We can't see anything in this valley. It's like being at the bottom of a ski resort, in the lodge, and guessing what the trails are like on the far side of the mountain."

Baeran said, "Dad, look a deer up on the ridge."

Cole eased way into the cab of the truck and grabbed the shotgun. Kay whispered. "Cole, take Baeran, we'll follow you."

Cole and Baeran moved from tree to tree following the deer, tracking up a hill. At the top there was a clearing where the buck stopped. Cole dropped to one knee and lined up his sights. He pulled the trigger. The shot reverberated in the valley. The deer buckled and limped forward before moving out of their view. Cole jumped to his feet.

"Dad, I think you got him!"

"Let's go see."

Baeran and Cole jogged up the hill and stopped at the crest. At their feet, lay the deer, lifeless. They stared into the valley below. Flames blazed on the next closest ridge. Cole yelled, "Run!"

Cole shouted as he reached Kay and the girls. He pointed to the opposite hill. "Up the ridge as fast as you can!"

Behind Cole and Baeran, the blaze crested the hill, following them.

The family climbed the nearest ridge, hoping to outrun the flames. After thirty minutes, Cole stopped the group. He yelled to his frightened family as they caught their breath, "We'll rest for one minute. Baeran, how far is the truck?"

"The truck is at least two ridges away. We shouldn't have tracked the deer this far."

Cole replied, "We can't undo that mistake. We pair up and continue to run. Jordin, you're with me. Kay, you have Annie. Baeran and Lani stay together with Selene."

Cole pointed down the slope at the flames. "We can't out climb the Firegale. We'll head northward parallel to the Firegale until we reach the other side of this crest. Once we have a clear path down, we'll break for the valley. Downhill is our friend."

Kay kneeled, pulling the three girls and Baeran closer. Scanning their frightened faces, she spoke in her calmest voice, "Remember, traverse downhill, and head for a stream or another body of water."

Cole clutched Kay's hand and kissed her while pulling the children closer. "We can do this! Kay, you lead with Annie. Baeran and Lani, with Selene, you're in the middle. Jordin and I will take the rear. Now run! Go. Go! GO!"

Kay took off with Annie close behind, racing northward along the ridge parallel to the Firegale below. Kay chose a path with the fewest branches barring their way, but before long, scratches crisscrossed the Sheridans' faces and hands.

Baeran kept a close eye on the Firegale and monitored its relentless climb. After thirty minutes, he yelled, "Dad, we can't outrun the Firegale! We should break for the valley now."

Cole called for the group to stop, gasping, "Everyone take a sip of water. Baeran's right, we head for the valley now. Jog diagonal down the slope. Keep the Firegale on your left. Move it!"

This time Baeran, Lani and Selene led the way. Lani leapt over fallen logs and stones while Baeran used his birch wood stick to negotiate the rapid descent. Selene's ears flapped as she jogged alongside the brother and sister.

After ten minutes, Lani yelled between breaths, "Baeran, Mom's not behind us. She's off to the right with Annie. Dad and Jordin are farther."

"Lani, keep moving. We'll join with them at the bottom."

"Baeran do you see it? In the valley, there's the stream."

"Got it."

Baeran sprinted, passing Lani, urging her on for several hundred feet, until he heard her scream.

"Baeran!"

He whipped around. Selene left his side, galloping to Lani. He bolted after the dog.

Lani had caught her leg in the twisted debris of an old fallen tree. "My ankle's stuck."

Baeran yanked on Lani's leg for a few seconds. "Don't move while untie your shoe."

Baeran pulled at the laces, blindly untying them while focusing on the flames nearby. Lani wiggled her ankle and fell back when it came loose. Baeran tossed her the shoe. Lani tied it and the two sprinted away.

Baeran and Lani continued diagonally down the hill, but the wind shifted, blowing to their left side. The Firegale raced behind them and appeared on the slope. The blaze irregularly climbed and consumed the trees, racing through pines but slowing down at a stand of older growth hardwood.

Baeran yelled, "Stay out of the pines." He directed Lani and they ran through a grove of oaks. The flames surrounded the siblings on three sides. Baeran grabbed Lani's hand and charged toward the stream. He felt the super-heated air at his back as he traversed the downslope. Like a giant horse shoe, the Firegale raced to encircle Baeran and Lani. Trees fell behind them, as crowns, the tops of trees, exploded, and fire whirlwinds ignited. Baeran pointed to the stream less than a football field away. Fire jumped and sparked around the tree tops like lightning.

Selene raced ahead, plotting a path for the siblings. A hundred feet from the stream, Baeran stumbled, pulling Lani down with him. They rolled down the slope, bumping into each other, and brush, coming to a stop at an overturned maple tree.

Baeran stood, helping Lani. "Get up."

Lani stood, and the siblings raced toward Selene.

Selene reached the stream twenty-five feet ahead of Baeran and Lani.

At ten feet from the stream, Baeran and Lani tumbled, falling toward the embankment. They rolled over the stream bank into the water. Baeran dropped his stick and forced Selene under. Already like bath water, the stream steamed. Selene struggled, gasping for air. Baeran released her and rose to the surface with Lani. Blinding orange flames danced on the stream's edges. "Get down!" Baeran shouted.

Baeran forced Selene under. She struggled to break his grip, scratching and biting him on the forearm. Baeran seized Lani's hand, pulling her to the bottom of the stream, into the pebbles. The water turned reddish-orange; Baeran's blood mixed with the orange fire-haze lighting the stream.

Baeran held Lani and Selene in the stream bed, finding a strength he did not know he had. Drowning, the dog and girl fought Baeran. Lani scratched Baeran in the face and chest while Selene bit Baeran on the arm. Baeran held back the pain as he watched the orange flames dancing on the surface. The scorching stream water caused a wave of pain on his skin, but he held on until the orange glow above the water faded.

Lani, Selene and Baeran broke the surface and coughed, catching their breath. The Firegale climbed the embankment and blazed toward the next ridge.

Baeran warned, "Stay under as much as you can."

After thirty minutes, the Firegale scaled the far side of the ridge. Selene nuzzled Baeran, licking his wound. Baeran and Lani waded to the shallow end, hacking up black phlegm and stream water. Collapsing, Baeran fell to his knees. With his strength ebbing, he made out, "Stay off the shore for a while. The ground will be hot. Keep Selene in the water."

Lani nodded.

Above the burn line, Baeran saw Cole, Kay, Jordin and Annie, safe and frantically waving. When the wind shifted, Cole had ignored his own advice and climbed with Kay, Jordin and Annie, while the Firegale had burnt downward chasing Lani, Baeran and Selene.

Baeran fell to his side into the water. Lani grabbed her brother and kept him from going under, putting his head in her lap. Baeran groaned, "Wait in the water. Watch Selene. They're safe."

As Baeran closed his eyes, Lani replied, "Got them."

Cole shouted from the ridge, "Stay in the water. We'll be down after the ground cools."

"Where would we go?" Lani asked. "I can't even stand."

Baeran nodded.

Two hours later Kay, Cole, Jordin and Annie waded into the stream, gulping water and splashing each other. Kay knelt in the water and kissed Lani and Baeran. "Thank God you're okay."

Kay stood, helping Baeran to his feet, while the girls helped Lani. Jordin asked, "*Tiankong*. Lani, are you okay? Any burns?"

Lani replied, "*Tiankong*?"

"*Tiankong*. It means sky. You know, Lani means sky."

"I have no burns." Lani ran her hands over her body, searching. "But I feel like I sprinted a marathon. Baeran's wiped out, too, and he has bites and scratches."

Cole focused on the scratches on Baeran's face and the bites on his left forearm. "What are these?" Cole asked.

"It's nothing, Dad-,"

Lani interrupted, "Nothing? Dad the marks are from Selene and me. Baeran held us down in the water while the Firegale raced over. Selene kept biting him, and I kept hitting Baeran in the face. We couldn't breathe. We nearly drowned, but it saved us. The Firegale burnt right over the water."

Kay wrapped Baeran in a hug.

Jordin grasped Lani. "*Wo he gaoxing*. I'm so glad you are safe. *Ni yeshi*, you too, Baeran."

Baeran asked, "How come you guys weren't trapped?"

Kay replied, "I don't know why the Firegale burnt toward you two and not up the ridge."

Cole added, "Fire's unpredictable when abundant fuel, like trees, are everywhere. I guess the wind shifted to another slope the Firegale had left untouched." Cole helped Baeran stand, and they all headed back to the truck.

When the Sheridans returned to the car, Kay instructed Annie and Jordin, "Help Baeran, Lani and Selene into the truck while Cole and I find the medical supplies."

Cole and Kay walked toward the tailgate. Kay reached for her husband's hand, while placing another over her mouth. Tears streamed down Kay's face. "Cole, I can't lose our babies. I couldn't live," she said.

"I know, Kay. We can't always protect them," Cole said. "There'll be a time when we have to choose between saving us or the children."

"We choose them," Kay croaked.

Cole took Kay in his arms. They kissed and Cole wiped away her tears.

Kay released Cole and retrieved the medical kit.

After Kay attended Baeran's and Lani's injuries, the family drove westward to the Vermont border. Cole slowed down along a river bank. A dozen families had established a camp.

Kay said, "Let's make some friends."

THE SILVER PENTHOUSE
M16. Maximus plus sixteen days. Lexington, Kentucky.
SOLSTICE

SOLSTICE STOOD IN LINE WITH ELLE AT THE QUARRY, behind the ropes, near the bunker door. The fence by the highway had given way, and a crowd formed behind those with passes. Guards with machine guns flanked the line and blocked the bunker entrance, maintaining order. A guard sought out Elle and motioned her closer. Elle clasped Solstice's hand and they weaved through the throng.

"I can only take one," The guard confessed. "Is this her?"

Elle nodded and hugged Solstice, whispering, "Be silent. Be swift. Stay out of sight. Hide. The bunker people will be desperate at the end. The government did not have time to deliver all the supplies. Go with Chief, the head guard, he'll protect you for as long as it helps him."

The crowd surged, knocking Elle over. The chief stood over Elle, forcing the crowd back, He brandished his weapon, then stooped, reaching for Elle.

Elle grabbed the guard's hand. "Ask him, she's his."

"I'm sorry. I wish I could help you, too," Chief offered. "I will do my best to get her to the senator."

Elle got to her feet and raised the rope. "Ove-lay ou-yay," she stammered to Solstice.

Solstice hesitated under the rope, and Elle shoved her. Solstice stared at her mom, focusing on Elle's ridiculous forced smile, searching for what it hid.

Chief let Solstice pass, holding back the throng. "You sure, he'll want her? You sure he knows?"

"Yes, Chief." Elle replied, as she forced her daughter away with another shove.

The crowd surged as the guards fell back. Solstice struggled against the mob, falling to the ground. Chief lifted Solstice and pulled her into the doorway. He discharged his rifle into the air, warning the crowd. He stepped into the doorway and pulled a lever on the wall. The hydraulic hinges on the door activated, causing the crowd to panic.

As the door closed, Solstice glanced through the crack and she could see Elle, still smiling.

A shot fired and struck Solstice's new guardian before the bunker door sealed shut. Chief clutched his chest and toppled to the ground at Solstice's feet, his life waning. Solstice fell to her knees. She leaned against the door, seeking cover. Chief moaned, "The old man doesn't know you're here."

Solstice reached for the chief, but his head slumped, and blood ran from his mouth onto the cold concrete floor. She stood and kicked the door. She screamed, "Mom!"

Two guards grabbed Solstice with their brawny, gloved hands, and pulled her from the bunker door into the darkened bunker tunnel.

"Put her with the others."

"Which ones? The test subjects or the tunnel rats?"

"The doctor needs a few young ones. Put her with the test subjects."

"Why did the chief help her?"

"I don't know, and it doesn't matter. The doctor is in charge. Process her now and take the chief's body. Clean that blood, too. Senator Adena won't like it."

Solstice squirmed and fell to the ground, breaking the guards' grips. One of the guards reached for Solstice and she kicked him between the legs. He fell, groaning. The second guard struck Solstice in the face. She fell to the ground and back-pedaled on her hands and feet.

"Don't move."

Solstice bumped into the tunnel wall. She grabbed a handful of loose dirt in her left hand, stood and flung it at the guard. He put his hands to his face and Solstice squeezed by him, dashing into the darkened tunnel.

Solstice crept among the shadows until she found an unlocked room. She entered it and closed the door, listening to the guards' chatter as it grew louder.

"Did they close the exit tunnel."

"Yes."

"What happened to the refugees?"

"We trapped at least a thousand in the Hillock Tunnel, but a few hundred made it into the main bunker complex."

"What will happen to them?"

"I'm not sure. It's up to the doctor and senator."

Solstice placed her head against the door, straining to hear more, but the door handle wiggled.

"This one is locked. Find the keys. Doctor Naetersen needs an accurate head count to ration the air, food, and water."

Solstice retreated from the door. She scanned the room. What were her options? She couldn't hide under the bed or desk, or in the closet. The guards would find her in those spots.

The guards banged on the door.

Solstice ran to the back wall. She pressed her shoulders against the cool concrete and slid to the floor. Her shirt caught on the cold metal corners of an air vent, scratching her back.

A guard fumbled with the door handle. "Is this the key?"

Solstice dashed to the desk, searching for a tool. She grabbed scissors and raced back to the vent.

Solstice jammed the scissors into the vent cover, catching and cutting the webbing between her thumb and index finger in the process. She bit her lips. Tears formed in her eyes, and her blood dripped onto the vent cover. She banged her palm against the rounded handle of the scissors, and the vent cover opened.

From behind the door a guard declared, "The knob's jammed."

A second guard barked, "Try the dead bolt."

Solstice removed her shirt and wiped the blood off the open vent. She peered into the duct. Three-foot-by-three-foot ductwork extended upward. She climbed in face first, scratching her exposed stomach. She pressed her back to the duct wall and stood, noticing the open vent near her feet. She crouched down and reached for the metal grate, straining and pressing her face on the cold ductwork until she caught the vent cover edges with her finger tips. She popped the grate back in, crooked. The door opened.

Solstice rose inside the duct and held her breath, hoping the skewed cover would go unnoticed.

The guards paced around the room, opened the closet, and scanned under the bed and desk. The lead guard said, "Room's clear, she must have gone into the one next door," and exited the room.

Solstice exhaled and straightened the vent cover with the scissors. She stood on her tippy-toes and peered into the junction. The tubing widened into three-foot-by-three-foot ductwork branching off into several directions. Cool, fresh air pushed Solstice's hair back. She put her shirt on and climbed into the wider duct before stopping to rest. She laid on her side, stretching on the cold metal ductwork. Sighing with relief, she closed her eyes and slept.

RELINQUISHED

M17. Maximus plus seventeen days. Lexington Bunker Complex.
SOLSTICE

Solstice awoke to the cool-dry wind circulating in the air ducts. She sat, clutching her shins with her head tucked between her knees, desperate to warm her body and wet her parched throat.

Elle had told her, on their walk to the quarry, that the government constructed at least two hundred bunkers across the country, in the 1940s and 1950s, to protect significant government personnel like senators, judges, Presidents, and cabinet members.

Elle warned that once the bunker door closed, it wouldn't open for a long time. Her mom had described the one-hundred-day protocol, but Solstice had forgotten the details.

Solstice explored the dully lit three-foot-by-three-foot metal ventilation system, crawling down the galvanized steel horizontal shafts. She found the cold on the first night intolerable and set about to find a blanket. She tested the strength of the tubing every few feet by extending her hand forward. She estimated that the duct hung eight to ten feet off the ground, suspended from the rock ceiling.

Solstice found a down chute and followed it to the lower level. She waited behind the metal grate, making sure the room was empty before she popped open the vent cover. She crawled into the room. Six washer and dryer stack units were arranged along the wall near the grate. She found a chemically sanitized blanket but could not quench her thirst. She turned a valve on a utility sink, but no water flowed.

Solstice remembered hearing the guards say that water was being rationed. She clutched the blanket and hurried back to the vent. She hesitated a moment. *Is this the best way?* She heard a voice down the hall and crawled into the ductwork. She replaced the vent cover and pulled herself into the main duct line. Wrapping the blanket around her shoulder, she leaned against the ductwork wall. "Eww. I hate the smell of the pine disinfectant. I hate wool. Why, Mom? What am I supposed to do?" She took the blanket off her shoulders and flung it down the ductwork.

"Stupid blanket. Stupid windstorms. Stupid Firegale. Stupid bunker. I hate you all. You too, Mom. Why did you leave me?"

UNKERBAY

M18. Maximus plus eighteen days. Lexington Bunker Complex.
SOLSTICE

SOLSTICE LAID ON HER BACK staring at the silver ductwork, shivering. Cool dry air blew across her body. The stress from her first two days in the bunker brought the headaches and flashes back. She crawled to the closest loud fan and despite her parched throat she sang.

"Unkerbay Omplexcay"

You worked off in D.C.
The wind's blowing, the Firegale's burning
Alone at the condo it's me
My world's spinning, now it's turning

Made the call
Leave work, Mom, come home to me
Take the plane
Time to go, it has to be

Ditched the Scout
We did along the way
Hiked the trail to
Unkerbay omplexcay

Doctor and senator
Those men can't see
High above in the ducts
Crawling, it's me

THE BURNT SUNSET

Fire's burning
My poor Lexington
Riots and the dazed
City's broken, done

Ditched the Scout
We did along the way
Hiked the trail to
Unkerbay omplexcay

Elle, where are you?
You left me at the door
Sacrificed yourself
Oh, Mom, what was it for?

My back, my head
They hurt so much, they ache
Can't take it anymore, Mom,
Soon, so soon, I'm gonna break

Ditched the Scout
We did along the way
Hiked the trail to
Unkerbay omplexcay

Melody's back!
Singing, begging to stay
Lost you, Mom, at the
Unkerbay omplexcay

276

M20. Maximus plus twenty-two days. Lexington Bunker Complex.
SOLSTICE

SOLSTICE PEERED DOWN THROUGH AN OVERHEAD VENT. She watched the doctor as he wrote in his notebook. The cover had the imprint USMC. In his right hand, he held a pencil, and with the other he held back his wavy black hair. Clean-shaven with gray near his ears, the rugged and muscular Doctor Naetersen, appeared comfortable at whatever he set his mind on doing. Solstice lay on her belly and read the doctor's notes from her perch.

276 people. Unsupportable population for a bunker this size. The senator let too many in.

But not her mom.

Over a thousand tricked into the Hillock tunnel. Trapped by locked doors on both ends and left for dead. The rest of us are confined in the bunker to ride out the Firegale and the riots. At least we have food and water, but not much. The timer is already set. No override until after one hundred days. Standard protocol requires two primaries to override. There are forty-eight guards stationed here but twelve are already dead.

Naetersen lowered his pencil. He had calculated the numbers twice. "Months to go, and about two hundred and fifty must die."

He continued writing in his notebook, jotting down ideas.

Disposal? Incinerator? Options: disease, crowd control, suffocation, starvation. Controlled die-off. Three deaths every two days are needed to prevent the supplies from running out. The Hillock tunnel is sealed for at least one hundred days. Segregate those who forced their way in: The UDs. Could be solution to Dazer pathogen question.

Knock, knock.

LBC

M20. Lexington Bunker Complex.
SOLSTICE

Solstice inched her way back from the vent opening. Her throat was parched, but she focused on the man entering the room. The doctor closed his notebook. "Senator Adena, come in, sit, please."

Solstice remembered the senator from an old picture. The silver fox, Elle had once called him, tall with flowing silver hair and piercing blue eyes, he wore a coat and tie.

Naetersen spoke when Adena sat. "I'll get straight to the point. Before the Firegale and riots, three hundred and twenty million people lived in the United States. About eighty percent lived in cities. This is where the real trouble is. The air toxicity over our urban areas, combined with a massive release of spores, is affecting our urban population."

The senator leaned onto the table as his left-hand shook. "Doctor, toxicity and spores?"

"The tremors are getting worse."

Adena ignored Naetersen's comment. "Tell me about the air problem."

"Toxicity—building materials, chemicals, human remains, and many other things are burning, releasing ash and poison into the atmosphere, and yes, spores. Trees and plants release spores in response to fire. The combination has created a pathogen that is causing failure in the body's filtering organs, like the kidneys, liver, intestines, lungs, skin, or lymph nodes. Single or multiple organ failure is the cause of the psychosis."

"Damn."

Naetersen continued. "I need to examine the affected. About

two percent of the urban population—if we extrapolate that out, five point two million people—have become docile and are congregating. For a lack of a better term, those people are herding. In fact, they've lost their ability to converse. They're stunned and dazed."

"Haven't the cities been evacuated?"

"Not fast enough. I estimate half our urban population will die from riots, fire, panic, exposure, disease, malnutrition, and thirst in the next thirty days. We can expect the countrywide elimination of our urban populaces within six months."

"Do you have everything you need to begin the tests?"

"Not yet."

Adena asked, "Regardless of what happens outside, we are safe in the bunker, correct?"

"No. If we manage to remain undiscovered, we will exhaust the fuel, food, and water supply, or our carbon dioxide scrubbers will fail."

"Doctor how long is the timer set for?"

"One hundred and twenty days, but together you and I can override the system and shut the timer off after one hundred days. But we'll be dead long before if things don't change. The Department of Defense designed food stores and life support systems for an army platoon, not the three hundred plus we have in the complex. Not to mention the thousand refugees we locked in the Hillock tunnel. We need to address the population problem in the bunker complex."

The senator stood. "Are you sure?"

"Yes, we need to pick soon."

Solstice gasped and crawled back from Naetersen's room vent. Considering the war, riots, and fire, her new home wasn't too bad. She'd hide, bide her time, and find a way out when Lexington was safe. The Fort Hillock tunnel would be her escape route. But first, Solstice needed to find water. It had been days since she had a drink.

DAZE

SEASCAPER

M45. Maximus plus forty-five days. Western Vermont.
BAERAN

BAERAN AND LANI SAT BY THE CAMPFIRE with Selene, while their parents spoke to other families around the campsite. Lani asked, "Are you okay? You've been quiet since the valley fire."

Baeran replied, "I'm fine."

"Seriously?" Lani asked. "You haven't spoken in days."

"I'm drained. I've been dreaming about the Firegale."

"Have you written down your thoughts? That helps."

Baeran kicked an ember back into the fire. "Says who?"

"My guidance counselor in high school."

"Is he like a therapist?"

"*She's* a person who helps you organize your thoughts."

"Like a therapist, for high schoolers."

Lani stood, hands on her hips. "Whatever Baeran. Fine. But it worked for me. I was nervous the whole first week of freshman year. Annie remembers. But Ms. Neiman helped me and encouraged me to write in a journal. I still do. But nevermind. You're set."

"Chill, Lani. Sit. I'll try it."

Baeran opened his sketch pad and jotted down his observations on the back page, while Lani stoked the campfire.

The Firegale haunts my dreams, as a burnt orange sky.

Refugees are crowding the road. Travel is slow.

Burnt out vehicles and bodies litter the road.

We wait for days until traffic clears. People are running out of gas. Abandoned cars. Abandoned gear. Abandoned lives.

I exercise the dog and scoop the poop. Don't let Mom step in it.

Everyone is searching. Seeking. Seascaping. Escaping from

the fire born near the sea. Dad's finding other searchers. He calls them "Seascapers." People seeking a way out, an escape. People seeking safety. People seeking a new life. People seeking Lincoln, Nebraska. We are waiting for more Seascapers. Dad wants to team with other families. Too many jackasses and thugs around.

Stores are running out of food. Money's about worthless. There is no more meat. We must learn how to hunt.

The family took a day off from the unending super-slow drive to nowhere, jumping off the panicwave ride.

There was one tiny pocket of cell phone coverage left, and I found instructions on how to construct traps. The family spent a day downloading apps, maps, and survival tips. We broke the Internet and the cell towers. There's no reception now and radio is gone too. We are all missing the chatter.

The generator keeps our phones charged. Everyone has their phones in airplane mode, no Wi-Fi or Bluetooth. We check once a day. Quickly. Rumor is the Japanese, Mexicans, and Germans are tracking us with our phones to maximize bombing runs.

Dad says that's stupid talk. There are no dumb questions, he says, but plenty of dumb comments. He says the war, if it exists, will bog down on the West Coast and in Texas. He says don't worry. Attrition and standstills will protect us. No way anyone will bomb this part of the country. Why bother? The Firegale and the riots are doing the work for our enemies.

Why would Japan, Germany, and Mexico attack us? Resources, unfair trade practices, worldwide influence, immigration, unemployment—you name it. Old grudges die hard, Dad says. Is it true? No way to know, but he says he wouldn't want to be on the west coast or in Texas. No way Dad could know about the war, but I bet the government knows in Lincoln.

Playing it cool. Got my Wayfarers on. Dad's playing it cool, too. But beer has run out in this part of the country. Dad swore beer shortages alone will cause riots. Thank God for Jack Daniel's whiskey. Dad traded his cot for it. Money well spent. Stuff is the new money. Dad wants Coke, popcorn and Cheez-Its for a movie night on a 4.7-inch display.

What could I trade? I have nothing except a baseball glove and *bat, phone, clothes, my old Boy Scout birch stick. I'm working with birch stick. Tossing. Twirling. Training. Selene's in on it, too.*

People are becoming sick and wandering away. Like the lady in the burnt-out neighborhood. Everyone makes lists now. Lists in their heads. Lists in their notebooks. Lists because they are afraid to forget and go crazy like the Dazers. They make lists of what they want, what they need, and where they can find it.

Been drawing the dream-voice girl and the sun non-stop. Remembered her name this morning. It only took forty-five days. She is Solstice. She sang that in the second verse of her song. Knowing that makes her real. Remembered, burn, daze and evolve from the song, too. The burn is the Firegale and the daze is the Dazers. What is evolve?

Lani interrupted Baeran's thoughts, "Well, is it working?"

"Yes. Lani, you're not evolving, are you?"

"Sure, my opinions do all the time. For example, since you agree with me about writing your thoughts down, I'm thinking that you are not such an idiot anymore."

BORDER CAMP

M50. Maximus plus fifty days. On the border of Vermont and New York.
BAERAN

BAERAN AMBLED ALONG A STREAM WITH KAY, noticing at least two dozen families spread out along the embankment.

"Anyone familiar?" Baeran asked.

Kay replied, "The big blond guy and the sidecar twins."

That night, Kay and Cole invited the two families to join them on the trip to Lincoln, Nebraska. Around the campfire, the stocky guy with yellow hair stood. His ginormous son sat near him, his jet-black hair matching his mom's. "I'm L.J. This is my wife, Tara and my son, Parker. We're from Dover, New Hampshire. We're low on food and fuel, but we have the truck, and two ATVs."

The two women with the twin motorcycles and twin daughters spoke next. "I'm Susan. This is Judy, my wife. Our daughters are Aileen and Megan. We appreciate the offer, but..."

Judy, straightened her glasses and pushed back her long brown hair. "Susan, how about we give it a night?"

She glanced at Judy, read her expression. "All right."

After the new families completed introductions, Lani stated, "Mom, I'm going to hang with the girls in the tent."

Kay beamed as her girls led Aileen and Megan into the tent.

Baeran sat next to Parker and asked, "What's up?"

Parker replied, "Do you have any games on your phone?"

"I have Super Kong Bros 9."

"Let me see it."

Once everyone sat next to the campfire, Cole commented, "Nice to see more Seascapers."

Kay leaned forward. "That's our name for people like ourselves heading to Lincoln. We left Portsmouth to avoid the Firegale. We escaped from the sea."

"Wanderers, the forsaken, escapees, refugees, exiles, the departed, drifters—we've heard the names," Judy stated.

"I like Seascapers," Tara offered, "since it started with that coastal storm, Maximus, and the dry lightning."

L.J. agreed. "Me, too, but what about the other guys, the thugs?"

"We hid from them on the road," Judy said. "They call themselves Jackers and are moving west also. They are joining together and strengthening as they pick off the weaker groups."

"What do you call those people who have lost it?" Tara asked.

Baeran replied, "The guy on the radio called them Dazers."

Susan pushed her shoulder-length pre-mature gray behind her ears, highlighting her hazel eyes. "What are we supposed to do?"

Cole replied, "I'm weary of running."

"What would the army or firefighters do?" Kay asked.

Judy replied, "I saw an episode once on The Weather Channel where firefighters dug in, allowing a fire to pass over."

"What if we dug in and let the Firegale pass over?" Cole exclaimed.

Susan stood. "You can't be serious. It would be impossible to bury our supplies, let alone us and the vehicles."

"Let's assume we could do it," Cole countered. "The Firegale would burn over us and scatter those Jackers."

Susan raised her voice, "Yes, but even if the Firegale never doubled back, our resources would be consumed in the flames."

Cole said, "We can't run forever. We're long past hoping the Firegale will burn out on its own."

"What if we hid in a concrete building?" Baeran asked.

"No, there are still too many flammable materials in those structures." Cole replied, "We need for the Firegale to pass over us while we hide underground or underwater."

"You can't be serious," Susan groaned.

L.J. countered, "Back off Susan, let Cole speak."

"Shut it, L.J.," Susan yelled.

Kay held up a calming hand. "Let's take it easy and talk this out."

"I have an idea." Baeran offered. "We had a close call a few days ago. We survived the Firegale for a minute in a stream-,"

Susan interrupted, "I'm glad you're fine, but a minute is not long enough. You were lucky."

"What if we did both?" Baeran countered. "We could be underground and in water. What if we hid under a bridge?"

Parker mumbled, "Assbrain."

"You got a better idea?" Baeran asked. "Hand me my phone. I saw you creeping through my photos."

"Here you go, Assbridge."

Ignoring the boys, Cole said, "We would have water at our feet, protection over our heads, and river rock to build the sides."

Judy added, "Based on what you told us about the valley fire that trapped Baeran and Lani, depending on the wind or the foliage, the Firegale can surge without notice. Eventually, we won't be able to outpace the Firegale."

The group voted, with the results being nineteen for hiding under a bridge and two against. Hours later, after Baeran's idea won the day, the group shared food around the campfire, but Susan and Parker stared daggers at Baeran for the rest of the evening.

JACKASSES

M52. Maximus plus fifty-two days. Border Campsite.
BAERAN

BAERAN, PARKER, COLE AND L.J. LEFT THE BORDER CAMP in the morning,
to look for a bridge. In the afternoon near an old railroad depot,
Baeran found a stone railroad overpass. The Vermont park service
had repurposed the rail line as a hiking trail. The bridge ran flat with
the forest floor while a stream flowed along a steep embankment.
L.J. noted the location on the map, and the group headed to the
border campsite.

About halfway back, L.J. signaled for Cole to stop.

Cole and L.J. pulled the ATVs off the trail and shut them off.

Cole asked, "What is it?"

"Over deeper in the woods, look, Jackers." L.J. pointed.

Cole pulled out his binoculars. "I see bikes and men, at least
two dozen, and three bikes are running. We can't hear them, so
they can't hear us."

"We'll have to find another way back," L.J. said.

Cole instructed the boys, "Stay with the gear, while L.J. and I find
another way to the border campsite."

"And stay out of trouble," L.J. warned.

Parker pleaded, "Dad, I want to see."

"Stay with the ATVs and Baeran." L.J. replied. "Watch each
other's backs. Cover the ATVs with downed branches. Stay out of
sight. We'll take cover behind the hill to the right. You won't be able
to see us, but neither will the Jackers."

Cole and L.J. left the trail and dashed into the woods.

Parker waited until he could no longer see the dads. "This sucks.
I'm leaving."

Baeran said, "Come on. Let's wait."

"Don't be such a candy-ass."

"I'm staying here, I'm not stupid."

"Fine, see ya."

Baeran sat next to the ATVs, alone, with his thoughts. *Damn, what was his problem? We've known each other for like twelve hours. I'm a candy-ass? You're an idiot. What's your plan? March into the Jacker group and make friends? Prick.*

Baeran hadn't finished the argument in his head before he saw Parker approach, with a knife to his throat.

A fat Jacker sneered at Baeran. "Step back from the ATVs. Lie face down on the ground."

The second Jacker released Parker and kicked him in the butt, knocking him over. "You lay down, too."

To Baeran's left, Cole crashed through the underbrush. Shotgun raised, he struck the fat Jacker in the neck. The man fell over, stunned. The second Jacker hit Baeran in the face, and he drifted in and out of consciousness, catching only glimpses of the fight. Cole tackled the second Jacker and subdued him, but the fat Jacker knocked L.J. to the ground. Parker attacked L.J.'s assailant with a stone, smashing it into the Jacker's skull. Parker stood and screamed, until he vomited on the bloody stone.

Later, at the border campsite, Baeran awoke, and saw Kay and Lani glancing down at him. His head rested in Cole's lap. Ten feet away, L.J. and Parker argued. Baeran rubbed his eyes. "Dad, where are we?"

"Take it easy. We are back at the campsite."

"What happened?"

"L.J. and I took on your abductors, but Parker had to save his father," Cole replied. "He killed a man."

"What are they arguing about, Dad?"

"How you boys were captured, whether Parker should have killed the man, and if I should have let the other man live," Cole said. "I knocked him out and tied him to a tree."

"What are we going to do now?"

Cole replied, "We leave soon, before the Jackers find our camp. The ash snow is back, and the wind has shifted. The Firegale can't be far behind. We need to construct the shelter."

"Why don't we escape in the truck?"

"We don't have the fuel, and we can't outpace the Firegale."

"Okay." Baeran sat up.

"Give Parker space." Cole patted Baeran on the back. "He's convinced you caused the fight."

"Dad, he charged off on his own, and he gave me up."

"I figured that happened. His story didn't ring true. But stay away from him. He's a hot-head. Rest for a while, the adults will watch the campsite tonight. Tomorrow we'll find more help."

CAMPFIRE TALES

M54. Maximus plus fifty-four days. Border Camp.
BAERAN

BAERAN SAT WITH LANI BY THE CAMPFIRE while two new families introduced themselves. The Firegale was visible to the east for the first time in days. Small amounts of ash whirled in the wind. The short guy with the gray hair rose. "Hi. I'm Mitch. This is my son Ethan. We're from east Vermont. We've been on the road for two days, which is enough for me. We brought with us an ATV and moped. I'm not sure how Cole and Kay and their family have survived for a month and a half."

Cole responded, "We were lucky. We're glad to have you."

Mitch replied, "People make their luck; you've done well."

Next a redhead stood. "Hi I'm Heather. We spent the last ten days hiking here. This is my son Deven and my daughter Reese."

"Dudes." Deven smiled.

Heather's freckles, neck-length auburn hair and tiny frame made her appear years younger than her age. Her green eyes watered as she spoke. "I am so glad to see people with trucks and supplies. And to be honest, I'm glad to see single men. We come from a small town and there wasn't any action..."

Reese yelled, "Mom!"

"Sorry. I'm nervous. Deven's strong. Reese is smart."

"I'm the smart one," Deven joked.

With a straight face, Reese said, "I'm the strong one."

Heather grinned. "We have no gear, but I have skills. I'm a waitress. I attended night school to be a nurse and I worked as a life guard in high school after cheerleading practice. I can fix you dinner, bandage a cut, or do a cheer. I'm sorry. I'm nervous-,"

"OMG! Sit Mom," Reese shouted.

Heather sat as the adults and kids laughed. Kay rose. "Welcome, Heather, Deven, Reese, Mitch and Ethan."

Baeran read over Lani's shoulder. He watched her record the following in her journal:

Cole & Kay—Lani 16, Baeran 14, Annie 16, Jordin 14

Susan & Judy—Aileen 12, Megan 12

L.J. & Tara—Parker 17

Mitch—Ethan 14

Heather—Deven 15, Reese 18

Cole stood. "Kids, the adults want to talk about tomorrow. We'll be over by trucks."

"Who wants to have their hair done in the tent?" Annie opened the tent flap.

The twins responded, "Meeeeeee!"

Annie smirked at Jordin. "It's nice to have girls who appreciate my talents."

Parker stood and stumbled over Baeran's outstretched legs. He kicked Baeran in the foot. "Watch it, assholio." Before Baeran responded, Parker said, "I'm smashing crap down by the stream. Who's in?"

Ethan said, "Sounds good," and slipped away with Parker.

"*Shenme yu Paike?*" Jordin asked, "What's with Parker?"

"It's the bruises," Baeran replied. "We both had our asses kicked bad the other day in the woods by Jackers."

Lani asked, "Is it true he caused the fight? Who does that?"

"The Jackers had a knife at his neck," Baeran lied.

"*Weisheme?*" Jordin asked, "Why did Parker leave the ATVs?"

Deven leaned forward. "Dude, wait, what happened?"

Baeran told Reese and Deven about the Jacker attack.

"Parker sounds like a jerk," Reese whispered, "but I wouldn't piss him off. He's full of himself."

"More like full of crap." Baeran blurted.

Lani, Jordin, Reese, Deven and Baeran burst out laughing. Baeran laughed so hard he fell backward off his log seat.

"Baeran be quiet, he's back." Lani said.

Baeran landed on a pair of feet.

Parker stood behind Baeran, glaring, "Get off my feet, Asstwerp."

Parker kicked Baeran and stomped off with Ethan.

Baeran sprung back into a sitting position. "Crap."

The five teens burst out laughing.

When the laughter died down, Jordin and Lani told Reese and Deven about their escape from Portsmouth.

"What's your story?" Lani pried.

"We're halflings." Deven and Reese said simultaneously.

Lani giggled. "What?"

"Half-siblings." Reese put her arm around Deven.

Deven rolled up his sleeve. "Check it out. We have matching watches."

"Our dads served together as Rangers." Reese added.

Baeran asked, "What happened to your fathers?"

"Reese's dad died during a deployment," Deven replied. "His best friend from his platoon—my future dad—came to see our mom about a year later, and they got it going on, Marvin Gaye style.

"What?" Baeran snickered.

Deven quipped, "You know—the sexual healing."

Jordin and Lani burst out laughing.

"The Army deployed my dad after his visit." Deven continued, "Months later, KIA too, but after Mom sent word to him about me. My mom called me Deven, after Reese's dad, since he brought us together."

"I am sorry for you both." Lani put her hands to her face.

"Total bummer right. But at least the dads are hanging out together in the sky. It's cool," Deven said.

Reese asked, "Can I see your journal Lani?"

"Sure."

Reese flipped through the pages. "You did this? You've got notes on people, supplies, your route here and even how to build and make things. And the sketches, are those yours too?"

"The sketches are Baeran's. He gives me about one per week. He saves some for himself too. He's got a mystery dream-girl he doesn't want anyone to know about."

"Lani, you are the worst sister, ever." Baeran grinned. "You two better watch out. Lani will want your life story."

Lani countered, "Once Baeran's head clears, he'll want to sketch you, too. Did you know he can draw? He can draw like I can write. Baeran observes people, finding the spaces."

"Whoa. Like what space are we talkin' 'bout?" Deven asked.

Baeran replied, "The space between who you are and how people see you. That's where the truth is. That's your essence, who you are."

117

Deven, Jordin, Reese and Lani looked at Baeran.

Baeran said, "Wait till I sketch you. You'll see. It's like looking in a mirror but deeper. I'll focus on one or two features. You'll be surprised what I pick up."

The teens passed around the journal, and talked into the night, swapping stories until they fell asleep by the campfire.

In the morning, Jordin, Deven and Reese left to do chores while Lani and Baeran sat by the campfire. Selene laid at their feet.

"I hear Mitch wants to talk to you," Baeran said.

Lani replied, "I already talked to him. I'm adding to my journal. Writing down everyone's stories. Mitch came by this morning. Ethan plays hockey like you."

"Ethan told me that. But he's so tight with Parker," Baeran replied. "I'm not sure I want to be around Parker that much. We have our own friends. There's something about Deven and Reese that I'm drawn to, like I am with Jordin."

"I know what you mean about Jordin," Lani said. "It's like we are more than friends."

Baeran scooched closer to Lani. "Like sisters?"

"Yes, but there is something more." Lani deflected. "But what about your mystery girl? Can I see your latest sketches of her?"

Baeran handed her a pile of sketches. "Okay, but I want these back."

"Is that a tunnel? Is she in a box? Is she trapped?"

Baeran replied, "Honestly, it doesn't look good, does it? I hope she's okay. The thing is, I don't see her with my waking mind. These are things I see in my dreams. I don't know where they are coming from. Don't freak, but she's real. Sometimes, I hear her voice on the wind."

"Baeran, everyone is a little tired. You're day-dreaming."

Lani made a goofy face, twirling her fingers near her ears.

"There's more, Lani. I feel weird. I've got this tingling in my fingertips. Like static electricity trying to get out."

"That is weird." Lani grabbed Baeran's fingertips. "Nope. I feel nothing."

"I told Mom about the tingling." Baeran confessed, pulling his hands away.

Lani, having gone too far with the teasing, apologized. "I'm sorry. What did she say, Baeran?"

"She says it's Peripheral Neuropathy."

"What?"

Baeran wiggled his fingers. "Nerve tingles. Remember that time I smacked my head on the boards in hockey? And I was down on the ice for five minutes. I felt like my whole body was zapped with electricity. I felt zingers moving up and down my body."

Lani shivered, shaking her back, recalling the hit. "Yes," Lani replied, scowling as she recalled the incident. "Mom freaked out." It had been a blindside check, slamming Baeran into the boards." Kay had run to the glass and kept banging on it. Finally, she ran to the door behind the bench and the coach let her onto the ice.

Baeran grabbed a stick and tossed it. Selene jumped up from her nap and chased it.

"I know, so embarrassing. The game was stopped, a hundred fans staring at me, and Mom runs onto the ice."

Lani asked, "But the nerve tingles?"

Selene came running back holding the stick between her teeth. "Drop it."

Selene wagged her tail. Baeran gripped the stick, wrestling it from her mouth.

"Mom says I pinched a nerve in my neck when I hit." Baeran continued.

"Baeran, that was over a year ago."

He tossed the stick. "She says Peripheral Neuropathy can get worse. Maybe she figures the camping and laying on the ground is aggravating my neck and causing the tingles."

"But you don't think so?"

Selene ran back, skidding to a stop and smacking into Baeran's chest. "Easy girl." Baeran patted Selene. "Mom's wrong. My neck only hurt for two weeks after the boarding check. This is different. I'm changing somehow."

"That's called puberty." Lani replied, grinning.

"You are the worst sister ever!"

Baeran gripped the stick and tried to pull it from the dog's mouth.

Lani apologized. "Sorry. Want to hear L.J. and Tara's story?"

"No, Parker's the worst. How about Mitch's?"

Lani handed the journal to Baeran and watched him absorb her words. After a few minutes, Baeran asked, "How did you get him to reveal he was mad at his dead wife. Who admits that?"

"People want to tell their stories," Lani said, "even the parts they aren't quite proud of. It helps them relieve the burden of guilt."

"But you're a kid!"

"Sixteen."

"Still a kid."

Lani smiled, "You told me about your mystery girl, the dreams and the tingles, and I wasn't even trying. There's a lot of guilt going around about how the world went to shit and the adults dropped the ball, not to mention the uncontrolled fire and the Dazers. Plus, people are afraid they will be forgotten. There's no more social media, likes are few and far between, and so are friends. People are desperate to tell their stories."

"I haven't had anything good to read in months." Baeran complained. "Got anything more?"

"Sure, turn the page, Susan & Judy are next."

Selene dropped the stick, having lost Baeran's attention.

Baeran read the next account, stopping to make comments. "They know about the war? Dad wasn't sure if that was true."

"Susan and Judy were able to get radio longer than us."

Baeran let this sink in. He raised his eyes to the wind in the treetops.

"Lani, have you told Dad or Mom the war's not a rumor?"

Lani stood. "Yes. They didn't say much, and they were disappointed I found out. Dad insisted it didn't change the plan to find Lincoln once we let the Firegale go by. Mom frowned. The worry shows on her, she's lost weight and has those circles under her eyes."

"I know." Baeran rose. "I'm worried about Mom too."

THE CAVE

M57. Maximus plus fifty-seven days. Border Campsite.
BAERAN

BAERAN AND THE SEASCAPERS PACKED UP THEIR GEAR after ash snow fell on the campsite overnight. With the Firegale on the horizon, the group left for the overpass. They rode in pairs along a woodsy trail until they found the old railroad crossing.

As the Seascapers parked and examined the bridge, Cole read their disappointed expressions. He addressed the group, "OK, it's narrow. The trucks won't fit. The best we can hope for is to save the gear and the ATVs and bikes. I'd keep driving westward, if we have enough fuel. This is our best option."

Mitch responded, "Agreed."

"Let's build stuff," L.J. added.

Cole dove in. "Mitch and L.J., let's move the four ATVs under the overpass along the westward wall. Susan and Judy, place the motorcycles close to the ATVs. Remove the side cars.

"Parker, Baeran, Ethan, and Deven, strip material from the old depot to build a shelf to place the two mopeds, the ATV trailer and two sidecars on top of the ATVs and motorcycles.

"Kay, Heather, and Tara, we need a full inventory of the food, and we need the water jugs filled.

"Lani, Reese, Jordin, Annie, Aileen, and Megan construct a shelf for the eastern wall to hold the gear. Build it two feet high.

"Mitch, L.J., and I will work on water and air intake and exhaust ports once we set the ATVs into place.

"Kay, once your group is finished, build a floor using material salvaged from the depot. Parker, when you're done with the western shelf, supply Kay's group.

"Lani and Reese, once your shelf is complete, work with the other families to unload their gear and place it on the shelf."

Mitch added, "Kay, your group should add holes in the new floor, so we can draw water as needed."

"Got it," Kay replied.

"Now, if you have any questions," Cole continued, "Ask L.J.. He builds homes and will be able to answer structural questions."

The Seascapers removed corrugated metal siding and pipes from the railroad depot station. Kay, Heather and Tara laid the pipes perpendicular to the stream, with the metal siding on top, creating a floor. The group made two holes in the flooring to provide easy access to the stream. L.J., Mitch and Cole rolled the ATVs and the motorcycles into the west side of the cave, under a wide sturdy shelf. The Seascapers stacked the mopeds and sidecars on the shelf. The girls laid the sleeping bags and clothes on top of the bench on the east side, and the generator, propane heater, and tools underneath it.

The next morning Cole, Mitch and L.J. used a winch on L.J.'s truck and the plow on Cole's truck to roll into place two knee high boulders on the north side. The Seascapers placed a flat rock on top of the boulders to create an arch with an opening of one foot by one foot, ensuring the stream continued to flow into the cave. Cole, L.J. and Mitch built a similar arch on the south side of the cave. On the second day, the group used the trucks to push rocks toward both sides of the overpass opening, placing the hefty rocks at the base of the mound. Later the Seascapers placed river stone, and sand on the top of the pile to finish the walls.

Cole helped Baeran install a pipe high along the wall as an exhaust port. They secured the two pipes with railroad ties.

Baeran whispered, "How come we won't suffocate, Dad?"

"The cave won't be airtight. Our concern is the carbon dioxide we exhale and not the oxygen we inhale."

"What about smoke pouring in through the pipes?"

Cole responded, "The cave is ten-feet below the forest floor in the stream bed. The smoke will be high above the cave."

Mitch interrupted, out of breath. "Cole, the Firegale's close. We have half a day at best."

"Let's finish walling off the north side and place the stone to finish the south side into the cave." Cole said.

At dusk on the second day, Baeran placed the last rock in the south wall. Within thirty minutes, black smoke clouds yielded to the orange glow of the Firegale.

H$_2$O

M22. Maximus plus twenty-two days. Lexington Bunker Complex.
SOLSTICE

SOLSTICE SAT IN THE BUNKER DUCTWORK, straining her eyes in the faint light. Four days prior, her water supply ran out. She had done the quarry swim with five things in her sling sack: her phone and lyricbook in a zip-bag, a water bottle, and a pink Sharpie. The phone didn't survive the swim to the shoreline. The water lasted about a day. She longed for a drop of water to quench her thirst, but her mind wandered, and she struggled to focus on the task.

Where's the water? The cafeteria, bathroom and laundry room have sinks, but the laundry room had no water, *only imitation pine scent. How about lemon?* Naetersen had the water shut off. *Solstice checked when she found the blanket, but the blanket's long gone. Where is it?*

No, where are the rooms? Not the blankets. Solstice needed a map, but she couldn't see anything. Unless she kneeled near an overhead vent. *Overhead to the occupants but underknee to Solstice.* To draw a map, Solstice needed to be able to keep track of distances. *Seconds or crawl-steps? No use shoes.* Measure distance with her shoes. *Because they were feet.* Solstice removed her left shoe. Size 6. *How long is a six? In inches? What's an inch? Worm. About the distance from the joint in her thumb to the end of her nail. How many thumb inches in a shoe? Feels like nine. Can't see crap. Feel is the new sight.* One shoe equals nine inches equals three quarters of a foot. *What's a standard unit in ductwork?* Solstice laid on her back, feeling and stretching. Every one and half body lengths, Solstice felt a seam. *One section of ductwork is how many shoes?* Solstice placed the heel of her shoe down

124

at the first seam, marked the toe of her shoe with her finger, and she leap-frogged her finger. Solstice repeated this process until she found the next seam. *More than ten and half size six Solstice shoes equaled eight ducklings. Quack. Quack. No. Eight feet equaled one duct length.* Every time she felt a seam, she had traveled eight feet.

Solstice rolled over and stared at the silver ductwork overhead. *The Chapstick she had on tasted nasty, like iron. Why was she here? For water. No. Why live in the ducts? Because of the culling. Because the guards are already killing people. No bodies. Simply disappearances. What's more important? Isolation or closeness to supplies, water and fresh air. Air sounded important. She shouldn't live on the return side of the ventilation system. Water. Return side. Return slide. Cha Cha slide. Because the designers expected a platoon to occupy the facility, not a battalion. Too many people snuck in. Focus.* Solstice had central air in the condo. *Spirograph. Same concept.* At the condo, the return side was near the floor. *That's how the ventilation system removed used air, while clean air came from the ceiling vent. But if she stayed in the air conditioner discharge line—the fresh air side, she'd have trouble climbing down. Roll over. Do it again.* She needed a rope. *Because she liked to skip. One two buckle my shoe.* How do you fabricate a rope. *Oops? When you're asking questions in your head do you need a question mark?* Rope resembled braids. She could braid rope. *Every fourteen-year-old girl can.* How could she move from the return side to the discharge side? *In a room. If she could reach a ceiling vent. Seal invent while no one watched.* But she needed rope and a map. And water.

Find the water. Find a home. Calculate distance from water source to home. Find way to transport water. *How come if too many people snuck in, Elle didn't? If she asked him and I was his?* Assemble a rope. *Sheet strips braided? Like Armenian String Cheese. Um.* Find food. Move from return line to discharge line. Solstice knew she had forgotten another important item... Bathroom. *Tinkles and deposits. Bathroom important too. But she hadn't tinkled in days.* Prioritize. Water. Rope. Food. Water. Bathroom. Move to fresh air/ discharge side of system. Water. *Move to the left. Move to the right. One more time. Clap your hands.*

Crap. Where does the used air go? The CO_2? Don't camp out near the intake of the filtration system. Avoid condensation too. Sensation. Sensational. Woot! Woot!

But Solstice needed water first.

Water. Cafeteria. Bathroom. Laundry. Damn. Solstice made the list in her head. *Too risky? Too many guards in those rooms. Where does water come from. Lakes. Rain. In buildings? Pipes. Find pipes. Pipes! Butt Cleavage Gardener from the condo had fixed her sink once while Elle worked in D.C. Butt Cleavage Gardener from the condo had fixed her sink once while Elle worked in D.C. Did she already think that? When Elle worked in D.C. Pipes. Blue equals cold. Red knobs equal hot and have insulation. Pipe insulation. Cold water pipes had water droplets. Condensation. Who's sensational? You are baby!* Solstice had been standing in the kitchen at the condo, washing dishes when she turned the hot water knob and it sheared off, sending a spout of water to the ceiling. Mrs. C. scurried from the kitchen, through the front door and down the hall, screaming like she had seen a rat. *Rat! Mrs. C. should see my new condo. The rats are like beavers.* A minute later Solstice met Butt Cleavage. His real name was Buttster. No. Buster. He scooted down and opened the doors under the sink, revealing his plumber's butt in its glory. By Glory, Solstice meant hairy peaks. He reached in and the water stopped flowing. Mrs. C. spread out a bunch of towels and kept thanking him. Solstice wanted to know how he fixed it.

"Can you show me?" Solstice asked. *Not the glory.*

"Sure. See the blue plastic pipe? Cold water. See the lever on the end? That's the valve to shut it off."

"Like the sink handles." Solstice replied.

"Yep. Now, see the copper lines? Those are for hot water. Occasionally, the cold water has copper lines too. See the lever at the end of the line? That's a shut off valve too."

"How do I tell them apart when both lines are both copper, without touching them?"

"Cold will be wet. Hot will have insulation."

"What's this red handle? It's like an outdoor faucet."

"That's a draincock."

Solstice smacked her head on the cabinet. "What?"

"It's to drain the pipes if you are doing work or leaving for a long time. You could use it to get water. If the valve is open and the valves are open downstream, you'd have plenty of water."

Find pipes. Elle and Solstice arrived too late. Because Solstice didn't swim fast enough. Because Elle had to summit a quarry mountain carrying frozen Solstice. Stupid interstate. How about turning off the quarry lights at night! Only a humongo sign would have been worse—something like Come to Quarry Highway Refugee People! Pipes are noisy. Like a pan flute. Puzzles played a pan flute. No. Rattles. Find rattles. Follow the noise. Where are the pipes? Next to the ducts. I'm sorry Mom. Follow the ducklings. Make way. Find noisy spots in the ductwork. Most rooms had concrete ceilings with exposed ductwork and pipes. *Too exposed. Find a noisy spot in the ductwork over a room with a drop ceiling hiding the ductwork and pipes. Because that's the best way to form a band. You need a man on the ductwork and another on the pan flute. Who had drop ceilings? More cowbell. Hit it TwoDogsSmiles-A-Lot.* But the nice rooms had ceilings. *Like the doctor's and senator's.* She had found Naetersen's room on the first day when she escaped into the ventilation system. *That's how she got her groove on.* That's why no one had a key once she locked it. But Naetersen had the key, *key to her heart, baby.*

Find the doctor's room. Search for a valve. What the hell did Buttster call the valve? How would she leave the ductwork to access the water pipe? Access panel. Find the access panel closest to the doctor's room. Naetersen had his own bathroom sink and toilet, and kitchenette.

She had it. Solstice stood in excitement. *Smack!* Ugh. She lay back down rubbing her forehead. *Sit. Don't stand.* Solstice sat. *Three feet by three feet, dumbass. How often must I tell you?* She closed her eyes. *Or where they already opened. Damn this Chapstick is nasty. When's the last time she tinkled? Naetersen's room. It's in the direction her feet are pointing. Did Elle escape to Lexington? It's been days. Or is it months. Is she outside banging on the door? Bang a gong. All night long.* She spun around and crawled toward the doctor's room. *And she counted seams. Solstice pulled out her pink Sharpie and put an arrow at the first turn. Wait how did she know the Sharpie wrote pink. Did pink exist in the dark. Oops nasty question mark. ??? For the ones, she forgot.* Underneath the arrow, she wrote *doctor. Without the unnecessary O's.* Later she would write the directions under his name. *Left. Five seams equal forty feet. Right. Thirty-two feet. Left. About ten feet.*

Stop. Important.

Don't crawl any further. Who's in the Derby this year? Yes. Whisky. No wait. Kentucky Bourbon. Neat please. I'll take Sir Gallopsalot to show. Thank you.

How did she enter the ductwork? Dammit. The Derby was last month. Through the side vent. In front of her should be a six-foot drop to the wall vent. Retreat. Can't see anything when his lights aren't on. On the base. Now on the sides. What's this? A panel? Solstice felt around the edges. Pulled. Pushed. To the right. Nope. To the left. Yep. It slides. *Everybody clap your hands now. Seal around the edges. Seal. Seadog. Arr. ArR. ARr. Wooo!* Solstice felt a strong breeze in her face. Fresh air. Clean air. *Access panel between the return and discharge lines! Connected by a maintenance duct two-feet-long sealed on both sides.* Solstice stuck her hand in, feeling around. She crawled, spun and closed the access panel. *Swoosh. There it is. Whoop.* Pressure normalized. To her right, Solstice could see light shining through a vent opening. *I have seen the light. Did she finish the bourbon already?*

She crawled to the vent. *Yep. Doctor's room. Overhead vent. Underknee vent.* She laid her head flat on the grid of the vent. *I have waffle face. I should switch sides so my waffle cheeks match. #waffleface. Straining to see the layout. Desk. Door with deadbolt— must be entrance into his room. Deadbolt saved her ass days prior. Another door. A slide door—must be bathroom. Bathroom means plumbing. When's the last time I tinkled?*

Solstice crawled backward and put her head to the side of the ductwork. *No noise. Pipes are loud when in use.* She'd have to wait. Solstice laid down on the ductwork. She reached into her sling sack and took out her water bottle. Shook it. Took off the cap and tapped the end. Bone dry. *Why did the doctor and senator have to lock everyone in? Why did Elle have to leave her?*

Click. Click. Clock.

Who's in the room?

Solstice crawled to the vent over the doctor's room. Peered in. Naetersen. *Now. Wait for him to tinkle... What's he doing? Drip. Drip. Coffee. He's making coffee? ...Waiting. Waiting. Bathroom trip. OMG. Deposit! Flush. Flush. Flush it! What? Wait. Where's he going? Wash your hands! Nasty. Turn around. Good God man wash them hands. Water on.* Solstice inched her way to the main duct junction in silence. Back four feet. Ear against the ductwork. Clunk. Clunk. Clunk. Rattle. *Don't be a tattle.* Solstice moved back two feet and put an X with her pink Sharpie. *Can't see those X's. Add to the mental list: flashlight. Hadn't answered the pink question yet. Does the color exist in the darkness or does it change to pink when it's in the light? Not a dumb question when you consider refraction.*

Find another access panel. Access panel. Can't see anything in the dim light. That's why you count, dummy. That's why you feel for seams. Why would they need an access panel for a ventilation system? Cleaning. Filters. Maintenance. Solstice would bet her life the doctor had a good filtration system near his room. Turn on the fan! Flush it! Why put an access panel connecting the return and discharge ductwork? Solstice moved back from where she thought she made the X, counting seams. One. Two. Three. She could see the light shining through Naetersen's overhead vent. *Three times eight equals eight times three equals two times twelve equals six times four. Twenty-four feet. Factorials are the rage. Flash cards please. Too far. Had she gone too far? Or Two far? The room is twenty by twenty. Crawl. Three seams. Everybody clap your hands. The vent to the doctor's room is off to the left. One seam. Eight feet. Crawl. Hand on right side. Put your right hand out. Do the hokey pokey and shake it all about. What's this? Another panel? Dammit. Screws? No, welded nuts. Reasonable. The panel would be accessed from outside the ductwork. How do you remove bolts facing the wrong way? Feel it. A seal. Like the other panel. Foam seal—quarter inch thick. How do I turn the bolts? Tear the seal. Mom, why am I in the bunker? Why aren't you? Are you well? I love you Mom. Wow. Mom upside down is woW. Or is it a 180? See if I can fit my fingers in and grip the bolt. Peel seal. Peel n seal. Fingers. Too tight. Need pliers. Fat chance. It's my last dance. Tonight. For love. What do I have? Empty water bottle. Sweatshirt. Leggings. Shoes. Sling sack. Shoe laces.*

Wrap shoe lace around bolt between panel and welded nuts. Wrap it. Wrap it again. Pull down on left side of lace. Nothing. Wipe gooey red Chapstick on the lace. Pull down on right side of lace. Movement! Ten minutes later. Or a week? First bolt... Second bolt... Third bolt... Dammit can't remove it. I don't remember red nail polish. Ugh. It's wet. Red nail polish tastes like iron. Stupid fourth bolt. Dam you fourth bolt. Get your stinking hands off me! Said Rusty the Bolt. Top right corner bolt. So far. So, close. Gonna make by bright eyes shoe. Where did the other three bolts go? Downtown. Ape. Or nowhere. Damn. Need those to close this panel. Bunker door sealed for over one hundred days. Is that what Naetersen meant? Plenty of days left to go. Togo. Bogo. You go girl. Buy one. Get one. Need water. If panel had bolts, it wouldn't be on a slider. Wrap fingers around edges and push down and to the right. Panel should pivot on the remaining bolt. Love you top right hand bolt. You're my vaforite.

Success. In a dress or leggings.

Feel with hands. No floor. Spit. Wait for it. Splat. Da dat. Do it again. Thank you. I'm hear or is it here all week. Or am I weak. Okay long drop out this panel door. Climb above ductwork. Damn. No space. Two inches clearance between ductwork and bunker rock ceiling. Bunker Rock Ceiling. Live! One night only. Why would Clearance be there? Chilling with Clarence of course.

Reach. Nothing. Loop sling sack strap around a ductwork support and grasp other end with right hand. Reach farther with left hand. Reach. Reach to the beach.

Pipes! Pipes! We have pipes! Feel to the left along the pipe. Ouch hot. Wait, a second pipe. Not hot. What's the opposite of hot? A lemon. Because a vest has no sleeves. Reach to the left. Run hand along cold pipe. Reach to the left run hand along cold pipe.

Valve! Contact. Bearing three six-mark point four. Dive. Dive! DIVE! No wait, withdraw.

Solstice pulled herself into the ductwork, to give her arm a rest. Eventually she would connect a hose from the draincock to the ductworks, so she didn't have to stretch. *Am I narrating in my head? Is he drunk? Has he drunk? When's the last time he drunk? Wait is the narrator a man or a woman? Hate to fall. And lose it all. What the hell lay at the bottom of the chasm? Cereal. Oil cans filled with cereal. And used sneakers.* Elle explained that the bunker was a bunch of tunnels eight feet deep. *Deep feet. Or not.* Otherwise Elle said bunker was a bunch of tunnels eight feet deep. *Crap am I doing it again.??? There are you satisfied stupid question mark in the head police.* Tall people would hit their heads on the special rooms with doorways...

Water. Solstice searched for water.

Could you narrate in Australian, please?

Can't see down into chasm. Don't want to fall. Access panel goes to a maintenance room. Because that's where the action is. Along with the action.

15. 16. 14. Seer, harbinger, oracle or presage. Dawning. Burning. Brand. BACK OFF MELODY YOU BITCH! No wait. Come back. Have you seen my left shoe? The counting one? You know, it's nine thumb inches long.

How many days without water? Three. Four. How many steps... no how many seams to this junction.

Water. Need to find water. Solstice licked her lips. *Check the Pfitzer valve.* Her tongue felt like sandpaper. Her lips, crackled, but were moist. *Tasted like metal or blood! When's the last time she tinkled? How did Solstice enter this room? Who sells blood flavored chap stick. Diggin' the accent mate. Dingo ate her baby.*

Water. Solstice searched for water. *Try doing a Canadian one now. Dallas you're my vaforite. Discuss amongst yourselves.*

Ball peen hammer.

What... Reaching. Reach for the pipe. Focus. *Tie off sling sack to ductwork support leading to rock ceiling. Loop sling sack around waist. Bow to the crowd. Thank you.* Find water bottle. Put in right hand. Lean. *I'm flying!* Turn valve on with left hand. Don't spill too much. *It's water stupid. It doesn't grow on pipes.* Steady self with left hand on pipe. Not the hot one. *Because you're the hot one baby.* Put bottle under valve with right hand. Fill it. Good. Shut off valve. Lean into ductwork. Smell water. *Is it clean? Smells better than Solstice. Drink. Drink. Drink. What did Buttster call the water valve? Lean back on ductwork wall. Drink. Fill bottle. Repeat. Lean back. What was the valve called?*

Solstice drank her water. The valve was called a...

Draincock!

RULES AND LISTS

M23. Maximus plus twenty-three days. Lexington Bunker Complex.
SOLSTICE

Solstice awoke in a puddle, drunk on water. Her face rested on the ductwork. She could smell the contents of the puddle under her: pee, blood and water. She opened her eyes. *Okay don't get dehydrated.* If Solstice wrote a rule book for bunker survival, after Don't Get Caught would be, Always Have Enough Water. She'd call it Rule 1b.

Solstice sat. The access panel door remained open. *Thank you bolt number four.* She stretched to pivot the panel to the left, to close it. She slipped on the puddle and caught herself on the sides of the ductwork. *Hate to fall out through the access panel. What was down there? Right. Cereal.* She'd name it, the Great Chasm.

Solstice closed the panel, sliding from the puddle. She needed to: drink water, fabricate a rope, find food, find a bathroom and find an isolated spot to establish her home base. Later, she'd need to find containers for the water and build a pantry for emergencies.

Solstice couldn't find her water bottle. She reached to her right and to the left. The bottle lay in the pee-blood-water puddle, with the cap next to it.

Solstice pivoted the panel open. She pulled down on the sling sack. She put the sling sack over her head and around her chest. She leaned out of the ductwork over the Great Chasm. Her shins touched the ductwork edge while the rest of her body remained suspended. *This is twice as scary as I remember it.* Solstice steadied herself on the cold-water pipe and opened the draincock. She rinsed the water bottle and cap. She filled the water bottle, capped it and backed into the ductwork, removing the sling sack from her body.

Solstice sat back against the ductwork and drank. Five minutes later she repeated the process. When she satisfied her thirst, Solstice untied her sling sack from the ductwork support and closed the panel.

Solstice crawled in the direction she guessed she had come from yesterday. After crossing the puddle, she found her right shoe lace. She leaned back against the ductwork. Solstice knew it was the right shoe lace because she was not wearing a left shoe. She closed her eyes. It didn't change the lighting, but it helped her think. She thought about her left shoe. She had used it to count panels and to draw a map in her head.

Solstice had crawled the wrong way, sixteen to twenty-four feet. She spun around and crawled toward the water access panel. Her hands and knees sloshed through the puddle. She crawled to the duct turn leading to Naetersen's overhead, Solstice's underknee, vent. She couldn't resist and crawled toward the doctor's room. She peered through the vent cover, but no one was home. Solstice retraced her steps, back into the main duct, until she came to the first access panel, the one with the sliding door. She stared into the opening. *Why crawl into the return line? Because she wanted to find her left shoe.*

Solstice slid open the panel door, this time the air in the return line pulled her hair into the ductwork. She crawled through the opening and slid the panel shut behind her. Solstice crawled for a few paces and felt nothing with her left hand. She reached with her right hand to steady herself but felt the slippery sides on the down chute. Solstice toppled over the edge, her head and her back smacking the duct sides. *Ouch!* Face down, Solstice stared to the right at Naetersen's return air vent. This vent cover had saved her ass on the first day. *Thank God, no one was home.* She pulled her knees to her chest and did a summersault, slide-landing on her butt, as she thought of a new rule. Rule number two, stay out of the return lines.

Solstice stood and stretched, her finger tips reaching the main duct above. She had fallen about six feet. If Solstice wrote down a third rule of bunker survival, it would be: don't leave home without a rope. Solstice pulled herself into the main duct.

Solstice crawled five crawl-steps and found her shoe. She put her left shoe on and crawled to the intake/discharge connector access panel. She slid open the panel, crawled through into the short connector ductwork, and closed the slide panel behind her. *No more return duct lines. Because you can't see the downchutes.*

Solstice stopped for a minute, sat and leaned against the ductwork. She had forgotten the next item on her list. Number one: water. Number two, unknown. Number three: food. Number four: bathroom. She had rules now too. Rule 1a—don't get caught, because they'll kill you. Rule 1b—stay hydrated, because you'll go crazy otherwise. Rule 2—stay out of the return lines, because you can't see the downchutes. Rule 3—don't leave home without rope, because that's how you climb back in when you fall out. Which reminded Solstice of number two on her list—create rope. She needed a long piece of cloth for the rope.

But number three on the list—find food—was important.

Solstice spent the rest of the day making maps in her head, and leaving pink sharpie arrows on the ductwork, in case she found a flashlight. She crawled down endless ductwork, lost her way, and retraced her steps, following voices until she found a cafeteria. Solstice saw the guards in the cafeteria through the underknee vent, and she waited for them to leave. She found another access panel between the intake and discharge lines and lowered herself into a downchute, in clear violation of rule 2 and rule 3. The kitchen guard had locked the pantry, so Solstice tiptoed to the trash and removed the least-foul scraps. She placed them into her sling sack, crawled into the side vent, replaced the cover and climbed the downchute. She slipped through the access panel and into the discharge duct line.

Solstice crawled to the cafeteria underknee vent to have light and laid out her spoils. *Can I eat what's left of the banana meat on the peel? Are the banana strings edible?* She examined a wheat roll with two bites removed. *Score!* She pulled wilted lettuce and a cherry tomato out of her sling sack. *Doable.* She opened a crumpled paper towel revealing gravy with three chunks. *Is that beef? Was the meat in a mouth already? You need the protein. Otherwise we're making rat stew.* She removed two full water

135

bottles from her sack and had a sip of water. *Two bottles plus her Kissani bottle... She needed five more to equal eight per day. Fill them at the draincock.* The biggest find of the excursion was a half-eaten sleeve of saltines. *I'm saving you for the pantry.* Solstice sat, eating her breakfast-dinner with her tears providing the seasoning. When she finished, she crawled from the vent and fell asleep.

LURK
M24. Maximus plus twenty-three days. Lexington Bunker Complex.
SOLSTICE

SOLSTICE AWOKE INSIDE THE DUCTWORK to the sounds of the cafeteria opening for the morning. Eighteen guards shuffled in for breakfast, which meant at least the same amount elsewhere on duty running the complex.

Solstice had asked Elle near the top of the quarry hill, "Who are the guards you keep talking about?"

Elle had replied, "A special secret military branch, working in plain sight, as body guards, or training in places like the bunkers, preparing for a disaster."

"How many, Mom?"

"At least a platoon for each important government person, like senators, cabinet members and judges or even academics—like scientists." Elle replied, "Most of the guards didn't receive their assignment until the last minute, for secrecy. The guards trained offsite for the skills they would need in the bunker."

"How do you know this, Mom?" Solstice asked.

"Remember when you called me, before I flew home? I worked on bunker preparation for the senator."

"It sounds smart, Mom."

Elle said, "The government made a mistake, they forgot about the people. Who will do the stuff? Who will do the living? Why save thousands of men and a handful of woman across the country? There's no need for a continuance of government, if there is no one to govern."

"Mom, you're scaring me."

"I'm sorry. We need to join the line by the bunker door..."

Solstice stared through the underknee vent at the bustling

cafeteria, as Elle's words echoed in her mind. *What about the people? Elle was people, Solstice too.*

Solstice had been silent for days. She inched her way back from the vent and in a breathy whisper she sang, not for Melody, not for the future, but for herself, mocking her predicament.

"Lurk"

Lie in wait
Skulk, loiter, conceal
Out of sight
Bended back, must kneel

Can't find me
Creep 'n' crawl
Never seen
Slink, sneak, prowl

Tortoise, spider, rabbit
Hamster, snake, groundhog
Mole, squirrel, boar
Racoon, skunk, and dog

Fox, gerbil, otter
Badger, mole, meerkat
Ant, mongoose, chipmunk
Ferret, worm, and rat
Tunnelers, they are
Watch me be like that

Above the rooms
Take cover
Lurking
I hover

Don't look up
I lurk

PRIVY
M24. Maximus plus twenty-three days. Lexington Bunker Complex.
SOLSTICE

SOLSTICE TACKLED HER LIST written on the ductwork interior after the guards left the cafeteria. *Water. Check. Food. Check. Rope. Do it later. No check. Place to sleep. Home base. Who cares? Check. Bathroom. Colossal empty spot, where a check should be.*

With her pink sharpie, Solstice made notes on the ductwork in the dimlight of the cafeteria vent. The senator and doctor had private bathrooms, while the guards had public unisex bathrooms. *Did female guards exist? Unknown.* Plus, there were civilian bathrooms for workers and staff. *The guards closed the door before the civilian staff showed up but imagine having a civilian job in a military complex at the end of the world. Your life must be worthless. Kids are worth even less. And if you snuck in, the guards must herd you into a corner and... The guards have the guns, but not the power because brains were important, too. Guards must know they need the doctor and senator, to operate the place, because those two men have the secrets and the way out. Did female guards exist? Likely, but not many, given the lifetime supply of courtesy napkins left out in the open.*

Solstice closed her eyes and focused on the bathrooms she had seen in the Lexington Bunker Complex. *Today was about bathrooms.* The voice, echoing in her head, was getting harder to block out. The thoughts and the ideas that came from her inner voice, seemed less like her own, and more like someone else's. And yet those ideas were born from the same experiences. There was only one answer to Solstice's question, "Who is the voice?"

I am the voice, it's Melody, let me help you.

Solstice opened her eyes. She needed help, and she was lonely, but this was a line she wouldn't be able to step back over.

Solstice closed her eyes, letting Melody in.

How often did she tinkle per day? Eight times. How often did she drop off a deposit? At least once per day. Make the deposits and two tinkles at night while everyone sleeps. That leaves a half-dozen tinkles. Bottles, buckets and pans. None sounded reasonable.

Solstice needed to investigate a bathroom to explore her options. She crawled along the long ductwork shaft, counting seams and leaving arrows until she found the nearest bathroom vent. She crouched over the fan in the center of the showers. The bathroom lights shone between her legs and into her face, and the idea came to her, between her feet. *Disable the fan, and tinkle into the shower through the fan vent over the drain.*

FIRENIGHT

M59. Maximus plus fifty-nine days. In the Cave.
BAERAN

Baeran spied the Firegale between the cracks in the Cave rocks. A giant wall of fire moved through the surrounding forest. Embers and ash rained from the sky, while trees crackled, burnt, and fell around their shelter. Black smoke danced with the flames, while the falling trees screamed like jet engines. In the valley fire, beneath the surface of the stream, Baeran had only glimpsed the power of the

Firegale. Already the stones lining the cave were hot, but Baeran was transfixed, awed by the fire twins—danger and beauty—swirling like a tornado.

Cole interrupted Baeran's thoughts, "Everyone take your positions!"

Kay, Susan, Mitch and Parker lowered buckets into the north and south floor holes, filling them with water and handed them to

Deven, Ethan, Baeran and Judy, who in turn handed the buckets to Cole and Lani at the south wall and Tara and L.J. at the north wall. Cole and L.J. dumped the water on the cave walls, while Lani and Tara returned the empty buckets to the front of the line.

In the earliest hours of the morning, a lofty pine tree fell on the north side of the cave, causing rocks to fall inward and open a hole, striking L.J., knocking him unconscious. Tara screamed, calling out for help.

Kay, Judy, and Tara moved the unconscious L.J. to the shelf opposite the ATVs and laid him down. The group's gear, including tents, sleeping bags, and clothing, ignited. Mitch and Cole doused Susan, Parker, Ethan, Baeran, and Deven with water as they worked with the ax and garden tools to hack at the tree breaching the north wall, and place fallen rocks into the hole.

Aileen, Megan, and Jordin hid under the bench with Selene, displacing the equipment. Lani and Annie stood close to Kay near the south side of the cave and took turns relieving Susan and Judy in the bucket brigade.

Near dawn, the stream ceased to flow because of an obstruction beyond the cave walls. Cole called Kay to him. "Sweetie, I have to crawl under the metal floor and remove whatever is damming the stream."

"Cole don't."

Cole recalled, "Remember after the Firegale chased Baeran and Lani into a stream and I said, '...there'll be a time when we must choose between saving us or the children-,'"

"We choose them." Kay interrupted.

Cole kissed Kay, wiping her tears. He addressed the group, "Deven, Ethan, and Judy, repair the wall. After I clear the obstruction, Parker and Baeran, you fill the buckets and hand them to Kay, Susan and Heather. Lani, Annie, and Jordin, you have Selene and the twins, and L.J.. Mitch, you have my back."

Baeran clutched Cole's wrist. "Be safe, Dad."

Cole instructed Baeran, "Mitch will help me, once the stream is free of the obstruction, if I don't return, work with Parker to fill the buckets, so the others can spray down the walls."

"You mean *when* you return."

Cole whispered into Baeran's ear, "Protect the family and anyone else you can. Remember, no problem is so great that you can't find a solution for it. Break it down. Examine the possibilities. Be ready to make a sacrifice, family first, then self."

"Dad?"

Cole embraced Baeran. "Got to go, Son."

Before Kay and Baeran could protest, Mitch handed Cole the ax, saying, "I'll crawl in behind and splash water on you."

"Got it. I won't have much air to breathe, I'll move fast."

The Sheridans watched Cole disappear under the floor.

Pine boughs obstructed the water. Cole broke off pieces of branches and stuffed them under his submerged chest to Mitch, who fed them into the cave via the north hole near Cole's feet.

As Cole moved material out of the way, the end of the tunnel opened, and Baeran could see the water glowing orange. Baeran rose, sped to the cave wall and peered through a crack. He watched Cole crawl out into the stream beyond the cave. Blackened by heavy smoke, the night sky appeared darker than Baeran had ever seen, but at the forest level, fire engulfed limbs and jumped from tree to tree. The wind blew the fire in mini-funnels, carrying flames and sparks from plant to tree to grass. The Firegale died out in one spot and appeared in another, ten-feet away. Leaves, cones, limbs, and branches fell from their host trees, raining debris down onto the forest floor. The Firegale, shockingly frightening and stunning to behold, burnt as bright as lightning, and the dying forest sounded as loud as thunder.

Cole froze for a moment, before plunging into the shallow water and soaking his body. He removed fallen branches from the stream, tossing them left and right. He worked feverously, stopping only to pat down flames on his clothing. The Firegale raged around the forest floor and stream embankment.

As Cole cleared the last of the sizable branches, a twenty-five-foot-tall maple tree succumbed to the fire raging around its base. The scorched trunk buckled and toppled over, crashing to the ground. It struck Cole from behind burying him in the flaming leaves. He struggled under the weight of the tree. Spent, Cole dropped to his stomach, and fell into the stream.

Baeran yelled, "Mitch! He's trapped. Dad's trapped. Mitch! He's under a tree." Baeran dashed to the hole and jumped in, but Mitch held him from crawling under.

"Baeran—wait. I have this! Do your job."

Kay came over and pulled at Baeran. Tears streamed down her face, as Baeran lashed out, desperate to enter the hole. Kay held back sobs. "Baeran, Mitch has this. That's the plan."

Mitch stepped into the hole. "Kay be ready to help me pull Cole out. Baeran and Parker, you have the buckets."

Parker followed Mitch's instructions and filled buckets in the south hole and passed them to the bucket brigade. Baeran knelt on the floor near Parker, oblivious to Parker's shouts for help, while he watched for signs of Cole's return.

Mitch crawled out from under the cave floor and into the stream. He stared at the fire for a moment. A flaming branch fell near him. He stepped aside and scurried toward Cole. He stuck his shoulder into the tree, pushing it onto the stream bank. Mitch's coat caught fire and he threw it into the stream. He pulled the coat out of the water and patted down the flames on Cole's jacket. Cole lay face down in the water.

Mitch seized Cole, pulling him from under the armpits toward the cave hole. Mitch dove into the stream and crawled backward into the cave pulling Cole with him. When the two men resurfaced, Kay and Tara reached into the north floor hole to help pull the lifeless Cole out.

Kay screamed. Lani and Baeran rushed toward their fallen father and embraced their mother. Kay shook Lani and Baeran off, forcing them into Tara's outstretched arms. As Tara held the children, Mitch moved in and elevated Cole's head. Kay brushed the hair from her husband's forehead. Kay sobbed, "No. No. No. I love you. Don't leave."

Mitch scanned the room and he saw her red hair, like flames calling to him—the waitress-former cheerleader and lifeguard-studying to be a nurse-searching for a man, Heather. Mitch shouted, "Heather, help!"

Heather rushed to Cole, placed her head on Cole's chest and her ear to his lips. With Mitch's help, she rolled Cole onto his side. Blackened water dripped from Cole's lips. Heather pushed Cole onto this back, listening to his heart and mouth. She glanced at Mitch, unsure of what to do next, or frightened to do it.

Mitch whispered, "You can do this."

Heather bent over, elevated Cole's head with her hand, and placed her lips on his. She forced air into his lungs. She listened, hoping to hear breaths but heard nothing. She placed her hands on Cole's chest, opened his jacket, and counted his ribs. Instructing Mitch, she moved his hands under hers onto Cole's chest and told him, "Press on his chest every three seconds."

Heather removed her hands from Mitch's and listened to Cole's breathing. Heather timed her breaths into Cole's lungs with Mitch's compressions. She listened. They repeated the compressions, but she heard nothing. Heather glanced at her watch. It had been too long. She moved Mitch, and crawled onto Cole, straddling his waist.

Kay sobbed and reached for Cole, but Mitch held her back.

Heather locked her hands together and raised them. She brought both hands down onto Cole's chest with everything she had. His body buckled. Kay screamed. Heather raised her hands and hit Cole in the chest. Kay screamed, *"No!"*

Heather leaned back, raised her arms, swinging her interlocked hands down. This time she yelled, and her scream joined Kay's. Blackened water projected from Cole's lungs through his mouth, spraying Heather. Heather moved to Cole's right side, and with Mitch's help, she rolled Cole over. Water spilled from Cole's mouth and nose as he coughed. Heather stood, turning her back to Cole. Her hands shook, and she moved them to cover her face as she cried. Mitch grasped her hands and pulled them downward. "You did it!"

Kay knelt next to Cole and placed his head in her lap. Between coughs, he smirked, "I left my right eyebrow outside."

Kay wrapped her arms around Cole. She brushed back his hair and kissed him on the eyebrow and shoulder. "No more chances," she begged, and she moved her lips to his.

FIRE AND WATER
M60. In the cave.
BAERAN

BAERAN STARED AT HIS PARENTS. Parker hit Baeran in the shoulder. "Asscave, snap out of it. Fill the buckets faster. Our dad's will be fine if we keep those walls wet."

Baeran filled the buckets and followed Parker's lead. Deven and Ethan attacked breaches, while Mitch replaced fallen stones. Annie watched the twins. Kay, Lani and Tara tended to L.J. and Cole. Judy and Susan dumped the buckets onto the walls. Jordin sat with Heather wiping the blood from her knuckles.

When a rock fell out of the wall and rolled past everyone else, Reese moved to take care of it. She hadn't noticed Mitch's, Deven's and Ethan's heavy gloves. Reese screamed and dropped the stone as her right shirt sleeve ignited.

Jordin rushed the older girl, knocking Reese to the ground and smothering her and the flames. Lani joined Jordin, and the two girls dragged Reese by her good arm to the waterhole.

"*Wo de shanghen!* My scars! Keep her arm under the water," she told Lani, thinking of her own skin burning, so long ago, when the boiling water had struck her. "Don't pull the clothing, you'll tear the skin."

Lani held Reese down while Jordin submerged her arm. The other Seascapers had seen the scars on Jordin's neck, shoulder, and arm. Jordin never hid them. The girl with the water-burn scars knew what to do. Reese writhed in agony. But Jordin waited, holding the arm in the water until it was cool to the touch. She cut the sleeve and peeled the shirt away. Several fingers on Reese's hands had fused. The arm turned red and puffy, and blisters formed. Reese screamed until the pain took her and her eyes closed.

147

"*Ganxie shangdi.* Thank God. It'll be easier this way, now that she's passed out," Jordin sighed. "I've had training in the burn center. While I healed, I helped others. I want to be a doctor, in a trauma center for children." She massaged Reese's arm underwater, allowing the water to cool the muscles and skin. "I need Vaseline—not cream or lotion. It must be Vaseline. And I need sheets, not towels."

Kay yelled, "Vaseline's in the med kit! Will a silk blouse do?"

"*Shi.* Yes."

Jordin dried the arm with the shirt, coated it in Vaseline, and wrapped it in a silk fragment.

As he held the last fallen stone in his gloved hands, Deven asked, "See it? The Firegale is moving on. I'm amped and bushed. I got a bad case of the noodles. Can I check on Reese?"

"Yes, and place the last stone on the ground," Mitch replied. "We'll leave the opening, so we can watch the Firegale.'

Baeran stepped out of the hole and checked on Cole. Kay whispered, "He'll be okay. Let him sleep."

Deven darted to Reese and placed her good hand in his. Baeran stepped back from his parents and sat on the floor next to Lani, Jordin, Deven and Reese. He put his hand on Lani's shoulder. Jordin had one hand on Reese and reached for Lani, connecting the five of them. Baeran pointed to the hole in the cave wall, and the five teens watched as the Firegale and rising sun melded into a burnt sunrise.

BREAKING THE GIRL

M28. Maximus plus twenty-eight days. Lexington Bunker Complex.
SOLSTICE

Solstice stood in a vertical down chute to relieve the tension on her back. She had spent most days in a crouched or crawling position. The problem with living in ductwork was the height. Being tiny helped, and lying down brought relief, but not enough. The three-foot-by-three-foot main duct allowed her to sit without stooping, but a dull pain had settled in Solstice's back and refused to leave.

Solstice had few options. She was locked into the Lexington Bunker until the doctor and senator opened the doors, and she couldn't risk joining the general population. She had heard the rumors. People had gone missing, never anyone important, mostly those people who rushed the door on day one, like Solstice.

Solstice scavenged for supplies at night, lowering herself down through the underknee vents. Since the guards did not search the trash before incineration, Solstice continued to select her meals from the refuse.

Once Solstice liberated over a dozen canned goods in a single night from a counter in the cafeteria. She lugged them into the ventilation system. But it dawned on her, the guards or the kitchen staff would notice the stolen food. Solstice returned the spoils, except for the peaches. Thereafter, she stole one can and one water per week, stocking her pantry while she continued to eat from the trash.

Solstice hadn't found any medicine yet and her back killed. If she was making a list, after aspirin, she'd take a friend, too, anyone besides Melody.

Solstice was broken in body and spirit. For four days, she lay on her side, rising only to drink, eat and use the fan bathroom, and it wasn't until the ductwork air got hotter, that she awoke from her stupor.

OF BRAIDS AND BURNING

M32. Maximus plus thirty-two days. Lexington Bunker Complex.
SOLSTICE

SOLSTICE COULDN'T REMEMBER THE DUCTS BEING THIS HOT, a balmy seventy-five degrees. She welcomed the change and the project laid before her. *It's nice to be busy.* She had stolen a sheet and a knife and began construction of her rope.

Solstice separated the sheets into two-inch wide strips. *Two-inches equaled the distance from the edge of her thumb nail to the webbing.* She'd need at least eight strips. Each strip was nine size6Solstice-feet long, which made it about eighty inches long. Solstice needed at least eight-feet plus four-feet of tie-off slack to reach from the underknee vents to the room floors. If Solstice connected two lengths of the sheet, she'd have over thirteen feet.

Solstice laid three strips side by side in the ductwork and she tied them together on one end. She twisted each strip individually from the tied end to the loose end. The three strips looked like licorice. She named the three strips from left to right one, two and three. Like braiding hair, she crossed one over two and three over one, and she crossed two over three, and one over two, and three over one, and two over three... 1-2-3. 2-1-3. 2-3-1. 3-2-1. 3-1-2. 1-3-2. Repeat, easy as one two three, if you're a girl.

Solstice repeated the pattern until she reached the end and tied off the final strands in a knot. She duplicated her work until she had four rope lengths. She tied two knots in each rope, for foot and hand holds, and she tied the four lengths together.

Solstice dripped with sweat as she finished the 123-rope. The normal operating temperature of the bunker hovered around sixty-eight degrees. She'd seen a thermostat dial on the senator's wall, days prior. The ventilation system was working fine because she felt the breeze blowing at her. The temperature of the bunker had increased from the outside, not within. *With the shortages in the bunker, why unlimited power and no exhaust? That's what they mean when they talk about the geothermal system.*

Solstice closed her eyes, despite the darkness, the act helped, and she opened the map in her head. *Home base was near the cafeteria and bathroom showers. Naetersen's room and the draincock were in opposite direction. What had she missed?*

Solstice scurried along the cool metal of the ductwork until she found the turn near the doctor's vent. She crawled over the underknee vent, continued straight and made another right turn, finding another vent. She proceeded with caution and peered into the room. A guard manipulated a joystick as he stared at a black-and-white screen. A fuzzy line ran through the video display. Solstice recognized this guard. Burly and kind, she called him Bill for no reason. Another man watched the screen with him. Solstice recognized him, too, as Gangly George.

Burly Bill said to Gangly George. "Get Naetersen, we're losing the video feed. The Lexington Firegale is burning this way."

Solstice frowned at the TV monitor. The fuzzy line grew, and the entire screen filled with static.

THE AURORA BRAND

M35. Maximus plus thirty-five days. Lexington Bunker Complex.
SOLSTICE

Solstice camped out near the cafeteria underknee vent. She liked to hear the voices of the guards talking during the day. Watching everyone eat took a while to grow accustomed to but eating trash scraps became the new normal. Besides the voices, the cafeteria vent had the best lighting in the ductwork.

Solstice removed her pink Sharpie from her sling sack. Although not much of an artist before her world had ended, now she attacked drawing with a passion, spreading graffiti across the ductwork interior. At first, it didn't matter what she drew, landscapes, cityscapes or people.

After a while, Solstice focused on drawing the natural world. She longed to be out in the fresh air. Trees, animals, and stars became her new favorite subjects. Eventually, she became fixated on the sun. The sun had special meaning to her. She drew it often as a child. She added the letters ICE inside the circle. Lesser dancers at Ms. LaMerde Femme's Academy called her "Ice" in whispers behind her back. *More like Princess Ice Meangirl.*

In the cold dimlight, the nickname Ice suited Solstice. She called the combination of the three—the circle, the rays, and "ICE",

her sign. After hundreds of drawings, she perfected its shape, and marked the ductwork junctions. Far from her sleeping area, Solstice imagined she claimed territory as she marked it with her sign, calling it, The Aurora Brand.

SUMMER CAMP
M60. Maximus plus sixty days. In the cave.
BAERAN

BAERAN HELPED MITCH AND ETHAN PEEL ROCKS from the north Cave wall at dawn. Mitch yelled, "The Firegale's moved on!"

Cheers rose amongst the group. Parker, Ethan and Mitch leaned on the north wall and knocked the upper stones into the stream. When half of the north wall crumbled, the trio climbed over the top and jumped into the water. Aside from Cole, L.J. and Reese, the rest of the Seascapers followed. Selene was the fourth one out, followed by Baeran. The dog knocked Baeran over in the stream. The rest of the Seascapers joined in and spent the next hour splashing in the stream and exchanging hugs.

As the day wore on, Baeran, Mitch, Deven, Susan, Ethan and Parker took turns removing wall rocks from the stream and stacking them on the embankment, leaving the cave floor and the south wall in place. Jordin, Lani, Kay, Judy and Heather chose a flat spot near the stream for a campsite and removed fallen debris. The Seascapers assembled the tents overlooking the stream and rolled L.J.'s and Cole's burnt trucks into the woods.

As Mitch finished moving stones near the north entrance of the cave, he surveyed the new campsite. Ash covered the ground, and the Firegale had incinerated the fledgling trees but many of the older trees still stood after the blaze.

Distracted, Mitch dropped a stone on his foot. "Crap."

From within the cave a voice uttered, "Not in the stream."

Mitch peered in the cave, and saw Cole and L.J. laying down. "Boys, enjoying the rest? How's the noggin and the eyebrow?"

"Fine."

"Super."

Mitch continued, "Are you ready to join us outside?"

"Yes."

"Yes."

"Me too, this bites." Reese jumped in.

"I didn't see you in the corner, Reese." Mitch waved. "I'm sorry that stone burnt you. I hope you feel better soon. Jordin did a fantastic job. You should be proud, Cole."

"Jordin did do a super job, but it has nothing to do with me. She learned the skills on her own, years ago."

"Your mom saved me." Cole grinned at Reese. "No question. I felt dead. I could see myself floating."

"You too, Mitch, you saved my ass."

L.J. interrupted, "From what I heard, you saved us all."

"Okay, but it was a team effort." Cole replied, sitting up from the bench.

"Why don't you guys peer out the entrance?" Mitch asked. "The campsite is coming together, and the lofty trees aren't too burnt."

Cole hobbled to the north cave opening and replied, "I've seen this before. Kay and I visited Yellowstone National Park after we married. The park had a huge fire the season before, but the rangers found less than three hundred dead animals. The park rangers figured most of the animals hid or out-ran the wildfire. Elder trees in the park survived the wildfire because of their thick bark growth, too. We met this ranger and she said the vegetation regrew in Yellowstone because trees release their spores after being heated, and the ash rich soil provided for excellent germination."

Mitch smirked. "Did you say fermentation?"

"Oh, that hurts." Cole laughed.

Kay heard the laughter. She ambled to the cave, and said, "Mitch, you leave those boys alone, they're healing."

"Yes, ma'am," and he quick-stepped away, passing Deven on his way to the cave.

"How are you feeling, Sis?" Deven asked. "You dinged your hand bad. You should have bailed on the rock."

Reese replied, "I feel like a mutant. It hurts like hell. Everything's fused—like a scorched flipper—it will never be good for anything. I acted without thinking. I'm an idiot."

"You totally helped out and tried to save us like everyone else." Deven exaggerated. "You were cranking it until you went after that piece of magma. Let's leave the cave. Mom's waiting for you and the Sheridans have powdered lemonade. I'm amped. I haven't had anything sweet in forever."

With Deven's help, Reese stepped out into the stream.

Jordin saw Reese and yelled, "*Bie.* Don't wet the wrap."

"Yes, doc, thanks."

"*Mei wenti.* No problem."

"You saved me Jordin," Reese said as she approached Jordin. "I'm grateful, but how long will it hurt like this?"

"*Chang shijian.* Sorry but a long time. Let's check in with Kay, she has Advil and lemonade. I think you can take three at most. That's the best we can do."

"I know this is sick, but the pain makes me feel a bit alive." Reese said. "I don't want to be burnt, but it's a rush."

"That's the 'drenalin. It doesn't last," Deven said.

As the teens strolled to the tents, a hawk flew overhead.

"Whoa. Sis, did you see the bird?"

"Yep. Cole says the birds and other animals will be back because they outran the Firegale or hid underground." Reese replied. "Plus, the grass and the larger trees will come back. Apparently, nature's way smarter than us and recovers from catastrophes all the time."

"No way."

"Way." Reese smiled.

When Reese, Deven and Jordin made it out of the stream and into the camp area, Mitch and Kay called the group over.

Mitch spoke first, "Glad to see the walking wounded. Everyone did a fantastic job fighting the Firegale and building the campsite the last couple of days."

Kay stood next to Mitch. "It's nice to have the stream flowing and tents set up, but not everyone has gear. L.J., Tara and Parker, Heather, Deven and Reese don't have shelter besides the cave. We have three choices: return to our burnt homes, stay in place or head back onto the road toward Lincoln, Nebraska."

"I want to ride home to Portland, Maine." Susan retorted.

"Ah, Mom we like camping." Aileen and Megan whined.

Judy said, "Girls, it's been two days. Wait till you have chores, and what about school?"

"Mom!"

"We'll stay a bit longer, give the authorities time to restore order back home," Judy offered.

Cole spoke, "I'm not ready to travel."

"Tara and I agree, I'm not ready," L.J. added.

"I'm not going anywhere," Mitch offered. "Ethan, you in too?"

"Yep."

Heather said, "My family is not leaving until Reese feels better."

"Of course, we're staying with Mom and Dad," Lani said. "We saw Portsmouth burn—it was not pretty. Dazers are even worse. You should check out Baeran's sketches of them. They are nasty, so no thank you. I vote we stay put, and hopefully no one finds us."

"We stick with Kay, Cole, Baeran and Lani." Annie added.

Parker interrupted, "This sucks. You want to camp out in this burnt-out crap hole? Fine, everybody is hurt and bushed. But I'm with Susan and Judy. The second we feel better, we leave. They could have put the Firegale out ten miles down the road."

"Who's they?" Baeran asked.

"They, the government." Parker replied. "What do you care?"

"Parker, we understand." Tara soothed. "You raise a good point. Civilization could be found somewhere else."

Cole struggled to his feet, and Baeran stood behind him. "I recommend we spend the next several weeks preparing to travel. We don't have enough vehicles to transport everyone. My family is not leaving till everyone has a ride. When we are ready and have scavenged enough food and fuel, we will head to Lincoln, Nebraska. Agreed or do we vote?"

"Vote," said Parker and Susan simultaneously.

Cole counted after a show of hands. "Nineteen yes, two no."

After two days, Cole, L.J. and Reese left the cave to watch the activity. While Reese sat with Deven and Heather, and L.J. with Parker and Tara, Cole rested against a tree. Kay took a break from cleaning debris from the stream, came over, and placed an arm around Cole. She kissed him and let out a sigh.

"What are you thinking about?" Cole asked.

"I was thinking about home. You know, it's not too bad, now that the Firegale has passed us over. But I miss Portsmouth and fresh veggies, yoga class, and my friends."

Baeran and Lani sat in front of their parents. The siblings sipped water and listened to them reminisce.

Cole interrupted Kay, "Beer."

"What?" Kay asked.

"I miss beer." Cole blurted out, "and the Bruins."

Kay gave Cole a peck on the cheek with a grin.

Baeran looked downward. Bruins, Red Sox, Patriots, and Celtics, he missed watching them on TV, too. But he avoided the stadiums. Unsuccessful attempts to enjoy live games littered Baeran's life. He hated the crowds. The thought of that many people at a game surrounding Baeran, was enough to get him breathing hard, and he whispered to himself as the anxiety crept in, "Break it down. Inhale. Exhale. Hold. Six-nine-four."

Baeran composed himself and smiled, he had a gift for his mom and dad. Mostly for his dad. Originally, he had saved it for himself. Either way, he'd wait till his parents wanted it. Baeran kept it in his backpack.

"We'll do fine for a while at this campsite," Kay said. "But I hope we head on to Nebraska soon."

"I know. I haven't forgotten." Cole responded. "Our long-term future lies in Lincoln, Nebraska. I'm not ready for the trip. We're better off traveling fast in the fall."

Kay agreed, "Hmmm, beeeeer."

The couple had plenty to grin about. The Seascapers couldn't see the Firegale off to the west, and they had finished constructing the campsite. For the first time in a long time, the group had achieved a tiny measure of safety.

SCOUT

M65. Maximus plus sixty-five days. Outside the cave.
BAERAN

BAERAN SAT WITH THE SEASCAPERS AROUND THE CAMPFIRE at breakfast. To the west, the Firegale continued to burn away from the cave. The trio of walking wounded, L.J., Cole and Reese, sat last with those who helped them, Tara, Kay and Heather. Kay grinned at the group. "First recognition is in order," and she listed at least two items each Seascaper had done to contribute, touching on the firenight in the cave, and on constructing the campsite. Kay continued, "We are staying near the cave for the near future. Yes, hunting is important. We are down to a bit of food. But we have other 'ings' to worry about. Scavenging for supplies, and harvesting wild plants has to top the list."

"I'm sorry Kay, but what about learning," Judy interrupted. "We need school for the kids, and wilderness skills."

"You're right."

Susan interrupted, "We're forgetting about the other 'ers'. While we Seascapers entrench, let's not forget, Dazers and Jackers survived. We've seen it, patches of forest and land untouched by the flames. Hell, Cole, you saw it happen, when the Firegale chased your kids into a valley stream but not you and Kay."

"Susan's right." Cole added, "We need another 'ing'—prepping. Prepping for an attack and our journey to Nebraska."

Baeran raised his hand. "We should trap."

"Okay, but no guns." Cole replied. "I suggest we save any ammo for whatever befalls us in the future. L.J. and I have shotguns and about one hundred rounds. Guns are loud and attract attention. Small game will be the first to return, and shotguns and squirrels don't work. It'll be weeks before the underbrush grows and attracts

160

animals like deer."

"I brought a handful of books from Portsmouth," Kay said. "I worked with the Scouts. I've been researching wild plants, and I'll be foraging."

Susan said, "I'd like to do foraging and scavenging."

"I'll teach," Judy declared.

"I'd like to work with Judy and the twins," Annie said.

Aileen and Megan beamed.

Heather spoke for the first time, "If she agrees, I'd like to work with Jordin to create med kits for injuries and illnesses."

"*Dangran*. Sure," Jordin replied. "I'd love too."

Kay added, "Great, you and Jordin have the skills."

"I'd like to work on the prepping, once I'm better," Cole said. "We must develop a way to transport gear with our ATVs and other vehicles."

L.J. agreed, "I'm with Cole."

"I want to work with L.J. and Cole too." Mitch said. "I know we need food, water and shelter, but this should be the single most important task we do. We need to be able to leave at a moment's notice. Jackers attacked Cole, L.J., Parker and Baeran less than two weeks prior, and likely survived the Firegale."

"I know this is stupid and I'll help out with school or water or foraging or whatever or... ahh nevermind..." Lani stammered.

Jordin put her arm around Lani and said, "*Shuo ba*. Say it. I want to hear your idea, Lani."

"Thanks, J." Lani murmured. "I would like to keep track of our goals and accomplishments, people's stories and instructions on how to spark a campfire or building a structure or treat water. I want to create a database, a history for us..."

Parker interrupted, "You have to be kidding me, a historian? That is a colossally stupid idea."

After one second of stunned silence, Baeran hopped to his feet, and challenged Parker. "You're a freakin' jerk."

Before Parker could stand, L.J. held his son down by the shoulders, knocking Tara over. Cole struggled to stand but Mitch stood first, grasping Baeran.

"Sit, Baeran!" Kay yelled.

Baeran shook his head and sat near Lani.

"Apologize, Parker!" Tara insisted.

Parker's face flushed red. He snapped, "Sorry."

"I'm sorry too. Lani, you're right, we need to learn from each other," Tara reiterated. "I'd like to help you, and Kay with the foraging."

Reese spoke, "I feel like totally useless. I have this webbed-flipper for a right hand. Thank god Dad's watch didn't burn."

Heather sighed. "Oh honey, I'm..."

Reese waved her hand, for all to see. The fingers were nearly melted together. "It's true Mom. I'm useless."

Baeran interjected, pointing to a thick-bark tree. "How about a lookout post?"

"I like it." Reese replied.

"No one has volunteered for hunting and trapping." Kay asked, "How about it boys?"

"Trapping," Baeran and Deven said.

Parker and Ethan replied, "Hunting."

"Three rules: no guns, let an adult know where you are and don't leave when the scavengers are gone." Kay smiled at her son. "Baeran, you know how to construct traps, bows, and arrows from Scouts. Spend time with Deven, Ethan and Parker and teach them."

Parker interrupted, "No way." He shook his head.

"Oh yes, Parker, work it out." Tara said.

Parker relented, "Fine, but Baeran's not in charge."

Kay gazed at Baeran for a peace offering.

"You're older. "Baeran said. "Once you know your way around, I'll follow your lead."

Tara said to Parker, "See, that worked out."

"Lani, post the volunteer lists." Kay continued.

The Seascapers dispersed, but Baeran lingered with Kay.

"Mom, why do it? Why stick us together?"

"So, you boys can work it out before it's a problem. This isn't the first-time you have clashed heads."

"Okay. I'll do my part."

"Do it now."

Baeran hesitated but left to speak with Parker. He approached

Parker from behind and put a hand on the older boy's shoulder. "Parker, wait a minute."

Parker spun around and hit Baeran's hand away. "What?"

Baeran said, "Let's build traps."

"Asstrap, let's do bows."

"We'll have better success with traps."

"Fine what's first, assmunch?"

"You know what Parker, like you said, you want to be in charge. Fine. But I guarantee there's not one adult back at the campsite now saying, 'We put teen boys in charge of getting the meat? We're gonna be eating tree bark before those boys catch anything.' We could spend like two days constructing bows and arrows, and shoot, miss and kill nothing. Have you seen how fast squirrels move? Because the deer are gone, since there's no underbrush to eat, but if we even had brush, deer are super-fast. And we'll lose like what is the best job in the camp and be stuck lugging water, or gathering campfire wood, or emptying the crap buckets. No one volunteered for shit duty, did they? That's what will happen to us. We have two days to succeed, because people are gonna be hungry real soon. So, Parker, what are we doing? Making traps or the Shit-Show?

"Traps." Parker agreed. "As long as they are not shitty."

Parker and Baeran constructed their first trap using an old stovepipe from the railroad depot rubble near the cave. Baeran cut the pipe to two feet and punched holes into the bottom. Baeran wove spare shoelaces in a grid pattern through the holes at the pipe base. Parker placed food from his pack on the lace grid. The boys hung the pipe trap from a burnt tree limb.

The boys returned later in the day to find the food gone. Parker glared at the empty trap and said to Baeran, "Nice. Like you said, we have two days. Tomorrow, we do it my way."

For their second attempt, Baeran chose an older tree along the stream's edge with minimal fire damage.

Baeran suggested changes to his original trap design and made the trap a foot longer with a wider stove pipe. He added a wood cover secured with a salvaged spring. Baeran sketched the improvements in his pad and donated his dinner scraps as bait.

The next morning, the trap yielded a squirrel. Parker approached

163

the trap. "I have this. It was my idea and my food."

Baeran remembered it differently, but he let Parker climb the tree and remove the trap. On his way down, he slipped and fell, rolling into the stream.

Baeran grinned, and Parker saw it. Parker stood and shook the trap to stun the squirrel. Parker removed the squirrel and snapped its neck. He flung it at Baeran. "Here."

The squirrel hit Baeran in the face, and he fell backward over a log into the stream. Baeran stood in the water, murmuring, "Prick."

"It's about time you had a bath," Parker said and stomped away.

THE TROUBLE WITH BAERAN

M67. Maximus plus sixty-six days. Summer Camp.
BAERAN

BAERAN AWOKE EARLY THE NEXT DAY AND BUILT ANOTHER TRAP. When he finished, he gathered his black backpack, his bowie knife, his birch stick, and Selene. With his Wayfarer sunglasses on, he hiked back out to the first trap along the streambank and re-set it with sunflower seeds on a bark piece. The Firegale was barely visible on the horizon. He hiked downstream, found a similar tree and set the second trap.

Baeran lost two interested squirrels to Selene's excitement. He patted the dog. "Like a fuzzy gray tennis ball with feet, huh?"

By noon, Selene understood, and Baeran trapped three squirrels. He couldn't contain his excitement and jogged to the campsite with his catch. Congratulations greeted Baeran as he showed off his catches. He beamed, until he saw Parker.

Parker complained, "Nice, this was our job and now you take it for yourself. You're an asshat. I hunt tomorrow."

"I thought, I'd just test it out," Baeran apologized.

"But you didn't think. You're on your own now asshero."

Parker slogged off, treading into the burnt-out forest. Baeran followed, and after ten minutes, the older boy stopped and said, "Hey Ass-trapper, are you going to follow me all day?"

"I wanted to apologize."

"Fine, since you are so smart, show me how to make a bow."

Baeran stepped forward and extended his hand.

Parker grabbed Baeran's hand and pulled him closer, while raising his knee into Baeran's gut. Baeran fell to the forest floor gasping for air. Parker jumped onto Baeran and punched him in the ribs. Parker had several inches and forty pounds on the younger boy, and Baeran lost the ability to defend himself. Gasping for air,

165

he cried out. Selene pulled at Parker's pants, but Parker answered her with a kick to the head.

At blow number twenty-five, Parker stood and sneered, "Hey asswipe! How's that for a Shit-Show? Think that was bad? Say a word to anyone, and next time I go after your sisters."

Baeran lay on his back, watching Parker stomp off. He gazed at the tree tops, catching his breath. A slight breeze loosened the burnt bark from the branches. Ash fell, floating, like tiny gray leaves. The ash flakes slow-danced an elaborate waltz as they dropped to the forest floor. By his side, Selene whimpered.

What were Baeran's options? Could he tell everyone? Sure, they knew Parker was a prick. The other Seascapers would accept Baeran's account, but it's not like the Seascapers would exile Parker or tie him up. Eventually Parker would attack Annie, Jordin or Lani. Even if Parker left to avoid punishment, the damage to his sisters would be irreversible, and there's no coming back from that. Could he tell Cole? Sure, but there was no way L.J. would keep his son under lock and key. Parker would play nice long enough to fulfill his promise.

Baeran stared into the sky, weighing his options, while by his side, Selene nuzzled his neck. Baeran couldn't risk unleashing Parker's wrath on his sisters, and he would remain silent concerning the fight. Soon Parker would realize that fact and the power he had over Baeran.

PRESAGE

M40. Maximus plus forty days. Lexington Bunker Complex.
SOLSTICE

SOLSTICE STARED AT THE DUCTWORK, and the words she had written earlier. Words she wrote on the cold metal in the dimlight of the underknee cafeteria vent. Words that had no meaning. Words represented by colors in her mind and by music. Words that formed from between the flashes, before the increasingly painful headaches.

Solstice closed her eyes and lay on her side in the ductwork. She blocked the flashes, moving the pain to the ends of her hair, fingertips and toes, and she weaved the words into a tune. A dreamvision formed and Solstice pictured Melody, laying on her side facing her, and the pair sang.

"Presage"

Star, herald, sign
Omen, forerunner, message
Melody, signal, portent
Seer, harbinger, presage

They come to me
With flashes of light
Glimpses of tomorrow
Revealed in plain sight

Soon will rise
As the world is dwindling
A pentad of
Ancient elements kindling

Just one so far is true
The rest waiting on time
No one accepts it
Opposite of paradigm

Sun igniting
Aether throwing
Air whirling
Earth growing
Fire burning
Water flowing

Soon will rise
As the world is dwindling
A pentad of
Ancient elements kindling

A way forward, a way out
Seascaper searching
Safety while
The Fire's burning

Abandon, hid
Retreaters running
To underground
The flee-ers flying

Soon will rise
As the world is dwindling
A pentad of
Ancient elements kindling

FLASHES

M41. Maximus plus forty-one days. Lexington Bunker Complex.
SOLSTICE

SOLSTICE STOPPED HUMMING, FREEING THE WORDS. But this time the song didn't stop the flashes that felt like lightning firing behind her closed eyes.

She saw the familiar shape. The jagged lines like her sign. The sun with rays melding into an aura. Solstice curled into a ball. It was happening, like it did seven years prior. The aurora flashing behind Solstice's eyelids represented more than the shape of her sign. Years prior, on the date of her birth it had appeared in the sky.

From the depths of Solstice's mind, Melody spoke. "Remember, on our sixth birthday, Mom explained it. Think hard. Remember her eyes—like blue glaciers. Remember her hair—like sunshine. Remember what she smelled like, her perfume—like lavender lilacs. Remember pinky binky and your baby book."

TOTAL SUMMER SOLSTICE ECLIPSE
June 21ˢᵗ. Eight years prior. Lexington, Kentucky.
SOLSTICE

SOLSTICE LEANED UP IN HER BED AT THE CONDO. "Mom, read it to me."

Elle climbed under the covers with her daughter. "Okay, because it's your sixth birthday. My Baby Book. Birthdate: June twenty-first. Height: eighteen and a half inches. Weight: six pounds, nine ounces. Head circumference: thirteen and one quarter inches. Features: blonde hair with blue eyes."

"Now tell me what happened," Solstice pleaded, holding on to her tiny pink unicorn blanket.

Elle replied, "I gave birth to you in Lexington, six years ago."

"More Mom, please."

"Sure, Honey." Elle closed the book, placing it on the night stand. She clasped Solstice's hands, smiling. "When I arrived at the hospital, I had to push for seven minutes. I gave birth around noon under a darkened sky."

"Why Mom?"

"You were born on the longest day of the year when a total solar eclipse occurred. That makes you special."

"Tell me why." Solstice begged.

Elle picked up pinky binky and draped it over the lamp on the nightstand, muting the light. "Because solar eclipses occur on summer solstices every twenty years and after three in a row—they disappear for two centuries."

Solstice asked, "How dark was it?"

Elle switched off the light, "This dark. The blinds were wide open in the birthing room and while I pushed, I could see a black hole in the sky with a ring of fire around it. It was a solar corona."

Solstice asked, "But the sun came back?"

"You saw it today. Yes, of course it came back, after your birth. The moon caused the eclipse, when it moved between the earth and the sun. Later at night, we had an aurora corona, too."

"What's that?"

"These weird yellow-green lights in the night sky," Elle replied. "Like an aurora borealis but with rays shooting out from the same location. It looked like a star with fifteen points."

"Call me it, Mom."

"What?"

What you used to call me as a kid."

Elle tossed pinky binky on Solstice's head. "You're six. You're still a child, my *SolStar*."

"Where'd you find the nickname SolStar?"

"Our sun, it's a star and its name is Sol," Elle replied. "And it's what the newspaper called the aurora corona."

"Tell me more."

"It's late. Time to close your eyes."

"Ah, Mom."

"Good night."

Solstice giggled, "Butterflies. Eskimos."

"Sure. Love you, my SolStar."

HYDRO

BAERAN PRESSED HIS HANDS TO HIS SIDES, probing his injuries, as he did chores around the campsite. He hadn't seen the Firegale in four days, not since Parker kicked his ass. *How long do bruises last? How long till bruises stop hurting?* Baeran considered himself lucky his ribs didn't break. He had seen Parker around the campsite, but both boys avoided each other. Baeran continued to have success with his traps, and taught Deven everything he had learned. When Baeran and Parker crossed paths, Parker said nothing, and smirked at Baeran.

Parker said it all with his eyes. *Remember—the girls.*

Baeran replied with his eyes. *You have me. I understand.*

Despite the pain, Baeran wanted to be around the girls, and helped them with their chores.

Baeran, Lani and Jordin lugged buckets of water from the stream to the campfire. Baeran took his bucket and filled the pot over the fire pit but water spilled, flashing off in the flames.

Cole watched as a puff of gray steam enveloped Baeran. When the cloud cleared and Baeran stopped coughing, Cole said, "Remove the pot with the heavy gloves and fill it on the ground."

Baeran asked between coughs, "What's the point? Does boiling work? Doesn't the debris settle to the bottom of the pot? And does boiling kill the germs? Lugging buckets is the worst. Could we fill the water bottles straight from the stream?"

Cole answered, "I figure we're at least killing the germs. But you're correct, it doesn't remove debris like harmful minerals. If it's too cloudy we can strain the water with a piece of cloth or use a cup and draw water from the top of the pot."

Baeran asked, "What about the bleach, Dad? We used to drop three drops of bleach in the water containers when we first left New Hampshire. How about tablets? Does Mom have those treatment tablets we used to use hiking?"

"Baeran, those don't work for the quantity of water we need, for the group, we have now."

Baeran continued to question Cole about the purification process, as he lugged buckets of water. "Dad, what are our choices besides boiling?"

Cole replied, "We have our pump filters and we have chemical tablets, but I'd save those until we're in a jam."

Baeran asked, "Can't we drink from the stream or a spring?"

"Baeran, the problem is we never know what's upstream, whether it be a carcass, other people using the stream as a bathroom or to wash, or animals tracking, eating or peeing."

"What if we are in a jam, Dad"

"You'd drink the water to avoid dehydrating, but I'd look for fast moving water, and avoid any signs of man-made activity and animal tracks, or I'd search for a spring."

Baeran asked, "What's the risk?"

Cole replied, "A bad case of the runs, like a two-week version. While we are camping, it would be intolerable."

"Dad, when we are on the move, we can't be expected to lug more than two water bottles around per person. Eventually, we'll have to drink unpurified water."

"Baeran let's wait before we chance anything."

"Wait for what Dad?"

"A better source of TP."

HEROES

M73. Maximus plus seventy-three days. Summer Camp.
BAERAN

BAERAN STARED AT THE PITCH OF HIS TENT, as he lay on his sleeping bag, waking. The girls had left, and only Selene lay at his side.

Cole spoke from outside the tent, "Baeran, I need your help today. We need to go on a scavenger run for the girls."

Baeran unzipped his tent. "What for?"

"It's Aileen or Megan's first time. Don't ask. It's worse than when our girls complained about peeing on the roadside."

"Where will we find the stuff?"

Cole replied, "L.J. heard about a town before we moved into the cave, before the firenight. It's a three-hour trek, about twenty miles from the campsite."

Baeran wanted to avoid Parker, so he jumped at the opportunity to go on the scavenger trip. "What about food or other stuff?"

"The mission today is FHP, feminine hygiene products."

"Why us Dad? We're hardly experts. Why not send a mom?"

"Because your mom asked me to," Cole replied. "Occasionally, women or girls ask us, men and boys, to do tasks that make no sense. And to be honest, I can't tell if your mom is screwing with me or testing me or if it's nothing. Maybe, she thinks I need the exercise or she thinks it's time I leave the infirmary in the cave. Maybe your mom has no hidden agenda. It's like when your mom used to leave me money on the counter in Portsmouth, but it's like twenty bucks less than the previous week. Is that an accident or statement? I have no idea.

"Baeran, we never know what the hell women are thinking. There's no point in asking. I can bug your mom and receive cattail harvesting duty by the stream or I can take a hike with my favorite

174

son. If you see like a year's supply of Hershey bars in the pharmacy or Cheez-Its or Coke, you can take whatever will fit into your backpack, but the mission today is FHP.

"To make it worse, I know your mom is already planning the same hike to the pharmacy in two days for some other supplies. Why doesn't she do this herself, now? Who knows?"

"Geez Dad, what kind do they want?"

"I hadn't thought about that. I'm sure everyone is different. We'll grab what we can."

"What about if we find beer?" Baeran asked.

"We screw the FHP and lug the beer!"

"Dad, you will fail. That's the Mom test: FHP versus beer."

Cole laughed, "So be it. Let's leave."

Baeran gathered his birch stick and his black backpack, and added two water bottles, his Wayfarer sunglasses, his bowie knife and dried squirrel meat. He whistled for Selene to join him.

Cole and Baeran traveled north and found the town within three and a half hours. During their journey westward, the Sheridan Family had seen selected areas of forest untouched by flames while other areas were scorched. Like a tornado, the Firegale distributed its destruction without a pattern. This town was no different.

"I know it's tempting but we avoid everything else." Cole said. "Straight to the pharmacy to retrieve the FHP."

Cole saw Baeran glance at the sporting goods store. "Stay on target. I want to be gone in fifteen-minutes tops. I'll watch for Jackers"

Baeran peered into the pharmacy. The shelves were stocked in the abandoned building. He bolted to the snack aisle and collected several Cokes and Hershey bars. Cole yelled in while guarding the pharmacy door, "Do you see them?"

Baeran scrambled from the snack aisle, reading the signs, "I found the aisle. Give me a minute."

Baeran surveyed the aisles. There were so many items he wanted to take, like water bottles, batteries, shampoo, soap, toys, games and Cheez-Its. But the girls couldn't live without the FHP. "Remember the mission," he jokingly said to himself. Besides he

175

knew his mom planned to come back in two days. Baeran said, "Do I want the white Nerf bullets or the giant Band-Aids?"

Cole peered into the pharmacy door and said, "Take it all, regardless of type and size. As if we could figure out sizes. We'll be heroes and at worst the extra FHP could be used as currency."

Baeran replied, "At least the boxes are lightweight. Mankind's finest scientists must have been focusing on developing lightweight FHP during the last couple of decades."

"They should've focused on fire protection and prevention technology." Cole laughed.

Baeran smiled as he exited the pharmacy.

"Good work. Let's head home."

When Baeran returned to the campsite, he felt like a conquering hero. FHP even surpassed the popularity of squirrel.

Later that day, Baeran tried to change his clothes in his parent's tent. Kay caught him, and asked, "When's the last time you changed your underwear?"

"I'm changing them now." Baeran replied.

His mom glared, "No way. Not in my tent. You're covered in dirt and grime from your hike with your dad. Go wash in the stream first and come back."

Baeran wanted to avoid the cold stream water and stripped in his own tent. Moments of privacy were fleeting, and Lani, Jordin and Annie strolled in to see him in his underwear. If the girls had been a minute sooner, they would have seen the family jewels. The girls outnumbered him, and they relished it, despite the fact Baeran had liberated and delivered a lifetime supply of FHP. When the giggles died down, Baeran vowed he would never change his underwear again.

CATTAILS, CALADRYL, AND THE SNEAKER
M74. Maximus plus seventy-four days. Summer Camp.
BAERAN

BAERAN FOLLOWED KAY DOWN TO THE STREAM at midday for her latest lesson on foraging. He had avoided a confrontation with Parker for seven days. The bruises on his ribs had healed. He kept his promise to not say a word, and so did Parker. For their safety, Baeran shadowed the girls, joining in with their activities.

Kay, Susan, and Judy brought the children down to the stream bed to search for edible plants. Baeran gripped a cattail and swung it at Lani. He owed her. The girls were giggling about the dome tent show and "Baeran Underwearin'." The brown tip of the cattail fractured, sending thousands of tiny white floaties into Lani's hair, and she yelled, "Mom!"

"Baeran Sheridan, put the cattail down," Kay said.

"She's fine, Mom."

"I'm not worried about your sister, that's your dinner."

"Mom, Baeran's being the worst, and you're talking about dinner." Lani groaned. "I'm not eating that. So, whatever, as long as Baeran doesn't smack me again."

Kay addressed the entire group. "Back when Baeran was in Boy Scouts, I became a den mother, and we learned about what we could eat or not eat, touch or not touch in the wild. We used to do overnight camps in the White Mountains. My ancestors, the Native Americans of this region—the Abenaki—once harvested cattails, integrating them into their diet. They ate the roots raw, but we'll cook them. The edible stem is tasty closest to the root. Cattails are loaded with vitamins and minerals: C, K, B-1, calcium and sodium."

Kay removed her pocketknife and cut off a six-inch piece closest to the root. Kay bit into the stalk and smiled. "Hmm, tasty, and for the ladies, twenty-five calories per cattail serving. The brown fuzzy tips at the top of the plant are edible, and taste like corn. We'll harvest tips and boil them over the campfire."

Kay picked a dandelion that had sprouted through the ash on the floor of the former forest, and said, "The entire plant is edible but bitter. I've experimented by boiling the dandelions. The bitterness faded through the boiling process, and after being strained through water it made for a tolerable tea."

The kids' mouths hung open.

Lani spoke first, "You can't be serious, Mom! OMG. Chicken, that's what I want and bagels, and pretzels with that orange dipping cheese. I want lemonade. I could drink a gallon of that. And I'd brush my teeth for like two hours. That's what I want. So, no way. No way, you can be serious."

"I am serious Lani," Kay replied. "The world has already changed so much and will continue to change. Your father, myself, L.J., Susan, Heather, and Mitch will continue to scavenge. But it's dangerous. What should we do: learn to like a new vegetable, or continue to put our family and friends in danger?"

"Mom, that's not a fair choice." Lani complained. "It's not like the adults are searching for fruit and veggies. We need gas, equipment, and other stuff."

Baeran interrupted, "As the one person who has been on a scavenging mission with Dad, I can tell you without question he is laser focused on beer, now that the FHP has been located and delivered. I hear Dad talking to L.J. and Mitch about a beer quest all the time."

"See Mom. Beer Questing!" Lani pleaded. "Why can't we quest for jam or cucumber sandwiches like Wàigōng's?"

Annie smiled.

Jordin grasped Lani's hand and whispered, "*Wo hen gaoxing.* I'm so glad you still remember."

Kay grinned. "Okay, but we are already looking for canned goods like jam and fresh vegetables, and we haven't found much. We need to change the way we think about food. We've never considered the choices. Let's try the cattails tonight."

"Now, certain plants should be avoided. Baeran knows about

this," Kay continued.

Baeran involuntarily stared at his crotch.

Baeran had no idea how he spread it over his body, years prior. It had burned like a wildfire. Worse than when he zipped it in his pants. But Baeran could think of one thing worse than the itch of the poison ivy: his mom putting Caladryl on his privates. He had been ten. The lotion brought relief with its application, but tons of embarrassment.

"When gathering plants," Kay reminded the group, "avoid three-leaf, reddish-green and oily plants, telltale signs of poisonous or dangerous plants. When exposed to poison ivy, remove your clothes and double wash your skin to help stop the spread of the oil. In a pinch, river sand could be used instead of soap."

Kay grinned at Baeran and the rest of the children, but Jordin had tuned out. Kay said, "Jordin, honey, why don't you ask Baeran about his poison ivy?"

Baeran interrupted, "No thanks. I want to go set the traps."

"Okay, but stay close, I'm going to the abandoned pharmacy in a little while with some of the adults."

Baeran set the traps in the woods, and an hour later he saw the adults going to the pharmacy, aka, PharmaTown. Everyone took turns scavenging, and he already had his chance with Cole, but he didn't care. He left Selene with Jordin, and he slipped into the forest. Staying within sight of the adult's backs, he followed them in secret to the edge of the woods overlooking the town. He climbed a tree, and watched the adults walk to the first house.

Kay pointed to the far end of the town. "Damn, a fire!" She pulled out Cole's binoculars. "Crap. It's the pharmacy."

Mitch and Heather glanced at Kay for instructions.

"That sucks. What a waste, but it doesn't change the mission." Kay said. "It's more important now. We won't be coming back. Another group hit this town, looting and burning. We check the houses and we leave."

Mitch and Heather entered the houses and searched while Kay watched their entry points for signs of trouble. Kay said, "Search the medicine cabinets and gather pain medicine like Tylenol or Advil, and any prescription medicine ending in 'cillin.' The antibiotics may come in handy."

After the sixth house, Kay noticed activity near the pharmacy. "There are Jackers. It's time to leave."

Kay, Mitch and Heather left for the campsite.

Baeran climbed down the tree. He studied the moss and the angle of the sun. He remembered what direction he had come from, but he checked the natural signs. He outflanked the scavenger party and made it to camp three minutes before the adults did.

Later, Baeran ate a couple peach slices around the campfire, with the entire Seascaper group, while Kay lamented the loss of the pharmacy.

"At least we have the FHP. Nothing could be more valuable." Cole smirked.

Baeran chimed in, "Dad I didn't want to tell you this when we were in PharmaTown, because you kept going on about the mission, but the pharmacy was full of beer."

"Baeran you are my least favorite son," Cole replied to a chorus of laughs.

Kay added, "Beer aside, this is significant. Jackers are on the move. That means there are other survivors of the fire night, possibly Dazers. Remember them?"

Susan replied, "I'm gathering my family's gear. We won't be backed into a corner. There will be no more cave hiding from the Firegale or any other horror, whether it be Jackers or Dazers."

Susan hastened to her tent.

Judy stood. "I'll delay her a bit, but we'll be gone in a week."

Judy followed Susan to her tent with Aileen and Megan.

"What do we do?" Kay sighed.

Cole replied, "We prepare for anything. We'll be fine."

SOLSTAR

M49. Maximus plus forty-nine days. Lexington Bunker Complex.
SOLSTICE

Solstice let Melody sing in the ductwork near the loud fan. The migraines, aura and flashes had come on suddenly a few hours ago, forewarning the impending dreamvision. Solstice closed her eyes, and she pictured blackness. At the center of the void, a bright light blinked on and slowly intensified, revealing itself as the sun. Solstice, looked away from the light, noticing the planets, moons and the space in between. Sol was the star at the center, and all revolved around her. The Solstar gave light and life, but promised destruction and darkness, and Solstice realized she was the sun, doomed to kindle or kill.

"SolStar"

White, when the colors are joined as one
They mix together, bleeding in our sun
Fused Hydrogen melds forming helium
Greater than the earth by times one million

Nuclear electron beware of anti-particle positron
Gravitation and magnetics, forces second to none
Sending unseen rays, wind, flares and photons
In the night sky, aurora corona it will become

Everlasting Sol will consume in an eon
Mercury, Venus, Earth and Mars, swallowed, gone
While gas giants and ice titans live on
Yellow dwarf will die, and the red will be drawn

THE BURNT SUNSET

SolStar, predicted, seen, future foregone
From the sky, comes to earth a phenomenon
Born under the ring of fire, the eclipse spawn
Kindler, keeper of the solar light, Seer of lexicon

Solstice sun ignites ancient powers on the horizon
Throw, whirl, grow, burn and flow in the Elementum
Aethi, Aero, Terra, Pyro and Hydro forces hereon
In sky, sunset, eventide and aurora will dawn

From the depths of Solstice's mind, Melody spoke. "There's more you need to remember. Struggles you need to understand, to give you strength for now and for the future."

Solstice closed her eyes and recalled events from half a lifetime ago.

ICE

June 21ˢᵗ. Seven years prior. Lexington, Kentucky.
SOLSTICE

Sᴏʟsᴛɪᴄᴇ sᴀᴛ ᴜᴘ ɪɴ ʜᴇʀ ʙᴇᴅ ɪɴ ᴛʜᴇ ᴄᴏɴᴅᴏ, screaming into the darkness, "Mom!"

Elle flipped on the light. Her six-year-old daughter sat in her bed with the covers pulled high on her chest. Her tiny white knuckles gripped the pink unicorn blanket, pinky binky. "What is it, honey?" Elle asked.

Solstice replied, "She won't stop. The voice in my head."

"Any flashes?" Elle asked, sitting on the bed.

Solstice scooted toward her mom, slipping her arm in Elle's, "A few—not too bad."

"What did you see?" Elle ran her fingers through Solstice's long blonde hair.

"The same," Solstice replied. "Pictures, numbers and words with color."

Elle pushed Solstice's long blonde hair from her eyes. "Sweetie, you need to write it down in the journal. Writing will help you release, and help you remember and later understand."

Solstice said, "OK. Can you help me? Fourteen equals fire, fifteen equals presage, sixteen equals catalyst, no—more like kindling."

"Sure, honey." Elle grabbed her daughter's journal, flipping it open to a blank page.

"The words, numbers, and pictures, Mom, have a tune, too."

Elle asked, "Like a song?"

"Yes."

"Songs can't be too bad." Elle smiled. She hugged Solstice. "It's a soundtrack to your dreams."

"Mom!"

"Write it down." Elle offered her the journal. "If the pictures have music, pretend you are writing a song, in your Lyricbook."

Solstice asked, "But who's singing the song, Mom?"

Elle moved deeper into the bed, leaning against the wall. She grabbed a handful of Solstice's hair, dividing it into three. "How about Melody? Melody is singing." She crossed one handful over the other starting the braid.

"OK, Mom. I like her name, Melody. Makes her less creepy." She grabbed the journal from Elle and slipped it under her pillow. "I'll write it down in the morning."

"Good idea. You need to close your eyes."

"Can I sleep with you, Mom?" Solstice squeezed Elle with both arms.

Elle replied, "Okay, because we have major plans tomorrow."

"Birthdays!" Solstice giggled. "Number seven for me and for you…"

Elle stood, leading her daughter into the next room, but Solstice pulled away.

Solstice ran back for pinky binky, jumping on the bed to retrieve it.

"Don't push your luck. Come to bed."

"Mom will Dad visit tomorrow?" Solstice bounced onto the floor.

"Honey, you know he won't, ever." Elle bit her lip, censoring herself.

Solstice said, "But the vision, Mom, from last month. I'll meet him near my birthday." She placed her hand in Elle's and they walked a few steps down the hall to the master bedroom.

"No, not this year, but you'll have many other birthdays. Go to sleep, Solstice. In the morning, we will have a special guest."

Elle lifted up Solstice and placed her in the bed. She pulled down the covers and Solstice squirmed in, holding pinky binky. Elle climbed in next to her daughter and switched off the light on the nightstand."

Solstice closed her eyes and dreamt that the special guest was her father, despite her mom's assertion otherwise. When Solstice rose, she rushed to the breakfast table. A woman she had never met sat across from Elle.

"Who's this Mom?"

Elle said, "Honey, this is Maria Pilar Consquento."

Solstice sat warily at the breakfast table. "Hi."

Elle said, "She's here to help around the house when I'm gone." She slid a bowl of Cheerios and some milk in front of Solstice.

Maria pulled her chair closer to Solstice. "Hi, dear, you can call me Mrs. C."

Solstice ignored the strange new woman in their kitchen. "Mom, I don't want you to go."

Elle reached over the table, for Solstice's hand, but her daughter moved back in her chair. "We talked about this. Mrs. C. will stay with you when I'm gone. She has a place down the hall, unit 209."

"But Mom..." Solstice pushed away her cereal.

"Honey, I need to work. I want to work. You have school, and Mrs. C. will meet you afterward. She'll help with homework and cook dinner. And I'll be home Wednesday nights, and weekends. You'll see. Give it a chance. It will work."

Solstice stood, crossing her arms. "Mom!"

Elle said, "Mrs. C. sings in two languages. She can help you with the songs, and with your friend, Melody."

Solstice replied, "Mom! That's our secret." She stood, stepping away from the breakfast table.

"Not from Mrs. C., honey. She's here to help. She starts next week."

Solstice whined, as tears formed in her eyes, "Mom, how could you?" She didn't wait for a response and stomped out the room.

Elle stood, making a move to go after Solstice.

Mrs. C. said, "Miss Elle, let her leave. We'll figure this out."

The two women sat back at the table and Elle and Mrs. C. discussed Elle's schedule. After they planned for the next visit, Elle thanked Mrs. C. and showed her to the door. "I'll see you next week. She'll be better next time."

"I'm sure she will. She is a lovely girl," Mrs. C. said.

After Mrs. C. left, Elle found Solstice in her bedroom.

"Solstice, I didn't like how you treated Mrs. C." Elle sat on the edge of the bed.

"I'm sorry." Solstice hugged her mom.

"Okay, how about you and I have a special day today? Do you want to do some shopping?"

"Can we get birthday pie?"

"Yes."

Solstice scrambled to get dressed. She raced into the kitchen, gulping down her cereal.

After breakfast, Solstice and Elle left for the mall in the Scout pick-up. Solstice sat in the back seat, imagining treats, gifts and the surprise party Elle failed to conceal.

Elle negotiated traffic making small talk with her daughter as they drove to the tumble gym.

Solstice was all smiles, until she heard Melody's voice:

> You are Solstice, the Sun
> Singing, kindling, sighting
> A seer with visions
> Of powers igniting
> Watch out for the mailbox
> Sorry about the lightning

Solstice closed her eyes, unable to bear the sudden and severe pain. Lightning flashed behind her eyes, and thunder echoed in her brain. She yelled, "Mom, pull over, you are going to crash!"

Elle swerved the curb. Solstice screamed. Elle whipped her head to check on her daughter in the back seat. The Scout bounced over the curb, striking a blue mail drop-off box. It tumbled through the air, crashing through the windshield, striking the steering wheel and Elle in the arm, while she sought to protect herself. The Scout crashed into a lamp post, coming to a stop.

Solstice hit her head, glancing off the seatback, and slid to the floor, shaking. She bit her tongue and blood squirted onto the tan seats. Her head thrashed back and forth, smashing between the front and back seats. Her arms and legs shook violently, like she was being electrocuted by a lightning bolt. The blood from her tongue mixed with vomit, and then pee. The tremors continued, and she twisted, spreading the warm liquids all over her body. Her eyes darted back and forth, desperate to find relief, but her vision was fading from the corners. Her last image was Elle, leaning over the seat screaming.

Elle woke up in daze, her arm shattered. She squeezed out from under the drop-off box. Elle pulled herself up with one arm, struggling to peer over the back seat.

"Oh my God! Solstice!"

SOLARIUM

June 28th. About seven years prior. Lexington, Kentucky.
SOLSTICE

SOLSTICE DRIFTED IN AND OUT OF CONSCIOUSNESS during her first days at the hospital. But by her eighth day at the hospital, Solstice was strong enough to meet her new physical therapist.

Solstice watched the physical therapist strap her into new leg harnesses. She was flat on her back, in the hospital bed. Her therapist had to be three times her size, but he had dark kind eyes.

"I'm Dallas. I played for the Cowboys for about two weeks, until I tore my knee up. I'll be your PT for the duration of your recovery." Dallas smiled, extending his enormous hands towards Elle. "You must be her mother, Elle. Nice to meet you. Elle if you want you can stick around for a bit, until you and your daughter are comfortable, but I like to do the sessions with children without their parents."

"Nice to meet you Dallas. Why?" Elle asked.

Dallas replied, "I find the kids work harder when they don't have their parents to lean on. The door will stay open and you can listen from the hallway." He tightened the straps on the braces and moved Solstice legs to test the mobility of the devices. "Each day we will walk to the Solarium. As she progresses, we will move onto a closed PT room with other patients. You can watch from behind the glass on the balcony overlooking the PT floor." Dallas taped the metal the sides of the braces, smiling. "Is that okay with you?"

Elle replied, "Yes."

"And you, Miss, is it okay?" Dallas asked.

Solstice replied, "Yes. Are you a giant?"

"No, but I hear you're a seven-year-old singer and a dancer."

Solstice struggled to sit up. "I am."

Elle reached for Solstice, to help her.

"Let her do it. She needs to find those core muscles." Dallas said. "So, you are a dancer? That should make my job much easier. Dancers are hard workers and singers make everyone smile. What kind of music do you like?"

"Radio stuff."

"Can you Rap?" Dallas asked.

"Sure. Here goes..."

I need to pee
Let's try them braces
I want to tie
my own shoe laces

Dallas is on the job
Assigned them tough cases
Working with the young Miss
So, she can get back her graces

Dallas grinned, "Nice. We'll get along fine. How about it, Elle?"

Elle smirked at Dallas and nodded.

"I'll be down the hall, Sweetie." She lingered for a moment, hand on the doorway, judging Dallas with her eyes.

Dallas waited for Elle to leave. He glanced at his clipboard.

"It says in my notes you are seven years old. Do you do anything besides sing and dance?" Dallas said.

Solstice replied, "Yep. Walk with these braces, today, right now. Later, I'll return to dancing."

"I like the attitude. Let's get you out of bed and fitted into the crutches first. Don't set your expectations too high. Standing today would be an accomplishment."

Solstice twisted herself in her bed, so her toes pointed towards the edge. "Dallas, you want to know a secret?"

"Does your mom know?"

"She knows." Solstice replied. "We're a team. We don't have any secrets."

"Miss let's hear it."

"I'm gonna glide out the hospital, soon." She swung her legs over the edge of the bed.

Dallas cautioned her, "Wait a minute, how do you know?"

Solstice replied, "I can see the future."

"Really?"

"Yep Dallas. Scares my mom, but it's true."

"How many fingers am I holding up?" Dallas asked.

"Doesn't work like that."

Dallas was intrigued. "How does it work?"

"I can't control it yet. I see numbers, words and colors. The predictions come to me in my dreamvision, after flashes behind my eyes and headaches. The dreamvision turns into a song, and she helps me sing them."

"Who helps you sing? Does your mom?" Dallas leaned forward, whispering.

Solstice replied, "No, Silly, Melody does."

"Who's Melody?"

"A name my mom invented for the voice in my head."

Dallas put both his hands-on Solstice's hips. "Is that so? I'm going to lift you now and stand you up. Is that okay."

"Yes."

Dallas lifted Solstice, placing her feet on the floor. He waited a moment for Solstice to find her balance. He released one hand. "Tell me about the voice."

"Don't worry." Solstice replied, "She's not another person. Doesn't take over or anything, but she's louder than other people's voices. She's louder than your voice."

"My voice?" Dallas let go of Solstice, so that she supported herself only with the braces.

"Yes, Dallas. The one that keeps you going, helps you work harder, and care more for the kids you help."

"Take one step towards me." Dallas extended his arms out serving as a safety net.

Solstice took a step forward, struggling under the weight of the metal frames. "I feel like a robot." She joked. "Beep. Boop. Bap. I. Am. Dancer. Robot. Beep. Beep. Beep." She took another step with her arms extend and locked at the elbow.

Dallas laughed. "Good. That's really good. Tell me more about

Melody."

"I've seen myself, older, dancing with a boy under the moonlight, after the flames." Solstice replied. "I've seen that dream a few times plus the one with all the numbers"

"What? I'll take your word for it. Let's ensure you don't miss a date with the boy. When is it?"

"Seven years from now." Solstice smiled. "I hope he sings and dances, too."

"Let's shoot for walking in seven weeks." Dallas declared. "That's our goal." Dallas backed up.

Solstice took two more steps forward, struggling, exhausted from the handful of steps. Her body, weak from accident, wobbled. "Dallas, I'll do whatever it takes." Her legs gave out and she fell into his arms.

Dallas supported Solstice. "Alright, that's a good start let's make our way back to the bed."

Dallas helped Solstice back into bed. He found Elle and updated her on the progress from the doorway of the hospital room.

"Tomorrow, they'll be moving you to the rehab wing. I'll see you there after lunch." Dallas smiled. "Great job today, Dancer Robot. Remember, the Solarium is our goal."

There were one hundred steps from Solstice's room to the Solarium, a room at the end of the hall, surrounded on three sides by glass walls. Potted fruit trees—a lemon and a lime, ornamental grasses, goldenrod and a yellow poplar sapling, the latter two, the state flower and tree, rounded out the room, surrounding a fountain.

The next afternoon, Solstice grinned when she saw Dallas. She swung her legs off the bed, and for ninety days, her day began the same way...

Solstice had been in the rehabilitation clinic all summer, and the long ordeal was ending. The strolls to the Solarium had been littered with failures and tears. But she made it, and she found her grace, thanks to Dallas.

Elle and Solstice sat on the hospital bed discussing Solstice's discharge. A nurse poked her head in the room. "Ms. Dayton, Dr. Johnson would like to meet with you across the hall for a moment."

Elle stood and walked over to the nurse. "Solstice, I'll be back in a moment." She closed the door halfway. "Just call for me if you need me, Solstice."

"No problem, Mom."

Solstice sat on the edge of her bed eavesdropping.

"If you'll come with me, please." The pair stepped across the hallway. "Dr. Johnson will be along in a moment. Ms. Dayton, I wanted to tell you, your daughter has been a ray of sunshine for the other patients. Given the condition in which she arrived, her progress has been remarkable."

"Thank you." Elle said, "That's kind of you to say."

"Here's Dr. Johnson now." The nurse extended her arm through the doorway, inviting Elle into the Blue-Sky Room.

Dr. Johnson said, "Hi Elle, how are you feeling today?"

"Fine. Thank you. We are excited to get home.

Dr. Johnson sat. Elle sat across from him.

"Good. The tumor we detected three months ago after the seizure, has shrunk to undetectable levels. This morning's MRI confirms that."

Elle leaned forward in her seat. "Without any treatment?"

Solstice hopped out of bed and tiptoed to the door jam. She ducked her head into the hallway as quick as she could to steal a glance of the doctor and Elle. She leaned back into the jam and caught her reflection on the glass window the half open hospital room door. She looked old and young all at once. She could see Elle's reflection off the door to the Blue-Sky Room. Solstice angled her head such that she could see the doctor and her mother. The double reflection was transparent and ghost-like.

The doctor tapped on his computer screen, waking it from sleep mode. On the display was a black and white MRI scan of Solstice's brain and skull. Dr. Johnson said, "Yes. Honestly, I don't know why. See here." He pointed to a region in the back of Solstice's brain. "There's nothing. I don't think we'll ever know without exploratory surgery—which I wouldn't do. The mass, a cyst-like fatty tumor has dissipated."

Elle slid her chair forward, scratching the legs on the floor. Dr. Johnson rolled his chair aside such that only his arm was visible to Solstice. Elle touched the screen and asked. "What about the seizures?"

"As you know, the seizure occurred on June twenty-first, over ninety days ago."

"Yes, Doctor, it was her seventh birthday. We were driving to the tumble gym to meet her friends."

"Right. I'm sorry for not asking. How's the arm?"

Elle waved her arm. "Cast comes off this week."

"Excellent. That was one hell of a break. I am not sure how you stopped a mailbox with your arm. So, there is no reason to presuppose she will have any more seizures. In fact, the human body, more so a child's, is remarkable. She won't remember this years from now. The mind has a way of blocking out unpleasant events."

Elle moved back from the screen, separating herself from Dr. Johnson. She asked, "What about the predictions?"

Solstice glanced down at her toes. Her mom was giving away her secret again. She didn't want to be different, not today, not ever and she promised to do everything in her power to suppress Melody. She leaned back against the door jamb, closing her eyes and focused only on their voices.

Dr. Johnson leaned back in his chair. He rubbed his chin. "Are you talking about the accident?"

"Yes, before we crashed she told me we would crash," Elle whispered as she leaned forward.

"Tell me what happened."

Elle said, "On the way to the party, in the back seat, she had a flash. She told me to pull over, to avoid the crash."

"And what happened next?"

"We crashed." Elle replied, "The car hit a mailbox and a light pole. Thank God no one stood near it."

"Did your daughter predict the crash or cause it by distracting you?"

Solstice opened her eyes and glanced at the double reflection again. Elle stood. She gave the doctor a look usually reserved just for her—anger and incredulousness combined with a partial eye roll.

"Doctor, she's seen more. Dark visions of the future, flames and people she doesn't know. Places she's never been."

"Elle have any visions come true besides the accident?"

Elle put her hands and her hips. "No, not yet, but she doesn't tell me everything."

The doctor reached for Elle. "And the visions are preceded by the flashes of light?"

Elle backed away. "Yes, and the headaches."

Doctor Johnson stood, stepping toward the open door. "Elle, bear with me." He peered into the hallway. "Nurse, can you bring in today's paper? Is it in the plastic like I asked?" The nurse brought in the paper. Doctor Johnson continued sitting, "Good. Thank you. Elle take note I haven't opened today's paper yet."

"Sure."

"Elle, do you read the horoscope?"

"Doctor, I don't think..."

"Elle give me a chance. What's your birthdate?"

"Same as my daughter's: June twenty-first."

"Do you share..."

"No. She prefers pie, chocolate mousse. I like lemon cake with white frosting and mini chocolate chips."

The doctor opened the paper. "Section E. Your zodiac symbol is Cancer. The horoscope says: 'Your feelings are related to your experiences. You will receive good news today.' Ha! I'm sorry for laughing. Honestly, I could have not asked for a better example."

"Doctor?" Elle scooted forward, trying to read the text.

He handed the paper to Elle and she sat.

"Predictions, Elle, like the one in your horoscope, are often vague enough, we feel they apply. Secretly, we want to believe."

Elle leaned back in her chair, tossing the paper to the seat next to her. "Doctor, she's predicted other events."

"Elle, I don't have a good explanation for what she saw." He tapped on his mouse and pulled up a hospital directory on the computer screen. "I could recommend a colleague. We have excellent psychiatrists in the attached wing."

"We don't need another doctor."

"Fine, let's focus on a schedule." Dr. Johnson tapped on the mouse and switched the display back to the picture of Solstice's brain and skull. "I want to see your daughter once a month for the next six months."

Elle replied, "Understood."

"And Elle, if she has another seizure, your first call is 911, and your second call is me. Your daughter's progress has been remarkable these last three months." He handed Elle a business card. "Keep this with you. Remember, it's important we stimulate her brain. I'm talking about math, art, music, dance, and singing. Have her keep writing songs. We need to engage the body and mind and consciously link them."

"Will dance help her recover from the paralysis?" Elle asked. "She used to be such a bundle of energy."

Dr. Johnson replied, "Yes. If she continues to progress, the average person won't know of her physical struggles."

"Will she dance again?"

"Your daughter will glide out of the rehabilitation wing today. She's shown extraordinary progress. After the seizure and rehabilitation, she remains graceful, but Elle, you'll have to push her." Doctor Johnson stood, extending his hand. "The therapy won't be easy, and later the exercise and the dance. She may hate you for it. Elle are we clear?"

Elle rose, accepting the hand shake. "Yes. Anything for her."

Solstice tiptoed from the door jamb to her bed. Had it been ninety-two days in the hospital and rehabilitation wing? The first seven days had felt like a year, strapped to a bed, hearing everything around her but seeing only a portion. Her one open eye was glassy, yielding blurry versions of her surroundings.

The braces had come off the previous week, her eleventh week in treatment, and the bruises from the straps on her thighs were fading. Solstice stared at her toes, wiggling them on the hospital bed, until she saw a familiar face.

Dallas poked his head into Solstice's room, knocking on the door frame. "Ready to leave?"

Solstice replied, "Yes, thanks to you, Dallas."

"You did the hard work."

"I won't forget what you did Dallas. Hopefully, I'll attend dance class this week and soon, school."

"You want to return to school?" Dallas asked.

"Yes. Dallas, let's do one hundred steps for fun." Solstice hopped off the bed and hugged him.

"Where to, Miss?"

The dancer robot replied, "Beep. Boop. Bap. To. The. Solarium. Beep. Beep."

LITTLE HOLES BIG PROBLEMS
M79. Maximus plus seventy-nine days. Summer Camp.
BAERAN

"BAERAN SHERIDAN, GET YOUR ASS OUT THE TENT and take care of your dog."

Baeran rose at the sound of Cole's voice and trudged into the burnt-out forest with Selene. It had been twelve days since the shit show with Parker. What was Parker waiting for? Was he out of ass-names? Wasn't it time for his second beating?

Baeran looked away as Selene made a deposit. He had slacked on the dog poop pickup for about a week, one time. He remembered when Kay stepped in it. The consequences had been swift and severe. Baeran didn't want to hear about his mom's poop-shoes again. He used a tiny garden spade to dig the holes, transfer the poop, and bury it. Picking up poop sucked, and Selene made it three times a day. The Seascapers lived in the wild, but he had to scoop poop because his mom didn't watch where she strolled. So Baeran dug three mini holes per day, and picked up the poops, topping the holes off with dirt.

Poop duty sucked, but it was tolerable, until today. He tripped and got crap on his shirt and on his chin, too. Baeran rose and wiped off his shirt, spreading poop on his hands. He shook the poop off the tiny shovel and scraped his shirt. But he itched his nose, and smeared poop on his face. His face burnt red. The blood rushed to Baeran's cheeks, his ears clogged, and his pulse quickened when he heard laughter over his shoulder. Parker was doubled over, a few feet away, unable to contain his mirth.

Parker said a joke about a bear and poop and the woods and he added, "Your sisters will shit their pants when I'm done with them."

Baeran darted at Parker, tackling him. Poop landed on Parker's shirt, as Baeran pinned him to the ground. He punched Parker in the chest and asked, "How do you like this shit show, Parker?"

But Parker was older, stronger, and better fighter. He flipped Baeran over onto his back and held him down with his knees. He hit Baeran where their dads wouldn't find the bruises, and he ripped off his shit-shirt and rubbed it in the younger boy's face. "Keep the shirt, assface."

Baeran rolled to his side, turning to watch Parker leave. He rolled onto his back and stared into the trees. His face burnt. Anger yielded to shame, and Baeran whispered to himself, "Idiot. Loser." He closed his eyes, and felt the anxiety kicking in. Was he no longer safe anywhere? He modulated his breathing and counted. Six-nine-four. Inhale. Exhale. Hold. Baeran tried to break it down and find a solution, but he was overwhelmed, and he let the shame take him. He had started the fight, but the bully finished it, leaving behind bruises, and a boy no longer sure of his place in the world.

CAGED

M83. Maximus plus eighty-three days. Summer Camp.
BAERAN

BAERAN SAT IN THE LOOKOUT TREE WITH REESE, watching Susan and Judy ride out on their motorcycles.

"Do see the dust to the west? What is that?" Reese asked.

Baeran scanned the horizon. He pulled out his binoculars. "It's refugees about two football fields away. They're coming out of the trees."

Reese cupped her hands over her eyes. "They don't look right."

"Shit! It's Dazers!"

Baeran climbed down and ran to Cole. He found Cole near the campfire and skidded to a stop. "Dazers are coming!"

Cole barked to the Seascapers, "We have company. Everyone move into the cave!"

As the adults rolled the ATVs in front of the cave, the Dazers stumbled into the campsite. Their leprous skin peeled in patches. The refugees were grimy, exhausted, and hungry with bloody sores, boils, burns and ripped clothes. They were unshaven, with broken arms, sprained ankles, ripped flesh, and missing teeth. The Dazers meandered through the campsite toward the stream, like grazing cattle, ignoring the Seascapers gathering near the cave.

Baeran focused on his mom and Lani, holding hands. Lani put her head on Kay's shoulder. Lani's eyes widened, and her head drooped. With her other hand, Lani grasped Jordin's hand. "Oh, J. Look at them. Look at the little ones. Mom, can we do anything?" She stared in horror.

What was wrong with their skin? Yellow eyes stared out from their bleak expressions, and blisters dotted their faces and arms.

The last time Baeran had seen this many people, he had been

exiting a New England Patriots game. Sweat rolled off his chin, and his eyes darted from the back of the cave to the front, searching for an escape.

Mitch spoke to the refugees from the cave: "Hello. You are welcome to use the stream. We have no supplies to spare. We have guns and will remain here until you pass on."

A half-dozen heads poked up. But they didn't care.

They were Dazed.

Baeran's raised his shoulders and squeezed his arms to his chest and he counted, "Six-nine-four."

The Seascapers remained huddled in the cave for the day and night, taking turns observing the refugees, whispering, "We should have left like Judy and Susan."

The Dazers swarmed to several hundred, fouled the stream, and consumed the vegetation. They knocked over the tents, bathrooms, and the cooking area.

Hours after having eaten, Baeran could taste his last meal rising in his throat. The newest Dazers appeared sicklier. Like animals, the Dazers were starving and grouping together for support. They communicated without words, grunting back and forth. They gathered by the stream like a herd, dazed and stunned. As the crowd grew larger, the Dazers grouped closer to the cave entrance.

Baeran leaned against the cave back wall. His face flushed, reddened by anxiety and shame. He heard his dad mention shooting their way out, opening fire on the herd, on the Dazed. His ears clogged, and his dad's words were the last he heard. He leaned back and fell to the ground. He had to escape. He rested his head on his knees. His eyes darkened, but outside the cave, he saw a familiar face approaching. In a stupor, Baeran mumbled, "Susan?"

The late-afternoon sun shone through the dust clouds and into the cave. Susan and Aileen rode on a motorcycle with no sidecar. Metal hung from the bike, dragging on the rough ash dirt. Susan road in circles, creating dust swirls with the motorcycle, kicking dirt, forcing the Dazers back.

Susan stopped near the cave at the stream embankment. She ran into the water with Aileen, choking back sobs. "We both were wrong. We shouldn't have left, but you shouldn't have stayed. Yesterday, Jackers attacked Judy and me on the road." Susan gasped between words. "Judy died in the crash after being shot. Megan's gone, too. It's my fault. Judy and Megan would have never left if I hadn't insisted."

"We're leaving!" Kay shouted. "We'll head west along the rail trail."

Baeran rose and backed into the far cave wall. No way he'd let those Dazer freaks touch him. What the heck was wrong with them? They were like cattle. What if they stampeded? He took one step forward, smelling the Dazers. They smelled like dumpster juice spilled onto hot asphalt baking in a noonday sun. Should he run or hide? Baeran leaned against the wall and slid down onto his butt. He placed his head between his knees, hugging his sore ribs. He couldn't breathe. The stink burnt his nose. He couldn't move. He closed his eyes. The groaning echoed in his ears. He had to hide.

Lani knelt and spoke to Baeran. She put her hand on him. He swung his birch stick—the one from Boy Scout Camp back in Portsmouth—hitting his sister. Lani held her ground, undeterred. She called for Kay and screamed at Baeran as he clutched his knees and pulled them to his chest, rocking back and forth.

Kay screamed at Baeran, "Remember what your father taught you. You can do this—break it down."

But Baeran couldn't move. He couldn't breathe—their stink overpowered him. He couldn't hear—the Dazers moaned too loudly. The number sequence six-nine-four had no power, and he had no breath.

Kay shook Baeran, but he wanted her to back off. He didn't want anyone touching him. There were so many people.

Lani slapped Baeran. His ears popped, and the sound around him rushed in. Kay screamed at him, "Baeran Sheridan, you get off your ass and run!"

Baeran couldn't move. He needed to be rescued. He couldn't break it down and realized what he had become: a damsel.

CAPTIVITY

M55. Maximus plus fifty-five days. Lexington Bunker Complex.
SOLSTICE

SOLSTICE LAY FLAT IN THE DUCTWORK AND CLOSED HER EYES. She felt the song forming, but there was no headache, aura or flashes. No dreamvision came. Melody was silent. The song belonged to Solstice, and she sang alone.

"Captivity"

Sunny days in the park
Run, laugh, play
You and me
Sing, dance, sway

Fire burning in the road
Run, scream, cry
You left me
Steal, hide, die

Pieces of me gone
Abandoned, you left me
Losing myself
Here in captivity

Culling
Bodies
Rats
Incinerator

Choose
Die
Eat
Burn

Pieces of me gone
Abandoned, you left me
Losing myself
Here in captivity

Sick men
Feeding off
Sick men
Killing

Living like kings
Starving
Sick kids
Culling

Pieces of me gone
Abandoned, you left me
Losing myself
Here in captivity

Die, dying, died
Lie, lying, lied
Cry, crying, cried
Try, trying, tried

You all will die!
The old men lie!
Tears for you I cry,
Save you, I don't even try!

Pieces of me gone
Abandoned, you left me

THE BURNT SUNSET

Losing myself
Here in captivity

You are killing them!
You're sick, you're killing me!
Losing myself
Here in captivity

UNDESIRED

Solstice eavesdropped from her ductwork perch. Adena disagreed with Naetersen's plan to eliminate two hundred and fifty excess bunker inhabitants to preserve food, water and air. Naetersen called it culling.

Solstice didn't doubt she fell into the "undesirable" category and being caught meant being culled.

Guards led out undesirables every day. Solstice had seen the bodies. The bunker had six major branches, with the most important people separated from the undesirables.

The undesirables were removed under the guise of getting their own quarters, but no one came back. The guards stacked the bodies like cordwood in the incinerator room at the tunnel end.

Why didn't the doctor open the bunker doors? Why not give people a chance in the outside world? Couldn't they reset the timer? But Solstice remembered the doctor's words to the senator. There was no override before one hundred days. The bunker designers built the complex to wait out a catastrophe. The timer saved the survivors from themselves, and removed choice, freeing their minds.

Those who forced their way into the bunker and had no job or function were labeled as Undesirable or "UD" by the guards. The UDs were like sheep, hoping to survive the next slaughter. Solstice lived in a palace compared to them.

Solstice didn't understand why Naetersen didn't give the immediate order to kill them. The UDs consumed precious resources like food, water and air, and they stunk, worse than Solstice. The guards had shut off the plumbing in UD Land. The UDs were closed off from other bunker tunnels and given food and water on a weekly basis.

Solstice remembered the quarry swim. Wasn't there water near the bunker entrance? Everything about this place screamed self-contained and limited. She guessed the water supply was finite and located within the bunker to ensure its purity. Not every disaster was a wildfire. The designers had wanted to protect the survivors against nuclear fallout, a pressing concern seventy-five years prior. It wouldn't do anybody any good to drink glowing nuclear water, would it?

The doctor understood resource limits, and Solstice did now too. *Kill them now to give us a chance.* Ice cold, like her mom, Elle, who abandoned her with a nod and a smile, Solstice's heart had hardened, too.

The doctor and senator had agreed on a schedule for the culling. But the senator delayed, hoping to save more UDs. Solstice had heard the two men argue about Lincoln, Nebraska. Naetersen needed information. The senator had it, doling it out, saving crucial details to be chess pieces.

At least Solstice didn't have to live with the UDs. She was content and cold-hearted in her silver palace, as the master of her own frigid domain. She was the ductworks' ice princess.

VOLUME 4

M63. Maximus plus sixty-three days. Lexington Bunker Complex.
SOLSTICE

Solstice crawled through the ducts beyond the cafeteria, the shower stalls, Naetersen's room and the control room, looking for activity. She pressed onward to the Senator's room. She stopped when she saw Adena standing at his desk.

Silverfox. Solstice watched through an underknee vent as the senator pulled a thick leather-bound book off the shelf. She read the title: *The Fourth Term of the Senior Senator from Kentucky, Volume 4*. He opened the book, as his left-hand shook, flipping through the pages, and stopped at the section titled "Staff."

The senator pushed back his silver hair and opened his desk drawer to remove a box cutter and a ruler. He pressed the book flat and used the box cutter and ruler to meticulously cut a three-inch-by-three-inch square from a page. He removed scissors from the desk drawer and trimmed the edges. He held the square to the light. Satisfied, the senator meandered to the corner, and placed the cutout in the wastebasket. He used his foot to push the wastebasket to the air vent. "I like it better here."

The senator returned the ruler and box cutter and placed *The Fourth Term of the Senior Senator from Kentucky, Volume 4* back in its place. He shut off the lights and exited the room.

Solstice scampered from the underknee vent and found the access panel connecting the return and discharge lines near Naetersen's room. In clear violation of Rule 2, Solstice crawled into the return line and located the downchute for the senator's room. She tied off the 123-rope to a ductwork support and she slid down the chute. She stared through the grid-like metal grate into the wastebasket. Her eyes welled, and she popped open the vent cover. She reached into the wastebasket and retrieved a picture of Elle.

DADDYLESS

M67. Maximus plus sixty-seven days. Lexington Bunker Complex.
SOLSTICE

SOLSTICE HUDDLED HER KNEES TO HER CHEST IN THE DUCTWORK. Talking to herself and remembering old conversations. Reliving them to remain sane. She pictured her mom stroking her hair, when at age five should couldn't hold a pirouette. "Don't define yourself by what you are not. You are not your weaknesses nor are you the sum of your missing parts."

But what if the sum of your present parts didn't equate to a whole person? What if you were missing half? What if you were daddyless? A tune formed, and Solstice sang. She sang a song for herself. Melody remained quiet and no dreamvision came.

"Daddyless"

Daddyless daughter
Pieces missing
Never complete or whole
For him wishing

Motherless daughter
Once filled me up
With your parts
Where to, Mom, 'sup

Summing up pieces and parts on today
It's time to find it, my own way
Not yours anymore, never his anyway
Singing, dancing, that's my forte

His pieces, your parts
All missing from the equation
No longer balanced
Can't face the facts, evasion

Daddyless daughter
Him never knowing
Says goodbye to a mother
Her love bestowing

Summing up pieces and parts on today
It's time to find it, my own way
Not yours anymore, never his anyway
Scavenge, survive, outlast, purvey
My own destiny, my own new way
Daddyless daughter, killin' it, slay

THE CYLINDER

M70. Maximus plus seventy days. Lexington Bunker Complex.
SOLSTICE

SOLSTICE CRAWLED DOWN THE DUCTWORK BEYOND NAETERSEN'S ROOM, the control room and the Senator's room to an unexplored underknee vent.

Naetersen faced a screen built into a desk. The doctor pressed a red button in the middle of the console. He raced to the center of the room and stood on a metallic disk. A thick cylindrical glass chamber lowered over Naetersen. Air escaped with a hiss, sealing the chamber with the disk. Hydraulic lifters raised the chamber, and Solstice heard another hiss as it rattled the ductwork. She lost sight of Naetersen as the chamber ascended into the ceiling.

Solstice sensed the chamber stopping on the same level as her ductwork. She pressed her ear against the cold metal, and heard another hiss, followed by a pop. The room was quiet for thirty minutes until the chamber lowered with the doctor.

The disk mated with the floor. The glass cover separated, and it rose into the ceiling. Naetersen stepped off the disk and hastened to the console. He opened his notebook. Solstice pressed her face to the vent, straining to see what he wrote.

Naetersen scribbled. Solstice couldn't read the words as he leaned over the notebook. He filled a page, then two more.

Naetersen paused and flipped to the first page he had written. He retraced four words. He leaned back. Solstice could read the words now: Periscope. Firegale. Riot. Sickness.

Seeing Elle's picture had broken Solstice, and despair overwhelmed her. Solstice opened her lyricbook. She had four words, too. Homeless. Neglected. Abandoned. Waif.

HIGHLAND CAMP

M84. Maximus plus eighty-four days. New York State.
BAERAN

BAERAN SAT ON THE GROUND NEAR COLE'S ATV in front of the stream embankment, where Susan had left him. Fed up with Kay and Lani's pleading with the boy, Susan had grabbed Baeran and dragged him from the cave. His head lay in his chest, slumped down. Twenty-five feet away, the Dazers regrouped, slogging toward the Seascapers.

"Mount up!" Kay yelled, "We take the rail trail west."

Kay propped Baeran between her arms and the moped's handle bars. He leaned into her, and she whispered, "Snap out of it. We're leaving them behind. I need you to hang on."

The Dazers broke into a trot, closing in on her. Kay felt hands on her back and legs touching her and she hit the gas hard, accelerating toward the rail trail. In her rearview mirror, Kay saw the herd slow, and meander away toward the stream.

After traveling west two miles on the trail, the Seascapers stopped. Deven hopped out of the rack behind Ethan, and yelled, "I'm nixin' that. Mitch, could you have hit anymore holes! You were junkyard doggin' it, and my cornholio is dinged up."

"Sorry I bruised your ass, Deven." Mitch smiled.

Mitch looked at Kay. "Is everyone accounted for? How's Baeran?"

Kay shook her head, scowling. "He's fine."

Baeran released his hands from the handlebars and slid off the seat of the moped. He glanced at his dad.

Kay addressed the group, "Rest. The Dazers aren't interested in us. They wanted to graze by the stream, and we spooked them."

Cole treaded to Baeran. He put his hand on his son's shoulder. "Remember what I taught you last year at the Patriots game? You can do it." Cole rubbed Baeran's hair and ambled off.

But I can't break it down, the Dazers are different.
Baeran stared at his feet.

Parker walked by Baeran, and whispered, "Assfreak."

Cole gathered the group together. "We need to take an inventory of our supplies and find out what made it out from the cave."

A half hour later, Lani reported the good news: "Except for Susan's motorcycle, the vehicles are close to full on gas, and we have twenty-five gallons of fuel remaining in the spare cans. The blue water jugs are full. We have the generator and our tools, plus a day's worth of cattails, dandelion greens, and dried squirrel. We lost clothes, books, and electronics, but we have our tents and sleeping bags. It's fortunate we packed the equipment while trapped in the cave. We have spare parts for traps, too, we should be able to construct more."

As the group dispersed, Lani came over to Baeran. "Cheer up brother. Don't worry, I packed your black backpack and stick in the ATV trailer between Selene and the generator. Don't lose it again. We need you. I need you."

Baeran cupped his hands behind his neck. He stared at his feet. "Thank you."

Baeran owed Susan, too. He wandered toward Susan with Selene at his side. She was off on her own near the edge of the trail. "Thank you, Susan."

Susan glared at Baeran. "Smarten up kid or next time you'll get us killed. It's bad enough we've got the Firegale and Jackers but now Dazers are coming after us, too. Next time I'll leave you or let your parents worry about you. I can't take it anymore. Judy and Megan are gone, and Judy didn't die right away. The Jackers took her. It would have been better if me and Aileen were dead too. But I'm going to choose when our lives end. The Dazers, the Firegale or the Jackers won't make that choice for me. My life and my daughter's life belong to me, and not some new horror, and not to you. Next time keep it together."

Baeran sat alone, stunned, avoiding everyone except Selene. She laid next to him and rested her head in his lap. Baeran wasn't sure what was worse: Susan throwing his phobia back in his face or declaring the merits of a mother-daughter murder-suicide. He didn't move for an hour, forcing himself to forget Susan's tirade.

Later, Kay found her son. "Baeran, time to leave. Ride with your father on the ATV."

The Seascapers loaded the gear, found another rail trail, and headed toward western Vermont. This time Baeran rode in front of Cole on the ATV while Lani sat in the rumble seat behind. Jordin rode with Kay. Again, poor Deven rode on the rack behind Ethan.

Cole whispered to Baeran as they drove, "Are you okay?"

Baeran responded as the ATV bumped along the trail, "I don't want to talk about it. Lani can hear."

"She can't hear anything behind me."

"Fine, I'll talk, but Lani can hear even if she says she can't. Lani can hear anything."

Lani yelled over the roar of the ATV, "I can't hear you!"

Baeran cracked a smile and continued, "I was overwhelmed."

"I thought you fixed this last year."

"Dad, this is different, the Dazers are nasty."

"You have to face this." Cole replied.

"I'm not ready."

"We may not be so lucky next time. The Dazers are gross and incomprehensible, but you can't freeze again."

"I know, Dad."

Baeran cleared his mind of Dazers, and instead focused on the trail. A crow darted between the off-road caravan, and he envisioned his next project.

215

FEATHERS

M89. Maximus plus eighty-nine days. New York.
BAERAN

Baeran and the Seascapers traveled on the ATVs, scooters and motorcycles west into eastern New York, seeing no sign of the Jackers or Dazers. When they had consumed half of their fuel, they made camp on a hill off the rail trail.

Baeran assembled new traps. He descended into the valley and found an older tree near the stream. He hung his traps. Hours later, the snares yielded a crow. Baeran unhooked the trap from the branch, removed the crow and snapped its neck. He examined the crow in his hand, and he thanked it. He hadn't done that before. But this crow reminded Baeran of himself. The crow, once proud and strong, now lay broken. Kay had told him that Native Americans thanked their kill, releasing the animal's spirit. His mom's ancestors had long ago walked these woods, hunted in them and lived in them. Baeran took comfort in completing the circle, touching the same earth as his descendants. Like Kay, his sister Lani had the same coloring as the Abenaki, and while Baeran, inherited only a slightly tanner version of Cole's Irish heritage, the spirit of the Abenaki resided in him.

Baeran de-feathered the crow and placed the plumages aside. He removed the head, claws, and entrails, and he wrapped the breast meat for later, like he did with squirrels.

Baeran had been waiting for the feathers to fabricate arrows and a bow. He found a one and half-inch diameter yew branch and cut it to a length of sixty-inches. He debarked the branch and used his bowie knife to carve out a one-inch by six-inch handle at the center of the bow. He tapered the wood from the handle to a half-inch on each end. He carved a notch perpendicular to the bow at the ends to attach the string later. At the center of the bow, Baeran made the bow grip and arrow sight by attaching a one-inch by three-inch by three-eighths-inch rectangular piece of wood to the center of the bow using sap and a strip of fabric. But he struggled with how to braid the fishing line to achieve the desired strength and diameter needed for the bow. He leaned against the tree and made a poor attempt at braiding four fishing lines together. In disgust, he threw the line, and sat mumbling to himself.

After a few moments, Lani walked by and examined the pile of fishing line at Baeran's feet. "I could see you huffing and puffing from a mile away. What are you making, a bracelet?"

"A bow string. Can you help?" Baeran replied.

Lani ran the tangled mess of line through her fingers. "How long?"

"I need four strands of fishing line braided, fifty-four inches long including a two-inch loop on each end."

"Baeran, that'll take me hours. That's like a six-foot long piece of line. The pattern would make your head spin: line one over line two, line one and line two over line three, then cross it with line four."

"Lani, that's why I need your help, and I need this now."

"What's wrong Baeran?"

"I freaked at the cave," Baeran replied.

Lani dropped the tangled line to the ground. "I understand that, but you've been weird for like ten days, even before the Dazers chased us out of the summer camp. I hardly see you around. It's like you're avoiding everyone."

"I need some space." Baeran picked up the snarled line, groaning as he detangled it.

"Is there a problem with you and Parker?" Lani continued, pressing.

Baeran stared at his toes. He lied, "Nope. I'm avoiding him."

"What about sketch-girl, how is she? Have you had anymore dreams?" Lani smiled, "Are you still feeling the electricity ripping through your limbs?"

Irritated, Baeran replied, "You're exaggerating. I could feel tingles, like static electricity. I still can, but it's worse. Like the electricity is trying to get out. Electricity is not the right word. It's more like space, or the space in between. The space in between is trying to separate. Something I can't see, like Aether. That's the word. Yes, that's freaking me out, and I'm still drawing sketch-girl and she's still in trouble. It gets worse every time. But who cares? I need this bow. And we need the game I catch. Can you teach me how to braid the bow string or not?"

"What the hell is Aether?"

"It's an old Greek word."

"Sure, brother, I don't know what you are talking about, but I'll trade a chore for the bow string."

"You are the worst sister ever."

Lani replied, "It hasn't been easy for me either. I'm changing, too. There's something about Jordin. I'm drawn to her. I've got these feelings. At first, I thought it was the love between friends or the special bond between special sisters, but it's more." Lani stooped and looked directly into Baeran's eyes. "Promise you won't tell."

Baeran scooched closer. "I promise, Lani."

Lani fiddled with her ponytail. She had this weird look on her face, like a smile was battling a frown. She spoke slowly, choosing her words. "I know you feel it too. Tell me you haven't adored Jordin since we were kids. I like how she mixes in some of Wàigōng's Chinese words. I know it was to make her grandfather happy when she was young, but it's cute how she keeps doing it in his memory. It's not the same with Annie."

"You are right. I've got a thing for Jordin. But it's not love. I've got a thing for Reese, too, and Deven, but in a Matt Damon kind of way." Baeran replied.

"Matt Damon?"

"Yes. I have a little man-crush. I could watch him read the paper."

"What?"

"Forget about Matt Damon, everybody loves him, like Tom Brady. But I agree, I feel a bond with Deven, Jordin and Reese, plus you too. But love isn't the right word, not for D, J and R. It's more like magnetism."

"Okay. I feel the magnetic attraction because we are super

awesome friends now," Lani replied, stalling. "Or like how Deven would say, 'We are crankin' as bros and does.' But with Jordin, it's more for me."

Lani's heart raced, hoping Baeran would ease the passage of the next few words. She kicked the ash-dirt at her feet.

"Like what?" Baeran asked, gazing into her eyes, offering reassurance.

Lani paused, desperate to speak the next few words. Tears welled in her eyes. "Baeran, I'm a lesbian."

Baeran reached for his sister and hugged her, as she cried. Lani cried the tears of a sixteen-year-old secret. The emotion from years of questioning was released, and the burden left her. Her tears mixed with a smile, and she laughed joyously.

Baeran pulled away from Lani and used the hem of his t-shirt to wipe her tears.

Lani's grin grew. "See, I told you. Like with the journal I'm keeping, people want to tell you their stories. I feel so much better but promise not to tell."

"Who?" Baeran asked.

Lani wiped her eyes. "Don't tell Mom or Dad yet. They'll understand. Maybe, they even knew before I did, but I want to tell them in my own way. And definitely do not tell Jordin."

"Why not tell Jordin?"

"Because, she likes you, idiot, like everyone else."

"Who else?"

"I bet Reese, if you were older."

"But still, Lani, why not tell Jordin?"

"Because we are like sisters, except, I've always loved her."

"Oh. Well, you'll never know till you talk to Jordin. She could feel the same way. But it doesn't change anything. I couldn't have asked for a better older sister. And listen, because I won't repeat this, ever. I love you for who you are, Lani."

"Thanks, bro."

"You should talk to Susan. She was a teen once."

"I will, but not till after I talk to Mom and Dad." Lani wiped her eyes and smiled. "Enough talk about me. How about doing my chore for a week while I make your bow string?"

Baeran agreed, and hugged Lani one more time.

After a week of doing Lani's chores, Baeran had his bow string. For arrows, he selected three-eighths-inch by thirty-inch long straight oak sticks. He cut a quarter-inch deep notch in one end. He sharpened the other end of the arrow and hardened the tips in the campfire.

Baeran divided each feather in two along the shaft using his bowie knife. He trimmed each of the half-feathers to a length of six-inches, discarding the wider top parts of the feathers. He trimmed the angle from one-eighth-inch to a half-inch. He cut two perpendicular slits in the dull end of the arrow, applied sap and inlaid the feathers about a half-inch from the notched end. Baeran completed six arrows and he practiced with his bow in the valley below.

Later back at the campsite, Baeran sat with Reese in the new lookout tree with their feet overhanging the edges. Baeran told Reese about the bow and arrows he had made and how he thanked the crow. Reese laughed. He opened his sketchbook to show her a drawing of the bow. As he flipped the pages, another sketch caught Reese's eye.

She placed her hand on the pad. "Can I peek?"

"Sure. Didn't I show you? This one is you." Baeran heard a stick snap below and said, "What's that?"

"A squirrel, let me see your sketch book." Reese put her hand on the pad.

Baeran let go.

When Reese saw Baeran's sketch of herself, she lost her breath. After a moment of silence, she kissed Baeran on the cheek. "This sketch is wonderful. It makes me feel beautiful. Lately, I've felt like a mutant, with my webbed hand. Baeran Sheridan, I can't tell you how glad I am after seeing your sketch."

Baeran grinned at Reese but couldn't speak.

Reese kissed Baeran on the cheek, smiling, "Too bad you're not Parker's age, we could date. You know he's such a creeper. I swear I've seen him staring at me. Should I tell Deven or would you talk to Parker for me?"

"He's stubborn."

Reese laughed, flipping through the pages of sketches. "That's putting it lightly."

Baeran heard another stick break from under the platform. He rolled to his side to find the source of the noise.

Reese looked up from the sketch pad. "What is it?"

Baeran lied, "Nothing." Underneath the platform, Parker creeped into the woods.

THE MEADOW

M95. Maximus plus ninety-five days. Highland Camp.
BAERAN

BAERAN AND ETHAN TOOK COLE AND MITCH TO HUNT, and Selene followed. They surveyed the forest during the hike and Baeran pointed to a grove of trees. "See Dad, not everything is burnt. The Firegale skipped certain areas."

As they came to the edge of a tree stand, the group examined a clearing. The regrown meadow had a matted-down path worn through the center. Baeran whispered into Cole's ear, "Dad, it's Dazers, let's see what they are up to."

Baeran noticed his breath quickening, and he forcibly modulated it. Six-nine-four. Inhale. Exhale. Hold.

Cole replied, "Okay, let's be careful."

Cole, Mitch, Baeran and Ethan followed the worn meadow path until they found fifty Dazers bedding down. They paused and dropped to the ground. Baeran peered at Cole and Mitch, desperate to find courage as he remembered the last day at the cave.

The herd became agitated and took off running northward through the meadow and into the woods.

The Seascapers gave one another a nod and followed the Dazers across the meadow. From deep within the woods a shot rang out. Cole held up his hand, stopping the group. "We should go now, it might be Jackers."

The Dazers closed ranks and charged away from the threat of the shotgun blast, becoming a stampede. They raced through the woods, toward the Seascapers.

The foursome sprinted into the meadow as the Dazer herd bore down on them.

Mitch yelled, "Split up!"

In the confusion, Ethan and Baeran sprinted left while Mitch and Cole dashed right. From over their shoulders, the dads watched in horror as the Dazers followed their sons and the dog.

At the center of the meadow, Ethan tripped and fell near Baeran's feet. Ethan yelled for help, pawing at Baeran's legs, but Baeran froze as the Dazers overtook him and Selene. Fifty Dazers surrounded the boys. Like mad fans rushing the stage at a concert, the Dazers slammed into Baeran and Ethan. The Dazers swirled and crashed into each other, like a mosh pit gone horribly wrong. Ethan could not regain his footing and he screamed as the Dazed stepped onto him and over him.

Baeran was at the epicenter of the Dazer's wild, spastic movements as they collided and smashed into him and each other, forcing him away from Ethan. Their oozing sores dripped onto his face, and he felt the panicwave rising within himself. Baeran closed his eyes, ready to let the Dazed take him down, but he remembered his dad's words: "Break it down."

Baeran opened his eyes and ignored the crowd of four dozen, intent on focusing on the four Dazers closest to him. Baeran pushed left, right, behind and in front, desperate to maintain his ground and hold his space while moving and turning toward the edges of the herd.

Selene fell, and crawled into the mess of legs. The dog broke through the stampede and galloped toward Cole, barking.

Black circles formed in the corners of Baeran's vision, and he fought to find Selene and Cole. The Dazer's moans and Ethan's screams filled his ears. Baeran counted. Six-nine-four. Inhale. Exhale. Hold. But he couldn't do it, and every time he tried to fill his lungs, the Dazers closed in, smothering him.

Baeran struggled to maintain his balance. He tripped and fell into the crowd. As he clutched at the frayed cloth of the nearest Dazer, her head exploded and covered him with red ooze. Baeran pushed her and she tumbled to the ground. Blood dripped into his eyes and mouth, and he vomited. Another head close to Baeran exploded. The Dazed momentarily backed off. Baeran doubled over, sucking in air until his stomach heaved.

Baeran saw Cole and Mitch cracking heads. The fathers

alternated between firing rounds and using the butts of the shotguns as clubs. The Dazers stopped their advance. A loud moan resounded through the herd and they bolted from Ethan and Baeran, retreating from the meadow, and into the far woods.

Baeran collapsed onto the fallen bodies. Blood dripped into his mouth and his nose, he vomited for a final time.

Mitch and Cole had killed at least two dozen Dazers. The men held back the bile in their mouths while they overturned the bodies, desperately searching for their boys.

Mitch shouted, "I've got Baeran. He has a pulse."

Cole waited a moment. He had found Ethan. The Dazer mob dislocated Ethan's jaw, broke a leg and arm, and collapsed his right eye socket. Cole called his friend over, "Mitch, come quick."

Mitch rushed to Cole, saw his son, and fell to his knees. "My boy, my beautiful boy," he cried.

Ethan's left eye blinked. Mitch bent down and kissed Ethan's bloody forehead, and his son breathed his last breath.

Mitch grasped Cole's hand. "Take Baeran."

Cole put his arm around Mitch and hugged him. Both men cried. Mitch pushed Cole away. "Go."

Cole put Baeran in his arms and carried him to the campsite. Selene trotted by their sides with her tail tucked and head bowed. Baeran shook the entire way as he grasped onto Cole's arm. "I tried Dad, I couldn't hold back that many Dazers."

Cole replied, "I know, son. I'm grateful you're alive. You held your ground. You stayed upright. That's what saved you. You kept your head for as long as you could. That's why you break it down. Remember what I taught you. Remember where you learned it. Close your eyes. You are safe now."

Cole carried Baeran back through the woods to the Highland Camp. Kay saw Baeran covered in blood and screamed rushing to her son. Cole put Baeran on the ground. "Kay, it's not his. He's okay. It's Dazer blood."

As Kay knelt next to Baeran, Jordin and Heather approached with a med kit, water and cloth. Lani and Annie joined them.

Heather probed Baeran for injuries as Kay looked on. "Heather grasped Kay's hand. There are no punctures, and nothing seems to be broken. Cole's right, the blood isn't his."

"Baeran Sheridan," Kay admonished, "If you weren't so nasty, I'd kiss you."

Baeran forced a smile, waiting for Cole to speak the next few words. It was his fault. He looked to Jordin and grasped her hand as Cole pulled away.

Cole stood, found L.J. and his son. "Take Parker and find Mitch. Ethan is dead."

Parker asked, "What?"

"I'm sorry. He's dead." Cole choked out, "The boys were overrun by Dazers."

"Not Ethan!" Parker screamed.

"Son, we need to help Mitch." L.J. put his arm over Parker's shoulder. "He can't do this alone."

Deven, L.J. and Parker hiked toward the meadow to find Mitch and Ethan's body.

Pointing at Baeran, Parker said under his breath to Deven, "Assboy is dead."

Susan and Aileen approached Baeran and watched Kay, Heather, Reese, Annie, Jordin and Lani attend to him. Horrified at Baeran's bloody appearance, Susan grabbed Aileen's hand. "That will not happen us. I get to choose."

Susan stepped back, pulling at her daughter. She put her hands to her face, and said, "No, I choose—not the Firegale, not the Jackers and not the Dazers."

Susan's eyes darted at the ground, glancing back and forth desperate for answers, while rocking her upper body. "This is my choice, and we're out." Susan pulled a gun from her waist. She grasped it with two hands, pointing the weapon at the forest floor.

Cole yelled, "Gun!"

Kay and Heather dove, shielding Baeran and the girls with their bodies.

Cole raised his arms. "Susan, put that down."

"Won't happen Cole. There will be no more Firegale, Jackers and Dazers for me or Aileen. We're done."

"Susan, wait." Cole extended his right hand, motioning to Aileen to join him. "Put that down."

Aileen pulled away from her mother and moved next to Cole. "Stay there, Aileen."

Susan raised the weapon, waving it. "Cole, do you know what those Jackers did to Judy before she died? No? I do. Every night, I go to bed with her screams echoing in my head. And they killed my Megan. Now the Dazers are killing us. I can't live like this, not anymore and not without Judy. My daughter will not see any more of this world."

Susan aimed at Aileen and fired the handgun.

The bullet struck Aileen above the left eye. Cole stood, stunned, as blood splattered his face. Flesh and bone rained down on the others.

Aileen's body collapsed to the forest floor.

"Oh no. God no." Kay cried out. She left the girls and crawled toward Aileen's body, desperately searching the forest floor for pieces of the girl's skull to replace. Kay reached for Aileen's head, holding the pieces together as the girl jerked back and forth. Kay leaned in to cradle the girl, as Aileen's blood flowed between her fingers.

Aileen gasped, and her body stopped shaking.

As tears streamed down her face, Susan pointed the 9 mm handgun at Cole's chest. "Back off."

Cole darted at Susan.

Susan raised the gun to her temple and pulled the trigger, muffling the sound of the discharge. Her body collapsed into Cole's out-stretched arms, with a grimace frozen on her face.

Kay reached for the girls as did Heather, pulling them into an embrace, shielding them from the revulsion.

Cole fell to his knees, clutching Susan's body, turning away from her face.

A chorus of wails and screams filled the forest.

Baeran pushed his sisters off himself. He rose, wiping the bile and Dazer blood from his lips.

Three deaths, two pre-meditated, and they were Baeran's fault. But he couldn't grieve, nor let himself take the blame—or more deaths would follow. He had to act.

Baeran stepped away from the fallen bodies and the howling

Seascapers. He knew the Seascapers would abandon the Highland campsite after laying Susan, Aileen and Ethan to rest, and they would never speak of this day again. But Baeran knew what he had to do next: face the Dazers, face Parker and face the Jackers. He couldn't be a kid anymore. The horrors of the new world wouldn't allow it.

Baeran scowled at the setting sun, knowing what he had to do. He murmured, "Break it down."

DOMAIN

M80. Maximus plus eighty days. Lexington Bunker Complex.
SOLSTICE

SOLSTICE SURVEYED HER DOMAIN. The three-foot by three-foot silver ductwork spanned a hundred feet in either direction. Downchutes, T-junctions and underknee vents populated the rectangular conduits spanning the ceilings and the walls. She had found vents to the senator's office, the cafeteria, the control room, the cylinder, the laundry room, the shower bathroom and Naetersen's lair, plus the draincock, the Great Chasm, return lines, discharge lines and access panels.

Solstice had claimed it, marking the insides of the ducts with her sign, the sun with rays and I-C-E. Vertical shafts, horizontal tubing and circular channels were hers except the UD tunnel and the incinerator tunnel. The rats ruled those ducts.

Solstice wanted more and made a list: a brush, a nice dress, rockin' kicks, a smartphone, to dance, a bagel and cream cheese, a tooth brush, a good rat exterminator, a safe place to sleep, a decent night's rest, a place where guards didn't leave bodies to rot, a friend, her mom, a way out and hope.

THE ICE MAIDEN

M87. Maximus plus eighty-seven days. Lexington Bunker Complex.
SOLSTICE

SOLSTICE GAZED AT HER LIST ON THE DUCTWORK. Had she made it a week prior? Was time slower or faster now? Time had no meaning. But the lists and rules that governed her survival did. Even if time had no meaning, Solstice had no time for little girl lists and baseless hopes. She didn't need it. Or she couldn't have it. Or she couldn't find it. It didn't matter. She took her Sharpie and crossed it out.

Get over it. It was her and only her.

Solstice had jokingly referred to her ductwork home as a palace, high above the UDs below. She ruled the grand silver metal palace, and her dominion was shiny and cold. And for a while, she reigned as its ice princess.

But Solstice had time to think, and princess didn't suit her, not anymore, not since the Firegale. Princess Ice Meangirl, the determined ruthless double threat singer-dancer, with her own condo and nurse maid, who unleashed tirades on the likes of HolesInHerTights, had checked out.

Maiden suited her. Princesses had fancy dresses and servants and food, but not Solstice. Princesses took baths, not Solstice, not for a long time.

Princesses had princes rescue them. Maidens didn't need boys and didn't need to be rescued. But a maiden could like the right boy, and even rescue him, on her terms, if he was cute and nice.

Maidens were warriors and could be defiant. Maidens kicked butt when they wanted to. Princesses were too polite for Solstice. Princesses sang to birds and talked to their animal friends. Solstice had no friends, but she liked to sing.

Princesses were beholden to their king, prince or subjects, and

229

Solstice would never answer to anyone. No way. Never. Not the guards. Not the UDs. Not the senator. And definitely not Naetersen, unless her life depended on it, because he was smart. And only if Naetersen was the last one left.

She'd still be a maiden, though. A kick-ass one. She'd be the toughest Ice Maiden the Silver Palace of the kingdom of Bunkerland had ever seen.

SLAYED

M94. Maximus plus ninety-four days. Lexington Bunker Complex.
SOLSTICE

SOLSTICE LAY FLAT ON THE DUCTWORK, submitting to the sudden pain behind her eyes in the silverdimlight unable to tell what time it was, because it didn't matter. Days mattered, but not the hours. There was no dawn, noon or dusk. The flashing intensified, until it yielded to a migraine aura. Melody beckoned and a dreamvision formed, and Solstice welcomed the release.

In the darkness of her mind, Solstice imagined herself alone on a snow-covered mountain against a black sky. She wore a flowing white dress that melded into the snow at her ankles. Solstice outstretched her hands and leaned her head back, facing the dark night. Beams of light shot from her palms upward and Solstice sang.

"Slayed"

Hope, screw it, it's gone
Hide, be silent, beware
They'll find you
Watch out, avoid the snare

The kingdom, it's hers
Horizontal, vertical shaft
She has no equal
Except for the rats, they have half

The Princess, she's gone
Slayed, stuck the blade in

THE BURNT SUNSET

From the silver palace
Here comes the Ice Maiden

"Avoid the UDs,"
You're the new Ice Maiden
In the tunnel
The bodies decayed in

Some of them are sick,
Rotting in their cramped holes,
No food for them
Dying, gone are their souls

The Princess, she's gone
Slayed, stuck the blade in
From the silver palace
Here comes the Ice Maiden

Glistening, glowing
Can't contain the light
Oh, my God
Too worn out to fight

Get out of my head
Where's it coming from
Leave me alone
The banging, the drum

The Princess, she's gone
Slayed, stuck the blade in
From the silver palace
Here comes the Ice Maiden

Seer kindling.
Air. Water. Earth. Fire.
Suffocating. Drowning. Buried. Burnt.
Aether. Sun.

Fractured. Eclipse.
Presage.

What the hell you lookin' at?
Melody, get out of my head
I didn't ask for that!

Wayfarer dawning
What the hell is that?
Melody, get out of my head

The Princess, she's gone
Slayed, stuck the blade in
From the silver palace
Here comes the Ice Maiden

THE SLATE SHREW

M109. Maximus plus one hundred nine days. Lexington Bunker Complex.
SOLSTICE

Solstice couldn't put her finger on it, but she had to be violating a new rule: Rule 4.

Solstice took a chance and lowered herself into a back room in the UD section. She blended into the shadows and listened but took nothing. She searched for hope and for information but didn't become involved.

Until she did. Solstice stepped forward, into the light. "Leave her alone!"

An older woman, her torn clothes hanging from her body, and a tiny girl with hollow cheeks, fought over an apple. Into a dark and dank corner, the girl crawled, pulling her knees to her chest as the older woman struck her. The girl, seven or eight, tucked the apple between her legs and absorbed the beating, until Solstice had intervened.

"Who are you?" the old woman asked.

"No one." Solstice replied.

The shrew towered over Solstice ready to strike, her silver hair blended into her tattered gray cloak. The old woman had a brittle voice and light charcoal-like skin. Everything about the woman reminded Solstice of the slate pavers in the gardens at the condo.

"The apple's mine. She stole it." SlateShrew seethed.

"She needs it more than you," Solstice replied.

SlateShrew didn't hesitate. She raised a wooden dowel, from an old chair, and struck at Solstice in the forearm and back.

Solstice recoiled covering her face, but only for a moment, finding her resolve. Solstice stood, facing SlateShrew. "Back off."

The Ice Maiden Rises.

The girl rolled her apple to SlateShrew.

SlateShrew retreated. "You bruised it. I'll be back to teach you a lesson."

Solstice extended her hand to the girl. "Let me help you."

The little girl shook her head, "No."

Solstice bent down, "Don't worry, I have more food."

"You shouldn't have made her mad."

Solstice lowered herself more, kneeling. "What's your name?"

"Mavourneen. Who are you?"

Solstice replied, "You haven't heard of me? I'm the Ice Maiden. You want to know a secret?"

Mavourneen's face glowed. "Yes."

Solstice beamed back, "I have a way out of this section of tunnel."

Mavourneen replied, "You do?"

"You bet. I'll show you too. But first, tell me about SlateShrew?"

"Who?"

Solstice replied, "The woman who hit you."

Mavourneen replied, "I call her Meany. She says she's in charge, along with her son. But she's like me. No one can leave the tunnel. It's locked from the outside. Once a week, the guards bring us food, but don't take the bodies anymore. But they take people and give us a little water. The bathrooms don't work."

"Listen, Mavourneen, I can take you, but we have to leave now. Are you with anyone?"

Mavourneen shook her head, "No."

"How did you enter the bunker?"

"My dad snuck me in with supplies before the doors closed."

Solstice asked, "Where is he now?"

"I don't know where, but he never made it in."

Solstice took Mavourneen's hand. "I'm sorry I lost your apple. It's best we disappear without a fight. I have food and ways to find more. Trust me."

"It's been awhile." Mavourneen pulled Solstice's hand, forcing her to stop. "I wanted to eat."

"Don't worry, Mavourneen. I have food for you, once we leave."

Solstice tiptoed to the corner of the back room and stared at the doorway, to ensure SlateShrew had left.

Solstice said, "Mavourneen, see the vent in the ceiling. I live in the ductwork. You can too."

MAVOURNEEN

M109. Maximus plus one hundred nine days. Lexington Bunker Complex.
SOLSTICE

Solstice put Mavourneen on her shoulders and the girl popped open the overhead vent.

Solstice pushed Mavourneen higher. "Climb in. "

Mavourneen peered into the ductwork, straining to see in the silverdimlight.

"Get in. It's plenty wide and sturdy." Straining, Solstice shifted her weight. "When you crawl into the shaft toss down my rope, it's tied off to a support."

Mavourneen scrambled into the ductwork and tossed down the 123-rope made from sheet strips.

Solstice climbed the rope and replaced the underknee vent cover. She crawled into the ventilation system and removed a telescoping broom handle from a sleeve on her back. The broom handle had a coat hanger wire duct-taped to one end.

Solstice caught Mavourneen's perplexed expression. "It's how I lift the vent covers and retrieve my rope. This is a handle from the cleaning supply closet. It telescopes—gets longer. I don't always have little girls to help me, and I can't leave dangling ropes or open vent covers."

"Are you really an Ice Maiden?" Mavourneen asked.

"My name is Ice," Solstice replied, "And this is my place, my castle."

"You live in the ductwork alone? Your name is Ice?"

Solstice laughed, "I do. And yes, Ice is my nickname from when I danced, because I was beautiful, cold-hearted and ruthless. The nickname was meant to hurt my feelings, but I liked it, because I've got a weird first name, and Ice is kind of an abbreviation of it."

"Aren't you lonely, Ice? Aren't you frightened?"

"Yep to both. I miss my Mom too. She never made it in."

Mavourneen stared at her toes. "I'm sorry."

"Me too. But now I have you Mavourneen. If you don't work out, I have my imaginary friend."

"Who?"

"Her name is Melody, and she sings with me."

"Really?"

Solstice spun in the ductwork, on her butt, to face Mavoureen. "Yep. We sing tons of songs." She placed her hand in the girls. "Write new ones too. I have markers, and I draw everywhere."

"Oh."

"Listen, Mavourneen are you hungry?" Solstice pointed down the ductwork. "I'll show you where my supplies are and how to find more. Follow me. I know it's dark. You'll adjust to it. I count."

"What?" Mavourneen asked.

"I count the seams in between the underknee vents." Solstice grasped Mavourneen's hands and moved them onto the seam between them. "Do you feel that? The seams are ten point seven size6Solstice-feet—sorry eight feet—apart."

Mavourneen asked, "Is it scary, in the dark?"

"Not too bad but watch out for the beavers." Solstice replied, putting her front two teeth over her bottom lip. She moved her head side to side over her hands, like she was chewing on an imaginary log.

"Beavers?"

"JK. There are no beavers, but you must watch out for enormo rats." Solstice spread her arms out wide. Mavourneen leaned back against the duckwork wall. Solstice ran her fingers in front of the other girl, pretending they were a rat scurrying by. "Let them pass and they won't touch you."

"I can't, Ice. I'm not tough like you."

"I'm not tough either, Mavourneen. I count. There are seven seams to the next vent opening."

"You count?" Mavourneen asked.

"Yes, my mom taught me once, when we swam for a long time." Solstice replied. "Focus on the numbers. Do it. Breathe. And before you know it, you'll be wherever you're going."

"Ice, you first. One. Two..."

Solstice counted with Mavourneen as they crawled to the closest vent, "...five, six, seven."

Solstice wiped the sweat from her brow and directed Mavourneen beyond the underknee vent, to the next bend in the ductwork.

"Sit. Put your back against the metal. Rest." Solstice lowered her voice. "Speak in whispers."

Mavourneen whispered, "Ice, aren't you afraid of falling? How come the ventilation system doesn't collapse?"

"The supports are screwed into the ceiling of the cave."

"Oh."

"Mavourneen, there's a few items you need to know. Not every room has a ceiling. The ventilation ductwork is suspended down from the cave roof. About six rooms have walls and drop ceilings. You need to be aware of where you are. And you need to be quiet out in the open like this." Solstice pointed downward. "Speak only in whispers. Underknee, further down the ductwork are maintenance rooms and other places where you can be louder—even sing, because of the equipment—heaters, fans or air scrubbers."

"Okay, Ice."

Solstice continued, "There are four rules of bunker survival you need to follow. Rule 1a—don't get caught, because they'll kill you. Rule 1b—stay hydrated, because you'll go crazy otherwise. Rule 2—stay out of the return lines, because you can't see the downchutes. Rule 3—don't leave home without rope, because that's how you climb in when you fall out." She counted on her fingers, stopping at her thumb. "I'll explain them more later. I need a Rule 4—but I can't figure it out yet." Solstice wiggled her thumb, then peered down the ductwork. "Let's move. We have about twenty-five duct seams to cover. Try counting to seventy-five in your head. This duct doubles back and branches off. We'll be heading over the UDs."

Mavourneen asked, "UDs?"

"Yes, the undesirables." Solstice answered. "Sorry, where you used to live."

Solstice grinned as the exhausted girl panted. Sweat poured down Mavourneen's face and soaked through her light shirt.

Solstice opened her sling sack. "Mavourneen, let's sit for a while longer. I have water and crackers. These are special crackers. I've saved them for eighty-six days for a special occasion. I have canned peaches too, we can share."

"Thanks, Ice. I could use a break. I've had a cold for days."

Solstice sat as Mavourneen consumed the entire sleeve of crackers, most of the peaches and the water. Solstice's belly growled but she resisted eating more than two peach slices. Mavourneen needed the food more than her.

Solstice did the math in her head. Mavourneen had consumed at least three days of rations. It would take at least a week to steal three comparable items from the cafeteria and not invite suspicion.

As Mavourneen finished the last drop of water, Solstice realized friendship would have its costs.

"Ready?" Solstice asked, as she closed her sling sack. "Did you have enough to eat?"

Mavourneen replied, "Sure, Ice. Thank you. It has been two days since I ate."

"You're safe now." Solstice continued, lying, "I have plenty of food."

"Count to seventy-five, to the next vent?" Mavourneen asked.

"Yes, Mavourneen. This time you lead."

The girl hustled ahead, eager to find the next light source, high on the sugary peach juice.

Solstice whispered, "Mavourneen, slow down."

"Ice, where does this turn lead?"

"Wait for me." Solstice scrambled to catch Mavourneen, sweating, feeling woozy. At least ten crawl-steps ahead, Solstice saw Mavourneen crash through a hinged underknee vent into a darkened room.

Solstice approached the vent opening and peered downward. She whispered, "Mavourneen?"

Solstice opened her sling sack, pushed aside her lyricbook and removed her 123-rope. As she tied the knotted sheet rope to the nearest junction support, Solstice heard voices.

Solstice hung her head upside down and peered into the vent opening. She tasted peaches in the back of her throat as she heard footsteps. She wiped her soaking wet face.

Solstice inched backward from the opening and closed the hinged underknee vent cover, gagging.

Solstice recognized the voice in the dark.

"What's this? It's that nasty Neeny." SlateShrew poked Mavoureen with her foot. "I told you she was sneaky. She's sleeping. Wake her son. See what else she has stolen."

Solstice bit her lip. She could see the outline of SlateShrew's son through the grid-pattern of the vent. He appeared massive in the shadows.

Mavourneen opened her eyes, "Ice?"

"What's that, Neeny? I don't have any ice." SlateShrew poked the girl with her dowel. "What are you doing in my tunnel? Stealing more of my stuff?"

SlateShrew seized Mavourneen by the hair as the girl screamed. Mavourneen held onto the roots of her hair as SlateShrew dragged her into the doorway. Mavourneen cried, holding onto her head, and she coughed, spitting blood onto SlateShrew's feet.

SlateShrew clutched her son by the arm. "What's this?"

Solstice leaned closer to the vent, spying down on the conversation. Her left hand slipped, and her face slammed into the cold metal of the ductwork. She felt weak.

SlateShrew glared into the darkened room to find the noise's origin. "Neeny's sick. Leave her, son."

Solstice glanced at her soaking wet hand. She shivered as sweat poured down her forehead. She leaned back against the duct. She felt faint, tasting peaches as she vomited onto the ductwork. Dizzy, she placed her hands at her side, slipping in her own vomit. Solstice fell onto her ribs, her head splashing in the warm puddle. She gazed at Mavourneen through the grid-pattern of the vent.

Solstice closed her eyes and slept.

DAZERS

M99. Maximus plus ninety-nine days. New York Highland Camp.
BAERAN

Ash fell as Baeran gazed at the three graves in the meadow. The Seascapers had promised to bury the horrors of that day with the bodies, but Baeran had to face the Dazers.

Even when he wasn't avoiding Dazer stampedes, Baeran hated crowds in general. He loved attending Red Sox, Bruins, or Patriots games, but he hated walking out. At Gillette Stadium, home of the Patriots, an ocean of people, seventy thousand freakin' people, exited through maybe twenty exits after a game.

Last year Baeran had held Cole's hand when he left a Patriots game, like a thirteen-year-old crybaby. The Patriots had smacked the Ravens. Tom Brady had torched them by like five touchdowns. The Ravens were a bunch of cheating whiners, like the Colts. Baeran loved beating the Ravens, and he hated whiners, as much as he hated crybabies.

After the game, back in the car, his dad had said, "Break it down," as the stadium crowd streamed along its sides. "Baeran, you need to break it down." Baeran stared at Cole, and his dad repeated, "Break it down."

Baeran didn't understand Cole. He had wanted to say to his dad, "Are you challenging me to a dance-off?"

But his dad had the serious expression on his face. Cole put both his hands on Baeran's shoulders. "It used to happen to me, too. Still does. I don't like crowds, either."

"What do you do?"

"Break it down," Cole replied. "Let's do the math. Seventy thousand people are in the stadium and there are twenty exits. That equals three thousand and five hundred people per exit. But you have slackers and the bathrooms peel off a bunch, so it's like three thousand people per exit ramp slogging out of the stadium."

"I guessed like five thousand. But you're not helping, Dad. Thinking about it makes it worse. How do we even know that's the right number of exits?"

Cole replied, "Wait. Listen. The number of exits doesn't matter. You can still break it down. Each exit ramp might have ten levels. That makes three hundred people per level. Imagine we are exiting in a grid. There are thirty rows of people per ramp leaving."

Baeran had lowered his head, Cole put his hand under it and raised the boy's chin. "How many people per row are exiting?"

The ramps were the worst part of exiting. Baeran did the math. "Three hundred divided by thirty equals ten."

"Right, there are ten people in your row." Cole smiled, encouraging Baeran. "And who is next to you?

"You, Dad."

"And who is on the other side? And in front of you and behind you?"

"They are strangers, Dad, three of them total."

"Right. You are exiting the stadium, and you know twenty-five percent of the people next to you. You have to break it down."

Baeran did the calculations at church, at the movies, at school and at stadiums. He broke it down. Counted the people. Did the math and modulated his breathing. Six-nine-four. Inhale. Exhale. Hold. Baeran broke it down and conquered the fear back in the world that once was.

The Dazers had bested Baeran twice, in the Firegale scorched new world, when he forgot the system, their vileness shocking him. The crowd, the moshing and the stink bothered Baeran the most, and he needed a three-part solution to conquer them.

Tame his fear of the crowd. Cole taught him a system, and Baeran had to apply it like he had back home. He had to pick a herd, count how many there were, and plan an exit strategy. He had to choose a smaller herd first, and infiltrate the herd, from the outside, with one side of his body next to them. Next, he needed to move to the center, count them, and modulate his breathing. Six-nine-four. Inhale. Exhale. Hold. Baeran needed to break it down,

like he had in the old world.

Tame the herd. Baeran couldn't let the raging mosh begin. What do Dazers do to chill? What do Dazers do when not stampeding boys and caves? They meander, moan and stink up the place. They daze and graze. Dazers like cattails. Cattails have nutrition, like vitamins and minerals. Dazers eat their cattails and chill. He needed to apply cattail cologne and daze.

Tame the stink. Their stink alone, could send Baeran into a full on panicwave. Like blood, crap and vomit rolled into one, the Dazer smell overpowered the senses. He needed to block the smell of their rotting leprous flesh and the body odor from ninety-nine days without a shower. How could he block the smell? Mask it with a stronger scent. Or never smell it—block his nose. Or do both. How did his mom remove stink back home in Portsmouth? The bathroom and Baeran's hockey bag stunk. How did his mom or dad clean the bathroom? They used lemon scented pine cleaner sprays. Abundant old heavy-bark pine trees stood in the forest. How did Baeran absorb the stink in his hockey bag? Kay put charcoal briquets sewed into a sock in with Baeran's equipment. There was plenty of charcoal in the forest, from the smaller trees. Baeran needed to stick pine sap up his nose and rub charcoal on his face.

Baeran broke it down, counted, and conquered the fear.

He trekked alone into the woods, without Selene, rubbed cattails on his body and ate several raw, the way the Dazers like them. He found charcoal and rubbed it on his face. Baeran found a pine tree and cut the bark, harvested the pine sap, waited for it to become gooey, and stuck it up his nose. Next, he found a Dazer herd near a stream, eating cattails. He counted. There were twenty-five. He broke it down. He snuck to the outside of the herd. He stood with one Dazer to his left, with an escape route on three sides. He ate cattails and he dazed. Later when the Dazers had their fill, he ambled his way to the middle of the pack. When the Dazers stopped at a meadow, and bedded down, Baeran did, too.

As Baeran lay in the meadow with a herd of Dazers, covered in cattail-charcoal-pinesap Dazer body spray, he calmed his mind, regulated his breathing, six-nine-four, and thought of one thing: Parker.

PARKER

M108. Maximus plus one hundred eight days. New York State. West of the Highland camp.
BAERAN

BAERAN AND THE SEASCAPERS LEFT THE HIGHLAND CAMPSITE on the ATVs, motorcycles and scooters the day after he infiltrated the Dazers. As the ash clouds moved back over New York, the Seascapers raced west along utility right-of-ways and rail trails. The skies grayed, and the temperature dropped, yielding the first snow in early September. The hope of one day reaching Nebraska, finding winter shelter and the new government spurred them onward. They avoided Jackers and Dazers and made it through unpopulated areas in New York, Pennsylvania, and West Virginia while observing burnt-out forests, dead cities, and towns from afar. Eventually the Seascapers no longer had enough fuel to continue and constructed a campsite in West Virginia.

After the group unpacked, Parker asked Baeran to join him on a hunt. "Baeran, let's put an end to this stuff. I want to learn more about trapping, and I can show you about hunting."

It had been thirty days since Shit Show #2 and Baeran wanted to end the conflict. The sleepless nights, the wise-ass comments, the fear for his own well-being, and of his sisters', and the shame he felt, had to end. Parker's answer to Baeran's next statement would let Baeran know whether the end to the conflict would be by peace or war. Baeran looked back at the campsite. "I'll find Deven."

Parker replied, "Let's hunt as a pair, like I used to with Ethan. Three's too many."

War it is.

"Let me gather my gear and Selene."

"I'll meet you by the woods." Parker's face lit up. "I'll see you in five."

Baeran collected his gear from his tent as Lani stood by protesting. "I don't want you in the wild alone with him. I don't trust Parker. That day when I made your bow string and asked you about Parker, you never answered me."

Baeran laid into Lani, deflecting, "I know. It's time. I'm ready. Thanks, but this is my problem. Have you talked to Mom and Dad or Jordin? You should worry about that. You haven't dropped the lesbian bomb yet, have you?"

"No."

"Well I've got a double L-bomb. I've got that eighteen-year-old prick pounding on me and I've got this stupid phobia of crowds, and what happens? God hands me a new world where crowds circle the countryside seeking me out to cause me torment. I'm done. You know what I did last week? I hung out with Dazers. That's why I stink so much. I walked with the Dazed, and even took a nap with them. So, Parker the prick wants to go adventuring with me today? So be it. It ends here. Don't worry about me, I'd fear for Parker's fate."

Lani stood motionless, and for the first time in a long time she had nothing to say.

Baeran grabbed his backpack, bow and birch stick, and he trekked toward Parker with Selene.

Lani watched the boys fade into the woods. Dumbfounded, she remained motionless and contemplated Baeran's words until Deven wandered by. Lani explained her concerns, and she bolted to find Cole, while Deven followed the two boys into the woods.

Baeran walked with Parker deep into the woods, allowing the older boy to take the lead. The older trees were charred, but stood strong and solid, while fledgling trees were burnt to the ground. A light gray snow fell from overcast skies.

After an hour Parker spotted an elevated rock outcropping. Twenty feet high above the ground, the stone had a wide view of the forest. "Wait, stay here, I want to sneak a peek. By the way, you smell like wet pine logs dragged through ass and tossed in a campfire. If I could bottle your stink, I'd call it Asspine Body Spray Repulsion."

Must be the cattail-charcoal-pinesap Dazer cologne.

Baeran smirked.

Parker climbed the bare rock face to a plateau. He stood and surveyed the forest. "Come up, Asspine. We need a better view of the valley."

Baeran climbed the rock face until he mounted the top of the outcropping. Selene watched him ascend from below.

Parker extended his hand. "Come see." And helped Baeran to the plateau.

Baeran traversed to center of the plateau. "What did you want to show me?"

Parker extended both arms, urging Baeran to engage and sneered, "Welcome to Shit Show #3."

Baeran lowered his backpack and stick, glaring at Parker. Parker rushed Baeran. Baeran planted both feet, with his left foot in front of the right. He leaned back with his right shoulder as his left elbow pointed at Parker. Baeran raised his left leg and stepped toward Parker. He twisted his hips and he swung his clenched right hand, landing a right cross on Parker's nose and mouth. *Crick!* Blood squirted as Baeran broke Parker's nose. The older boy fell to the ground. Baeran towered over Parker staring at the two teeth embedded in his knuckles.

Parker scooted away from Baeran and stood. He licked his missing teeth. "Ufth fweakin athpairan."

AssBaeran?

Baeran stepped back from Parker toward the edge. Parker darted at Baeran. Baeran side-stepped to his left. Parker grasped at thin air, his momentum propelled him, and he fell over the edge of the outcropping to the ground twenty feet below.

Parker screamed as he struck the ground.

Baeran removed the teeth from his hand and put them in his pocket. He collected his pack, bow and stick and climbed down the outcropping, weighing his options. He could leave him, kill him to protect the girls or help him. He shocked himself, weighing the middle option for a moment. What would his dad do? He would help Parker.

Baeran treaded from the base of the outcropping with Selene. He watched Parker from a step away, while he wrapped his hand with a strip from his shirt.

Parker clutched his ankle, yelling, "You stole Reese!"

Baeran responded to Parker in his thoughts. *She hates you, creeper. You're gonna lead with that one?*

Parker pulled a knife and stood, but he collapsed under his own weight. From the ground he cried, "You tricked me! Crouching around and tracking. You were scaring away the animals."

That's all you have. I can feel your power over me leaving.

Parker sobbed into his hands, in tremendous pain, tears mixing with the blood flowing from his nose. "That time we were captured by the Jackers, it was your fault, Baeran!"

Not. Cry baby.

"You killed Ethan!" Parker screamed as spit and blood spewed from his mouth.

Baeran nearly admitted he deserved the beatings for Ethan's death, but Parker had beat him twice before Ethan died.

Wrong again.

Baeran stepped toward Parker and kicked away the knife. "Let's be clear. You will never hit me again, ever. You will never touch Reese or my sisters. If you do, I will kill you. If Shit Show #4 ever begins, it will end in your death."

Baeran choked on his own words.

Kill you.

It had come to this.

Parker cried into his hands.

"We can work this out later." Baeran kneeled, offering his hand. "Let's hike back to the campsite."

Baeran put on his pack and helped Parker to his feet. The boys and Selene hiked toward the campsite, but Parker's strength ebbed after twenty minutes. He collapsed. "It's no use. Leave me."

"I won't." Baeran sat, resting. "Let's take a breather."

"I can't keep hiking." Parker gasped.

"Fine but I can't carry you. I'll run for help."

Baeran raced with Selene to the campsite without caution. Branches slashed his hands and face, while rocks rose out of the ground and strove to trip him. When he returned to the campsite, he collapsed from exhaustion, covered in sweat and cuts.

L.J., Tara, and Kay rushed to meet him. Between pants, Baeran asked, "Where's Dad?"

Kay asked, "What's the matter, Baeran? He's off with Mitch searching for you and Parker."

Baeran glanced at Kay, wanting to confide in her about Parker's treachery, but L.J. asked, "Where's Parker?"

"He's in the woods." Baeran replied, "He fell and twisted his ankle. I couldn't carry him any longer."

"Where, Baeran? Tell me!"

After Baeran recalled trail markers, L.J. hopped on an ATV and took off to search for Parker. But by evening, L.J. had returned alone. He had found Parker's trail and his boy's belongings but nothing else.

A while later, Deven came into the campsite and saw Baeran.

Baeran asked, "Where have you been?"

"Setting traps." Deven replied. "You're lookin' flat."

"Parker and I went hunting, he was hurt, and we can't find him."

"Chill. We'll tread back to the trail tomorrow. He doesn't even sleep in a tent. He'll be fine in the woods."

In the morning, more Seascapers returned to the woods to search for Parker. Deven and Baeran followed L.J. to where the boys had parted and found Parker's trail.

Deven called Mitch over as Baeran stood near. "Mitch, see—overturned earth—there was a total wipe out here. P-man's tracks are littering the trail, plus animal tracks, lots of rovers."

"Dogs?" Mitched looked around and lowered his voice. "Have you told L.J. yet?"

Deven shook his head. "No. But L.J. has already guessed. Wild dogs attacked Parker. He's dead. See the blood?"

Mitch put his arms around both boys, pulling them closer. "Okay, but we keep searching, until we find a body. Deven, what time is it?"

"Sorry Mitch, no dad watch."

"You don't have your dad's watch?" Mitch grasped Deven's wrist.

Deven pulled away, "I must've left it back at camp tent city."

"Okay, let's split up and continue the search."

As they searched, Baeran told Deven about the three fights

culminating in the attempt on his life, Parker's threat against his sisters and Parker's lust for Reese.

"Bummer. The P-man's a prick." Deven smiled. "If he was like a dinosaur, he'd be an Assasaurous Rex. Damn. I was tryin' to make sure he didn't get his mits on the sis. When we find him, I'll slay him, if you bail. I'll show him a Shit Show."

Baeran stopped. "I didn't say *Shit Show*."

"You totally did. You're drained, and the old rules don't mean jackshit anymore." Deven kept walking. "Parker could kill you in your sleep or take Reese. Don't think for a nano he'll let you live. Don't think for a milinano, I'll let him live."

Baeran stepped in front of Deven, cutting him off. "You are not killing anyone, and you don't mean that, whether he was a prick or not. Let's find him first and we'll talk to Cole and Mitch."

"Okay. We find the P-man and cash him out."

"Cash him out?" Baeran asked.

"Make him pay for it."

But after one week, L.J. acknowledged what everyone saw, the blood and the paw prints. It took a while to convince Tara. When she relented, the group stopped the search.

Later at night, back at the campsite, Cole and Baeran had a quiet, long, overdue talk by the campfire. After the rest of the Seascapers turned in, Baeran came clean about conquering his fear of the Dazers and his struggles with Parker over the last forty-five days. As he spoke, Selene lay across his legs, and he scratched her.

Cole put his arm around Baeran's shoulder. "Your mother and I have given you important responsibilities. It's a different world now and we know we can't keep you tied down. I'm glad you've worked it out on your own, but I am saddened you did not come to me or Mom. You know you can tell us anything, right?"

"Yes, Dad."

"No more laying with the Dazers."

"Yes," Baeran lied.

Cole stoked the fire and added a burnt log. "All right, now Parker, we don't know if he's dead or alive and you tell me seven days later you punched his lights out. Parker could be dead. Is that what you want?"

"Honestly, that's what I wished for the last month and half. I wanted him dead. But once I had beaten him, I saw him for the coward he was, and I pitied him. Once I broke his nose and knocked out his teeth, I knew I wouldn't kill him."

"How so, son?"

"I put his teeth in my pocket." Baeran smiled. "I thought we'd stick them back in."

"Baeran, why didn't you tell me?"

Baeran pushed Selene off his legs, pulling his knees to his chest. "Because, Dad, he threatened to attack Lani, Annie and Jordin if I said anything."

"How did it feel beating Parker and laying with the Dazers? I can already see a change in you."

"It's weird, Dad. I felt calm, free, liberated and in complete control, like Parker and the Dazers had no power over me."

Cole stood. "Baeran, I'm glad you're safe."

They sat by the fire for the rest of the night, a calmness in the air.

In the morning, Baeran wanted to build new traps. He sought after Deven with Selene. He stopped at Reese's and Heather's tent. They hadn't seen him. Baeran checked with Mitch. Mitch hadn't seen him either. Baeran asked Kay, Cole, Lani, Annie, and Jordin, and he asked L.J. and Tara. No one had seen Deven. An hour later, the entire Seascaper group hiked into the forest to search for Deven. By nightfall, Deven hadn't returned.

For the next seven days Heather, Mitch, Cole, Baeran, and Selene returned to the woods each morning in search of Deven. They wandered through the woods each day until on the seventh day they found a fresh trail of blood and paws. After tracking the trail, Heather, Mitch, Cole, Selene and Baeran found a pack of wild dogs consuming a fresh kill. Cole and Mitch chased the dogs into the woods. As the last dog darted, Baeran got a clear view of the dog's meal: a human skull. Heather screamed. Baeran dropped to his knees and he crawled toward the skull. Baeran gazed at the bloody scars on his knuckles and at the skull—it's two front teeth were missing.

Parker.

Baeran reached into his pocket and removed two teeth, placing them near the skull.

Cole whispered to Mitch and Heather the skull was Parker's. Baeran rose. Mitch knelt to get a better view of the skull. Parts of the soft pallet and tongue were still present, but something was stuck in the skull's mouth. Mitch put his fingers in and removed a black watch. Baeran recognized the watch, as did Heather.

Heather gasped. "Oh no."

Mitch wiped the blood off the watch. "Heather, Deven's not dead, the watch was placed in the skull."

Mitch handed Heather the watch.

Baeran recounted Parker's threats to Mitch and Heather, as well as their fight and the conversation he had with Deven, when Deven threatened to kill Parker if Baeran didn't. Baeran added, "Deven must have followed me and Parker into the woods the morning of our final fight, and confronted Parker after I left."

Mitch put his hands on Heather's shoulders, running them down to her elbow. "Heather, he left seven days ago, and his gear is gone. Deven's not coming back, and he lied the whole time we searched for Parker."

I know." Heather sobbed.

Mitch added, "We have to lie, too. We tell everyone Deven is dead. He's not coming back. The group won't survive if they know Deven killed one of our own, no matter how justified he felt. L.J. and Tara can't know. There is no point in telling them. Reese can't know. She can't have this on her head. We hide the watch. We lie."

Baeran, Heather and Cole agreed.

JACKERS

M122. Maximus plus one hundred twenty-two days. West Virginia.
BAERAN

BAERAN REMEMBERED HIS VOW TO FACE THE JACKERS. When the Seascapers stopped for more than one day, he left the new camp and headed into the woods alone to set his traps. The world had changed, and kids handled adult jobs. Fourteen was the new twenty, and solo hikes into the woods were common.

The Firegale was visible on the horizon. Snow fell at night and burnt off in the daylight. Gray snow, a mixture of ice crystals and ash, left its residue everywhere. Gray dim light ruled the day as the ash clouds blocked the sun.

Baeran spotted a town through the woods and investigated. Like with PharmaTown, Baeran crept to the houses closest to the forest, but Jackers had overrun the neighborhood.

Despite his vow, Baeran couldn't face the Jackers. These savage men had guns. He scurried into the woods, climbing a tree. A snow squall covered his tracks, and he hid until the Jackers left.

Baeran stayed in his treetop perch too long, and his frozen hands lost their grip on the high branch. He tumbled to the ground. His knee hit the ground first, followed by his face. Minutes later he awoke covered in gray snow, shivering. A voice in his head called out lyrically, "Wayfarer, this is not your death, it is your dawning. Look for me in the full moon's shadow spawning."

By afternoon, the sun broke through the cloudy skies and Baeran could stand. Rising, he supported his weakened knee with his stick and trekked back to the Seascaper campsite, convinced he had to prepare for the next Jacker encounter.

Baeran had to become a better fighter, and he knew how to do it. Parkour, hockey, and baseball were the key, as was Solstice.

THE LEGION OF DOOM

M110. Maximus plus one hundred ten days. Lexington Bunker Complex.
SOLSTICE

Solstice sat in the ductwork, with her knees to her chest, coughing. She had lost Mavourneen but was too sick to worry about her. Solstice hacked, and blood spattered onto the duct panel inches from her face. She had crawled down to the ducts closest to the fans, to conceal her cough and to breathe cool air, hoping to break her fever. But it didn't matter anymore if the fan with the loose bearing concealed her constant hacking, she'd be dead by morning.

At first, she struggled to breathe, fighting the headaches and the muscle pain. Five days later, the fever attacked. Solstice had vomited on herself, and soiled her underwear, too. She curled into a ball and shivered as her sweat soaked through her clothes. The nausea passed after day seven. She drank water, but each droplet

scorched her throat like a spicy sauce.

Solstice had done her best to keep two weeks of water and food on hand, but by tomorrow, the water would be gone, and she'd shrivel up, in violation of rule 1b—stay hydrated, because you'll go crazy otherwise.

Through the underknee vent, Solstice watched as an argument raged between the guards and their superiors. Behind a table, two higher ranking guards distributed white oval pills.

Solstice heard a guard in line say, "Forget about giving us pills, let us out, we need fresh air."

A guard from behind the table pushed a tablet forward. "Not yet. Take the pill."

The man in line stepped closer and coughed, vomiting blood. When they saw the blood vomit, several guards rushed for the door, while others dove for the pills, overturning the tables. Solstice alone noticed a bottle roll off the table, onto the floor, and get lost behind the wastebasket in the corner.

"Everyone cool down! We'll try this again after lunch. If you want to live, come back in an orderly fashion to get your pills." The head guard cleared the room, locking the doors from the outside.

Once she was sure the room was empty, Solstice dragged herself to the nearest T-junction, crawled through a discharge/intake access panel, tied off her 123-rope, and slid down to the vent opening two feet off the ground. She doubted she'd have the strength to climb the downchute later. "One problem at a time," she told herself.

Solstice popped the grate and crawled to the wastebasket. She clasped the pills and used the last of her strength to crawl into the vent and close the cover, resting for a moment.

Solstice read the label. Azithromycin. Treatment for Legionellosis. Take one per day for three to five days. A dosage of one per day recommended for five days for individuals who are immunocompromised.

Solstice took two pills daily for seven days.

On M122, Solstice's mind wandered, and she thought of the boy. *He's in trouble, again.* She pictured him, like she had on the day

Superstorm Maximus first struck the Atlantic Coast. As her strength returned, she called to him, "Wayfarer, this is not your death, it is your dawning. Look for me in the full moon's shadow spawning."

She smiled at the thought of her imaginary boyfriend, and she joked, "I need to clean myself up, in case we ever meet."

Later, she found bleach to clean the ducts and ill-fitting replacement clothes, but it wasn't enough. She'd do anything for a belt, and the Silver Palace in Bunkerland still stunk.

THE BELT

M124. Maximus plus one hundred twenty-four days. Lexington Bunker Complex.
SOLSTICE

SOLSTICE SAT IN THE SILVERDIMLIGHT OF THE DUCTWORK freezing in a stolen pair of granny panties and a pit-stained v-neck t-shirt. Naetersen could have overridden the timer at M116, after one hundred days. What was he waiting for? The Ice Maiden of the Silver Palace in Bunkerland needed a new wardrobe. Her pair of oversized underwear was held up by a knot in front.

Solstice followed the ductwork until she found an underknee vent near the incinerator. She couldn't see through the vent opening, but she could smell the bodies, and she could hear the rats. The rats had a kingdom greater than hers, and she couldn't find the courage to lower herself down.

Solstice stared through the underknee vent, gagging. She lowered herself flat onto the ductwork, straining to peer through the hashmarks of the vent cover placing her upper torso onto the vent. The cover gave way when Solstice hit the latch with her elbow. She fell, in clear violation of Rule 3—don't leave home without rope, because that's how you climb in when you fall out.

The rotten corpses provided a squishy landing for Solstice, but the bodies weren't the worst thing in the incinerator tunnel. It was the beaver-rats.

The oversized-rodents focused on the juicy bodies until the floor angled upward. A conveyer belt on the floor moved and bodies tumbled down an incline. The rats climbed on the one thing ascending the avalanche of bodies—Solstice.

Solstice was convinced the beaver-rats were the worst, especially the ones hitching a ride, until a door at the end of the

incline opened and illuminated the entire tunnel. Definitely, the incinerator flames were the worst. Solstice turned her back to the fire, and she climbed the avalanche of bodies. As she reached the top of the heap, a belt came loose from a small body. She grasped the belt and shook off the rats. She found a concrete foothold on the side of the conveyor, stepping onto the beaver-rats on the steps. The rats screamed as she crushed them under her bare feet. She climbed the access ladder on the wall and saw a metal hook in the vent opening. She had to use her new belt to snag the hook and climb through the vent, because she had forgotten Rule 3.

Solstice closed the underknee vent panel and scurried to her ductwork home. She sat with her back against the cool metal. She pulled her knees into her chest and she sobbed, staring at her new belt and the word scrawled on it: Mavourneen.

DEAREST

M128. Maximus plus one hundred twenty-eight days. Lexington Bunker Complex.

Solstice sat in the ductwork and wrote in her lyricbook: Rule 4—don't make friends, because you'll lose them.

Solstice ran her hand over her body. Thick calluses had formed on her knees, elbows, and palms. The cuts, less frequent now, served as a reminder of those first weeks in the air ducts along with her dried blood streaks on the cold metal. Her eyesight had changed, too. She spent most of her time in the ducts, leaving them only to forage for food in the rooms below. As energy was rationed, the lights were shut off in nonessential areas, and the ductwork became darker.

Why didn't the doctor open the bunker to the outside world? What was so horrible topside? Naetersen could have overridden the timer twelve days prior, but Solstice remained trapped.

Solstice's teeth and gums hurt. It had been a month since she had had a decent piece of fruit. She risked lowering herself into the senator's room. She needed fruit before her back teeth wiggled out. She couldn't handle being sick again.

The senator met with Naetersen after lunch each day. Solstice overheard the two men talking about why an individual they favored should live or die. It was a lottery no one wanted to win. It sickened Solstice to know the senator and doctor determined people's fates on a full stomach.

When Solstice was sure the senator had left to meet with the doctor, she entered the room through the underknee vent with her 123-rope tied to a support. She tiptoed across the floor. It took a minute for her eyes to adjust to the night-light in the corner. After the darkness of the ducts, even faint light blinded her.

Two cans of oranges, a bag of dried pineapple, a light stick—the kind found in a car emergency kit, and a 7-oz. bottle of red wine were arranged on a table in the center of the room. Solstice tiptoed to the table and loaded the pineapple, light stick, and oranges into her sling sack. As she placed the wine in her bag, a folded piece of paper fell from the table to the floor. Solstice snatched the paper and placed it between her lips. She climbed the 123-rope and replaced the underknee vent cover behind her. Her heart pounded as she crawled to her main hiding spot near the cafeteria vent.

Solstice placed the sling pack down and opened the paper. She pulled a shirt over her head and snapped the light stick, flooding the shirt with fluorescent light. Her eyes burnt like she had stared into the noonday sun. She adjusted the shirt, ensuring it blocked the light from escaping down the ducts. Solstice waited another moment. The blindness subsided, and the words came into focus.

My Dearest Solstice,
I suspect you'll be needing these items. I know you are desperate, and I will continue to help you when I can.
I remember your mother, Elle. I don't claim to have known her

truly, but I suspect she would be proud of your ingenuity. She spoke of you often in my office at the capitol.

I doubt you would understand this, but I have failed many people. I knew your mother and let her get locked out—dooming her to die at the hands of the Dazed or in the Firegale or the riots. Many people rushed the door that day. I could not choose. And now I am a party to the murder within these walls. The end game is near, and I am a witness to Naetersen's crimes. I doubt I will survive long enough to see the sun.

Solstice be wary. My actions toward you may seem unexplainable. It has been my intention to protect you. I know who, or rather, what you are, but the doctor must never know. Hide. Avoid Naetersen!

While I live, I will do what I can to help you.
Senator Adena

Solstice reread the note. Her imagination had gotten the best of her, desperate to have someone care for her. The note was much shorter and didn't even have her name on it:

Take this stuff. I suppose I owe you that much. I'll make sure the doctor doesn't harm you. Stay out of my room.

Silverfox. Solstice held the note close to her face, and tears poured onto the paper. The old light stick was already fading, and she curled herself into a ball. *Why let her rot in the ductwork?*

For over a month Solstice had shut the voice out and blocked her songs. She raised her head, glaring at the endless ductwork and spoke, "Open the door. Please open the door. Please."

When silence answered, the flashes and headaches overtook her, and Solstice cried, "Melody, take me."

EVOLVE

NITEWALK

M132. Maximus plus one hundred thirty-two days. Kentucky.
BAERAN

BAERAN'S BUTT HURT. He had been sitting between Cole and sister on the back of the ATV every day for about a month through West Virginia and into Kentucky. The Seascapers rode the ATVs, mopeds, and the motorcycle for hours on end. They zigged and zagged. They found trails and lost them. They rode under power lines, over gas lines, and on bike paths, avoiding tar roads. The adults took turns serving as scouts, and when they came back hours later, the Seascapers would ride off.

Each day the Seascapers would scavenge for food, water and fuel, slipping into burnt-out towns a few at a time at either dusk or dawn. Homes had been abandoned by those running from the Firegale, but the flames didn't scorch everything in their path. Supplies could often be found in a shed, detached garage or basement.

The wind shifted, and the sun made a final stand, beating back the gray snow. Autumn had been found. The gray mud hardened, littering the landscape. The Firegale burnt on the western horizon. The gray dim light faded. By day's end the sun had burnt off the gray clouds. By night, the moon approached fullness, and allied with the sun, before the ash clouds took over for the winter.

At night the families pulled off the road and camped together. While everyone slept, Selene awoke near midnight, and Baeran let her out. Selene became used to waking during the night, and Baeran let the dog venture farther into the forest around the campsite each evening. After several days, the boy and dog developed a routine to sneak away from the campsite under the cover of darkness.

Baeran acclimated to the sounds of the night and learned to explore by the moonlight. On the trip through Kentucky, Baeran

decided he would have a little fun, and planned a longer excursion
for him and Selene.

HILLOCK
M132. Maximus plus one hundred thirty-two days. Lexington Bunker Complex.
SOLSTICE

SOLSTICE WATCHED FROM THE UNDERKNEE VENT as three dozen guards assemble in the cafeteria before Doctor Naetersen and Senator Adena. While the guards licked their chops at a feast laid before them, Naetersen spoke, "Today is our last day in the bunker."

Cheers rose from the guards.

Naetersen continued, "We have fulfilled the initial part of our mission: survival. We've gone to ground, and we survived the riots and the Firegale. Tomorrow we head to the Presidential bunker complex in Lincoln, Nebraska."

The guards cheered again.

"I know we've lost men, a dozen, by my count, and we've had to make tough choices. The bunker complex was designed for fifty people: the two primaries, the senator and myself, and forty-eight dedicated men and woman." Naetersen pointed to the guards. "We had many challenges one hundred and sixteen days ago. Two hundred and seventy-seven individuals illegally entered the bunker, overcoming and killing twelve guards on the first day, not to mention the thousand refugees we trapped in the Hillock tunnel. As you know, we did our best, but resources and disease killed the refugees. Lest we pity them, let me remind you—their disease, Legionellosis, almost wiped us out, and we had to delay our deliverance after one hundred days had passed because of that same disease. You have done well. Be proud. Now the senator and I will leave you to it. Enjoy the feast, the last of what we have. Tomorrow we leave!"

The guards cheered for a third time.

The senator and doctor left the cafeteria, and the guards dug into the feast. She heard a buzzing and near the cafeteria door, a blast door lowered. The guards stopped and stared at the heavy metal door. The guards coughed, gripped their throats, and collapsed, falling at a rate determined by how much food they had consumed. Solstice panicked, collected her sling sack and 123-rope and scurried toward the control room.

From the control room underknee vent, Solstice watched the senator and doctor each place a key in the control panel. The senator's left hand shook uncontrollably. She heard the senator say, "Doctor, are you sure we had to do it?"

"Yes, you read the orders. After one hundred days, leave and kill everyone." Naetersen gathered his notebooks. "We stayed in the bunker complex an extra two weeks while you divined the intent of a clear and direct order. A directive the government preplanned."

Senator Adena put his quivering left hand in his pocket, clenching his arm to his side. "Wouldn't a platoon have been helpful in getting to Lincoln?"

"Yes, but it carries too much risk." The doctor shoved his notebooks into a gray backpack. "I have no illusions that the guards will continue to follow my orders in the wild without you and the directive was clear."

The senator asked, "Are you sure we are safe in the control room?"

"Yes, the poison was in the food, and if anyone survives, they are locked into the cafeteria. Please enter your part of the code senator to open the Hillock door."

Solstice had remembered Elle's words from the summer trail:

"Under Fort Hillock is the back door to the bunker. The back door faces the forest and beyond, the river. I've seen the disaster plans, by accident, in the senator's office. The tunnel is twenty-three miles long from the quarry to Fort Hillock. Six short bunker tunnels are located under Lexington, but the seventh tunnel leads from the city to the fort."

Adena asked, "What about the bodies in the tunnel, doctor? We trapped over a thousand refugees between the tunnel doors."

Naetersen replied, "I'll take the module to avoid the bodies.

Ingenious how we tricked the refugees into the Hillock tunnel on the second day. Unfortunately, they lasted for a week, longer if they resorted to eating... In any event, bodies will litter the full twenty-three miles. I'm glad I'll be in the module."

The senator stalled, "And what about the plumbing mishap?"

"We had to dump the waste into a new location after the malfunction, but I'll be shielded from the smell in the module." Naetersen replied.

The senator typed in a sixteen-character alphanumeric code with his right hand, his left no longer obeyed his mind. The doctor typed in a different sixteen-character alphanumeric code and hit enter. The doctor flipped through the channels on a display. He said, "The Hillock door is open."

The senator asked, leaning on the console, "Do we have a deal? Subject # 277 lives."

"Yes. 277 is immune to the Dazer pathogen." The doctor reached into his pocket and removed a pill bottle. "Based on what you've told me, she evolved seven years prior—the first of her kind. A pity you won't survive to see it."

The senator replied, "It is."

"Senator are you sure you want to do it?"

"Doctor are you sure about the images?"

"Yes, the tumor should have already killed you, and the tremors are worse." Naetersen pointed to Adena's left hand. "A pity we didn't have a surgeon and staff. If you had the tumor removed, it would have been survivable, it's nestled between the skull and the brain. From the scans, it appears to be contained. It's the sheer mass—size of it—that's killing you, putting pressure on the brain."

"Yes, but we both know I'm not made for the new world. Doctor, will you watch over 277 in my stead? I have too long avoided that responsibility."

"Yes." The doctor handed the senator a pill bottle.

"We have a deal." The senator handed the doctor a set of prints.

"These will work fast. Goodbye." Naetersen strode out of the room.

Solstice waited until the doctor and senator exited the room in different directions. She put on her sling sack and lowered herself into the room, leaving her 123-rope. She followed the doctor from a distance, into a tunnel she had never entered. At the end of the tunnel the doctor opened a door and stepped into darkness.

Solstice peered through the door into the eight-foot wide by eight-foot tall Hillock tunnel. The doctor sat in an egg-like capsule. The capsule was attached to a rail on the left side-wall of the tunnel. An illuminated hood came down over his head, and the capsule zipped away. Within minutes Solstice lost sight of the doctor. She stepped into the tunnel, and the door automatically closed behind her. She reached for a handle, but there was none.

It doesn't matter Solstice, we are leaving no matter what.

Solstice trekked into the total darkness and the horrors of the Hillock tunnel, determined to gain her freedom. Solstice climbed over a thousand bodies, through the raw sewage with the beaver-rats. She trudged twenty-three miles to her freedom through the backdoor at the other end of the Hillock tunnel. In the depths of the utter darkness, Solstice no longer heard her mom's advice, nor could she remember her bus-condo friends or Dallas, or the faces of Silverfox, SlateShrew, Burly Bill and Gangly George or Mavourneen. Everyone but Melody abandoned Solstice.

We can do this. Count with me. Sing with me.

Solstice had been stooping in the ductwork for months and struggled to straighten up, her muscles taunt. With bent back, she tramped twenty-three miles in twenty-three hours. With Melody, Solstice sang every song they ever sang, and they talked about the draincock, 123-rope, 4 crazy days without water, 5 rules, 36 guards gassed, being stuck on a count of 46 in the quarry water, 116 days in captivity, the 276 killed in the bunker and the 1372 bodies climbed over in the Hillock tunnel. And when she had done that twice, Solstice did the math with Melody as they slogged: 23 miles door-to-door equals 15,180 duct-lengths of Hillock tunnel horrors equals 82,800 mom-counts in the total darkness equals 161,920 size6Solstice-feet to freedom.

And then, Solstice emerged into the moonlight.

STICK
M132. Kentucky.
BAERAN

Baeran jogged through the woods as Selene trotted next to him. They'd have fun tonight. He could still see their campfire, but they had trekked far enough to make noise.

It took a while, but Baeran found flat, hard ground. He gripped his birch wood stick. The top end had a tiny bend. Baeran flipped it over, and it became a hockey stick.

Baeran pulled a can from his pocket and crushed it into a hockey puck. He challenged Selene, "Come and get it if you can."

Selene remembered the game and set upon Baeran. Baeran had his stick. Selene had her paws and her teeth. Once Selene captured the puck, the game digressed into Baeran chasing Selene with his stick in the inverted position, tapping the dog on the butt until she released the puck.

When Selene refused to yield, the chase devolved into a mock sword fight. Baeran twirled the stick over his head and passed it behind his back. Selene danced at his feet, dropping the puck and attacking the stick.

Baeran extended the stick, pulled it back, and tossed it into the air. He adeptly spun the stick and caught it one-handed. On the next stick toss, Selene jumped at Baeran, knocking him to the ground. Baeran laughed and wrestled with Selene while saying, "Who's a good doggy?"

After five minutes, the dog and boy rested together, staring at the stars and moon.

Baeran had practiced his stick moves since he was a boy while skating at the rink or in the backyard. Heck, any time he held a stick or bat, he'd twirl, toss, and strike. He used to dispatch imaginary

271

foes with ease. He had played hockey since the age of five, and baseball and soccer for almost as long.

Baeran had to be ready for the Jackers. He should have been ready for Parker. He should have fought off the Dazer stampede.

His hockey stick had once been a weapon, on and off the ice. Baeran rose and swung his stick in the air, and Selene backed off. He twirled the stick overhead and passed it behind his back. He hit a tree branch. He hit the tree again and broke off the branch.

Baeran swung harder, smashing another branch. He swung repeatedly. He hit the tree until the forest floor was littered with splinters and sweat poured down his brow. He fell to the ground exhausted. Selene lay at his side, nuzzling his neck as he caught his breath.

Baeran scratched the dog. "It's about hockey and baseball. I've already got the skills to be a good fighter, but I need to use them differently."

Selene wagged her tail and jumped up.

Baeran sensed the dog understood, and he rose, attacking another tree. He threw his stick into the air, catching, tossing and striking with rhythm. The stick was his instrument and Baeran made music, smashing branches. Selene joined in the game, attacking the broken branches on the forest floor.

The boy and the dog continued smashing imaginary foes until they were exhausted. When Baeran leaned his stick against a tree, Selene stopped, panting. Her ears pricked up, and she stared off into the woods.

Baeran looked at the dog and off into the direction that Selene was staring. "I hear it, too, girl. It's the wind."

Selene turned toward Baeran and cocked her head. Unconvinced, she trotted toward the direction of the sound.

DMR

M132. Hillock Tunnel.
SOLSTICE

SOLSTICE STARED AT THE MOON. She didn't remember it being that colossal. Every breath was sheer joy, as was every smell. The scent of charcoal, new plant life, water, and animals blended, filling the night air. It smelled like freedom. But she wouldn't stray too far yet. Walking hurt, and Solstice would have to find more supplies before she could leave. First on her list had to be a bath.

The day of Solstice's deliverance came on October 31, Halloween, one hundred and thirty-two days after her birthday. Solstice and Elle had left their condo about two weeks after the windstorm, Maximus, smashed into the Atlantic Coast. She had spent one hundred and sixteen days in captivity with no moon, stars or sun.

Naetersen had left the bunker with the hydraulic back door wide open, having learned what he needed from the senator. Now, the bunker inhabitants were all free, but they were all dead, except for Solstice, Melody, and Naetersen.

Solstice peered out of the Hillock Tunnel, searching for survivors of the Firegale and the Lexington Bunker Complex. At her feet, she found matches and clean clothes. *Where'd that come from?*

Solstice shivered. *We need to build a campfire, and to change.*

Solstice shook her head, trying to dislodge Melody's voice echoing in her head. But Melody was right, the heat from a campfire would feel good after shivering for months in the bunker. She'd enjoy the space, breathe fresh air, feel the earth, warm herself by a campfire, drink fresh water, and deal with whatever came her way. Aether, air, earth, fire and water, the elements that haunted her songs, now welcomed her return into the world.

After sitting by the campfire, Solstice found a stream and bathed. It was freezing, but it didn't matter. Solstice figured it would take at least twenty-three baths to wash off the twenty-three miles of the Hillock tunnel. But it was time for her new clothes. She had found a clean blue dress on the way out of the bunker and had slipped it over a long-sleeve white T-shirt. The moonlight danced on the shirt and shone through the dress. Solstice treaded on the grass. It tickled her toes. Her leg muscles hurt, but her back loosened as each moment passed.

I'm leaving now, Solstice. I will be back when you need me, and when you are ready.

Solstice arched her back and stretched. She spun, and the tall grass touched her fingertips. Her neck released from the imaginary rope that had been pulling it to the ground, and she straightened her back, as her muscles became looser. She spun. She imagined the studio, and her life before, without Melody.

Solstice remembered the summer performance piece. The meadow would be her stage. She rocked between her toes and heels, feeling the beat, and sensing the song. She closed her eyes and swayed side to side. Her muscles remembered, and the dance meadow rhythm began...

She ran through the meadow and leapt with legs stretched in the air. She stuck the landing with a smile.

Solstice bent her left knee and arched the left heel. She raised her hands in the air, like a swan. She lowered her wings by her side and raised her eyes toward the sky.

She arched onto her tippy-toes and twirled with one arm stretching for the moon and one arm brushing the tall grass.

She kicked her right leg. She kicked again, higher, and held it, touching her right knee to her nose while holding her ankle.

She spun and released the ankle, twisting into the ground until she sat.

Solstice lowered her eyes and hugged her knees. She released, extended the left arm and raised her head. She pointed her left leg to the sky and held it, touching the elbow to the knee.

Solstice lowered her leg and sprung up.

She extended her right leg even with her waist and arched her back with her eyes facing the sky.

Solstice swung the right leg, roundhouse-kick style and transferred her weight from left leg to right leg at end of kick.

She ran, leapt and rolled to the ground, stopping to kneel.

Solstice arched her back and bent her elbows, raising her hands to the sky.

She sprung up and balanced on her tippy-toes.

Solstice twirled through three rotations.

She stopped and breathed deeply before repeating the dance.

Solstice danced until the moonlight reflected off the sheen of her tears. She remembered the dance, freedom, and the girl she had forgotten.

MOON
M132. Kentucky.
BAERAN

Baeran watched Selene trot deeper into the woods, intent on finding the source of the noise she had heard. It sounded like words, but it was the wind, not ghosts.

Baeran smiled. It was Halloween and a harvest moon, but these weren't haunted woods. He chased Selene until she stopped. "Hold up, girl."

Baeran grabbed Selene's collar and held her back. He stared into the woods and saw a gleam off in the distance. The moonlight danced and shimmered on a metallic object. He grinned at Selene. Her tail wagged. She saw it, too.

"Okay, let's go see it."

DARKLITE
M132. Near the Hillock Tunnel.
SOLSTICE

Solstice lay in the meadow grass, watching the stars twinkle. She sang the song born from her mind minutes prior. She could hold off Melody a bit longer, but Solstice owed her at least one song. Solstice smiled, no aura, migraine or flash came. The words and tune belonged to Solstice and merely were a reflection on her time in the bunker, and not a vision of the future.

"Darkness and the Light"

Darkness and light
The girl is the sun
Caught in a black hole
Stuck with the evil one

Day and night
He held the key
Locked in a cage
Now she was free

Lost forever
Dancing with the moon so bright
The life that once was
Fading now in the twilight

Good-bye to everyone
All alone
They are dead

On her own

Which road to choose
Stay or go
Should she check on him
Whoa, whoa, whoa

Lost forever
Dancing with the moon so bright
The life that once was
Fading now in the twilight

Darkness and light
Was he still in there
The sun needs him
Back into the snare

The sun needs him
Can she find strength, does she dare?
Needs him to shine
Once more into the snare

Lost forever
Dancing with stars so bright
The life that once was
Fading now with the night

Lost forever
Dancing with the moon so bright
The life that once was
Fading now in the twilight

Solstice smiled. With the song, her memories returned. She could picture her mom, her bus-condo friends, Mavourneen and Silverfox. And Solstice remembered Dallas, and a dreamvision she described to him at age seven: *"I've seen myself older, dancing... under the moonlight, after the flames."*

QNA123
M132. Kentucky.
SOLSTICE AND BAERAN

Baeran saw the shiny object beyond a clearing. Already he was too far from camp, but he had to investigate and left the safety of the forest. The wind sang to him. His weary ears played tricks on him. He doubted his eyes, too, until he saw it. From the edge of the woods he saw a giant open steel door built into the hill. Discarded camouflage littered the ground near the entrance. He studied the contours of the hill and he couldn't contain his excitement. He and Selene had discovered a hidden fort! He'd show Cole in the morning, but first he had to examine the door. He dropped to his belly and crept toward it. Selene followed.

At the meadows edge, an acorn hit Baeran in the back, and he heard a sweet voice.

"Stay away from the door. It's not safe."

Selene jumped to attention. Baeran rolled onto his back and brandished his stick.

A girl in a tree sprang from the lowest branch and landed on her feet. She gleamed and twirled her blue dress. "Put your stick down."

Selene's tail wagged, and the dog ambled to the girl, lying at her feet. The girl bent down into the shadows and scratched Selene's belly. She stood with her back to the clearing. The moonlight shone through her blonde hair and into her blue eyes.

Baeran rose. He had never seen anything more beautiful. He muttered, "My name is Baeran."

The girl beamed as her dreamvision came true. "I'm Solstice."

"It's you isn't it? I wasn't sure if you were real."

Solstice smiled. "I'm real."

Selene rolled on her back, playfully waving her paws as her tail wagged.

Solstice asked, "What's your dog's name?"

"Selene." Baeran replied.

"Selene?"

"It means moon."

Solstice interrupted, "How come you named her that?"

"It wasn't me, my dad named her. My mom used to say that he loved the dog more than the sun, the moon and stars in between. Now, he won't even acknowledge Selene."

Solstice sat next to Selene and the dog curled up to her. As she scratched behind Selene's ears, Solstice asked, "Your parents are still alive? How'd you get here?"

Still standing, Baeran replied, "My parents, sister and I are camped a short walk away. I was sneaking out to have a little fun with Selene. We have other people there, too. Where's your group?"

Solstice replied, "I came from the tunnel. They're gone. I lost my mom a long time ago, twenty-three miles from here."

After a moment of silence Baeran sat on the ground across from Solstice. "I'm sorry about your mom."

"It's been one hundred sixteen days since we were separated." Solstice crossed her legs. "I can remember her face and I still hear her voice giving me advice, guiding me."

"You came from the tunnel and you are alone now?"

"Yes," Solstice answered.

"And that was one hundred sixteen days ago, twenty-three miles from here?"

Solstice replied, "Yes. My mom taught me to... to keep track... to help me... nevermind."

Baeran Everdork's curiosity ran amok. "Where does the tunnel go? How long have you been there? Is there food, games, movies or books? How about showers or bathrooms? Do you have heat or air conditioning? Coke, is there any Coke? How about beer? For my Dad, he would love a beer. Is there anything besides squirrel, cattails and dandelions? Where'd you come from? Where'd you used to live? I'm from Portsmouth, New Hampshire. We've been on the road for over four months."

"Slow down, it's been a long time since I've talked to anyone." Solstice smiled. "Let's keep it simple." Solstice reached over Selene and put her hand in Baeran's. "Sit closer to me."

Without releasing her hand, Baeran scooched over, inches from Solstice, but the dog refused to yield her space in front of the girl. Selene put a paw on Baeran's knee. He smiled and scratched the dog with Solstice. Selene's tail wagged as she snuggled closer to the pair of teens.

"It's the legendary double-scratch—dogs love it." Baeran smirked.

Solstice gleamed. The moonlight shimmered in the ruffles of her dress, and she said, "It's been so long since I talked to someone, but I don't want to talk about the bunker or tunnel tonight."

"What do you want to talk about? Do you want to know about

my group?"

"Let's play a game for now."

Baeran replied, "Okay, what is it?"

"It's called QNA123. I ask a question." Solstice touched her hand to her chest. "We count to three and we both answer at the same time." She put her finger on Baeran's chest. "Then you ask a question and count to three."

"Okay got it. Are there any other rules?"

"No. I've had enough with rules." Solstice scooched closer to Baeran. "Are you ready?"

"Yes."

"Okay, what is your favorite activity?" Solstice counted, "Wait, One, two, three..."

Baeran replied.	Solstice replied.
"Hockey."	"Dance."

Baeran asked. "Second favorite? One, two, three..."

"Parkour."	"Singing."

"Any siblings?" Solstice asked.

"One—no three."	"None."

Solstice cheated. "One, no three?"

Baeran replied, "No fair, my turn. How old are you?"

"Fourteen."	"Fourteen."

"Baeran, what's your favorite food?"

"Cheez-Its."	"Fresh vegetables."

"That's not definitive, but I'll allow it." Baeran chuckled. "What thing do you miss the most?"

"My longboard."	"Bus rides."

Selene stretched, putting a paw on both Baeran and Solstice. She looked at the new friends as if to say, "Less talking, more scratching."

Solstice scratched Selene. "Sunsets or moonrises?"

"Moonrises."	"Moonrises."

"Name something that people wouldn't guess about you?" Baeran moved closer and his glasses fell from his pocket.

"I sketch."	"I make up nicknames."

Solstice picked up Baeran's glasses. "You dropped these, Wayfarer."

Baeran countered, "I'm already sketching you in my mind."

"What is your biggest secret?" Solstice deflected.

"I hate crowds."   "A voice in my head sings."

"Okay, can I ask a follow up question?" Baeran asked.

Solstice looked away. "No, but don't worry, I'm not crazy."

Baeran smiled. "But that's what crazy people say."

"Too late." Solstice shrugged. "Speed round."

"Righty or Lefty?" Baeran waved his palms.

"Righty."   "Lefty."

Solstice quipped, "Color?"

"Gray."   "Yellow."

Baeran asked, "Favorite music?"

"Alternative"   "Show tunes."

"Birthdate?" Solstice asked.

"January 1st."   "June 21st."

"Favorite team?"

"Patriots."   "Bengals."

Baeran laughed, "Oh. I'm sorry..."

"Me too." Solstice replied. "Okay, it's time for the bonus round. You guess my answer for three questions in a row and you'll get a prize."

"What's the prize?" Baeran's eyes lit up. "Can I pick it?"

Solstice smirked, "Get it right and you'll find out." She looked around. She had nothing. "I'm not even sure yet, but it will come to me."

Baeran jumped to his feet. "Okay, here's the first question." He twirled in a mock ballerina pose. "Will you dance for me later?"

"Yes."   "Yes—if you Parkour."

"Can you sing a song for me?" Baeran grabbed a fake microphone and he warbled, "Will you?"

"Yes."   "Yes."

"No more yes or no questions." Solstice took Baeran's hand, pulling him back toward her. "You're cheating."

"Okay, but I wanted that prize." Baeran sat. "Give me a minute. I'm not sure of my next question. I don't want to mess this up. I need to break it down, to do the math."

Solstice's eyes widened. "What?"

"Nothing—it's something my Dad taught me." Baeran paused,

choosing his words. "Here goes. Final question for the prize. What do you do when you are scared? One, two, three..."

"I count."   "I count."

"What?"   "What?"

"Really?"   "Really?"

Solstice reached for Baeran's hand. "I've spent the last one hundred and sixteen days counting."

"I've been dreaming about you for one hundred and thirty-two days." Baeran smiled. He looked over his shoulder, back towards the way he had come. "I've got a pile of sketches of you in my backpack at the campsite."

Solstice responded, "I'm sorry about the dreams. I can't control them. Twice I've managed to call you. Back on the day the Firegale started, I sent you a warning and again ten days ago, when you fell out of a tree. Tonight, I knew it was you I had been calling, once I saw the sunglasses, Wayfarer.

"How do you do it? How do you call me in my mind?" Baeran spread his pinkie finger and thumb, raising them to his ear and mouth. "I'll be honest, I'd like to have the brain phone, too."

Solstice raised her hand, mock calling Baeran. "I was born with it, but it seems to get stronger every seven years. I have dreams of the future and I sing about them, or Melody does. That's the voice, my friend in my head."

"I'm not freaking out because I'm changing too. But I should be freaked out since I've been drawing you for months and I can feel tingles down my arms and legs."

"Tingles?" Solstice pretended to shiver. "Where?"

Baeran wiggled his fingers. "It's like static electricity right here, but more. Like if I tried hard enough, I could move something. That's weird, right?"

Solstice replied, "No, I've been expecting you, Aether."

"Aether? I was talking to my sister Lani about that. I feel like I can see the spaces between things. The energy that bonds things together. I've always noticed things, that's why my sketches are so realistic." Baeran flung open his fingers on his right hand, tossing an imaginary ball. "But now I feel like, if I could release the static electricity, no the kinetic energy, stored inside me I might be able to move something." Solstice was silent and Baeran grew uncomfortable. "Well? It's crazy, right?"

Solstice grasped Baeran's hand. "No, you are not crazy, nor alone. There are five of you. The other four should already be gathering around you."

"What other four?" Baeran rubbed his chin. "There are kids and adults at my camp."

"Air, Earth, Water and Fire." Solstice touched Baeran's hand. "And you are Aether."

"What does that mean?" Baeran asked.

"I'm not sure." Solstice replied. She waved her fingers and pointed at her head. "You'd have to ask Melody, but she's gone silent."

"What do you mean, Solstice?"

"Melody is the name for the voice in my head. I told you." Solstice closed her eyes, and put her fingertips to her forehead, smiling like she was drawing a vision forward at that moment. "I see things in dreamvisions. Plus, I see words and Melody makes them into a song. And the song, well, it predicts the future, but it's usually vague."

"Still, that's a neat trick." Baeran imitated Solstice with his fingers to his temples. "Nope, doesn't work on me."

"You're lucky, it comes with a cost. Each prediction hurts more." Solstice rubbed her temples. "I have flashes, auras and migraines. When I was seven, I even had a seizure. My dreams and songs, they are pointing to one date: my birthday next year on the summer solstice."

"Wow. I'm sorry. What will happen on your birthday?"

Solstice laughed, trying to lighten the mood. "Besides the total lack of ice cream and cake?" But her smile faded. "A prophecy, I suspect, for you, Aether, and the other four, and likely myself, too."

"Will you be okay?"

"I don't know." Solstice smiled. "But I won't be alone. You'll be there."

Baeran put his hands under his thighs, squirming. "Other people are changing, too, maybe for other reasons." He whispered, "Have you seen a Dazer?"

Solstice replied, "Are you afraid of summoning them?" Before Baeran could say, "Yes." Solstice continued, "Not in person, but a man in the bunker saw some through the cylinder—like a full body periscope—and I read his notes. Why?"

"Dazers are people that look like lepers. They've changed."

"I bet if you thought hard enough, you might know Air, Earth, Fire and Water already."

"My sister's name is Lani. It means sky, and she's breathless." Baeran laughed. "She talks and writes like the wind blows."

Solstice recognized the name. "Skyhaven is Lani. I've dreamt about her. I've seen one other, too: Water." Solstice pointed to her neck. "I've seen her scar. She loves both you and Lani."

"That's Jordin Brooks, her name means river water."

"Baeran listen to me, we weren't supposed to meet, not yet. It's dangerous. It's too early. Already you are feeling the kindling or the tingling, as you call it. We can't undo this: finding each other. But you can't tell the others. It's too risky. They need to be ready for the dreamvision."

"The one on your birthday, Solstice?"

"Yes."

"How come I can already feel the kindling?" Baeran wiggled his fingers.

"I don't know. But you're the glue that holds us together, the space in between the other elementals. You are the Aether, the space between the light—the sun—and the dark."

"Solstice, you are the sun, the light?"

"Yes."

"And who is the dark?"

"I have my suspicions." Solstice paused, thinking of Silverfox and Naetersen.

Baeran scooched closer, placing his hands in Solstice's. "How do you do it? How do you live with this knowledge? How does your head not explode with questions?"

"I feel like it might. I used to be a normal girl. I danced and sang, and Melody was quiet."

"I'm sorry."

Solstice sighed, "It is who I am."

"I want to know more, and I want my prize."
"Stay with me Baeran, tonight, and hold me."
Baeran reached over Selene and embraced Solstice.
Solstice gazed into Baeran's eyes. She gleamed, placing both hands on Baeran's chest, and she kissed him as the moon set.

MAIDENRISE

M133. Maximus plus one hundred thirty-three days. Hillock tunnel door.
SOLSTICE

SOLSTICE WATCHED BAERAN LEAVE AT DAWN after their moonlight meeting near the Hillock door. He had asked her to join his family, but Solstice had to check the bunker one more time, and she needed time to consider it. *Maidens didn't need boys and didn't need to be rescued.* Naetersen had opened the door a day before she had met Baeran, and Solstice desperately wanted to check on the senator. Not to ask why he never claimed her, but to meet him and to say good bye before he was gone.

Solstice had sat near the entrance of the Hillock tunnel at dawn, wiping ash flakes from her shoulders, while Baeran dashed to the Seascaper campsite to talk to his parents. She stared into the tunnel door questioning if she had the strength to hike the twenty-three miles back through the Hillock tunnel to the Lexington bunker to find Senator Adena.

Solstice stared into the open door of the tunnel and said, "Maybe there is a return line I could use."

Rule 2—stay out of the return lines, because you can't see the downchutes.

Return line or not, Solstice had to find Silverfox. When she resolved to take the day-long trip back through the Hillock tunnel of horrors, she sought Baeran. Solstice tracked east a half-mile through the woods following Baeran's directions until she viewed his campsite from afar. She could see Baeran arguing with a man. The rest of the Seascapers had mounted their ATVs, mopeds and motorcycles, and were ready to leave. The entire camp had packed. Even Selene sat in a trailer attached to an ATV. Solstice scanned the faces amongst the group and she remembered how Baeran described them: the redheads must have been Reese and her mother. The two girls with black hair, the tinier of the two girls had to be Jordin. The tall brunette and girl next to her, must have been Baeran's mom and sister Lani. The wind whirled around Lani's hair. Solstice had once called her Skyhaven, it suited her. An adult male on an ATV, that had to be Mike or was it Mitch. Nearby was the stocky yellow-haired guy and his wife. Solstice smiled, she could be content with them. She didn't bother with nicknames for them, already she had learned some of their real names.

As she contemplated this, Solstice heard the unmistakable sound of gunfire, and she dropped to the forest floor.

Rule 1a—don't get caught, because they'll kill you.

Solstice scanned to the north and she saw several men approaching the Seascapers on motorcycles. Baeran's camp was under attack. Baeran had called them Jackers. The Seascapers started their vehicles and rode eastward on a trail. Within a minute, Solstice could no longer see them.

The Jackers came to a stop at the campsite, choosing not to pursue the Seascapers. Solstice watched the Jackers from her prone position. They lingered, poking around the old campsite. When the Jackers discovered nothing of value, they rode off in the direction they came in.

Solstice hoped she could locate Baeran later. *On her terms, because he was cute and nice.* While she hoped Baeran would double back, Solstice knew Baeran abandoned her. Remembering the coping mechanism her mom taught her, she counted, "There are three thousand five hundred twenty size6Solstice-feet to the backdoor."

Rule 4—don't make friends, because they'll leave you.

Solstice put on her sling sack and she trudged toward the Hillock entrance determined to find Senator Adena. After hiking through the woods, she found the tunnel entrance. She stepped toward the open door, but a darkened figure stepped out. Solstice fell to her butt. Naetersen glared at her. "Solstice, I hoped you'd be back. A coat, warm clothes and supplies are near the door. I see you found the dress I left you. Prepare yourself. You're coming with me. Are you thirsty? Have some water."

Rule 1b—stay hydrated, because you'll go crazy otherwise.

Solstice stared at him in disbelief. Naetersen said, "Yes, I knew of you. I allowed the senator to feed his pet rat."

Naetersen poked her with his foot to emphasize the word "rat." He continued. "Keeping you pleased him, and I needed him to cooperate. And now you will help me. Carry that tube of prints, binoculars, the notebooks and the rope. We'll need them."

Rule 3—don't leave home without rope, because that's how you climb in when you fall out

Naetersen continued, "Adena's dead. He took pills. He was sick. Come with me."

Silverfox dead?

Solstice asked, "Why?"

Naetersen replied, "Why would you come? Or why would I want you to?"

"Both I guess."

Naetersen said, "Why would you come with me? Everyone from the bunker is dead. Armed men rule the countryside. You will need protection."

And definitely not Naetersen, never. Maybe if her life depended on it. Because he was smart, and only if Naetersen was the last one left.

Naetersen continued, "Why do I want you? I need a person with your skills. We have a new tunnel complex to infiltrate, in Lincoln, Nebraska."

She'd still be a maiden, though. A kick-ass one. She'd be the toughest Ice Maiden from the Silver Palace the kingdom of Bunkerland had ever seen.

Solstice stood, remembering Baeran wanted to find Lincoln, too, and he might need saving. *A maiden could like the right boy and even rescue him.*

Solstice said, "You brought clothes? Good, I'm cold."

How about sending the egg capsule back next time?

WINTER CAMP

M170. Maximus plus one hundred seventy days. Kentucky.
BAERAN

BAERAN SAT ON THE BACK OF THE ATV arguing with Cole. Baeran knew how to find Solstice but Cole had said, "It's too dangerous. We can't go anywhere near those Jackers."

Autumn had lasted for about three days. Gray snow returned along with the gray dim light. Gray mud re-hardened, this time it froze where it fell. With no sun and no moon, which way was west? Toward the Firegale on the horizon, the last permanent source of light remaining.

A month passed, and Baeran hadn't seen Solstice, or much else besides ash snow. Solstice had called him Aether during their meeting. She had said he would never be the same—she kindled an energy from within Baeran. He felt it. He was crushing on her, major-league, but already a change coursed through his veins, tingling his fingertips.

"Wait," Solstice had said, "Wait till my next birthday, your life will never be the same."

Baeran wanted to find out more, but the Seascapers raced westward, hoping to reach Lincoln before winter and avoid the Jackers. But after thirty days of gray snow, the trails became impassable. Ash clouds blocked out the sun and gray dim light ruled the day, like the promise of a new day that never dawned.

The Seascapers constructed a permanent winter camp off a rail trail, a half-mile into the woods in a meadow, no greater than Baeran's tiny backyard back in Portsmouth. In the center, the Seascapers constructed a raised campfire with stones harvested from a stream. They erected five tents close to the campfire. Kay and Cole; Reese and Heather; Mitch; Tara and L.J. occupied two-person tents, while Baeran, Selene, Lani, Jordin and Annie bunked in a single dome tent. The group packed gray snow against the sides of the tents to provide insulation and protection from the wind.

Superstorm Maximus had spawned a firestorm, littering the sky with ash. Now the ash clouds spawned a superwinter, blocking out the sun, coloring their world gray. Dawn, noon, and dusk became only slightly different from each other and the days only negligibly warmer than the nights.

Lincoln became a dream, fading with each falling snowflake. Cole had said to Baeran, about Solstice, "If she had a bunker, she'd be better off than the Seascapers."

As he shivered in his tent, with Selene at his side, Baeran thought of Solstice. If the international governing body of awkward teens had met to handout outstanding awards for dorkitude, he would have earned a gold blue-ribbon. He had talked non-stop for the two hours after the kiss, while Solstice talked sparingly about her time in Lexington. More than once, Solstice spoke but stopped, distracted, like she was talking to another person. But he talked on and on, while Solstice grinned.

The girl had her own bunker. She refused to talk much about it, but it must have been tremendous. It couldn't have been that bad. The doctor sounded creepy, but the bunker people must have had so much fun while Baeran had to outpace the Firegale. The bunkerites must have played roller hockey in the halls or had their own bowling alley, and movies and books, too. They probably drank soda and ate soft-serve ice cream. Solstice must have had it made. She likely had new clothes and friends, and everything she wanted. It must have been awesome. Not like the Sheridans. The Seascapers had the Dazers and Jackers.

As Baeran thought of Solstice, he felt the "tingles" race down his arms. His perception of the world was changing, as the kinetic energy kindled within his body.

Baeran unzipped his sleeping bag and pulled Selene closer. Selene settled against his side, and he re-zipped the sleeping bag. Baeran said, "Do you remember her? Solstice?"

Selene's tail wagged in response to the girl's name.

"We'll find her once the snow breaks."

SHIMMER
M170. Maximus plus one hundred seventy days. Kentucky.
SOLSTICE

SOLSTICE SAT WITH THE DOCTOR AT THEIR CAMPSITE around a campfire. Gray snow fell adding to the gray mud everywhere. The Firegale burnt on the horizon. She longed to find Baeran but assumed he had stopped along the way to Lincoln, Nebraska, to ride out the gray snow. Solstice and Naetersen were not subject to travel impediments. She had to hand it to the doctor. He didn't fool around. She could remember almost dying for a belt. *Mavourneen.* But now, Solstice had the gear she needed, including snow shoes and poles, goggles, a gray-white super thin insulated jacket and pants. Both the pants and jacket were reversible and could be worn with a pitch-black color outward, for night travel. She had a heated undershield—like tight-fitting leggings and a long shirt—that drew its charge from capacitors. The undershield charged its batteries while Solstice hiked, and if she was cold, she flipped a switch in her pocket and the heaters came to life. And if she was hot or sweaty, the undershield whisked away the moisture. Naetersen had even more gear. He rode the egg capsule to the Lexington bunker three times before they left and retrieved backpacks, super small dehydrated lightweight rations, razor sharp plastic knives, maps and this pop-dome tent that operated on body heat. Buttster had once explained about insulation in the condo basement; he'd rambled on about R values. The R value of the tent material must have been like one million because Solstice sweated at night. She didn't bother zipping into her sleeping bag because the R value on the bag was like one billion. The doctor had this Vaseline like cream they put on their faces to keep them warm in the wind. And the gear fit into two uber lightweight packs. The one item that weighed anything was water. Had Naetersen pulled de-hydrated water out of his pocket that wouldn't have surprised Solstice, but instead the doctor melted and purified gray snow with an ultraviolet laser pen. Solstice used to think the secrecy of the twenty-three-mile Hillock tunnel was impressive, no way, not now. The government had developed some seriously awesome secret stuff.

How come they didn't bother saving more people? Elle was people too.

Solstice missed Baeran and wanted to find him, but when her belly was full of super small dehydrated lightweight rations and she drank her ultralaser water from a lightweight collapsible cup in her undershield capacitor body suit, she was comfortable, and Solstice could no longer remember why she had once hated Naetersen.

Sure, the gray snow might put a stop to their hikes, or they'd lose an important item like snow shoes, but Solstice figured the doctor would pull rocket boots or a hoverboard out of his ass and they'd be saved.

So, Solstice sat by the campfire writing in her lyricbook, humming to herself as Naetersen pored over his prints, and she sang:

"Moonlight Meeting"

My glowing white hair
Glistening blue eyes
You saw me hiding
From under dark skies

Hello
Seeking a friend
Nice to meet you
Here at the end

Fast, almost racing
My heart beating
I saw you at our
Moonlight meeting

Your dirty-blond hair
Golden speckled eyes
Not enough time
Before our goodbyes

Parting
Under your spell,
Adios
So long, farewell...

Fast, almost racing
My heart beating
I saw you at our
Moonlight meeting

Leaving on your cheek
You're a sweet thing
First kisses at our
Moonlight meeting

Solstice closed her diary. She could see Baeran's face, his smirk, and how he moved—athletically. But the words stalled. Sometimes her songs were songs Melody didn't sing.

Those lyrics were the hardest to find.

FLC

M185. Maximus plus one hundred eighty-five days. Winter camp in Kentucky.
BAERAN

BAERAN WAS WEARY, COLD AND HUNGRY. He sulked in his tent. Selene and the girls slept to his right. The gray snow fell. He zipped his sleeping bag, until only his eyes showed, as he watched the shadows of the snowflakes floating onto the tent peak. He counted the flakes, like blows they beat him down, delaying his ability to search for Solstice.

Gray snow fell, like fallout. To the west, the Firegale burned, clinging to dense forest, protected by the canopy. It lay in wait, for the spring, smoldering.W

His dad had played it safe since Portsmouth—urging the group to camp out in the wilderness, away from the burnt-out towns and cities, Jackers and Dazers. But the wild had other risks, like freezing or starving to death.

What about Solstice? It had been fifty days since their moonlight meeting and three weeks since the Seascapers bedded down for winter. Baeran set traps every day, but squirrels became less plentiful. Lately, he had been trapping only the stupid skinny squirrels. The fat smart squirrels hid for the winter in their acorn-condos. Kay had supplemented the Seascaper's diet with pine bark jerky, pine needle tea and pine soup, providing ample fiber and vitamins but little protein.

Baeran had the daily routine down. Find campfire wood. Freeze. Check traps. Freeze. Eat nasty pine soup with funny squirrel parts—feet were the new "it" thing. Freeze. Contemplate the complete lack of the color spectrum—gray was the new gray. Freeze. Chew on tender inner pine bark till jaw breaks. Freeze. Sleep cuddling dog. Freeze. Repeat. Repeat. Repeat.

Cole had long since refused to double back to Solstice's bunker, so Baeran dwelt on the memories. He smiled. Solstice had hit him with an acorn in the back. Slender and graceful, she had floated down from a branch. He bet she could kick his ass at parkour. Selene liked her, too. And the twirl—he loved the ruffles of her dress, how they struggled to catch her hips as she spun. He caught a glimpse of her legs. Her ice-blue eyes glistened, and her blonde hair, whitish, glowed in the moonlight. Her voice floated on the wind as she sang. Later, Solstice had danced for him. She picked his Ray-Bans off the forest floor, and playfully called him Wayfarer. She had a thing with nicknames. Beaming, she held his hand and placed her lips on his. She cast her spell on him, and marked him on his arm with her sign, the aurora brand.

Solstice had marked Baeran on his heart, too. He weighed those four hours versus the last fourteen years. Four short hours with Solstice outweighed a lifetime with a loving family.

Baeran wanted to be with Solstice, but he needed to be with his family. He resolved to have them both, but he'd wait. Family came first, and self came second. He had heard that before in church. Baeran remembered more, The Trinity of the Graces: faith, hope and love. He had faith in his parents' leadership. He hoped Lincoln still stood against the Firegale, looting, riots, and anarchy. And he loved his family.

The Sheridans needed more, but Baeran had nothing left. He was weary, cold, and hungry: a trinity of sorrows.

Baeran closed his eyes and imagined his old home in Portsmouth. On the mantel over the fireplace in the den, he saw a palm-size brass four-leaf clover. In his mind's eye, he held the heavy keepsake. It covered most of his palm. His dad's grandmother had given the trinket to him as a child. He had seen it often in the house. He flipped the brass clover, and Baeran's mind strove to recall the inscription. It read:

> One leaf is for faith,
> One is for hope,
> One is for love, you know,
> And God put another in for luck

The Seascapers needed luck. He smirked.

Baeran was half-Irish, and luck would come along. The other half, from his Mom's side, was mostly Native American, and that would help keep him alive in the meantime. In his mind, Baeran placed the brass four-leaf clover back on the mantel, and his focus drifted back to the dome tent. He joined the peaceful dance of snowflakes and shadows on the tent's peak. He counted the flakes until he grew weary and slept.

JACKED

M185. Maximus plus one hundred eighty-five days. Kentucky.
SOLSTICE

Solstice sat by a campfire with the doctor, enjoying her ultralaser water in her undershield capacitor body suit. Gray snow fell in pale light of the evening. They had stopped for the night and hadn't assembled the tent yet. The packs were fifteen size6Solstice-feet behind herself against a tree. It had been fifty days or 4,320,000 mom-counts since Solstice met Baeran and left the Hillock tunnel with the doctor.

Naetersen became grumpier by the day. He could not solve the Dazer problem. Already the doctor indicated Lincoln, Nebraska would have to wait until he had more Dazer information.

Now, Naetersen mumbled something cruel under his breath, and Solstice remembered why she hated him.

The doctor said, "Mavourneen."

"What?" Solstice glared at him, pulling her gaze from the campfire.

"It's nothing."

"Please, what's that name?" Solstice asked.

The doctor replied, "Test subject #276, she was an interesting case. In fact, she was the last test subject. She was a female, age seven who survived Legionnaires disease. I wanted to determine how the Dazers came to be. I convinced myself the Dazed were infected with a pathogen created by plant spores and toxins within the wake of the Firegale. Of course, we were doing this to figure out a cure for the pathogen. The first two hundred seventy-five subjects succumbed to the various unbalanced percentages of the toxins. We thought we had a solution with #276. The key was surviving the toxicity of the initial exposure, but in the end, she had massive organ failure. The gas dosage exceeded the tolerance for her body

weight. She had been our most promising test subject."

Solstice asked, "You experimented on the UDs?"

The doctor replied, "Yes, the trials served as an effective means of population control with a bunker network that had limited resources, and it advanced our knowledge of the pathogen. But we were never able to create the pathogen synthetically. So, we'd give people a bunker upgrade. We'd bring the UDs into an isolated section of tunnel, one I'm sure you never saw—otherwise you'd be dead, and we tested their response to different pathogens. Like with the Hillock tunnel, we sealed each section of the Lexington Bunker Complex from the other sections. You explored section 1. We did the experiments in section 2. Section 3 housed the post-Lexington Bunker Complex supplies. Sections 4-6 had been walled off years prior."

"You wanted to create Dazers to find a cure?" Solstice asked.

"Correct. Why else would the government station me at the Lexington Bunker Complex?" Naetersen replied, "I'm a medical anthropologist. Finding a cure for the Dazer pathogen became the primary responsibility of the Lexington Bunker. Our staff never made it in, however, and what I hadn't considered was how genetics factored in. But like I said our best case was #276. She survived the longest."

Solstice stood and faced the doctor. "Her name was Mavourneen. I hate you. I hate this stupid fire-scorched ash-covered gray world. You can infiltrate the Lincoln Bunker Complex on your own. What does that even mean? Why not knock on the door? Why do you need me? It doesn't matter. She was my friend. Mavourneen was the last good thing in this awful world. I'm leaving."

Solstice clutched her sling sack and dashed into the woods. She jogged for seven thousand one hundred and fifty-three size6Solstice-feet. She imagined she could run to find Baeran. In the shadows of the moon that no longer pierced the clouds, Solstice ran. Through a burnt-out forest, she ran, for as long as she could until she found another campfire, stopping in time to remain hidden in the shadows.

Ten men sat around the campfire in a small clearing. Hardened by life of the road, Solstice caught glimpses of their scared and worn faces. She silently stepped backwards, creeping out of the shadows, back into the darkness of the burnt-out forest. She bumped into a tree stump and stopped to rub her thigh where a broken branch had poked her.

"Don't move." Behind Solstice, a man spoke.

She ran away from the voice back towards the fire, stumbling into the group of men, tripping near the campfire. The conversation stopped, and the men stared at Solstice, struggling to stand.

The man from the woods chased her into the clearing. He bent down and grabbed her by the arms, forcing Solstice up.

"Look what I found boys."

Rule 1a—don't get caught, because they'll kill you. Or worse.

Solstice struggled to break his grip. All but one man around the campfire stood. The man pushed her towards his compatriots. They ripped off her coat and pawed at her breasts. Solstice screamed, and the men continued to push her around the circle, laughing. One man, the grossest of all, licked her face. Solstice gagged, smelling his stench, as his rough beard scratched her face. She pulled away from Sir Lickalots falling at the feat of the one man not standing. He spoke, "That's enough boys."

Around the circle, the men cried out, "Come on, Stowe. Let us have our fun."

"Leave her alone," Stowe replied, helping Solstice to her feet. "We wait for the boss."

Stowe led Solstice to a burnt-out five-foot-tall tree stump away from the men, but in sight of the campfire. Solstice struggled, screaming. Stowe hit her in the face as he pushed her against the stump. He whispered, "Shut up. I just saved your ass."

"Toss me the rope." Stowe yelled back to the group.

Stowe tied Solstice to the stump, and she slumped forward. "Keep it quiet, and I might just save you."

Solstice counted two thousand seven hundred and fourteen mom-counts. She counted because she wished the Jackers would decide what to do with her. The waiting made it worse than anything else. She was tied to a tree, waiting for the boss to arrive. Her undershield capacitor body suit shirt had ripped. Her jacket, gloves, and hat lay at her feet, as she shivered. Blood dripped from her lips, and she slouched against her bonds, held up by a rope around a tree, stunned from the ordeal.

Solstice awoke from her stupor, shaking from the cold, when she heard a commotion around the campfire. She smirked when the doctor stumbled into the group of men. At least she wouldn't die alone. Served him right. *Because #276 was people too.* Unless he came to save her...

Solstice couldn't follow the conversation, but she could tell within minutes, Naetersen had made friends. This was not a rescue attempt. She put the full weight of her body against her bonds, and she let the cold take her, along with the exhaustion, hoping to die.

Solstice awoke to harsh voices in the dark. A campfire crackled. Around it sat twelve—no, thirteen men. The doctor sat with them, laughing.

Naetersen said, "Listen, boys, I have to leave. Take the girl. But I need the prints. She had some of them in her sack."

Solstice closed her eyes. She was too drained to fight, but at least she'd die of hypothermia first...

Voices haunted her dreams along with turkeys, but it wasn't Thanksgiving. It was closer to Christmas. *Gobble. Gobble. Gobble.* Rough hands lifted her and dropped her more than once on the cold ground.

Solstice awoke in the dark. She counted, like her mom had taught her, hoping to calm her fears. She lost count at forty-six, and Solstice was sure she had counted the number more than once. A man stood over her, cutting her bonds around her ankles. He said, "Stay still. This is your chance. Be quiet, and I'll save you from them for me."

Solstice heard voices shouting, searching for her. "Come on, Stowe! Let us have a chance, too."

Stowe said to Solstice, "Be quiet. Don't move. I'll be back. I'll keep you safe, regardless of what I say to them." Stowe retreated.

Stunned, Solstice didn't move. From a distance, she heard Stowe. "You idiots! We need the doctor. Did you listen to what he said? There is a city underground in Lincoln."

A second voice, rougher and older, said, "You're not in charge, Stowe."

Stowe pumped his shotgun and fired.

Schklict. Klikt. Pfoof!

The second voice screamed, "Stowe, you bastard!"

Stowe pumped the shotgun and fired a second time.

Schklict. Klikt. Pfoof!

"Anyone else have a problem?" Stowe yelled. "I'm taking over. Bring me the doctor. I'll give you the girl."

"Solstice. Where are you?" A third voice in the dark said.

It was Naetersen.

GIFT

M194. Maximus plus one hundred ninety-four days. Winter camp in Kentucky.
BAERAN

BAERAN STARED OUT OF A HOLE IN THE TENT. Dawn was only slightly less gray than the evening and negligibly warmer. Wonderful this winterland was not. The world was an old picture, like TV in the 1950s at 2:01 AM. Graydimlight ruled.

Baeran exited the dome tent and plodded to the center of the campsite. L.J. sat on a five-gallon pail next to the campfire. Baeran could hear L.J.'s teeth rattle. Kay and Cole sat close to L.J.. Without raising his head, Cole offered Baeran a steaming bowl of green water. Baeran sat between his parents and sipped the meager bowl of pine-bark soup on New Year's Day. Lani joined them.

Cole didn't bother with his soup, and Kay gave hers away. Both parents had the same red puffy eyes. Cole's were from lack of sleep and anxiety, and Kay's were from malnourishment. She kept giving her food to Annie, Jordin, and Lani.

Kay and Cole didn't remember Baeran's New Year's Day birthday. Often unable to tell day from night or new day from old day, the Seascapers overlooked holidays and birthdays. There were no words, no smiles, and no reassurances.

Lani had forgotten Baeran's birthday, too, but she was more concerned for her parents. Her eyes pled, "Help them!"

Cole and Kay stood and trudged to their tent. Kay stumbled, and Cole steadied her, holding her hand.

Baeran said to Lani, "Don't worry, I have a present."

Baeran left the campfire, following his parents. "Mom, Dad—wait. I have a surprise for you."

Baeran opened his pack and slipped a brown paper bag into

Kay's hand. He whispered into her ear.

Kay smiled and kissed her son. She told her husband, "Let's climb into the sleeping bags. I have a present for you, but I need to warm it by the campfire for a minute. It's frozen."

Cole waited for ten long minutes in the tent until Kay returned. "What is it?" he asked.

Kay beamed and produced the paper bag. Reaching in, she withdrew the contents and exclaimed, "This, my dear, is the last known can of Corona in eastern Kentucky, courtesy of one Baeran Sheridan."

Cole opened the sleeping bag, and Kay joined him.

Baeran had helped his mom from the tent to the campfire and back, and he lingered long enough to hear Cole shout for joy. His dad had once yelled while packing in Portsmouth. "Don't forget the beer." Three times, he had yelled it.

Cole had savored the Portsmouth beers for weeks, and Baeran had saved one for himself. He hid it in his pack for his fifteenth birthday, today. Old laws and rules no longer applied, and fifteen was the new twenty-one. But he'd find other beers and celebrate other birthdays. It was enough that his parents were happy for a moment.

VALUE
M185. Kentucky.
SOLSTICE

Solstice laid in the gray snow in the dark, choosing.

"Solstice," the doctor whispered. "Move. We're leaving."

Solstice hesitated. Should she choose Stowe or Naetersen? Both men were liars. Did she need either?

"Solstice, come with me. The Jackers will be back any minute. I have your sack. Your journal, the prints, and my notebook."

What about the ultralaser water purifier?

Why? Didn't Naetersen say the Jackers could have her?

She was nothing, worthless and abandoned, by her mother at the bunker door, by her father before her birth, by Mrs. C. on the evening before the Firegale, and by Naetersen, an hour prior.

Take the girl. But I need the prints.

She was nothing more than chattel to be traded. Her current value equaled a roll of prints. But at least Naetersen had come back for her.

Rule 4—don't make friends, because they'll leave you.

Except Solstice had violated Rule 4, not Naetersen. But he killed Mavourneen, coldly, without regret, and Silverfox, too.

But the doctor will protect you. Why would he? Because you are special, #277. You are the Ice Maiden. Harden your heart. Find Aether.

The Ice Maiden said, "Take me with you."

DOG
M225. Kentucky.
BAERAN

BAERAN HAD DROPPED THE "MAXIMUS PLUS THE NUMBER" CRAP. Exhausted and hungry, the Seascapers were efficient with their words. Two more weeks had passed since the now famous beer, and the entire Sheridan clan slept in the dome tent. The world was gray. Gray winter camp. Gray Kentucky. Graydimlight. Gray world. Gray snow. Gray dog.

The group had experimented with using blocks of snow outside the tents to reduce the wind chill. The Seascapers tried to build a sizable teepee to hold a campfire, with no success, and despair set into Baeran's bones with the permanent chill.

Baeran rose and exited the tent. The campfire had gone out. Thankfully, the Sheridans had packed dozens of Bic lighters back in Portsmouth. He gathered pine needles, kindling, and forearm-size pieces of wood. He relit the campfire and returned to the tent. He glanced at his parents. His father held his too-skinny mother. Kay had joked she had gone from a size 8 to a size 2.

Cole rose to keep the campfire going. He spoke to the children, doing his best to reassure them he would find food soon.

Baeran rolled over. He couldn't sleep anymore, either. He scratched Selene as she stretched in their shared sleeping bags. Lani, Annie, and Jordin shared two joined sleeping bags. Baeran felt the dog's ribs and his own ribs, and he could count them, sticking out.

As February dawned, other than Baeran, only Cole had the strength to rise and gather wood for the campfire. Only the occasional grunt of coughs emanating from the tents interrupted the silence. Sleepless for days, Cole gathered campfire wood.

As luck, would have it, Cole stumbled upon a feral German shepherd. Emaciated and weak, the dog strolled into the camp. Cole dropped his meager bundle of wood. The once proud dog cocked its head at Cole. The animal lacked the strength to attack, and the memory of a former life urged it to beg instead of bite.

The shepherd approached Cole and lay at his feet.

Cole withdrew his knife. He paused as his eyes welled. He patted the back of the German shepherd, and he spoke to the worn-out animal. "Thank you, girl," he said.

He took a deep breath. He extended the blade toward the animal and felt along the dog's protruding rib cage. He plunged the knife into its heart. The shepherd, losing its life, did not resist. No bark or bite came from the dog, just an expression of betrayal. Cole collapsed atop the shepherd and held the animal in its last moments.

Baeran heard Cole sobbing outside the tent. He rose and stepped outside.

Blood had splattered the gray snow around Cole. Baeran helped him stand and said, "Get L.J. and Mitch, I'll skin it."

After the Seascapers prepared the first portions of shepherd meat over the campfire, Cole brought a hearty stew to each tent. He cautioned each family to conserve the soup and eat slow, so their empty bellies did not heave from the sudden intake of nutrients. Last, he came to his dome tent and brought food to Lani, Jordin, Annie, and Selene. He consumed a portion for himself, and as she had insisted, he came to Kay last and served her.

Lani took her soup and Annie's from her father. Lani placed the stew on the floor of the tent near Jordin. Lani shook Annie, and said, "Morning, sleepyhead, we have food!"

Annie didn't respond. Lani rolled Annie onto her back but the girl was cold and stiff. Lani and Jordin screamed when Annie's lifeless eyes stared back at them.

After the scream, Jordin didn't even say a word. She climbed into Annie's sleeping bag and held her sister for an hour. Lani and Baeran sat at the foot of Annie's sleeping bag. At noon, Jordin left the body and asked Cole to take it.

Lani and Jordin made a wreath of pine boughs for Cole to place by Annie's body. Cole carried Annie, the wreath, and a marker alone into the woods. The turf was frozen, so Cole left Annie's body to nature.

Baeran didn't know how Jordin could have these many tears. Jordin cried for a day. Lani held her, and Baeran did, too. But it was still not enough. Jordin's mom and dad had died years prior. She had never known them. Her Wàigōng died on the bridge. Now Annie joined them. Jordin drowned in tears, and Baeran and Lani couldn't save her.

Baeran whispered into Lani's ear, "I'll be back later. Keep her close," and he lumbered from the two girls.

Lani held Jordin, outwardly comforting Jordin for the loss of her sister, while secretly thanking God for not losing Jordin, too.

Baeran followed Cole's trail toward the body. He had to see her. Baeran read the flimsy marker Cole had left on a tree. "Annika Elizabeth," he repeated. He had no idea. She had been Annie to him. Baeran crept closer to her body and studied the marker. He bent down and held Annie's icy hands. His dad had stripped her of any warm-weather gear, leaving her feet and hands exposed. Baeran fell to his knees and pawed at the ground. After he removed the snow, he found the ground, but it was rock hard. Baeran didn't want to leave her out like this. He searched around for stones to cover her but found nothing.

Annie had faded, slipping into the night with her friend and her sister close by. Her death appeared peaceful, unlike every other previous Seascaper loss.

Baeran gazed at Annie, and whispered, "Goodbye, sister." He leaned over and brushed the hair out of her face and kissed her cheek. A part of him found comfort in her passing. Annie would have never eaten dog, never, ever, while Baeran had eaten shepherd twice already.

He rose and trudged to the campsite. The early-morning sun warmed his face. Soon, the Seascapers could leave. Spring beckoned. Baeran said to himself, "Find the trail. Find Lincoln. Find Solstice."

BONDED
M205. Kentucky.
SOLSTICE

Solstice and Naetersen had escaped the Jackers twenty days prior and continued their relentless march in the gray snow westward to Lincoln, and hopefully answers. Dinner had saved Solstice from the Jackers. Half a dozen turkeys had strolled into the Jacker camp. One minute, the Jackers desperately wanted Solstice and the prints. The next minute, the Jackers wanted turkey. The Jackers had tripped over themselves chasing the birds, while Solstice and Naetersen, beyond the light of the Jacker campfire, escaped in the commotion.

Naetersen had saved the gear, except for the snow shoes. He had found Solstice's coat and their packs with the body heat dome tent, the ultralaser water purifier, and the super small dehydrated lightweight rations, which Solstice called supsdelite because no one wanted to say five words when they meant food.

Solstice had to make tough choices. Accepting Naetersen as Mavourneen's murderer was one of them. Acceptance didn't mean forgiveness. But Solstice had to find Baeran, her visions demanded it, and the doctor was the key to finding Lincoln, Baeran's goal.

Solstice contemplated her choices in the woods off a trail in an unknown location in Kentucky as she peeled the tender inner bark—the thin layer between the wood and the hardened bark—off a pine tree. The supsdelite would be running out soon and Naetersen wanted to supplement it. The Doctor had taught Solstice what to search for and sent her out. She stripped back the living inner bark from the hardened outer bark.

Naetersen had said the pine strips were rich in vitamin C, and

Solstice wanted to do everything she could to avoid another case of scurvy. She used a pocket knife to cut the cream-colored inner bark into one-inch wide strips. She stacked the strips and wrapped them in a ripped piece of cloth. Later, the Doctor would have Solstice cook them on a heated flat stone.

Solstice had tried eating the bark strips raw last week at Naetersen's insistence. An hour later, her jaw hurt, and the bark strip hadn't dissolved. It had been Solstice's idea to try frying the strips like chips. With pine oil and salt, the strips became crispy and edible, and Solstice didn't mind the taste anymore.

Solstice dropped a pine bark strip into the snow. She crouched down, and after retrieving the strip, she removed her glove and searched for the earth underneath. She turned her head sideways to reach lower and saw Naetersen approaching. The doctor sunk into the wet snow with every step as he struggled toward Solstice.

"Solstice, I need to know more about those men. We have not made much progress since you lost the snowshoes to the Jackers, and they could be close by. What were the Jackers planning? What did their leader talk about when he had you captive?"

Rising, Solstice replied, "Sure."

Solstice had made her choice—Naetersen over Stowe. Nothing could be gained by holding back.

"He called himself Stowe. He named himself after the resort that killed his girlfriend." Solstice said, "The Firegale cornered Stowe and his fiancé. We spoke for minutes. He said I reminded him of his girl, and he'd protect me. He wanted to convince me to leave with him-,"

Naetersen interrupted, "Solstice, you had to know he lied, to use you as bait for me."

Solstice ignored the doctor but secretly agreed and continued, "He had a scar stretching from his forehead down the side of his face. Stowe and his group of Jackers had been tracking a group of Seascapers for two days when we stumbled in on their camp. He knew what the Seascapers called themselves. It fit them, Stowe said. They were searching and never finding. Stowe added at least the Seascapers had resources he could take, far better than those aimless Dazers picking the country side clean."

"Did he mention more men than the dozen we saw?"

"Stowe didn't say, but he did call his group a re-con party."

"Excellent, Solstice, re-con implies a significant group was near. That is helpful."

Solstice placed the wrapped pine bark in her sling sack and stood with her head bowed. She waited for Naetersen to give the order to leave, reminding herself the prints she carried were far more valuable to the doctor than her life.

TODAY IS NOT THAT DAY
M215. Kentucky.
SOLSTICE

Solstice had heard him say it enough. She could do it. She built snow structures with the same body heat tent thingy every night for weeks. Snow fell daily in the graydimlight. Progress had been slow since Solstice lost the snowshoes. It was the same old routine. Build the shelter. Find the wood. Build a campfire. Pass out the last of the supsdelite. Eat pine bark. Passively accept ridicule.

They were bound together through the unending winter. She had the routine down, and kept her mouth shut. She needed Naetersen to find Lincoln. Finding Lincoln equaled finding Baeran. It was seven hundred miles from Lexington to Lincoln. Solstice had seen the map, and already done the math. The hike was five-million size6Solstice-feet if they avoided Louisville, St. Louis and Kansas City.

Solstice and Naetersen hiked in the woods north of Louisville. The ash floated like fallout from the sky. The Firegale burnt on the western horizon without providing any warmth in the frozen gray wasteland. Beyond the flames, both Solstice and the doctor hoped Lincoln still stood, and had defenses against the Firegale.

Leaving the doctor had been foolish. Without her undershieldcapbosuit, Solstice would have frozen. Without his supplies and gadgets, she would have never survived. So, she knew why she needed the doctor. And for an unknown reason, Naetersen needed her.

Solstice put together bits and pieces. The doctor had once said he needed her skill as a tunnel rat to infiltrate the Lincoln Presidential Bunker Complex. But if he led a mission for the government, why would he need to infiltrate the bunker? Why not knock on the door?

What made Solstice subject #277? If Mavourneen was the last at #276? But Solstice was special, the doctor had said. Solstice guessed during her first days in the bunker, she stumbled upon one of the synthetic Dazer pathogens, when she had been searching for the draincock. But she wasn't a true test subject for two reasons. Her exposure occurred outside the lab, and in the doctor's words, she had evolved around age seven, with a built-in immunity to the pathogen. Born with other gifts too, she was a seer and a kindler. Melody held a piece of the answers, as did Solstice's seizure at age seven. But Melody had been silent for weeks.

Lately, Solstice didn't feel special. She was a pack mule and lugged Naetersen's gear over frozen wilderness. Someday, Naetersen would see Solstice as more than a porter. Already she had learned much from him. But today was not someday.

Someday, she'd find Baeran. Recalling their night together made her smile, and smiles powered her through the gray world.

Someday, her belly would be full. She'd eat like three bowls of noodles.

Someday, the winter would end. She'd swim or wear shorts.

Someday, Solstice would be free of Naetersen. She'd do whatever she wanted.

Someday, Melody would return. She missed her, hating the deafening silence in her head. Gone since Solstice's night with Baeran. The songs Solstice sang now, like "Moonlight Meeting", were her own.

Today was not someday, and even Ice Maidens needed help. But Solstice knew nothing about him—his first name, or where he lived before the Firegale. She never asked. Solstice didn't speak unless spoken to. They had established that rule with harsh-worded responses. The doctor needed to jumpstart his self-described mission, finding a cure for the Dazer pathogen. He was missing a crucial piece of information and he struggled deep within his own thoughts. Solstice had spent days and nights in the bunker vents and listening suited her. If they didn't speak another word for the rest of the winter, Solstice would be fine.

But today was not that day. The good doctor had all sorts of advice for Solstice, and she would heed it.

THE PATHOGEN
M225. Kentucky.
SOLSTICE

SOLSTICE LEANED AGAINST A TREE. Close by, Naetersen studied the footprints in the gray snow left by a medium-size Dazer herd. They were in Kentucky, or not. Solstice was convinced they no longer traveled toward Lincoln. As Dazers became more common, the doctor became increasingly distracted by them. Naetersen could never know enough about the Dazed. What did the Dazers eat? Where did they sleep? How did the Dazers interact? What was the cause? Was it a virus, bacteria, or chemical agent? Did the disease have genetic markers? Could he be wrong about subject #276? Was it curable or reversible? Was it contagious?

Naetersen interrupted her thoughts, and said, "The Dazers are human."

Solstice nodded at him. It was the same kind of nod she had given her Algebra II teacher last year when he first introduced the concept of solving linear inequalities.

Naetersen smiled. A rarity. "I don't want to travel to Lincoln with an idiot. I'll explain it once, so listen."

"The Dazed are not zombies. Not undead, not werewolves, not vampires, or anything else you can imagine. They are dangerous. Like cavemen or apes without the extra hair and strange skulls. A long-forgotten gene has been activated after one hundred thousand years of dormancy. The toxicity of the Firegale combined with a release of tree spores has created a new pathogen that triggered a DNA switch."

"What is a DNA switch?" Solstice asked.

"It activates a hidden trait. Humans, as you know, as a species are called *Homo sapiens*. What you likely don't know is modern humans are in a subspecies called *Homo sapiens sapiens*, which means 'anatomically modern humans.' Another species, Neanderthals, disappeared thousands of years ago. They share about ninety-nine-point-seven percent of the same DNA as you and I and went extinct forty thousand years ago.

"The Dazed could teach us a thing or two. They've survived this winter with minimal clothing while foraging for their food. Their bodies are adapting to the cold and they are subsisting entirely on tree bark, cattails, shrubbery, and anything else not buried in snow or burnt by the Firegale. Where are they even sleeping at night? Do they have dens, or do they use the snow? Instinct—a long forgotten predisposition—is guiding them.

"What we are seeing with the Dazed is the emergence of a new subset of *Homo sapiens*. A *Homo sapiens armenta*, if you will. *Armenta* is Latin for 'herd.' This is nature's way of adjusting itself. Like with the Firegale, the correction is unstoppable. After the flames scorch America, changes in the weather and the environment will affect which plants and animals survive and thrive. America—no, the world—will be a better place after the surface is burnt clean and modern man and his devices fade."

Solstice interrupted, in clear violation of Naetersen's rule about not speaking unless spoken too, "Where is the government? Why didn't they put the fire out?"

"Were going to Lincoln to find out why."

Solstice asked, "How did the Firegale survive the winter?"

"Somehow, we must have reached a tipping point on an ecological scale. Like with the dawn of an ice age or rising sea levels, there is a point of no return. America is full of unmanaged forests, ripe for burning. The Firegale is self-sustaining, changing and creating weather patterns as it advances. First the ash snow blocking out the sun, later it will be a scorcher of a summer as carbon dioxide floods the atmosphere. It will get worse. Every time another forest burns down, we lose more of the earth's ability to process the CO_2. At some point, climate change will be self-sustaining. This is the dawning of an extinction-level event.

"This new subspecies, Dazers, is part of nature resetting the clock. Additional subspecies of humans could emerge. And these additional subspecies might not devolve like the *Homo sapiens armenta*. Other people out in the wild could be on the cusp of developing or finding new skills and abilities, secretly programmed into their DNA. Solstice, you could have a hidden power, waiting to come out." Naetersen laughed. "Exciting, isn't it? Soon, we will infiltrate the *Homo sapiens armenta*."

B-1
M235. Kentucky.
SOLSTICE

SOLSTICE WAITED AS THE DOCTOR STUDIED another herd in a burnt-out forest, trampling the gray snow. She reached into her sling sack and pulled out Naetersen's notebook and a pencil. He'd want to take notes. The Dazers creeped Solstice out, but Naetersen had extensive plans, and the Dazed figured into them.

Naetersen smirked at Solstice as she placed the pencil and notebook in his hand. He scribbled:

B-1. APS. Askerpy-Pereratus Syndrome.

First Askerpy encephalopathy develops followed by Pereratus. Askerpy is dementia, ataxia, and ophthalmalgia. Pereratus is amnesia, aphasia or apraxia, agnosia, and deficiency in cognitive control.

Solstice read over Naetersen's shoulder. Annoyed, he asked, "Do you want a translation?"

Solstice nodded.

Naetersen replied, "I've got it. APS could be what ails the Dazed. The *Homo sapiens armenta* are suffering from Askerpy-Pereratus Syndrome. Askerpy—a decline in memory or processing skills, and confusion, a diminished ability to control movement, and paralysis of facial muscles near the eyes. After, Pereratus kicks in—memory loss, and the inability to understand language, to recognize objects or people through the senses, and to switch between different tasks."

Visibly annoyed with Solstice, the doctor continued, "Rat, the Dazed are suffering from a thiamine deficiency. They don't consume enough vitamin B-1. It might explain the cattail cravings. Cattails are loaded with B-1.

"I suspect the ash toxicity and the spores have activated a genetic marker inhibiting the B-1 absorption. It must be the liver. APS can be common in alcoholics. We could be looking at liver damage on a massive scale, and a new subspecies created because their livers can't filter toxins anymore. The open sores, the bleeding gums, yellow skin and eyes, rotten toes, and distended bellies bruises—they are symptoms of liver disease.

"If the Dazed can degrade because of liver toxicity and a subsequent B-1 absorption problem, imagine what could happen to us. We could devolve like the Dazed or evolve into a greater species."

"Couldn't a substantial dose of vitamin B be used to reverse the damage?" Solstice asked.

"It's B-1, and no, APS must be treated aggressively in the preliminary stages of onset. The Dazed can't be cured now. There is no one to administer a treatment. Soon, more people will develop the disease. It might be years before the fallout from the Firegale clears."

Solstice said, "How come we're not sick?"

"It could be the bunker protected us from the initial scale exposure, or genetically we are not predisposed for liver disease."

Solstice countered, "Would B-1 thiamine help manage the Dazers? Would B-1 make them less sick or docile?"

Naetersen paused and chose his words, as if mulling over their meanings. "No. The best we could hope for with the B-1 would to be able to control them."

He smirked. "Control of the Dazed. Good, Solstice. Good. Have you seen them spooked, when the Dazed form up to run? The Dazers go from peaceful grazers to a stampede in seconds. Imagine if we could harness the rage and fear of the herd. The thrashing, colliding and wildly aggressive movement would be a formidable device if you could point the stampede in the right direction, like branded cattle.

"It's possible a cure is not the answer to the Dazer problem, after all. We must initiate tests immediately and develop a control mechanism."

BURDEN

M252. Kentucky.
BAERAN

BAERAN'S STRENGTH RETURNED as the group became more active around the winter campsite. Spring was coming, and plant and animal life returned to the forest. The graydimlight faded, yielding to occasionally patches of natural sunlight.

Stiff from inactivity but fortified by emerging greens, squirrel, and the last of the Shepherd soup, Baeran had been eager to stretch his legs. The skies became less gray and the snow melted. At night, Baeran left Selene behind, and hiked southward, scouring the burnt-out forest for utility rights-of-way, rail trails, and roads. The Seascapers planned on abandoning the campsite and would need a route to Nebraska.

Baeran traversed through the woods until he found a road, and a large puddle. Baeran stepped back and stared into the mud puddle in the ditch. The moonlight afforded a quick glance at himself. He barely recognized the grimy, fatigued boy reflecting back at himself. He hadn't slept soundly in a long time, and Parker's and Ethan's deaths hung on him, as did Annie's.

Baeran stepped into the puddle and stomped at his reflection. Except for when it was unavoidable, Baeran had been evading people for days on end. They all died around him.

Baeran fell to his knees. The mud soaked into his tattered clothes, covering his exposed flesh. The Firegale on the horizon burned off in the distance, and he knew Lincoln would be a lost cause.

He let his body collapse into the mud. Soon, it would be his family's turn to die.

The mud seeped into him. He rolled onto his back and stared

at the night sky. Trees waved in the breeze and blackened out the stars. Mud flowed between his fingertips, into his ears, and around his cheeks. It enveloped him. Baeran shivered as the cold mud took hold of him. The force of gravity—or the force of his own despair—pulled him deeper into the mud.

Baeran pictured his reflection from a moment prior. A different boy had left Portsmouth. The change showed in his face. He had come so far. It was time to replace despair with determination.

The mud no longer sucked him down. It blanketed him. Baeran regained his focus, waking from a winter of despair.

Gone was the boy, Baeran.

In his place, arose Baer.

The cool mud calmed Baer. Covering him from head to toe. He focused on the sounds of the forest, and voices, whispering close by.

Baer closed his eyes and held his breath. He heard a Jacker group making their way through the forest. The patrol stopped and gestured his way.

Baer remained motionless, hoping the mud would keep him safe. He relaxed his muscles and focused on a happy memory. He remembered playing ball with Cole back in Portsmouth.

The Jacker patrol crept closer to him. He opened one eye to catch the six-man patrol dropping to one knee.

A pebble bounced near Baer, tossed by the Jacker leader. A second pebble hit him, but Baer did not flinch. The Jackers exchanged whispers and stood. They hadn't seen him. A walkie-talkie crackled, and the sharp voices of the patrol retreated.

The mud calmed Baer. It gave him focus, strength. And stealth. Baer opened both his eyes and let out a breath. He needed to warn the other Seascapers about the Jackers, but Baer allowed himself one more minute of calm.

He focused on the mud hardening to his body. He had a plan. Beyond the Firegale had to be hope for his family.

Find the trail. Find Lincoln. Find the girl.

He let out another breath and whispered to himself, "Be prepared."

He repeated this pledge to himself—forcing himself to commit to it. At dawn, Baer strode into the campsite covered in mud and into the twin glow of the Firegale on the western horizon and the sun rising in the east.

MARKER
M253. Kentucky winter camp.
BAER

BAER LOOKED AT THE EMPTY LOG STOOLS around the campfire. Rumors, hearsay, and tales from other refugees about a group of teenage boys in the wild known as the Wolfpack, led by a boy named Deven, led to the departure of Mitch and Heather from the campsite.

Baer stared behind the campfire. On the horizon the Firegale had roared to life. Protected by dense tree canopies, it stood, waiting, smoldering throughout the winter, biding its time. As the temperature rose, so did the flames off in the distance. By midday, the sun broke through clouds at noon and the graydimlight faded.

Reese refused to search with her mother. She said to Baer, "Deven's dead, and now Mom and Mitch will soon be dead." She wrapped her arms around Baer. "I told her I would hate her forever and begged her to stay."

Baer sat with Reese and Jordin by the campfire until he saw Lani. Lani waved him over to their tent. "Reese, I'll be back in a moment," he said.

Baer walked over to Lani and she asked, "How's Reese? How is Jordin?"

"She's not great. Why don't you tell Jordin how you feel?" Baer replied, "It's nice to be loved. Jordin feels alone now. She might welcome the knowledge."

"Baeran, what if she's not gay? No, I lost Annie. I can't risk losing Jordin. I should have told her months ago, and Mom and Dad. But this moment's not about me, it's about our friends."

Lani clutched her brother's arm and ambled with him to the campfire. She whispered, "We need to help Reese and Jordin. Deven must be dead. Her mother's gone, and Jordin lost Annie."

Baer responded, "We could make a memorial."

Lani grinned. Jordin and Reese were close enough now to overhear and moved in to hug Baer.

Baer nudged the girls. "All right, now let go."

Using a Sharpie and a sheet of metal salvaged from an ATV sled, Lani, Baer, Jordin, and Reese made a sign. Reese struggled with the pen in her webbed right hand, but she insisted on writing in her family's names.

The teens left the sign on the border of the campsite:

M253
We left the Granite State as strangers.
We became friends in the Green Mountain State.
Those of us who continue on the road:
Cole, Kay, Lani, and Baeran
Jordin
L.J. and Tara
Heather and Reese
Mitch
Our faithful pet, Selene

Those we lost along the way:
Susan, Judy, Aileen, and Megan
Parker
Deven
Ethan
Annie

STRIKER

M263. Kentucky.
BAER

BAER SNUCK INTO THE WOODS AT NIGHT WITH SELENE. To the west the Firegale glowed on the horizon. The time had come to prepare himself for the next confrontation with the Jackers.

Baer faced a tree. He raised his birchwood stick and struck at the lowest branch.

Baer had excelled at baseball. When the time came, he would strike at the hands, the feet, the groin, and the head. He asked the tree. "Ever play catcher? A bat to the hand will put you down. Ever foul a ball off your foot? Try jogging to first base. Ever take a pitch to the balls? Try breathing. Ever stop a line drive with your head? Try living.

"Hands. Feet. Balls. Head."

Baer struck the tree. He broke it down. He struck low and quick. He jabbed and moved. He had to stay out of his opponent's reach. If he was too close, he'd dive under their legs. He would disable and finish. Finish meant kill.

He had seen what the Jackers did to the Dazed. He had heard Susan describing what the Jackers had done to Judy and Megan. That was the reason Susan quit living. They had no mercy. When the time came, Baer would not show mercy, either. He smashed his stick through a branch. These men were evil, and Baer would show no hesitation if they attacked.

But trees didn't hit back. Trees didn't bleed. Trees didn't have guns. Baer struck low and quick, while coaching himself out loud. Selene danced at his feet, attacking wood shrapnel as it fell to the floor.

"Jab. Move. Disable. Finish."

The trees didn't stand a chance. Baer struck low and quick.

"Jab. Move. Disable. Finish."

He had to work harder. He struck the tree. He had to be prepared.

"You're a kid. The Jackers will never expect it."

Baer struck the tree harder. "Don't ask questions."

He struck the tree and a branch yielded, sending splinters into the air. "Don't show mercy."

He struck the tree, focusing on a new branch.

"Don't hesitate."

Baer struck low and quick. Bark flew into the air.

"Jab. Move. Disable. Finish."

He struck the tree, smashing through another branch.

"The Jackers will kill Dad. They'll take Mom, Tara, and Reese. They'll take Jordin and Lani. They'll kill L.J.."

Baer smashed another branch and hit a thicker one.

"Strike low and quick. Jab. Move. Disable. Finish."

He'd be ready. He would never let them take the girls.

"Break the branch. Don't leave any Jackers alive. No mercy. Smash the tree."

The Jackers will take everything he had. "Strike harder. Harder. Harder. Repeat. Strike the branch. Strike the tree. No mercy. Harder. Harder. Harder."

Baer tossed the stick in the air and spun. Selene danced at his feet. He turned and faced a new tree. "Strike. Jab. Move. Disable. Finish."

With one blow, the branch shattered. Baer moved to his left and chose another opponent. "Strike. Move. Disable. Finish."

Sweat poured from his brow. Selene backed off. Baer struck a new branch and fragments rained upward. He spun and attached another tree.

"Strike. Disable. Finish."

Baer's voice rose, and he struck the same branch repeatedly, yelling out encouragement, "Strike. Finish. Finish. Finish the tree. Finish the Jackers. Strike the tree. Strike harder with the birch stick—with 'Striker'. Finish with Striker. Finish means kill."

Baer tossed Striker into the air. He spun, caught Striker, and knelt with his head bowed. Selene sat to his left. Baer raised his head and gazed into the rising sun, while behind him the Firegale burnt on the horizon. For the first time in months, the sun warmed him, burning through the ash clouds. Baer calmed his mind and he thought of her, calling her name. "Solstice."

SERIOUSLY
M245. Kentucky.
SOLSTICE

Solstice drank her ultralaserwater from a light-weight collapsible cup in her undershieldcapbosuit inside the pop-up body heat dome tent, which she now called the bohedote. The ash snow tapered off for the day, and Naetersen remained outside near the campfire.

Solstice crouched down and sang to herself, while she thought of Baeran and how he had left her. Did he even remember her? The words, not Melody's—because she had abandoned Solstice, too—came from her own heart.

"Seriously, You Suck"

Da da da, da da—da da
Da da da, da da—da da

I'm missing him, and I feel loathsome
Our friendship, blossoming
Just met you, and you're gone
Damn that sucks, seriously
I said I'd be back
How about waiting for me
Can't do it, can't keep going
Seriously, you suck,
Screw you!

Now I'm searching for you
Holding onto hope for you
Where'd you go, I said I wouldn't be long

THE BURNT SUNSET

That seriously bites,
When I see you, I'm gonna give you a smack
How about seeking me
It's bringing me down, it's bringing me low
Seriously, you suck,
Hate you!

I need something while I wait for you
To bring me back
To you, anything to pass the time
They haunt me
The doctor and the Melody

Da da da, da da—da da
Da da da, da da—da da

You're not the first to leave me
What's wrong, it has to be me
You split with the sun, right at dawn
It blows
I keep thinking of you, flashback
How about finding me
I'm losing it, forgetting me
Seriously, you suck
Miss you!

Da da da, da da—da da
Da da da, da da—da da

Seriously, you suck
Screw you
I hate you
I miss you
I want to see your face
One more time, forever

Seriously, you suck

I long for you
I think I love you

Come find me

Da da da, da da—da da
Da da da, da da—da da

SUNBUTTER
M253. Kentucky.
SOLSTICE

Solstice and Naetersen followed a trail in Kentucky until they came to the outskirts of a town. Not every building was burnt. Like with untouched tree stands in the forest, the Firegale, visible on the horizon, had been selective with the town. Still bitter about losing the snow shoes, Naetersen struggled with each step, falling behind, while Solstice practically glided on the snow, elflike.

Solstice stopped and closed her eyes, rubbing her temples as she waited for the doctor to catch up.

"What is it?" Naetersen asked.

"I keep seeing these flashes and I have blind spots." Solstice replied, "My vision goes blurry on the sides. Lately, my face tingles when it happens. My eyes hurt. I swear I can feel the tips of my hair burning."

"Have you ever needed glasses?"

"No."

"Let's check. Give me my notebook." Naetersen waited for Solstice to remove his log. He wrote five letters on a blank page and stood in front of her. "Step back. Read this."

Solstice said, "A-E-F-P-M."

"Perfect. Your eyes are fine." Naetersen said, "It's a migraine. Add ibuprofen to the pharmacy list. We're close. I can see it beyond the clearing. At the pharmacy, gather the B-1, your ibuprofen, water and peanut butter."

Solstice grabbed her throat. "I'm allergic to peanut butter." Falling over she fake-died in the ash snow.

"Okay I get it." Naetersen asked, "What did you eat at school?"

Solstice replied, "The cafeteria had sun butter." Solstice stood smacking her lips. "Actually, it was awful, but since I deprived the entire school of the pleasure of peanut butter—it was a peanut-free school—I had to pretend like I liked it."

"Sun butter, that's a thing?" Naetersen ripped a page out of his notebook handing Solstice the list. "Okay, get some sun butter or jelly to mash the B-1 into. Do you understand? I want you in and out. He pointed toward the pharmacy. "When I give the signal, sneak across the parking lot and head straight for the door."

Solstice peered across the parking lot and asked, "Do you see them?" She pulled away from the view spot, hiding behind a burnt tree stump. "What about the Dazers near the dumpster? I don't want to go anywhere near them."

"I see them." Naetersen replied, "Move slow and deliberate, and they'll ignore you."

"I don't want to."

"We've observed many herds from afar. Solstice, you will be fine. Keep quiet and stay out of their line of sight

Solstice glared at Naetersen.

"Solstice, this is part of the deal." Naetersen insisted. "All this nice gear you have, your safety, and your food comes from me."

Solstice wanted a few personal items and did as Naetersen instructed. "Okay but tell me if they get close."

With her head down, she glided from the edge of the woods across the parking lot to the front door. She stepped on the broken glass littering the sidewalk. The sliding door had been shattered from the inside. Bits of flesh and torn clothing hung from the shards of the glass lining the doorframe.

Solstice pulled out her penlight from the doctor. She pressed the top, sending flashes into the darkened interior. She rubbed her temples, hoping to relieve her pounding headache.

Solstice crossed the threshold. She snatched a handbasket from the overturned pile and scanned the interior. Except for the mess by the door, the shelves remained neat. Solstice read the list and loaded her pack and basket. She found the Advil, popped the top and chewed two of them, washing them down with ultralaserwater from her compressible canteen. She swallowed hard, the bitter taste lingered in her mouth. Chewing the Advil was an old habit long since learned that sped the release of the medicine into her blood stream. She stopped in the food isle, ignored the candy and chips, and added noodle cups to the basket. Solstice ambled down the empty feminine hygiene isle, finding a lone box of pads on the floor, kicked under the shelf. She whispered to no one, "How about the rest of us?"

Solstice checked the list. Satisfied it was complete, she tightened the straps on her pack and crossed the threshold of the doorway into the parking lot. She glided several paces, and with her free hand, she waved to Naetersen along the clearing edge.

The doctor waved back with two hands while bowing. Solstice smiled at the doctor's odd little dance, until she realized he was signaling her to withdraw. She looked left and right, but already the Dazers were surrounding her.

OTHERBOY

M253. Kentucky.
SOLSTICE

SOLSTICE REMOVED HER UBER LIGHTWEIGHT BACKPACK outside the pharmacy and placed it on the ground with the overflowing shopping basket. The sun's rays mixed with the grayness of the world, and everything looked tinted. The Dazers surrounded her, putting their hands in her hair and on her body. The Dazers pawed at Solstice, smelling and licking her face as they oozed on her. She could no longer see Naetersen in the sea of bodies. The smell reminded Solstice of when she had fought off the Legion of Doom back in the ductwork,

a combination of blood, vomit and feces plus a new smell—rotting flesh.

Solstice pulled her arms to her chest, protecting her body. Fresh ones, old ones, skinny, skinnier, men, women, girls and boys surrounded her.

Solstice felt hands clawing at her, turning her face toward a boy about her age. He stared into Solstice's eyes, remembering a sister or a girlfriend. He put his yellowed hands in hers, clutching her as he led her through the Dazer pack into the parking lot.

When she was a few paces beyond the herd, Solstice pushed the boy, separating their hands. He reached for her, and Solstice knocked him to the ground. His empty red-streaked eyes stared back at her.

Solstice fled with flashes behind her eyes. Across the parking lot, she saw stars. Right past Naetersen, she scampered with blurred vision. Into the woods, Solstice dashed with her head pounding, smacking into branches. She sprinted so hard, Solstice didn't see the hole. She stepped forward and for one second, like a cartoon bunny, she remained suspended and then she fell. She dropped ten feet. Her feet hit the earth first and her body crumpled until her butt hit the ground. Solstice checked her body for injuries, and smiled, finding none. The sinkhole was like a downchute from the bunker. She felt safe and at home.

SINKHOLE
M253. Kentucky.
SOLSTICE

Solstice sat on her butt. Apparently, Kentucky had a sinkhole problem. Naetersen yelled down, "Don't worry, sinkholes are common. I have your backpack and the basket, too. I'll find a rope."

Rule 3—don't leave home without rope, because that's how you climb back in when you fall out

"Shut up," she whispered to herself. "I'm comfortable." Sure, her ankle hurt, but it would be fine. At least the flashes had stopped with the impact, as did the headache. The hole, sized for a former tunnel rat, descended shoulder-wide about ten feet into the earth. It could have been a dry well or an abandoned mineshaft or an old fashion sinkhole. It didn't matter. Solstice liked it and she felt right at home, like back at the Silver Palace in Bunkerland.

Solstice was comfortable, it had been a long time since she had been in such a confined space. She preferred horizontal shafts, but a vertical shaft would be fine today. She missed the bunker ducts. Sure, the Legion of Doom thing, the UDs, and the incinerator incident had been downers.

Naetersen peered down the hole and asked, "Are you OK?"

Solstice pulled her knees to her chest and tucked her head between them, finding safety in the shaft. She was happy in her solitude, but Naetersen kept yelling to her.

Solstice could hear him fine. A minute later, she took the rope.

RAT

M263. Kentucky.
SOLSTICE

SOLSTICE AND THE DOCTOR TRAVELED ON A BACK-COUNTRY ROAD, heading westward for ten days. The sun was visible at dawn for the first time in months, competing with the glow of the Firegale in the west. Naetersen had grown weary of the road, and his time with Solstice.

As Solstice gazed at smoke billows on the horizon, Naetersen called to her, "Rat!"

Sinkholes were never around when Solstice needed them, nor were dance studios. There was no chance he would call her Solstice anymore. She had been impetuous and ungrateful to boot—running away earlier in the winter, losing the snowshoes and staying in the sink hole too long.

"Binoculars!" he shouted to the girl.

Solstice handed Naetersen the binoculars. She had pushed her luck and had paid for it with skipped meals. She needed to eat tonight so she would be on her best behavior. Odd at first, how Naetersen had refused to feed her, but after two days, she understood the message. She'd have to learn to scavenge in the wild on her own, but she had drained her supply of defiance. Exhausted and hungry, she'd behave.

"Rat, Jackers are ahead, attacking a group. We'll hike around."

Naetersen handed the binoculars to Solstice. She snuck a peek, but when he glared, Solstice returned them to the backpack.

"Could it be Baeran?" Solstice whispered to herself.

Naetersen waited. Solstice gathered the pack and moved off the road. Head bowed, she led Naetersen into the woods.

An hour later, the smoke billows from the roadside battle were no longer visible. Solstice glided across the melting gray snow, distancing herself from the doctor, focusing on the ground before her. But Naetersen quickened his pace to catch Solstice. With the sound of his footsteps drawing closer, she stopped and stood motionless facing her feet.

The flashes had increased in frequency over the last couple of days, blocking out reality and Solstice didn't notice a herd of Dazers grazing by a riverbank, eating cattails.

Naetersen caught up to the girl, pulling Solstice's hair, forcing her to the ground. "Get down, Rat, Dazers."

Solstice involuntarily trembled thinking about the Dazers touching her. She removed the pack and lay on her belly, shaking. She looked at the doctor and said, "I don't want to, not again. Keep them away from me."

Solstice reached for the doctor, desperate to hold onto anything or anybody, even him. Naetersen pushed her away, and said, "Take it easy. I did not expect you to react like that when I lured the Dazers to the pharmacy entrance. I'll inform you before the next Dazer immersion."

"You did that to me? Am I not special? Or am I worth less than the stuff I lug around for you?"

Solstice moved two feet away from the doctor while he examined the herd, ignoring her outburst. She laid her head into the gray snow, turning away from him, and let the tears flow. Each blink brought a new wave of bright yellow flashes and pain.

Solstice whispered, "Take me. Take me. I'm so tired. I'm ready. Is there no one who will love me? Why have you left me? Silverfox, Buttster, Mrs. C., Dallas, Mom, Baeran, is there no one?"

I am here, Solstice.

SOLSTICE SETTING
M273. Kentucky.
SOLSTICE

Solstice and Naetersen emerged from the bohedote in their undershieldcapbosuits on the spring equinox. They packed their gear along with the supsdelite and the ultralaserwater pen in their uberlightpacks and continued trekking westward toward the Firegale on the horizon.

Naetersen had not been overly cruel throughout the winter, but he hadn't been nice either. He had spent much of the season poring over his notes on Dazers, his blueprints of the Lincoln Presidential Bunker Complex, and making calculations in his notebooks. Spring had dawned, and Solstice and Naetersen had been on the move, uninhibited for days. Soon, Naetersen would want to infiltrate the Dazers.

Solstice scouted the trail, but the constant flashing, headaches and aura blurred reality. Her strength was ebbing, and her last hope lay with the kindness of a cruel man.

Near dusk, Solstice stumbled into a campsite. She felt the coals of the campfire; it had gone out hours before. A dog carcass, with split bones was off to one side. Solstice scanned the site one more time before waving to Naetersen. Ten feet off into the woods, illuminated by the setting sun and the Firegale burning on the horizon, a homemade sign beckoned her. Solstice glided toward it and removed a pine bough. She could hear Naetersen approaching. She read the sign, a marker for the people who survived the winter at this campsite.

The fifth line said: *Cole, Kay, Lani, and Baeran*.

Naetersen came behind Solstice and asked, "What's this, Rat?" He pushed her out of the way, and Solstice fell to the snowy ground.

She whispered to the snow with joy, "Baeran." *She'd still be a maiden, though, a kick-ass one.*

"These people are in their grave now," Naetersen said as he read the sign, failing to notice the warm coals.

Solstice rolled over, and Naetersen reached down. "Time to go," he said as he extended his hand. Naetersen saw her expression of disdain, and he allowed months of frustration with the girl to influence his words as he stated, "You know I killed him, Rat. You watched as I gave him the pills. He died in his bed, a weak man, the day I opened the bunker door.

"Senator Adena knew your mother, Elle. But he let her die. Why did he do it, Rat? And yet, Senator Adena let you live in the ducts. Why didn't he rescue you? Was he too ashamed to admit the truth out loud? Is his name too familiar? Was it spoken in whispers around your home? Would you have spied on him from the vents, knowing what you know now?"

Solstice cut Naetersen off with a scream, her heart broken, unwilling to hear the truth or to verify her long-held suspicions. But the doctor couldn't have her tears.

Silverfox. Ask him, she's his.

The late-day sun shone over Naetersen's left shoulder, lighting Solstice's face, warming her. Sorrow became resolve, melding into defiance. *Maidens were warriors and could be defiant.* Solstice pushed aside the doctor's outstretched hand. She was no longer the Rat. Her birth name had power, and she would claim it. There would be no tears for a father who never loved her. Her mother, Elle, alone deserved her love. The girl rose and faced Naetersen as the setting sun and the Firegale on the horizon framed his darkened shape.

Solstice was not beholden to him. She was the freakin' Ice Maiden from the Silver Palace in Bunkerland.

She glared at Naetersen. "My name is Solstice Dayton."

Solstice marched toward Naetersen, pushed him aside, and walked westward.

Naetersen stood motionless, staring at his hand.

Solstice made it two steps before the pain came.

Oh, no. Please, not now, not here.

Rhymes, alliterations, colors and numbers fought the flashes, preceding the dreamvision, pairing the words "elementa presage" with the number 15 in front of her. Each letter, a distinct color, burnt. The number was red, bleeding. The number 16 followed, paired with the words "kindling eclipse," wrapped in orange flames, oozing red.

Burning letters and bleeding numbers floated, blocking out the sun, blocking out Naetersen.

Blinding blood burnt in her right eye. Flashing fire filled the other eye. Her head was bursting, breaking, throbbing, and pulsating. She was spinning, swirling, and slipping. Vomit projected onto her coat and her feet. The ground rose to meet her, like a crashing wave, and she wet herself, warming her pants.

Flashing light yielded to a dreamvision.

Solstice was trapped in an airplane hangar, with Baer at her side, but she was powerless to control her body. Burnt-out planes littered the hangar. On the side of the closest one was the number 15. She watched herself weave six songs together while Baer and four other teens collapsed, joining her song.

The dreamvision swirled. Lightning crackled again behind her eyes. A new vision came into focus.

A building with a gilded, golden dome tower burnt, trapping Baer and his family on the summer solstice in the midst of an eclipse. Lightning flashed, and Solstice saw another image. The sun with triangular rays and ICE in the middle, Solstice's sign burnt on Baeran's arm, with the number 16 overlaid.

Lightning flashed again behind her eyes, and Solstice collapsed, falling to the ground, seizing.

Solstice's body stiffened, and her eyes rolled back as she shook, bleeding from the mouth. Her arms thrashed while her thumping legs churned snow, tossing dirt and breaking sticks. Her head whipped back and forth as she writhed, tearing, turning, twisting, and twitching.

But the moment was fleeting. Solstice felt herself floating, and it was freeing as she was finishing. The seizure was slackening, stagnating, slowing down, and stopping.

Solstice lay perfectly still, and her spirit-mind floated away with a lyric.

Naetersen, the doctor, Nether approaching
Softly to her, Presage Melody singing
At peace, now eyes closing, almost sleeping
Solstice barely alive, but still, she's clinging
Watch out, Aether, Darkness is awakening
To Baeran she calls, with her mind she's pinging

ENDDAY

M272. Kentucky. Winter camp.
BAER

Baer and the Seascapers gathered around the campfire. Cole called a meeting at the winter camp, on the final day of winter, when the trails were passable. He spoke: "It's been five and a half months since the snow's first fall. We've survived the Firegale, Jackers, Dazers, and the super winter. We've hidden in the wild, and had friends die and leave. We must be bold, too long has the winter trapped us. We will ride for Lincoln, in the morning."

Cole held a map up, showing the group a picture. "This is where we're going in Lincoln. It's a square building with a gilded-gold dome-topped tower."

Baer smiled. Find the trail. Find Lincoln. Find the girl.

Baer wandered from the campfire, pulling a folded drawing from his pocket, and beamed at a sketch of the girl in the woods. The moon shone brightly overhead, uninhibited by the gray clouds for

the first time in months. It had been a night like this when Baer had met Solstice, before the super winter.

Baer folded the picture of Solstice and leaned back against a tree. Deep in his own thoughts, he blended into the shadows along the edge of the forest.

Kay said goodnight to the group around the campfire, and followed Cole, catching him when he stopped at the forest's edge. Kay slipped behind Cole, placing two hands around his waist, easing them under his blue jacket. She hugged him until his shoulders loosened and Cole raised his head, leaning into her. Kay rested her head on Cole's shoulder. She pulled him tighter, and with her left hand she turned Cole around to face her. Kay embraced Cole and kissed him.

Cole grinned, straightening his back while maintaining the embrace, and Kay kissed him, again.

Baer waited for his parents to pass by. He slipped out of the shadows, glad his mom and dad still had a spark. It made life easier knowing Kay and Cole needed each other, because he still needed them.

Cole had said to the Seascapers around the campfire, "We will leave tomorrow. We ride fast and hard."

Baer added to himself, "Be prepared."

The adults had their guns.

Baer had his bowie knife, birch wood stick—Striker—his yew bow, and Selene. And he had the memory of Solstice.

MEADOWS SUCK
M273. West of Winter Camp in Kentucky.
BAER

BAER AND THE SEASCAPERS ABANDONED THE WINTER CAMP in the morning. Each member of the group packed a water bottle and their clothes in a backpack with the remainder of the previous day's greens and game. The group broke a long-held rule and rode westward on a direct route, abandoning the safety of the trails to traverse the distance with haste along a roadway.

Baer packed his black backpack, Striker, a trap, his phone, Wayfarer sunglasses, and his bowie knife. He put his yew bow over his neck and shoulder and a quiver into his backpack. He settled Selene in the trailer and mounted his ATV.

The Seascapers rode out: Cole on Susan's motorcycle, Kay and Lani on Parker's ATV, Baer and Jordin on the Sheridan's ATV with Selene on the attached ATV trailer, Reese on Mitch's ATV and L.J. and Tara on their ATV.

Jordin held onto Baer's waist, and they talked about Portsmouth, Kittery and Sumwhereorother. They chatted about the Border Camp, the Summer Camp, the Highland Camp and the slow painful despair of the Winter Camp. Baer recounted the Shit Shows, his ridiculous, but effective ccpDazer, cattail-charcoal-pinesap, body spray that he used to infiltrate the Dazers, and the construction of traps and bows. Jordin reminisced about saving Reese, and she spoke of Wàigōng, Annie and Deven. Baer spoke about Solstice about their moonlight meeting and his hope of finding her one day. They rode on, into the afternoon as the sun shone overhead, and Jordin and Baer talked about gray ash snow, gray clouds, gray mud, and the graydimlight, and the destruction of the forests and cities. Baer and Jordin talked about the rise of a different sky, like an old photograph, sepia in tone, a mixture of gray and yellow blocking out the blue. As the sun fell lower in the sky, they talked about Maximus, the hope of Lincoln, and the Firegale as it loomed on the horizon. Baer smiled, and Jordin laughed throughout the long day.

And it took Baer and Jordin a moment to notice Cole had led them straight into a Jacker ambush.

On the open road, armed Jackers jumped from their hiding spot in a meadow. Cole hit the brakes on Susan's motorcycle. The front wheel locked, and the motorcycle leaned to the left. The bike fell on its side, skidding to a stop in the center of the road after seventy-five feet. Kay steered into a ditch on the right side of the road, and her ATV rolled, tossing Lani and herself from the four-wheeler. Baer slammed on the brakes of his ATV, causing it to jack-knife and eject Jordin, Selene and himself. Baer hit his head, rolled into the ditch and blacked out.

The first thing he heard were Jordin's screams. "Baeran!"

Baer opened his eyes, facing the sky. Smoke billowed from the roadway. Kay and Reese laid next to him in the ditch, while Selene waited by his feet.

Baer was warm, wet, and red. He put his hands to his head, torso, and limbs, unable to find any holes. Kay lay next to him, gasping, and Baer realized it was his mom's blood covering him.

Baer rolled onto his stomach, and the sights and the sounds of the battle kicked in. Bullets flew. L.J. screamed. Cole yelled, arguing with a stranger. Kay labored, fighting for every breath.

To Baer's right, Reese cried to Jordin, "There's too many of them..."

Reese stopped midsentence as a rock struck her head from a bullet ricochet. Jordin gasped and pulled her friend closer.

Baer blazed at Jordin, "Get down! Protect Reese!"

Baer found Lani under his mom, unconscious, but not bleeding. He stared at the road and watched the battle unfold.

In the center of the pavement, a stranger, he called himself Stowe, stood over Cole shouting, punching and kicking Baer's father. Beyond the pair, at least two dozen Jackers moved east, toward the fight.

L.J. stood up from the rubble of his ATV, midway between Cole and Stowe and the larger Jacker group. L.J. fired seven shots, emptying the chamber as he took three Jackers down. The Jackers dropped to the pavement and returned fire. L.J. took a shot in the side and the right leg. He fell to his knees and looked to the ditch, at Baer. L.J. dropped his empty weapon, and the Jackers unloaded on him, peppering his body with bullets. L.J. shook spastically, and he fell onto the roadway. His face hit the pavement and he searched the bodies for his wife. Spotting Tara among the fallen; he closed his eyes.

Baer watched as the Jackers stood, traversing toward Cole and Stowe, trudging over bodies and around overturned, flaming ATVs.

Stowe kicked Cole and screamed, "Where were they when the Firegale wiped out towns? Where were they when we froze, and starved to death this past winter? The government doesn't exist. No one is coming!"

Sweat poured down Baer's face. He couldn't move from the ditch. He froze, like he did when the Dazed overtook the cave, or when Parker first hit him in Shit Show #1.

Stowe continued, "The government is gone. Lincoln, Nebraska is gone. The army or FEMA or the guard should have ventured out this far by now. You have no friends. There will be no help for you. Only one law exists now. We take what we want when we want it!"

Stowe kicked Cole in the side and spat, "You will die, without hope, knowing you led your family to their deaths."

Baer struggled to find courage as he glanced at Tara lying face first in the mud. She hadn't moved since the crash. Twisted metal protruded from her back and side. Her husband, L.J., was gone, too. In the ditch, Kay lay on top of Lani while Jordin covered the unconscious Reese.

Beyond the road, on the far side, Baer spied movement, but the Jackers fired into his ditch. Baer ducked down, forcing Jordin lower into the hollow. Kay let out a moan as another bullet struck her.

Baer struggled to formulate a plan as he dragged Lani and Kay to the bottom of the ditch.

Baer had to break it down. He counted six-nine-four. Inhale.

Exhale. Hold.

Baer took his gaze off what remained of his group and stared into the horizon. The glow from the Firegale mixed with the sun's setting rays.

Cole raised his head. Spat blood onto Stowe and shouted one last cry of defiance.

Baer yelled, "No!"

Enraged, Stowe jabbed at Cole with his knife. Cole seized Stowe's right arm and pulled it toward his body. The Jacker fell. As he toppled toward Cole, Cole bent his attacker's arm at the elbow, forcing Stowe's own knife into his chest.

Stowe gasped as the knife sunk deeper under his own weight—stopping at the hilt. The Jacker stumbled off Cole, removed his knife from his chest, and fell backward. He hit the ground and with his final breath gasped, "Stacy."

The twenty-one remaining Jackers rushed toward their fallen leader. They fired at Cole, striking him in the thigh and the opposite shoulder. Baer rose from the ditch, and watched Cole writhing on the pavement

Jordin clasped Baer's arm and pleaded, "*Meiyou!* No! Don't do it, Baeran. We can't save them!"

Baer gawked at the Jackers closing in on Cole, until he saw a barrage of arrows released from the meadow.

A familiar face rose and motioned Baer's way. The arrows from the meadow had taken down six Jackers.

JRB
M273. Kentucky.
BAER

BAER CLOSED HIS EYES, as the Jackers dropped to the ground under the salvo of arrows. He couldn't catch his breath. The blood pulsed in his ears. He had never seen so many bodies. L.J. and Tara were dead. Blood puddled in the street. Cole was in trouble and Kay was bleeding everywhere.

Baer gazed at his left arm. He could see the mark Solstice had left on him last fall—a sun with rays and the word "ICE" written inside the circle. As it faded during winter, he had retraced it.

Baer could see Solstice's face, framed by the moonlight, many months prior, smiling, and kissing him. But Baer couldn't speak as she left him and glided back to the bunker door. "Check in with your parents, and meet me by the tunnel," Solstice had said.

Baer had been stunned by the revelation of that moment: he loved Solstice.

Baer glanced at his dad and his mom. He needed to act, family first, then self.

Baer crawled from Kay and Lani. The movement from the meadow created a distraction, and an opportunity for Baer to act. He climbed over Jordin and Reese. Reese stirred. He noticed the right hand with the fingers fused. The cruel new world had done this to Reese. A world ruled by the Firegale, Dazers and Jackers.

Jordin said with watery eyes, "*Meiyou.* No. Baeran."

Baer replied, "Stay down and crawl to the right if you can. We have help."

Baer rose from the ditch. He grinned at Selene, rising to her feet. He pulled his yew bow over his head and found his quiver in his backpack. He strung an arrow and released it, striking down a fat Jacker rising from the ground. Baer strung another arrow and took down a second Jacker, and then hit a third Jacker

Cole forced himself up into a kneel. He found his shot gun. Twelve Jackers stood in the middle of the road and rushed him. Cole fired seven shots, knocking down six Jackers. At least a dozen more arrows flew from the meadow striking four Jackers. The two remaining Jackers rushed toward Cole with inverted, empty, bulletless shotguns. Cole struggled to remain on his knees, but his exhausted, bloodied, battered, and bruised body couldn't take his own weight. His leg buckled, and Cole collapsed onto the cracked pavement, hitting his head.

BAER RISING

M273. Kentucky.
BAER

BAER LOOPED HIS BOW OVER HIS HEAD as he prepared to leave the ditch. He pulled out his bowie knife. In his mind, he laid out instructions for his attack. The Firegale burned on the horizon and behind Baer's eyes.

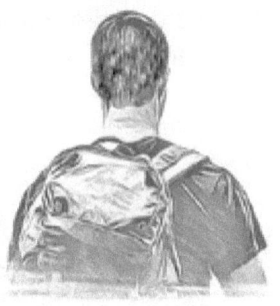

Break it down.
Baseball. Hands. Feet. Balls. Head.
Strike low and quick. Jab. Move. Disable. Finish.
Finish means kill.
Baer dashed into the road melee, and he slid on the loose gravel of the pavement to the right of a fat Jacker. Baer swung his bowie knife at the Jacker's foot. The fat Jacker doubled over, and Baer dove into a roll as he passed him.
Parkour.
Baer leapt to his feet and swung the bowie knife backward, striking the Jacker in the arm.
Hockey.

Blood squirted on Baer. On the pavement, a hand lay twitching. Baer stared at his right hand, the one with the blade, and his left hand, and the Jacker fell to his knees.

Move.

Too late.

The second Jacker struck Baer in the back with an empty rifle. Baer fell to his stomach.

Inside, dive under the legs.

Baer rolled over and raised a knee.

Baseball.

Balls.

Baer kneed the Jacker in the groin and rolled right as his assailant fell over.

Head.

Baer stood and placed the point of the blade into the back of the man's neck, pushing the bowie knife in. The blade found its way through the man's head and came out his jaw, stopping on the tar.

Finish. Finish meant kill.

Baer removed the blade and darted to the first Jacker. The man held his hand stump, crying, "No!"

Head. Finish.

Baer slashed at his opponent's face. The blade stuck, and Baer let it fall to the ground with the body.

No pity. Only wrath.

Don't ask questions. Don't show mercy. Don't hesitate.

Baer retrieved his bowie knife and surveyed the roadway.

Lani, Reese, and Jordin rose from the ditch, staring at Baer.

Baer ignored their glares. He heard a cry for help. Cole and L.J. had wounded many, but the dads hadn't killed enough. Across the battlefield injured Jackers stood, ready to clash with Baer.

Baer spotted his first assailant and broke into a jog, diving at the man's shins, upending the man to the ground.

Finish.

Baer knelt, and stabbed at the man's neck with his bowie knife. Blood squirted onto Baer's face.

Baer found Striker in the roadway near his feet.

Selene saw the stick, and snapped to attention, trotting into the road. She followed Baer, watching his back.

Baer listened and heard another cry of pain.

A man reached for Baer, knocking away the stick.

Baer bent over for the stick, his hand outstretched, and Striker moved six inches off the ground, closing the gap with his hand. A blinding flash of light stunned Baer, and he heard Solstice's voice:

I am Solstice, the Sun
Singing, kindling, sighting
A seer with visions
Of powers igniting

Baer raised Striker and struck the man.

Baer felt the spark run through his fingertips. Finally, after months of his nerves being on fire, he felt it, the release. The Aether came forth, and Baer wielded it.

Baer spun through the bodies littering the road, tossing the stick and swirling. Even Selene backed off. With Striker raised, Baer darted between the wounded, the able and the carcasses, finishing, probing and striking, smashing the skulls of dead and living men.

Finish.

Baer became a berserker, blazing a burning trail of blood through the bodies. With each blow, blood rained upward. Parkour, hockey and baseball melded into one, and Baer had no equal. Striker moved from Baer's hand, jabbing opponents and retreating into his palm. Horrifying and beautiful to behold at once, Baer struck, rhythmically without hesitation or mercy. Baer delivered death blows with lightning speed, anticipating his next target three or four moves ahead.

Striker moved in and out of Baer's hands, controlled by Baer's will, vanquishing any who stood before him.

When Baer took a breather, Lani dashed to him. Lani pulled at Baer, and screamed, "That's enough!"

But Air had no power over Aether.

Baer held Lani at bay, scanning the roadway for more wounded Jackers. He brandished Striker, jabbing another Jacker through the soft part of his head.

Finish.

Finish meant kill.

Baer had finished nine.

Baer stood amongst the bodies, calming his mind, forcibly slowing his breath, as he turned off the berserker.

Selene rejoined Baer.

From the tall grass beyond the far ditch, a friend rose, covered in animal skins. He removed the pelt covering much of his head. He wiped the grime from his face, and an older and wiser Deven emerged. Behind him, three girls and four boys stood, dressed like Deven, covered in skins and grime.

Baer darted into the meadow to greet his friend.

Deven gave Baer a wide berth but offered his hand. Blood covered both Baer and Selene. Baer took it as he held Striker in his left hand. Deven nodded at Baer while Selene sat peacefully at attention. Deven said, "Meet the Wolfpack."

Baer grinned and said, "Dude."

Baer released his friend's hand, rolled his sleeve and took off Deven's watch, handing it to him. *We know. Thank you.*

Deven reached in and grabbed Baer, hugging him and said, "I've got some tales to unweave with you."

Baer smiled, but turned to Deven's friends and said, "Thank you. We owe you our lives."

The Wolfpack teens held back, revealing their apprehension of Baer's bloodied appearance.

Baer nodded to the new group and strode to the roadway to examine the bodies. He needed to be sure. Selene followed.

Deven's sister stared in disbelief. Deven put on his father's watch and embraced Reese. Reese asked, "Have you see Mom or Mitch?"

Deven shook his head. "Nada. Negator. Nixo."

From the ditch, Jordin watched Lani help Kay stand. She rushed to join them.

"Where's your father?" Kay asked.

From the middle of the road, Cole called out for Kay: "Here!"

Kay coughed, and blood spewed from her mouth. She doubled

over, falling to the ground, slipping from Lani's grasp. Cole called out, and Kay dragged herself toward Cole. Lani stood frozen as Kay crept across the tar and over the bodies.

Cole pulled himself toward Kay, and they met in the middle of the road. Kay fell into Cole's arms. With the last of their energy spent, the couple embraced.

WAKE

M273. Kentucky.
BAER

BAER HELD BACK IN THE ROAD, CHECKING BODIES. He glanced west. The sepia sky yielded to the burnt orange of the sunset and the Firegale on the horizon. Lani, Reese, Deven, and Jordin rushed to join Cole and Kay. They knelt around the couple.

Cole held Kay's hand and gestured at the children to hug him. He lingered when it was Lani's turn. "Where's Baeran, Lani?" he asked. "Watch over him. Help him."

Kay gazed at her husband as tears dripped down her cheeks, and she called to him, "Cole."

Cole pulled Kay closer and kissed her.

Lani's tears streaked down her face as she reached for Kay's hand and Cole's.

Cole kissed Lani's hand and called out for his son. Baer approached his parents and knelt. Cole nodded and placed Baer's hand on top of Lani's hand. Lani pulled Kay's hand toward Cole's, and the four Sheridans' hands intertwined for a final time.

Kay scanned Jordin, Lani and Baeran's faces. "I so wish I could have seen who you become. Remember where you came from, and who raised you and then you'll know who you are."

Lani put her hands to her mouth, searching for words.

Kay looked at Lani and said, "My dearest daughter, be yourself. Embrace it. They will love you for who you are."

Kay looked at Jordin. "You are my daughter in more ways than one, watch over Lani."

Kay smiled at Baer and said, "The girl is the key. I see your face light up when you speak of her. Find Solstice."

Turning from the children, Kay gazed into Cole's eyes, and said,

360

"I'll be waiting for you, my love."

And Kay passed.

Selene bowed her head and crawled toward Cole. He petted her. "I'm sorry for ignoring you, girl." Cole regained his grip on Baer's hand. With a rasp, Cole repeated what he had said to Baer months prior: "Protect them: Lani, Jordin, Deven, and Reese, and anyone else you can. Family first, then self." Cole coughed blood and said, "Break it down."

Cole closed his eyes, and with his dying breath, he called to her. "Kay..."

Lani put her hands to her face, she had no words.

Baer rose. Lani, Jordin, Reese, Deven, and Selene gazed at him. *Find the trail. Find Lincoln. Find Solstice.*

Baer pointed westward to the Firegale and the setting sun, melding into one, and he said, "Rest now. Tomorrow, we ride into the burnt sunset."

JOURNAL
M273. Kentucky.
LANI

LANI CLOSED HER JOURNAL. The Firegale roared in the west, melding into the sunset, into the burnt orange colored the sky. The survivors gathered near the roadside battle around a campfire.

Lani sat with her back against a tree on the edge of the meadow near the Jacker roadside battle. Later, Lani would have to bury Cole and Kay, and words would need to be said, but for now, she wanted to remember. She wrote M273. She kept the count to honor the dead, her mom, dad, and many others, and to honor those who had survived beyond the early days:

Baer, herself, Jordin, Deven and Reese.

Aether, Air, Water, Earth, and Fire.

On the cover of the journal, Lani wrote the words *The Burnt Sunset.* She had combined tales from other Seascapers with her own journal entries and Baer's sketches to tell the events since the dawn of the Firegale. Lani smiled, Baer had handed her another pile of sketches of the mysterious girl, Solstice, a few days ago. For a girl Baer hardly knew, he remembered her face and shape, revealing more about his feelings, than sketch-girl. Someday, if Lani met Solstice, she would add the girl's story to the tale, as well.

Lani placed the journal next to her leg and leaned against a tree, keeping the first watch. Near the campfire, Baer slept fitfully with Selene by his side, muttering three words, "Presage, Melody and Solstice."

To Lani's right side, Deven rested with Reese while Jordin slept with her head on Lani's lap. Lani leaned over Jordin stroking her hair, and whispered, *"Wo ai lu."*

Jordin opened her eyes, she looked at Lani, smiled, and said, *"Wo ail u.* I love you, too, Lani."

BAER AETHER

M273. Kentucky.
BAER

Baer slept near the campfire with Selene as his mind broke it down. The glow of the Firegale battled the setting sun. Burnt orange colored the sky at dusk.

Baer was changed, as was the girl, and she called to him in a dream.

Solstice searched for Baer from the prison of her body, invading his dream, overlaying it with her dreamvision. She called to Baer, lyrically, like she had done thrice before on the wind, "Baer, it is time, ignore the broken body, and join my mind."

A blinding light filled Baer's dream. He shielded his eyes, as they burnt under the glow of a white-hot sun.

Solstice said, "Baer, open your mind. Melody is here. She will show us the way. Hurry, Nether is close."

Baer let Solstice into his thoughts. In the dreamvision, Solstice appeared and showed Baer *The Burnt Sunset*—the Firegale melding with the setting sun. It faded, revealing *The Eventide Blaze*—a gilded gold-domed tower in flames, burning on the horizon. The flames faded, and Solstice pointed at her sign on Baer's left arm—*The Aurora Brand*—the sun with triangular rays and the word "ICE" written inside the circle.

Solstice's eyes glistened, and her hair glowed. She grasped Baer's hand, and he was kindled within the dreamvision as Solstice sang Melody's Presage:

I am Solstice, the Sun
Singing, kindling, sighting
A seer with visions
Of powers igniting

363

THE BURNT SUNSET

Baeran Wayfarer
Kinetics spawning
This is not your death
It is your dawning

First among five, beware
The darkness fawning
And the Sun revealed
Without an awning

Come now with dog Selene
Find me, I have foreseen
Come now with Striker birch
With them, Seascaper, search

Sun igniting
Aether throwing
Air whirling
Earth growing
Fire burning
Water flowing

Soon will rise
As the world is dwindling
A pentad of
Ancient elements kindling

Baer awoke. Solstice was near, and he knew what to do next.

SOLSTICE SUN

M273. Kentucky.
SOLSTICE

Solstice had seized, and her spirit wandered in a dreamvision, leaving her body, searching for the Pentad. Solstice had envisioned her fifteenth birthday, about ninety days away, on the summer solstice, glimpsing hits of the Elementa Presage in the airplane hangar, a prophesy concerning the Pentad—five teens—who would develop elemental powers on Solstice's sixteenth birthday during the Kindling Eclipse at the gilded golden tower.

Solstice had to find Baer, the first of the five teens, to help her weather the coming storm, tame Melody and fight Naetersen. Baer's power, Aethikinesis—the ability to move objects and energy—had come over a year early, making it dangerous and unpredictable. It had awoken during their moonlight meeting near the Hillock Tunnel door and kindled in the road side battle with the Jackers. Solstice sensed without meeting the rest yet, that Baer kept the other four elementals close, while beginning to test his power.

Solstice sought Baer as she projected her mind in a dreamvision and found him between the light and the dark. That's where the dreamvision lived. Both sides called to Solstice. The part of her that was Solstice sought the light, but the part of her that was Melody sought the darkness. The darkness offered death and freedom from her pain. Solstice saw Baer in the middle, in the gray ash of the fire-scorched earth. Baer was the space in between the light and the dark, the Aether. Solstice was the light. Naetersen was the dark, and already Melody was lobbying to join the doctor's cause.

Solstice had sung to Baer with Melody earlier, "Wayfarer this is not your death, it is your dawning," calling to him in his dreams by a campfire.

The image of Baer faded, and she called to the other four teens one by one, revealing hints of her personality and power. And when she was done with Aether, Air, Water, Earth and Fire, Solstice returned to her body, choosing the pain of the fire-scorched world over the sweet relief of death.

Solstice involuntarily bit her tongue, as her body reminded her of its struggle on the forest floor, and she opened her eyes at dawn, returning to the world.

Solstice rose, wiping the blood from her lips. Her eyes glistened, and her hair glowed, like sunrays were blazing from the tips of her blonde hair and from her blue irises. She glared at Naetersen and said, "I'm going to find my friend, Baer, and you're coming with me. He is near."

Dumbfounded, Naetersen said, "Why would I follow you? You're not the one in charge."

THE BURNT SUNSET

Solstice interrupted, "Baer walks with the Dazers."

Without waiting for a response, Solstice hiked westward toward Baer. Naetersen frantically gathered their gear and fell in line behind her.

A lyric formed in her mind, and Solstice smiled as she sang with Melody, her two halves melding into one.

Dreamvision, flashes and the aura
Sunset, Eventide and Aurora
Find Baer Aether, the plan she is devising
The Ice Maiden, Solstice the Sun is rising

www.ingramcontent.com/pod-product-compliance
Lightning Source LLC
Chambersburg PA
CBHW021133260626
47169CB00005B/1586